N

JA̶ ̶
WINTERS

To Stevie,
Hope you enjoy
Kim & Evan's story?
Stay Scandalous?

Secretly
Scandalous

A WILLOW CREEK NOVEL

Jacquelin Winters

Other Books in the Willow Creek Series:

Sweetly Scandalous *

*All Willow Creek Series books can be read as standalone novels.

ISBN: 978-1-943571-05-5 (print)
ISBN: 978-1-943571-03-1 (Kindle)
ISBN: 978-1-943571-04-8 (ePub)

Editor: EJ Runyon
http://www.bridgetostory.com
Copy Editor: Brenda Letendre
Cover Design: RBA Designs
http://designs.romanticbookaffairs.com
Cover Photo: Lindee Robinson Photography
https://www.facebook.com/LindeeRobinsonPhotography
Cover Models: Ahmad Kawsan & Mikeala Galli
Formatting: Michelle Josette
www.mjbookeditor.com

Prologue

Kim Wilkerson trudged up the concrete stairs toward the church entrance. The bells clamored what her heart refused to believe. These past three days, an emotional tornado had carved its way through her life, targeting what strength she had left.

"C'mon, Kimmie." Her dad's large, calloused hand covered her shoulder. Chip Wilkerson trembled from his own grief. "Let's get inside."

"I . . . I need a minute." From the lower stair, she met her dad's tear-soaked eyes. The longer she postponed the walk through the double glass doors, the longer she could pretend this was all some horrible nightmare. "I'm just not ready." With each second she stalled, she hoped she might wake up in her once happy, perfect life.

"Of course, sweetie," her mom said, ushering Chip up the last couple of stairs. "We'll save you a seat."

The moment her parents vanished inside the church, Kim scurried down the stairs. She ran, following the narrow sidewalk behind the church, and stopped only when she found a deep alcove at the back of the brick building. Tears soaked her puffy cheeks.

Her cousin was dead. *Dead!* The man she loved had tried to save Jeremy, but he'd nearly died too.

"Kimberly, how you holding up?"

Kim spun around, feeling abundant relief to see Evan Rowe towering over her, blocking out the rest of the world with his broad shoulders. Here, out of sight of the street, they could embrace without raised eyebrows or whispers. She clung to Evan, pulled at the collar of his shirt so hard she thought it might rip.

Inhaling Evan's musky cedar scent, she wondered what she would've done if those flames had taken him, too. "I love you, Evan," she whispered against his firm chest. "I don't know what I would've done if . . ."

He tensed beneath her. "Kimberly." He kissed the top of her head, his tender touch allowing her the briefest smile despite the anguishing reality waiting inside the church.

Tomorrow Kim would be eighteen. Tomorrow they'd planned to let the town watch them slowly fall in love so no one would ever suspect they'd been carrying on in scandal these past few weeks. Their ten-year age difference was sure to raise eyebrows no matter what, but at least it wouldn't seem quite so inappropriate.

"We'll have to wait, won't we? It's too soon to tell anyone about us with . . . with . . ." The words refused to come. Until she walked through those glass doors, she remained in denial that Jeremy was really gone.

Evan cupped her cheeks with both his strong hands, drawing her lips to his. Their kisses were flammable. Their tongues mingled; Kim moaned. Then Evan pulled away, dropping his hands to his sides. "I love you, Kimberly. Please, don't ever forget that."

The warning hung in the air. "What are you saying?"

"My best friend is dead because I couldn't save him."

"This isn't your fault." Through the crack between the brick wall and Evan's arm, Kim glimpsed a couple walking around the side of the church. "You tried to save him."

"I failed." Evan's raised voice caught the attention of the nearby couple. Their heads turned toward the alcove as they passed.

"It's not your fault," Kim said again.

Evan ran a hand through his hair, his eyes studying the brick wall until they returned to Kim's. "I'm leaving. Tonight."

"But you'll be back, right?"

"No." Evan had an established life in Willow Creek. She couldn't imagine where he planned to go. "I can't stay here, reliving my failure every day."

"Where are you going?" Kim touched a gentle hand onto his forearm. "I'll come with you."

"No." Evan slipped her hand free from his arm, intertwining his fingers with hers. "Go to college, get your degree so you can open your store. I won't let you give up your biggest dream just to follow me to Alaska."

"Alaska?"

He kissed her forehead once. "There's an opening in Fairbanks. On a Wildland fire department. They want me up there right away." Against her ear, he whispered, "I love you. I always will." After squeezing her hand, Evan dropped it and disappeared around the corner, heading back toward the church entrance.

Her legs collapsed beneath her. Her hands and rapid tears slapped the pavement. Hidden in the alcove, desolation and disbelief twisted in her stomach. Kim couldn't bear to go inside.

Chapter 1

Five years later . . .

"That's it!" Kim slapped her desk with both hands and caused poor Doris to jump half a foot behind her. She should explain her outburst, especially since the frail woman already trembled in her squeaky rolling chair. But Kim was preoccupied with the ludicrous email on her computer. *Dry cleaning? I'm supposed to pick up his damned laundry for his executive trip to Alaska?*

She shoved away from her desk and glanced at the one reminder that this was all temporary—the purple and turquoise logo for her future floral shop, The Twisted Tulip. Her dream was so close to becoming a reality that she could nearly put up with anything to see it through.

"Stupid Alaska," she muttered. Rocketing from her chair, Kim took a deep breath. She had planned to wait two more months before quitting. It was the only full-time job she'd held, and her paychecks were funding her startup costs for her future store.

She locked eyes with a framed picture of her and her best friend, Allie. It and the logo of her future were the only personal items at her desk. She'd never planned to stay at Reddington Shipping & Storage longer than necessary. Certainly not long enough to decorate her sad little cubicle with homemade calendars, family photos, or trinkets.

Originally, she sought this position to gain valuable business experience. Kim liked that it was a smaller branch—four employees, five if you counted Jed, the janitor—of a larger company, one specializing in accounts receivable for customers all over the country. *Including a new one in Anchorage.* When thoughts of Evan fighting fires in the Alaskan wilderness tried to trickle in, she forced them away. *Time for action.*

Kim felt Doris peeking over the top of her cubicle as she stood, prepared to beat down Todd Crawley's door with her fists. For months she'd put up with his arrogant attitude and demeaning behavior. The urge to let Crawley have a piece of her mind grew larger every day that she tolerated the worst manager in the history of the corporate world. Her vision blurred to a hazy red.

She'd bitten her tongue, mostly, and now she felt nanoseconds from erupting.

Two inches from his door, Kim had an epiphany.

"Doris, hold down the fort. I have some errands to run. *For Todd.*"

She swiped her keys off her desk and whisked out the front door to her dependable Little Green Car.

Todd would be out in front of her desk demanding the end-of-the-month income report the second she pulled onto the main road to fetch his stupid suit, despite his delusional ideas—like Kim doubling as his personal assistant. She had been naïve enough to offer him help once with those reports when she was new and he seemed overworked. *Dry cleaning.* She seethed.

Racing through Norfolk, Nebraska's afternoon traffic, Kim shook her head. At one time, she believed the harder you worked, the further you'd climb. Even if the corporate ladder of Reddington's little branch equated to no more than a stepstool.

When she picked up Todd's suit, it was already zipped in its black garment bag. She didn't have long to pull this off, but if she was quitting, she was quitting with a bang, damn it. She owed it to those other employees crushed beneath Todd's bony finger. Even Jed, the janitor. If someone didn't take a stand now, those poor cubicle workers would never have the courage after she left.

Bursting into her tiny apartment, Kim nearly tripped over a box of old watering cans. She kicked it aside and rushed to the washer. Unzipping the garment bag, she dropped in Todd's precious black suit. Shoving aside a dusty basket she stored on the stackable washer and dryer, she found the bleach hiding behind it—and emptied the bottle into the washer.

Then she uncapped a red permanent marker and tossed it in for good measure.

"Where have you been?" Todd demanded the moment Kim walked past. His face and neck were red, his thin hair sticking up in the back from having run his hands through it so much. "I've been trying to reach you for over two hours!"

The end-of-the-month report was Todd's responsibility, but he seemed to have forgotten how to run them since Kim stepped up. What he hadn't forgotten how to do, however, was take the credit when he passed on those reports to the big boss in Houston. "Calm down, Stick Boy. Here's your precious suit." Kim hung the bag from one of his coat hooks, biting back an outburst that begged release.

"Excuse me?" Fire raged in Todd's eyes. Or maybe it was just red lines of stress. His report was due in ten minutes.

She forced a sweet smile. "You all packed for Alaska? I hear there are these giant grizzlies that eat scrawny men for snacks." Todd was tall, at least 6'3", maybe an inch more, and skinnier than a pencil. Kim was certain she had more muscle in her pinky finger than that man had on his entire skeletal frame.

Todd's face dropped. "There aren't any bears in Anchorage. It's a city."

Kim shrugged. "Guess sometimes bears get bored and wander into town. Take a picture if you see one, will you?" She patted him on the shoulder. "I better get *your report* done so the big boss doesn't revoke your vacation."

"It's a corporate trip."

"Sure it is." Kim spun around, flying back to her desk. She caught Doris' eye again. The timid woman caught her sliding glasses with her index finger and watched from behind the safety of her cubicle wall.

Todd slammed his office door. He couldn't stand not appearing the bigger, tougher man in all situations. Jed the janitor poked his head in from the hallway, halting his mopping and adjusting his worn ball cap.

"Ass hat," Kim mumbled.

"Did it really take you two and a half hours to pick up his dry cleaning?" Meek Doris asked with a voice so quiet from behind Kim it was barely audible.

Kim turned in time to watch Doris' oversized glasses fall from her nose again. "No, Doris." She suspected she had limited time before Todd unzipped his garment bag. He wouldn't be able to resist the urge to gaze longingly at his precious suit slotted for his fancy-schmancy trip. She needed to be miles away when that happened. "For future reference, Doris, *never* pick up your manager's dry cleaning unless your job title includes personal assistant."

Signing back on to her computer, Kim found six unread emails that she'd received from Todd during her dry-cleaning run. "And even then," she added over her shoulder, "he'd better be a millionaire."

The deadline for the end-of-the month report was now only seven minutes away.

Ordinarily, she sent the reports directly to Crawley. The CEO didn't know that anyone else ever saw those reports, much less generated them. Those reports were the reason Todd was chosen to join the select few on their trip to Alaska.

Earlier that morning, Kim had finished up the monthly report. She'd sat on it simply to let Todd sweat. Now, she mentally patted herself on the back.

In a separate window, she opened a new email screen, addressed it to the big boss in Houston, and copied Todd. Kim began to type:

Mr. Reddington,

Attached you will find your end-of-the-month income report for the Accounts Receivable branch in Norfolk. I apologize that you're receiving this report so last minute. Normally, I have them finished first thing in the morning, but today I had to make sure Mr. Crawley was all ready for his trip up north. Please note that beginning next month, he will be generating these reports himself. It's been over a year, but I think he will be okay. Our Todd is a man of many talents.

I regret to inform you that this will be my last day. Mr. Reddington, I appreciate the opportunities this company has granted me, but I can no longer work under the management of Mr. Crawley. I'm not his personal assistant, but he hasn't come to realize that.

Kim sat back, rereading the email once to check for typos. When satisfied, she hit the send button and powered down her computer.

Shoving her minimal belongings in her purse, she looked over her shoulder. "Doris, remember what I said."

At the receptionist's desk, she paused.

"Leaving, Ms. Wilkerson?" Alice asked with a tilted head, ignoring a ringing phone. It dawned on Kim she might not see this woman again outside of a grocery store or post office after today.

"For the last time—and I do mean last—it's *Kim*, Alice. And yes, I'm leaving. Not coming back."

The receptionist looked down the hall toward Todd's office as the phone continued to ring. "What are you waiting for?" A worried expression washed over her freckled face.

Not to disappoint, Kim heard the ear-piercing scream, one that could rival a little girl's in a horror movie. She smiled, victorious, as she flew out the front door and raced to her car.

A box of chocolate cupcakes from Kim's favorite bakery sat open on her passenger seat as she zipped through town, headed home. It'd been a long time since she had an entire afternoon free and she wasn't about to waste it. She planned to binge watch *The Next Great*

Baker and conduct an inventory. Her tiny apartment had become overrun with possible floral arrangement containers, ribbons, pins, and odds and ends she'd picked up from garage sales, thrift stores, and even a few found while Dumpster diving. *Not that anyone needs to know that.*

Taking a big bite of cupcake at a stoplight, she jumped at the shrill ring of her cell phone. *I really need to change that ring tone.* Her realtor's number flashed on the screen. Inhaling the cupcake with free her hand, then swallowing, she answered her phone on speaker and set it on her leg. "Talk to me, Debbie." In her mirror, she spotted a smudge of chocolate frosting smeared along her cheek.

"Who's the best realtor in the world?"

"Shut up!" Kim squealed. She swiped the icing from her cheek. "Shut up!"

"That space you've been eyeing on Norfolk Avenue is finally coming on the market in two months. Okay, I'm not just the greatest realtor in the world. I'm the best damn one in the universe. They're willing to let you make the first offer two months from now, before they even announce it's coming up. You and me, we're the only ones who know anything."

Kim felt like fainting from her delirious excitement. *Could this day get any better?* "You. Are. Amazing!" At the next stoplight, she banged excitedly on her steering wheel, scaring a child in the next car over.

"They won't consider any other offers until late October. They promised you a two-week exclusive window to negotiate terms."

She wondered vaguely what had become of the blue-haired woman who ran the gift shop in the space. "Did you have to murder someone to make this happen?" Kim asked. She jokingly hoped Debbie hadn't done anything illegal.

"Let's just say I have connections."

She heard a beep on the other end and glanced down at her phone to spy her sister's name on the screen. Macy would surely want to ramble on and on about her precious Alaska, trying to convince Kim to come visit yet again. *Stupid Alaska. Takes everyone away from me.* She ignored the call. "Debbie, I can't thank you enough."

"Can you meet me at the space in ten?"

Kim squealed so loudly, she startled a dog this time. The Doberman barked as if Kim was coddling a cat he wanted. "Really? I get to *see* it?" Kim rolled up her window in delight and stuck her tongue out at the dog as the light turned green. "I'm on my way."

Spinning a full circle in the empty commercial space, Kim shrieked. "This is perfect!" She faced Debbie. Her realtor was always fashionably dressed in one pantsuit or another. Today a dark teal number showed off her slender waist and shoulders broad enough to take out a linebacker.

Debbie worked out twice a day in a CrossFit gym, whatever that was. Sounded terrifying to Kim. If the rumors were true, the woman was as ambitious and aggressive in commercial real estate as she was in the gym. It was a trait Kim admired more with each passing second spent inside the building that would soon house The Twisted Tulip! *Her* very own store.

"They're bringing some things up to code right now." Debbie motioned around the space. A couple of ladders and a padlocked box of tools sat in one corner, a stack of two-by-fours piled in another. "That's why it won't be on the market right away."

For the past six months, Debbie had taken Kim to exactly fourteen different storefronts in Norfolk, either for lease or purchase. Each had its perks, but in the end, none were right. None of those spaces were *this* one. A few months ago it had been a shock to see the

Going Out of Business Sale signs. But there'd been no word on what the owners planned to do with the building when it emptied. Until now.

"Can I take one more look around?"

"Of course." Debbie's phone vibrated, and her eyes shot straight to the screen. "I've got to take this. I'll meet you outside?"

Kim's eyes traveled around the space again. The high ceilings, the tall storefront windows perfect for her unique floral displays, the stained concrete floor—everything about it screamed modern with a rustic twist. Already, she imagined her shelves along the walls.

Dashing to the back room, she envisioned it filled with accessories and the long table for assembling her arrangements. She knew which table she'd purchase to fill the middle of this room. One day, it would allow four people to work at once.

In the far corner, she spotted plumbing hookups—the ideal setup for a deep sink. It would save her money and time not having new plumbing to install.

To the right, Kim slipped through the door of a large office. An old oak desk still stood in the center of the room, proud though alone in the office. She planted her hands on the polished wood and leaned forward.

What would it be like tracking my business in this office? My *office?*

Kim's phone rang again. Mom this time. She considered ignoring it, but decided that she could perhaps share the good news with her. "Mom, you'll never believe where I'm standing right now!"

"I'm sure it's lovely, dear. Listen. I was hoping to ask for a favor."

Kim deflated. Leave it to her mom to get right down to business. Penny Wilkerson wasn't a woman who dabbled much in small talk when she had a point to get to. Still, today Kim wished she'd take the extra minute. *Should've talked to Macy instead. At least she would pretend to listen.*

"I was wondering since you stopped working at the radio station a couple of weeks ago, if you have any free time to help out at the store."

Kim tensed and tried not to squeeze her phone. She busted the plastic case of the last one that way. "Not interested. Tell Dad to stop trying to change my mind. Especially if he's not going to apologize."

"Honey, it's not your father asking."

Sure it's not. Kim hadn't been to see her parents in over two months. The last time she stopped by for supper, her dad bombarded her with his patented guilt trip. *She was the only sibling not in the military, and wouldn't she want to carry on the family legacy?*

"Sorry, Mom. I'm busy. Opening my own store soon. I have to run. My realtor's outside waiting." She hung up before Penny could try another angle. Kim didn't want her discovering she'd quit another job, freeing up additional time.

Spotting Debbie still outside, Kim slipped out the door. Once she was off the phone, Kim grinned. "It really is perfect."

"Glad you think so." Debbie offered Kim her best smile in return. "Look, you're going to have to make a strong offer. A little higher than what we talked. If you don't go in aggressive, you'll get beat out in the competition to follow."

Kim felt a slight panic creep under her skin. "Debbie, you know what my limit is. Anything more means I'll need a larger down payment."

Shoving her phone into her Kate Spade purse, Debbie eyed Kim with her signature intensity. She imagined it was the same look the woman used in the gym or when negotiating with hotheaded clients. "This is your dream space, Kim. You just need a couple thousand more. You have two months to come up with the down payment and a preapproval letter. Then this place is as good as yours."

Kim managed a weak smile and wondered if it was too late to get her job back at Reddington's.

Chapter 2

It was back. Evan gasped and shot straight up from his narrow bed. Sweat poured down his face as if he'd run a marathon. His breath was ragged, his lungs burned . . .

The nightmare replayed. Kicking in the front door, slamming into that wall of smoke. It had filled the living room like a thick, sweltering fog. Again those flames crackled as they incinerated the walls. "Jeremy, you in here?" he yelled, already coughing. Covering his mouth and nose with his shirt, he squatted below the cloud of dirty smoke.

He dropped to the ground and crawled through the carpeted living room toward the tile in the kitchen.

"Jeremy?" he yelled again.

If it hadn't been for Jeremy's old beater truck in the driveway, the one he'd been forced to drive since his Chevelle wasn't running right, Evan would've guessed he had taken the highway back to town.

Evan found him in the bedroom off the kitchen, sprawled on his bed and snoring. *Helluva time for a nap.* He didn't understand how Jeremy could sleep through smoke that was already making him sick to his stomach. Each breath seemed to fill his lungs with shards of glass. "Jeremy, let's go man!"

Shaking Jeremy proved useless. Evan hefted him onto his shoulders, crouching low and charging for the back kitchen door.

One end of a structural beam split the ceiling and crashed to the floor. Its diagonal landing blocked their exit. Flames licked every side. *Can't move it.* Evan spun, forced to find another exit.

Then everything went black.

He reached for the water bottle beside his bed and chugged. He told himself, like he did every time, that he wasn't in Willow Creek anymore. That Jeremy had been dead five years. "It was just a dream."

Before he had time to take a deep breath, a pounding came though his door. "Let's go, Rowe. Got a fire to put out."

The Casa 212 hummed as the crew of eight smokejumpers flew off south of Nenana. Some tourists had been a little too ambitious in their campfire-building efforts, the embers catching a high branch of a tree. At their last report, the blaze was still small—about five acres, maybe ten, at the base of a mountain that paralleled the river. If the crew arrived quickly and contained it, they'd prevent what could be a massive fire that would soon threaten remote homesteads.

Evan tried his best to focus on the task. In less than fifteen minutes, they'd be parachuting in. The Alaska terrain could be unforgiving if you landed in the wrong spot. In this area, there were narrow trees to avoid, and if they landed in the swampy area, the mosquitoes would make life extra miserable.

Despite trying to run through the jump procedures in his head—ones he knew in his sleep—he couldn't shake his earlier nightmare. It was the same every time. He'd kick the door in, find Jeremy snoring, start carrying him out to safety. Then, everything would go black. Just like his memory of that day.

Someone punched Evan's arm, though it didn't hurt. Their suits were like armor. It took quite a bit for anything to penetrate them, including a friendly nudge. "Let's go, Rowe," his jump partner, Carson, yelled. "We're up."

Smokejumpers always jumped in pairs, if possible. It was one way to ensure both made it safely to the ground. And another reason Evan had to shove that reoccurring nightmare out of his mind. Carson was counting on him. Maintaining full awareness, and not letting himself become distracted, were crucial.

Evan watched the spotter release a drift streamer into the air. The bright yellow crepe paper dropped, fluttered toward the east. The streamers were weighted to drift the same as a jumper might. Near the ground, the wind swept it up a bit.

Carson sat at the door first. After a pat on the back from the spotter, he let his body fall from the plane. Evan followed suit, tucking his body tight as he freefell into the air. Most would call him crazy for jumping out of an airplane near a fire, but it had become a way of life for him.

Evan counted to four. *Check canopy, check partner, check jump spot.* Deploying his chute, he maneuvered through the smoke, aiming toward the streamers that designated the landing spot. Carson was already on the ground.

The fire, though small, raged less than half a mile away. It looked like its own miniature weather system, dark gray clouds hovering over a concentrated area, orange flames sweeping through the vegetation at the bottom. The waft of smoke invaded Evan's senses, stinging his eyes.

Less than two hundred feet from the ground, Jeremy's face flickered before him again. One quick flash, a smile from that same morning. They'd been working together at Loomis Manufacturing. Jeremy clapped him on the back.

Evan tried to shake away the memory, but it was too late.

A patch of small, narrow trees stuck out like daggers; there was no way to avoid them. Evan steered toward the largest one. If he could maneuver his chute to the top of it, he could secure himself and repel down.

No luck. His lines caught on the pointed tops of two trees, leaving him dangling in the air between. "Damn it," he muttered. Every second he was stuck was two he was wasting.

He didn't need to tie anyone else's time up, and began swinging himself. Hopefully he'd arc wide enough to grab one or the other. Within three swings, he latched onto a small branch and managed to hug the trunk of the larger tree.

He unclipped himself from his chute. He'd have to come back for it later, once the fire was dealt with. Right now, there was work to be done.

Testing his footing, he felt confident climbing down would be little trouble. He increased his speed, knowing he had to hurry. They still had half a mile through marshy grounds to hike before they could start containing the fire.

Evan descended with such momentum that he didn't hear the branch snap beneath his foot. His fall landed him hard, a good fifteen feet below. He smacked branches on the way down. One pierced his thick suit, low on his leg. He cursed loud and thoroughly right before the wind got knocked out of him.

Lying on his back, he heard Carson coming for him. "Rowe, you all right, man?"

"Fine." Evan tried to stand, but he underestimated how hard a hit he'd taken. He nearly toppled. As it was, Carson had to steady him. "Just a little pride hurt." He grimaced. "That's all. Let's get going."

That first step sent a searing pain straight up from his calf. He bit back a scream that threatened to escape. Something wasn't right. Looking down, he saw it—a branch sticking out from his suit. He'd have to wait until the supplies landed. Now that the last jumpers had cleared the plane, the supplies would be next. He'd need the first aid kit to stop the bleeding.

"That looks like it might be an issue, Rowe." Carson pointed to the branch.

"It's fine." If there was one thing smokejumpers were, it was tough. Evan had met many who endured worse in the line of duty. Hell, he'd met one guy who put out a fire with a broken ankle. He wasn't about to complain about this small puncture wound.

When the supplies dropped, Evan dug through the box, discarding the food he should be grabbing. If he waited too long, he'd be left with the worst MREs in the crate. But the first aid kit was more urgent right now. Snatching it, he hobbled to a rock.

Evan bit down on his leather glove and pulled it off. With his other hand, he grabbed the branch and yanked it free before he had time to consider the painful after-effects of that move.

"Rowe, that looks pretty bad." Carson hovered, his eyebrows drawn.

"It's just a stick." Evan went to work, shoving a wad of gauze at the wound to staunch the blood flow. Within seconds, it was soaked red, leaving Evan a little lightheaded. He hadn't expected a stick to do *that* much damage.

"Then get it wrapped up and let's go," his partner said.

Fighting the dizziness, Evan cleaned up the wound the best he could and wrapped it tightly. Standing nearly caused him to go blind. It was a pain he'd never experienced before. Incredible and horrific, as if an icicle had shattered inside his calf.

"Rowe?"

"I'm fine." He pushed on, grabbed his pack and pulled his gloves back on. They had a fire to put out. If they didn't manage it now while it was still small, all it took was one gust of wind and the fire would risk lives. It might head right for the small village only a couple of miles away. "Let's go."

Against his will, Evan was chauffeured to the emergency room on Fort Wainwright, an Army post in the heart of Alaska. He'd helped put out the fire, and then hiked the three miles to the Parks Highway for their ride home. By that point, he had begun dipping in and out of consciousness.

"You're a tough son of bitch," Carson said when they found the road. "Your pack's got to be over a hundred twenty pounds."

A new personal record. Evan should have smiled at that prospect. Most jumpers carried obscenely heavy packs. They had no choice. Some fires kept them out for several days or even weeks. That pack had to contain everything they needed not only to fight the fire, but to survive in the wilderness while doing it.

"Rowe, when we get back, you're going straight to the hospital."

Evan wanted to argue, but it was all he could manage to fight back tears. The pain had grown increasingly intolerable. He wanted to show everyone, including himself, that he was tougher than this. But he passed out before they reached Fairbanks.

Chief Benson stood next to the exam table as the doctor returned with the prognosis. Evan wished it hadn't come to this, being escorted by his superior. If the news wasn't good, he'd prefer to keep it hidden. He was born to put out fires. But the look on the doctor's face was gloomy at best.

"Can he jump?" Chief Benson asked, straight to the point, as always.

The doctor stared, as if the chief had asked if Evan would grow a third arm. "Not anytime soon. Most injuries to this muscle involve athletes tearing or pulling it. But Evan here actually punctured a hole right through his soleus."

"What if I do?" Evan asked. "What if I jump again?" Because he had to know. It was only late August. The fire season wasn't over. There was still a month or more before the snow would fly to help lessen the threat.

"Jump? One *good* landing could cripple your entire leg." The doctor scribbled some notes on his clipboard. "Not only would you never jump after that, you'd be lucky to walk." Evan felt his stomach slam toward the table. "Look, if you take a few months off the muscle will heal over time. You'll need physical therapy, and you'll need to take it easy. Respect the healing process your body needs. If you listen, you might be ready to jump again as early as next spring."

Evan looked at the chief.

"Sorry, Rowe. As of right now, you're off jump status. I can't risk you crippling yourself indefinitely. I need you for the long haul."

"Chief, please. I've jumped hundreds of times. You know I know how to land."

"Not negotiable, Rowe."

"What am I supposed to do until next spring? Join a volunteer department?"

"No," the doctor interrupted, ripping the prescription from his pad and shoving it at Evan.

"I can't fight fires at all?"

"Not right now. You need a few weeks away from dangerous work. Any misstep at a fire call, no matter how trivial it seems, could be the end of your career. Take some time off." The doctor's words burned more than his ripped muscle. "I don't care what you do." The doctor went on, in spite of Evan's twisted expression. "Sit on the couch and watch TV. Learn to knit. So long as it's not causing your leg unnecessary strain."

He wouldn't hear of it. "I heard the department off the Steese is looking for help." Evan felt like fighting now.

"Listen to the good doctor, okay?" Chief Benson suggested, patting Evan's shoulder. "I'll make sure no departments up here take you until you're cleared."

"You don't have any desk work?" Evan knew he was grasping at straws, but the idea of sitting in his cabin, trapped with only his thoughts and those nightmares, made him desperate.

"No. Why don't you go home, Rowe? You said it's been a while. How long?"

Evan regretted ever talking about his family, but the group of jumpers was close. "Five years."

"Go home," the doctor chimed in.

"I'll take it easy," he promised. Returning to Willow Creek was out of the question.

Five weeks and several physical therapy sessions later, Evan tossed the last duffle bag in the backseat of his truck. It was amazing how little he owned, but as a jumper, keeping too many possessions had never made sense. The less he could survive on, the better. What few items he had—a mattress, a couch, and some heavy winter gear—he left behind in his small cabin south of Fairbanks.

The nightmares had grown unbearable, forcing his hand. If there was any hope of jumping again next season, he had to find a way to stop them. He couldn't afford that kind of distraction. Next time it might just get him killed. The only true hope he had for putting the horrific memories to rest was to go back to Willow Creek and face his past.

Turning onto the Richardson Highway, Evan tried to relax. He'd be able to return to Alaska in a few weeks. He knew a few jumpers in their mid-forties, giving him reassurance that the job would still be there waiting when he returned.

Evan thought the drive would help him prepare for what was ahead, but he was still tense. Other than his brother Alex, he'd not seen anyone from his hometown in five years. That was only because his brother came up to Alaska two years ago to go fishing. There were many people who would be happy to see him, he reasoned. And as many who wanted nothing to do with him.

His mom had let him know what she thought of his staying away from Nebraska for so long with each clipped phone conversation. His little sister Hannah, now a teenager, refused to talk to him at all.

As the miles of Alaskan wilderness rolled by, he wondered if Kimberly still visited Willow Creek. He imagined her sitting at the kitchen table in Violet Wilkerson's kitchen, eating a piece of cherry pie and tinkering with some flower arrangement. He let himself smile before the dark thoughts washed over him.

His leaving had hurt Kimberly most of all.

Chapter 3

In the past month, Kim had picked up as many extra shifts as she could, but it hadn't quite been enough. She stared at her latest paycheck from her last remaining part-time job at a floral counter in Norfolk's largest grocery store, wishing it contained an extra zero at the end.

She had too much pride to go back to Reddington's and ask for her job back. Todd had called her at least twice a day—every day—since she left. He'd filled her voicemail inbox two weeks ago. By leaving the old messages there, she prevented him from leaving new ones. But not from calling. Or texting. Or sending emails. *When's the carrier pigeon going to show up?*

Kim had two choices. The first: agree to return to Reddington's, demanding extra pay and less interference from Todd. Within a month, though, she'd just quit again. If she did go back she wouldn't feel bad about leaving Todd, but she'd send mixed signals to the others. She'd driven by the office two days ago and recognized Doris' car in the parking lot. She felt a small pang of sadness that the meek woman had yet to find her courage and walk out too.

The second choice . . . Kim took a deep breath and prepared to make the call. Maybe her sister would lend her the money. Macy had been bragging about all she'd saved from her last deployment, and about the four-wheeler she'd been able to buy with cash. Kim only needed a thousand more to make her down payment. Her brother, Kyle, had already admitted he'd spent all his money on his new flashy truck. Macy was her last hope.

I'll probably have to agree to visit her.

Before Kim could scroll to Macy's number, her mom's name flashed on the screen. Though eager for any distraction that meant prolonging this call to her sister, Kim pushed ignore. *Call you back tonight, Mom.*

In the kitchen, she snatched the last cupcake and set it in front of her on the counter. She could eat it *after* she called Macy.

Again, her mom's name appeared. Kim grumbled, and ignored the call again. "Sorry, Mom. I'm not coming back to Willow Creek to help out at the store. I know it's just Dad's secret ploy to recruit me."

Kim transferred the cupcake to a small plate and peeled back the blue polka-dotted wrapper. She dug a fork out of a drawer, in denial that she knew she was stalling.

Macy could be a little bossy, claiming her additional three years were packed full of wisdom since she joined the Army and became a Blackhawk helicopter pilot. If that didn't sound heroic and awesome enough, she also tended to brag about her wonderful life being stationed in freaking beautiful Alaska.

Kim took her time and sliced her cupcake in half with meticulous precision. Macy had a way of making her life seem like the ultimate accomplishment and Kim's life the epitome of failure. "Maybe just one bite, for motivation." *And tolerance.* She shaved a sliver from it with her fork and savored the bite as if it was her last.

The third time her mom's name blinked on the screen, Kim heaved a sigh. "Geez, Mom!" She swiped her phone from the counter. "Mom, can I call you back later? I'm—"

"It's about damned time you picked up your phone! Did you know your voicemail is full?" With the amount of irritation coming through the phone, Kim expected the lights in her apartment to flicker. Even at her angriest, it was rare for her mom to curse. Considering she'd lived with Kim's dad the past thirty years, that was quite the distinguishing accomplishment.

"Mom, what's wrong?"

"It's your dad."

Here we go again. "What now?"

"Something happened."

Her mom's tone caused her to set the fork on the counter. "What exactly?"

"Nothing major. Well, not really."

"Mom!"

"You'd better come down to the hospital."

Hospital? For the first time, guilt crept in. Her dad had a way of driving a person to the edge. She'd wanted to prove a point by making him apologize for his last outburst. But neither had wished the other into the hospital.

Plans to watch *Property Brothers* shoved aside, Kim considered packing an overnight bag. Though Willow Creek and its dinky one-story hospital were a short half-hour drive away, she knew it could be a late night.

"Let me grab a few things. I have to finish something." She eyed her cupcake, and decided the call with Macy would have to wait. *No sense in wasting a perfectly good cupcake, though.* "Give me an hour to get to Willow Creek. What room is he in?"

"We're here in Norfolk, honey. Your dad had a heart attack."

The last time Kim had stepped foot in the Norfolk hospital was the day she lost her cousin, Jeremy. It must have been more serious than Mom let on if Chip was transferred here, to this larger facility. Only critical patients were transported from Willow Creek. Clutching her binder to her chest, she asked for directions to her dad's room.

Knocking on the door of Room 103, Kim let herself inside in time for the doctor's lecture.

"Stress. Too much stress." The doctor, a man who looked more like a twelve-year-old boy playing dress-up, stood at the foot of the hospital bed. "Mr. Wilkerson, if you don't do something immediately to alleviate this burden, you're going to have another cardiac episode. And I'm afraid the next one will be much more serious."

"I've been telling you for months," Penny said. "You need time off."

A pang of guilt shot through Kim. She slid her binder onto the floral patterned couch. Her mom had asked for her help more than a month ago. Wanted her to come back to that tiny dot on the map.

Chip grumbled from his bed and refused to meet anyone's eyes. His wrinkles seemed heavier with his larger-than-usual frown. "Then *who's* going to run the store?" With an IV tube in his arm, he looked more vulnerable than Kim had ever seen him.

Kim had a feeling that comment had some special reservation for her. Another hint as subtle as a bomb that she was supposed to be the sibling that took over. But she tapered down the argument, the one they'd started weeks ago. There were more important things now than being right about Wilkerson's Grocery. Besides, getting kicked out of the hospital for causing another heart attack wouldn't help anyone.

Bags sat under Penny's worn hazel eyes. "Not you if the next heart attack *kills* you."

Chip Wilkerson could be hardheaded and downright grumpy on a good day. But Kim had never met two people more resilient than her parents. They'd run that grocery store for nearly thirty years, conquering any obstacle that arose. Seeing them now, both weakened and ragged, frightened her. Her dad could have died today.

Luckily, he's too stubborn for that.

"I don't care what you figure out, but you need to do something drastic now or there won't be a later to argue about," the doctor interjected into their grumblings.

44

"Mr. Wilkerson, I'm ordering you to take four weeks off."

"Four weeks!" Chip nearly flew out of his bed, but Penny jumped up from the couch in a flash to shove him back down by the shoulder.

The doctor sighed, exasperated from the circles he'd no doubt argued before Kim entered the room. "You're not to step foot inside that grocery store, understand?"

Chip sat up straighter in his bed. He yanked a paper cup from his tray, splashing some of its contents on his wrist. "No, I don't understand, Doc. And I don't think you do, either. Because if you did, you'd understand that four weeks away from that store means it closes."

Tears hung in Penny's eyes. "I won't let that happen." Her soft words were drowned out by the hum of the machines surrounding Chip.

"What about you?" Kid Doctor stared at Kim until she met his eyes. "Can you help your mom out at the store?"

"I'll pay you. More than your office job." Her mom grasped the metal railing of her dad's hospital bed, her knuckles fading to white.

"Showing up once a week for an hour won't cut it," Chip interjected. "Your mother needs someone reliable."

Willing herself to ignore his baiting, Kim said, "Of course I'll help, Mom."

Chip snorted at that comment. "Sure you will."

"I *will*. We're family." She'd avoided helping out at the grocery store for years, convinced even one day would somehow trap her there indefinitely. But she would not let her mom work herself into exhaustion.

Penny rose from the edge of the hospital bed, hugging her daughter in a vise-grip. *This is what it must've been like to wear a girdle.*

"What about your other jobs?" Chip wore a smug look, fishing for a moment that would unravel Kim's noble intentions.

She hadn't told them that she quit her full-time job. Her parents wouldn't understand the victory or practicality in that seemingly spontaneous and freeing decision. "I'll work it out."

"Thank you, Kimmie." Penny finally let go of her daughter and returned to her spot at the edge of her husband's bed.

"I'll stay in Willow Creek for a couple of weeks. I might need some time off to meet with the bank and make an offer on the building." Kim waited, hoping one of her parents would ask what she was talking about. She glanced at the binder sitting behind her. She'd meant to show her mom her plans for The Twisted

Tulip tonight, thinking her dad would be resting, maybe sedated.

"We'll work it out," Penny answered.

Even a glimpse at Kid Doctor was hopeless. She gave up on anyone feigning interest in her soon-to-be greatest life accomplishment. "I'll stay with Gram."

"Good," the doctor said. "Sounds like that's all settled. Now, I mean it, Mr. Wilkerson. You don't go near that store until I've cleared you in four weeks." At the door, he turned to Kim. "I'm counting on you to make sure he stays out."

Kim sent him a salute. "Roger."

Once the door clicked shut, leaving the three of them alone, Penny asked, "Honey, are you absolutely sure? I would understand—"

"It's fine, Mom. Someone needs to duct tape Dad to his recliner so he isn't trying to sneak into the store."

"That'll be Macy's job."

"Macy? You're not getting that girl out of Alaska, Mom." Kim's sister had been one of the smart siblings, joining the Army and escaping the family legacy by heroic default. She'd missed Christmas last year so she could explore some skiing town up there. Lucky her, watching the Northern Lights from a hot tub. Kim doubted her sister would sacrifice vacation time to come back now, especially when Kim had already volunteered.

"I called her earlier. She'll be on a plane Thursday morning."

"What about Kyle?" she asked. "I know he isn't doing anything." *Except probably sleeping his way through his new duty station.*

"Kyle has training for the next month. Somewhere in California. So it's on you girls."

"If I had known this was what it took to get you to learn the family business, I'd have had a heart attack years ago," Chip said now that the doctor was out of earshot. He reached for his cup of water. "Too bad I won't be around to teach you anything useful. Maybe from the house I can—"

"No!" both Penny and Kim shouted.

"Chip, I know that store as well as you do." Penny crossed her arms, offense glistening in her narrowed eyes. "We'll handle things just fine. The doors will still be open in four weeks."

"Maybe after that I can teach you a couple of things," Chip said to Kim.

"Let's make one thing clear." Kim forced a smile. "I'll help Mom out while you're on house arrest. But that's it. Sorry, Dad, but I'm not Jeremy. Owning a grocery store was never on my bucket list. After four weeks, I'm back in Norfolk. I have my own business to start."

Chip sputtered some kind of mocking laugh.

Kim yanked her binder off the couch, presenting it to her parents. "I actually have the perfect space—"

"That's nice, dear." Penny dismissed Kim's binder with its purple and turquoise logo. "We open at eight tomorrow. Can you be there that early?"

"I'll go home and pack a bag." Heading toward the door, Kim knew she should have given her dad a hug, but it'd just give him the chance to squeeze in one last jab. And that might finally set her off. "I'll see you at the store tomorrow, Mom. Dad—listen to the doctor. Because if you don't, Macy and I *will* strap you down to some heavy furniture. I'm sure the Army taught her how to tie a few good knots."

Slipping out the door, Kim practically ran to her car. "Just get through this," she mumbled to herself in the parking lot, dusk falling around her. "Get through these few weeks to save the last bit of money. That's all you have to do, Kimmie. Then wow the bank with the most epic business plan and vision they've ever seen."

Chapter 4

Kim parked in the small graveled lot off the alley behind Wilkerson's Grocery. Though twenty minutes early, she wasn't surprised to see her mom's Equinox stationed in its usual spot, left of the back door. No doubt Penny had been at the store for over an hour already.

With a yawn, Kim grabbed her half-empty coffee cup and headed inside through a heavy metal door she hadn't used since she was a teenager.

A straight path led directly to the store where the heavy saloon-style doors separated the back area from the customer side. The lights inside were still dim. "Mom?"

On one side sat stacked boxes of peanut butter, cake mixes, toilet paper, cleaning supplies, and a few pallets of cereal. On the north side, a staircase led to the office upstairs. Knowing her mom would be there, probably drafting the schedule or preparing to place this week's order, Kim headed that way.

"Mom?" Kim hollered at the top of the staircase, ensuring she wouldn't startle her. "You up here?"

"In the office."

The old brick building had at one time been two separate, narrow but deep storefronts on Willow Creek's main street. Several decades ago, Kim's grandfather purchased the second building and knocked out walls to expand the store space downstairs.

"I'm here. Put me to work!"

The office encompassed the entire back portion of the north side, the one that sat on the corner of Main and Sixth. On the south side, the open space behind a wall of brick collected old sale and product advertisements, holiday decorations, and dust.

"Mom, did you sleep at all last night?" Penny's normally perfectly styled hair was held back in a frazzled ponytail with a tied bandana headband.

Penny dismissed the concern with a wave of her hand. "Your father is worse than the three of you kids combined when he's incapacitated." Scooting back her rolling chair, the whine of metal wheels screeched through the otherwise quiet building. Kim remembered her grandfather, gone more than a decade, in that same chair when she was a little girl begging for free cream soda. "Today is inventory day."

A few years ago, Kim would've groaned at this assignment. The dreaded inventory day was one she used to avoid by faking the flu or insisting Gram needed help weeding her garden. Now that she'd been planning how to run her own store, the prospect didn't feel so daunting. *This might be better than an office job.* "Where's the clipboard?"

Pulling open a drawer on her old but sturdy metal desk, Penny drew out a hand scanner.

"Whoa, what is that?" Shocked, Kim let her mouth hang open. "Don't tell me you convinced Dad to join the twenty-first century!" Inventory, for as long as she could remember, had been printed out from an ancient computer with little blank lines she filled in by hand after manually counting each item.

"Let's just say your father doesn't know everything that happens in this store." Penny smiled, revealing laugh lines at the corners of her eyes. "I bought this two years ago."

"Two years?" Kim set down her coffee cup and reached for the scanner. "How have you hidden it from him all this time? Doesn't he do the books?" With a push of a button, the scanner flashed on. A fancy screen with multiple options appeared, one labeled 'inventory'.

Penny sent a cunning smile to her daughter. "We both do the books. I just filed it under a . . . different name."

"What? Mom!"

"I called it a feminine products order."

Kim burst out in laughter. "That's brilliant!"

"And true. Only women have ever used it in this store." Penny closed the ledger, dropping her pencil on the desk. "Welcome to our secret club. You just scan the label's barcode and enter the count on the shelf. Super simple." Penny shut the drawer and reached for her purse. "I have to stop home and make sure your dad's asleep. In a couple days, Macy'll be here to take over that duty."

Kim shook her head. "I can't believe you actually convinced her to come home. She's like the poster child for the glories of Alaska. I think she sold her soul to the state. Didn't she say something about never leaving unless it was in a casket or a straightjacket?"

"Doesn't mean she'd turn her back on family." Penny adjusted the strap of her canvas purse. "I don't think you give her enough credit, you know."

Sure, I *don't give* her *enough credit.* "Too bad Kyle couldn't make it." Kim emptied her coffee cup and dropped it in the trashcan.

"Well, the Army has other plans for your brother this month. I thought sending a Red Cross message might be a little over the top." Penny squeezed Kim's shoulder. "Thank you for helping, Kimmie."

"Maybe I could stop by tonight." Kim followed her mom downstairs. "I want to tell you about my new building. Well, it's not mine yet, but—"

"Let's do it another night," Penny interrupted, her tone soft. "Your dad is still getting adjusted to being home."

At the foot of the stairs, Kim bit the inside of her bottom lip. She wanted to share her exciting news with her family, but it'd have to wait.

"Wilma—Wilma Gentry, you remember her right?— she'll be here any minute to run the register." Penny didn't give Kim a chance to answer. "You focus on inventory until I get back. As long as Dad's resting, I won't be gone long." She stopped at the back door. "Oh, I have some errands to run, too. You'll be able to handle the store for a few hours, right?"

"What if something goes wrong?" *What if the customers fight over the last Digiorno or someone tries to rob the place?*

"I have my phone. Call me."

Kim nodded. The least she could do for her mom was accommodate some time off. She could show Penny

54

her binder in a few days, once they found a steady rhythm with the store and Dad's new home life.

At the bottom of the stairs, Penny swung around. "Whatever you do, do *not* call your father, understood?"

Sending her mom a salute, Kim asked, "What do I do if he shows up?"

"Shouldn't be a problem today, honey. I added a heavy dose of melatonin to his breakfast shake. Did you know they sell them in ten milligrams?" The twinkle in Penny's eyes was the first sign of relief Kim had seen this morning. "With any luck, he'll sleep through the evening news."

Half an aisle into inventory, Kim snapped a picture on her phone of the scanner model, already planning to purchase one for her store. As long as the register didn't break down or the place didn't start on fire, Kim thought she might just survive playing business owner today.

Evan was tired of driving. The throbbing in his calf had mostly subsided, or at least dulled enough that he barely noticed it anymore. *Thanks, Doctor Langdon, for all that painful physical therapy.*

From the highway, he wasn't sure whether he was happy to see Willow Creek come into sight or if he dreaded it. Five days on the road, most of it in Canada, was enough. But now that he was so close, he had the urge to turn around a mile from town and head back to Fairbanks.

An hour ago he'd called his brother, Alex, to let him know he'd be in town for a few days. Alex, a special investigator for the state patrol, had seen right through his unspoken anxiety about facing his past. "You'll be fine," he'd assured him as Evan rode a bridge over the Missouri River into the northern border of Nebraska. "No one blames you, you know."

Evan wanted to say *I blame me*, but instead he shuffled the phone to his right hand and read a sign welcoming him to *The Good Life*.

"I'll be in town tomorrow," Alex added. "Maybe we should have supper at Mom's?"

"Sure."

"Okay, now I know you're thinking of turning around. Even five years ago, going to Mom's for supper was something you avoided worse than a blind date."

I'm overdue. "What time?"

"She's not happy you've been gone this long." At Alex's long pause, Evan studied the miles of gently rolling hills filled with lush crops. The corn had grown

56

higher than he ever remembered seeing it. Or had he just been gone that long? "At least Russ won't be there."

Evan considered asking why his stepfather wouldn't be around, but he was too relieved to question it. He and Russ had never seen things the same way, especially when it came to Evan's little sister, Hannah. It didn't matter if they had different fathers, Evan would always consider her true family. Russ argued the latter.

Alex asked, "Where are you staying?"

"I'll figure that out in a couple hours. Got something to take care of first."

An hour later, when Evan turned onto Main Street, he cringed, then mentally berated himself. If he wanted to hide out for a few days, driving his big truck down the busiest road in town was probably the wrong approach. Not much hope of keeping people ignorant of his return while showcasing his Alaska license plates.

Crawling along at the reduced speed limit, Evan surveyed Main Street, noticing how much had stayed the same. One antique store had closed, and the front of the post office had received a facelift. But otherwise, the town of Willow Creek looked the same as it always had. Inviting and, well, *like home*.

Evan dismissed the thought. At one time, he'd planned to start a life here. But that time had passed.

He'd do well to apologize for the pain his abrupt departure had caused and be on his way.

He hoped his nightmares would stop once he made peace with those he deserted. He had another one only two nights ago, while sleeping in his truck in a parking lot of a Canadian Tire in Saskatchewan.

A few people gave him the index-finger wave from their cars. He wanted to believe their friendliness was a good omen, but people waved to everyone in this town. Even outsiders. Others tilted their heads from the sidewalk as they read his plate. He recognized one man, Tim Hollander. They'd spent time on the volunteer fire department together. In fact, Tim had encouraged Evan to join in the first place. Best decision he ever made. He'd have to tell Tim that before he left town.

At the north edge of Willow Creek, Evan turned west, away from the school, and drove until the pavement turned to gravel on Rural Road 865. Shortly after the skitter of rocks began to bounce off his tires, the familiar patch of trees came into view on the left side of the road. Violet Wilkerson lived a little less than a mile from town. A distance he'd walked or ridden on his bicycle many times as a boy, often with Jeremy after school let out.

"She never blamed you, either," Alex had told him during their phone call earlier, when Evan mentioned stopping by Violet's house first. "But she was hurt that you left without warning and never came back. A lot of people were."

Evan didn't have any surviving grandparents in Willow Creek. He did have a great aunt who everyone called Aunt Ruby, but it was no secret that Alex was her favorite. Almost by default, Violet became the grandmother he never had. He and Jeremy had spent countless hours taking care of her lawn, repairing her clocks and small appliances, and eating enough homemade pie to feed a small country.

Before Evan put his truck into park, he spotted Violet standing with folded arms. He glanced around the property, mostly to avoid whatever look was in her eyes. Evan noticed the shingles seemed a little ragged, and the west side of the house looked as if it needed a new coat of paint.

Cutting the ignition and opening his door, he forced his feet to shuffle toward Violet, who hadn't moved, waiting on that covered porch of her large square home.

She met him at the bottom of the stairs. For a moment, they simply stared at each other. There were a few more wrinkles around her eyes than the last time he saw her. She'd taken the stairs a little slower than he remembered, clinging to the railing with one hand.

But those eyes were still the same hazel and her wavy silver hair still just covered her ears.

"It's been a long time, Evan."

"Yes, it has. I'm sorry."

The sternness evaporated, and she opened her arms for a hug. "Come on inside. We have some catching up to do."

Evan followed Violet, nervously watching her climb concrete stairs. They had pulled away from the house near the porch, leaving the stairs angled. He'd have to fix that before he left. He'd never forgive himself if Violet slipped and broke a hip.

At the top step, she looked over her shoulder. "You're just in time. I have a pumpkin pie cooling on the counter."

Inside, the past came crashing down on him. He'd spent so much time here, preserving every inch to memory. The big house had all its living space on the main floor—the spacious living room with a fireplace and hardwood floors. Even the floral area rug in the living room was the same, looking as new as it did the day she'd bought it. Evan remembered because he and Jeremy had carried it in for her.

"Come on into the kitchen, have a seat. I'll cut you a slice."

On his way, Evan glanced to the top of the staircase. He could almost see seventeen-year-old Kim standing there in her cute little shorts and bare feet, daring him to sneak upstairs for a kiss. But they'd never been able to stop at just one kiss.

Falling into a wooden chair, he folded his hands on the solid white table sprinkled with blue specks. He'd thought about how to start this conversation for days while on the road, yet nothing seemed right.

"Doubt you would have heard, but Chip had a minor heart attack yesterday."

Timing had never been Evan's strong suit. Looked like he was picking the worst time to bother Violet about the past. *Guess it'll have to wait.* "Is he okay?"

"Yeah. They let him go home last night. That store's causing him too much stress."

"If I'm imposing—"

Opening the cupboard near the sink, Violet said, "Nonsense. It's nice to have a distraction." She pulled down a small plate and set it on the counter. The smell of pumpkin filled the air, making Evan's stomach rumble. He hadn't eaten since last night. "You remember what that store did to my Jim."

Evan didn't know what to say to that, so he stayed quiet. Violet's husband was the first Wilkerson to own the grocery store. He'd spent most of his days there, even the weekends. Jim had worked himself into such exhaustion that his body became permanently crippled with pain. It had forced their oldest son, Chip, to call off his three-month honeymoon trip to explore the country with his new bride.

"Where are you staying?"

"I thought I'd get a room at the motel off the highway." He didn't have to explain why he wouldn't be staying at his mom's house. Evan had spent enough nights at Violet's as a teenager when he fought with Russ. Anita always sided with his stepdad.

"No, you won't. You'll stay here. Bring your bags inside." She plated a piece of pie but didn't slide it toward Evan. "You know which room's yours. I put clean sheets on the bed just last week."

"Violet, I appreciate the offer, but—"

"I'll have a fresh pot of coffee ready in a bit. We can talk once you're settled in." A good-sized cup from her cupboard followed the pie plate to her table. "You're here to make things right about leaving after Jeremy died. You can start by *being* here. Stay as long as you like. The longer the better."

"Thanks, Violet."

Evan watched her open and discard three Cool Whip containers from the fridge before she found the right one. "I could use a little help, if you don't mind."

She motioned toward the window. "Some branches to cut down and so forth."

"Of course."

"Eat your pie."

Twenty minutes and three slices later, Evan lugged his heaviest duffle to the second floor. It was the bag that contained almost everything he owned.

At the top of the stairs he faced the bathroom, its door ajar. The mint green tile he remembered still traveled from the floor halfway up the wall. It was a little old-fashioned—even the countertop was green tile—but Evan found comfort in the familiarity of something as simple as an outdated bathroom.

A white wooden door sat behind a cozy sitting area. He'd only glimpsed inside that bedroom once, but it had been decorated heavily in flowers. Kim had always stayed in that room as a girl.

And as a woman.

He hoped he'd get a chance to see her before he left, to make sure she'd followed her dream. Knowing Kim, she'd probably not accept his apology no matter how sincere. He wouldn't blame her, either. They had something special, something real. And he'd walked so far away from the life they planned that she couldn't have followed if she tried.

Turning the opposite way down the hall, Evan found his usual room at the end. It held two twin beds, but he had never minded that. That he'd had a place to sleep when his mom and Russ kicked him out from time to time was enough. Evan slid his suitcase under the bed on the right and sat on the thin mattress. *Sure beats sleeping on the hard ground.*

He recognized the landscape painting on the far wall, and the rickety nightstand hardly sturdy enough to support its brass lamp. He surveyed the room with a bittersweet nostalgia that didn't stay. Homey as all this was, he'd rather be combating a raging forest fire right now than walking down those stairs back to the kitchen table.

How could he accept even a cup of coffee, much less a room, from the woman who'd been nothing short of a grandmother to him? Especially when he'd been responsible for the death of her grandson.

Chapter 5

With the handy scanner, Kim wrapped up inventory at a quarter till three that afternoon. "You're sure you don't want me to stay a little longer?" Kim asked, licking her fingers. She'd forgotten to grab a bite to eat and was relieved when her mom brought back a Styrofoam container from Willow Creek's only restaurant, the Saber Saloon. She'd nearly swallowed that cheeseburger whole.

"I have high-schoolers who show up just before four."

Her mom did seem less stressed after her errands.

"Only if you're sure, Mom."

"Go on and get settled in at Gram's."

"You're sure Dad's okay?" Kim shoved the scanner in the drawer, all the way in the back. "I didn't hear from him once."

"I swung by the house. He's snoring so loudly the dog's cowering in a corner."

"Poor Drifus." For being a giant bloodhound, that dog was scared of almost everything, including thunderstorms and his own shadow. "If something comes up, call me. I'm only a couple of minutes away." Kim balled up the burger wrapper and tossed it into the trash.

It was unexpected, but the once hated task of conducting inventory produced some ideas for her own store. Of course she intended to use technology rather than printed forms and penciled numbers, but she'd never given much thought to how she'd track everything. Or even arrange the shelves. *Maybe this gig won't be so bad after all.*

Zipping through town, Kim turned left at the end of the Main Street and drove until the pavement turned to gravel. At least Gram would appreciate the news about her space in Norfolk coming up for sale soon. Kim had snapped no less than a hundred photos the last time Debbie got her a sneak peek, and she was eager to share them with someone. Anyone who'd ask her where she planned to place the front counter and display cases.

Gram's boxy two-story house appeared through the thick mass of trees, the front stairs boasting pink thornless roses on either side. Kim noticed her grandma's Impala missing from its usual spot in front of the detached garage. Flowerpots filled with golden sundrops, velvety purple peonies, and striped oriental lilies brightened the covered porch, distracting from the chipping white paint.

Parking near a patch of trees east of the house, Kim dug her suitcase from her backseat, upsetting a cardboard box filled with tin watering cans. *Maybe she swung by Aunt Ruby's house or ran to the store.*

She let herself in when she found the front door unlocked, as always—something she never considered doing in the small city of Norfolk. But in a town of less than a thousand people, few bothered with locking up.

Kim dropped her suitcase onto the foot of the bed upstairs and retrieved her binder from her bag. Everything about her favorite room resonated flowers. She admired the purple iris wallpaper, and the bedspread that was a mixture of green, white, and rose colors with arrangements blending into one another. She might use those colors. Who knew? Even the sheer curtains that were embroidered with daffodils and draped over the canopy frame offered ideas.

Bag left askew on the edge of the bed, she slipped out of the bedroom and settled into a cushioned wicker chair in the sitting area. Flipping to the tab regarding store arrangement, she began making notes about paint swatches, inventory, and displays. She had scribbled nearly four pages before she heard the car.

"Gram!" She jumped from her chair and leaned against the window to see outside. Instead of the Impala near the garage, she spotted an enormous hunter-green pickup in its place—one that could make most cowboys jealous. The beast could probably tow a small house.

"Who is that?" she murmured to herself.

She watched someone in worn jeans and a black T-shirt exit the driver's side of the manly truck. The garage was a little far from this window, but Kim liked what she saw so far. What caught her eyes was the way that black T-shirt hugged and defined the muscles of his shoulders and back. If he was selling something, she was definitely buying.

Then the delicious man turned around, carrying a paper sack from what looked like Meyer's Hardware Store.

Kim shrieked in horror and jumped back, tripping over the wicker rocking chair behind her. Her fright and momentum sent her tumbling over it. The light chair landed on top of her. *I have to leave, now*! Her attempts to stand were hindered by the wicker chair's arm. Its rocker leg clenched her ankle like a bear trap.

After yanking her foot free, she hobbled down the hall. She threw the guest room door open and spotted a large duffle bag beneath the bed with "Rowe" stenciled on its side. *Evan?* Sleeping *here?*

Limping to the top of the stairs, cursing the wicker rocker for her sore ankle, Kim considered her best escape route.

Through the narrow floor-length windows on either side of the front door, she saw Evan heading up the steps like he belonged here. Without so much as a knock, the front door's knob turned.

Realizing a first-floor exit was out of the question, Kim retreated to her bedroom and shoved open the window. It'd been years since she snuck out and she suspected the latticework was in rough shape, but she took a chance anyway. She wasn't ready to face the man who'd left her behind.

She should be mad at Evan, but right now she wasn't sure she could manage anger. With him wearing that damn black shirt and a few days of stubble, she felt inches away from throwing herself into his arms. *Stupid. I need to get out of here.*

Halfway down the lattice, she heard the crack. One of the crisscrossed boards gave. Kim felt herself falling backward. "Crap!" She landed with a thud against the grass, pinned beneath the falling bits of board and vines that followed her down. Shimmying from underneath the scattered lattice, Kim untangled a paint-chipped slat from her hair and chucked it away.

Crawling low on Gram's lawn toward her car, Kim slipped in through the open passenger side window as Evan disappeared inside the house. Scrambling to right herself in the driver's seat, she cursed those NASCAR drivers who made this type of car entrance look easy. It was either curse them or curse herself for forgetting to use the car door like a normal person.

Keeping her profile low—not easy in such a compact car—she cranked the key and slowly backed up along the meandering drive. Once protected by the cover of trees, Kim whipped the car around, sat up straight, and sped away as if a crazed, shotgun-toting farmer pursued her.

"That's great news, Kim!" Allie Jordan held a paint roller in one hand, a smudge of beige on her cheek. "You've been drooling over that space for months."

Allie's little ranch house had looked pretty much deserted so she kept driving until she arrived at Allie's boyfriend's house. Everyone knew those two lovebirds were practically living together anyway. Kim should've known to head straight to Nick's mansion on the hill in the first place. It came as no surprise that Allie was heavily involved in renovating his home.

"How long before you meet with the bank about your loan?"

It was refreshing to have someone care about Kim's business. So many people had been treating it like it was a foolish dream. As if she'd gone away to college to learn the ancient technique of basket weaving. She'd studied hard for her degree, and was ready to put that knowledge to work. "Two weeks."

"That's so soon!"

"I know! I was hoping Nick might be willing to put together some of the furnishings. He's so good with restoring old dressers and stuff." Kim tried her best to stall. She glanced in the kitchen, noticing it no longer screamed *Brady Bunch* throwback.

Kim didn't want to admit to Allie that she climbed out Gram's window just to hide from Evan. "Is there anything in his barn I could see?" As far as Kim's best friend knew, she'd had a crush on Evan's younger brother, Alex, when they were teenagers. It'd been easier than explaining falling in love with a man ten years her senior.

But dammit, when Evan rescued that cat from a big, scary tree, she'd been hooked. Everyone else on the fire department thought it too dangerous. Not Evan. Kim watched him rescue the world's angriest cat, all because some little old lady couldn't live without her precious Butterscotch. Kim had fallen in love with him then, at fifteen.

"I could ask him," Allie said, the enthusiasm from earlier disappearing. "He's been a little preoccupied lately."

"Oh?"

"Yeah. But I'll check. Just let me ask him later, okay?"

Kim picked up an edging brush, studying its foam sponge. "No trouble in paradise, is there?"

A new smile washed over Allie's face. "No, paradise is . . . better than any romance novel I've ever read."

"Wow. Glad to hear it, Al."

"Speaking of paradise, I heard something interesting."

Kim twirled the brush between her fingers. "Yeah?"

"Heard Evan Rowe is in town."

The brush fired from her hands, smacking a paint can. "Oh?" She had intended to tell Allie all about Evan Rowe, five years ago. Until that fire. Everything changed that day, including her plans to visit her best friend in Omaha and tell her all about the man who'd stolen her heart.

By the time Allie came back from college to visit over Thanksgiving, Kim had given up hope that Evan would change his mind and come back.

"The whole town is buzzing about it." Allie brushed back a long strand of wavy hair with her wrist. "Of course, driving a giant truck with Alaska plates down Main Street tends to catch some attention."

The front door opened and a black German shepherd charged right at them. Norman nudged Kim for his usual greeting pat. "Hey, Norm!" She scratched vigorously behind his ears and won a few licks of approval.

Allie set down her paint roller and practically floated toward Nick as he came through the doorway. Kim envied her best friend, having found love with Willow Creek's new doctor. She looked away as they locked lips. *Guess asking to stay here is out of the question. I'd never get any sleep.*

Nick lived in the only house on the only hill in town. He'd moved from Georgia earlier that year, replacing the town's retired doctor. The house, though one of the largest in town, was in desperate need of remodeling. A project the two of them would probably never get done if they couldn't stop making out every two seconds. It was still a young love, and the pair seemed eager to make most romance novels jealous.

"I hate to interrupt Lover's Lane."

"Oh, hi, Kim. Didn't know you were back there," Nick said, a slight shade of red appearing on his cheeks. He whispered something to Allie, kissed her once more, and patted her on the butt before returning outside, Norman on his heel.

"Better than your precious romance novels, you say?"

Allie blushed. "Much better."

"I'm really happy for you, Al. You finally landed a good one. Better than that piece of shit Travis." Kim reached for her neglected glass of water. "Speaking of which, how are our favorite villains?"

Allie laughed. "You've been reading too much!"

"Says the queen of romance novel blogs." This past summer, during one of Kim's visits, Allie had taken Kim up on her advice to turn her passion for blogging about romance novels into something lucrative. Allie read those books like Kim inhaled cupcakes. After adding a website that offered advertising packages for authors, Allie had been able to quit her job at the hospital.

Picking up her paint roller, Allie said, "Travis is still on life support. There's enough brain activity that no one will let them pull the plug. They're still hoping he'll wake up to testify against his mom."

"For killing his dad?"

"Yep. I know what I heard from them both, Kim. It was a confession. But I'm told it's not enough. A jury won't convict Lesley for murder without Travis' testimony or Rich Meyers' body. They have neither."

"You mean, even after getting a warrant they haven't found a body?"

Allie shook her head. "Good news is that the judge won't post bail for Lesley. They're certain she's a flight risk. They're waiting for Travis to wake up, or—"

"Or die?"

"Yeah, basically."

"That's morbid." Kim reached for a stack of paint swatches, absentmindedly shuffling through the various shades of beige. "Can't they convict Lesley for attempted murder? You know, for Travis?"

"I didn't see who fired the first shot." Allie's voice was quiet now. "Alex thinks Lesley's lawyer will argue self-defense." Dipping the roller in the paint, Allie changed the subject. "Ed told me that Evan is staying at your grandma's house."

The change of topic threw Kim. "No one bothered to warn me."

"Warn you?"

"It's not fair. He just parades up to the door in that damn tight shirt like he owns the place. Not that I care or anything." Kim didn't realize she was fanning herself until Allie raised a challenging eyebrow.

"Right."

She knew she owed Allie the truth, but right now all she wanted was to escape Evan at any cost. Talking about him would conjure memories she'd worked hard to bury. "You want to catch a movie or something tonight?"

Allie parted her lips, about to say something. Kim watched her eyes dip toward the tray filled with Monroe bisque paint. "Nick and I are going to catch the tail end of an estate auction to look for some furniture."

"Mind if I tag along?"

"Sure," Allie said. "Amanda has a volleyball game afterward. But that might not be too exciting. She's been benched a lot this season."

"Benched? You mean that vulture Rachel Jamison is still holding a grudge against you? I can't believe she's set on punishing you because she didn't win Nick for herself. Amanda's got to be one of their best players!"

"She is. And rumor has it a UCLA recruiter'll be there tonight."

"Then we have to go! We need to make sure she plays."

"What do you have in mind?"

At Allie's concerned expression, Kim simply patted her on the back. "Don't worry, we won't get arrested. I don't think we will, anyway."

Suddenly, this new mission excited Kim. *It'll keep me away from Gram's house for one more night.* She doubted she'd be able to avoid Evan indefinitely, considering the size of the house. He'd probably be there almost nonstop, offering to rebuild the house from the ground up. Kim wished he understood that no one blamed him for Jeremy's death.

Well, no one except for her dad.

Chapter 6

Violet had been cooking a supper large enough to feed an entire crew of smokejumpers. It would've been rude to mention he'd be eating across town. So Evan was already full when he showed up at his mom's house.

He and Violet had talked for what seemed like hours—about old memories, funny stories, and sad ones. Eventually, the conversation grew serious. She assured him repeatedly, as many had before he left town, that Jeremy's death wasn't his fault.

"You tried to save him," Violet said as she cleared the dishes after their meal. "That means something, you know. Not everyone would have the courage to run into a burning house, trained or not."

"I failed."

"We all wish Jeremy was still with us. But he's not. You need to move past it, Evan."

Driving through the north edge of town, Evan knew she was right. He just wished it was as easy to accept

78

her words. He quickly found himself back in the country headed toward his mom's house. Half a mile before her driveway sat the old blue mailbox at the edge of Sue Wilkerson's driveway. Jeremy's old house.

As a boy, Evan had ridden his bike from his parents' farm down the rutted gravel road to Jeremy's farm. It was one of the reasons they'd been friends—they'd been the closest neighbors with any kids.

Pulling into the long driveway, he took a deep breath. When his dad was alive, he farmed the several hundred acres surrounding their two-story house. The barn had been full of chickens, a few cows, and some pigs. But his dad had been gone for over two decades, trampled to death by the only bull they ever owned. Later, while Evan was visiting his grandparents in Wyoming, his mom sold every animal except for half a dozen chickens.

Evan had expected her to sell the farm too, but instead she leased out the land and stayed put.

A few years later, when Evan was in the eighth grade, his mom married Russ Procter. When Evan was in college, Hannah was born. Evan doted on his little sister too much, and Russ let him know it. The farmland stayed leased to others, because Russ drove trucks. The absence of Russ' semi hauler in the yard now brought Evan relief.

He found Alex pacing in the driveway, finishing up a phone call as Evan parked his truck.

He expected things to be tense with his mom, but he wasn't sure how Hannah would react to his return. When he announced he was leaving for Alaska, Hannah was only eight. Her face had been drenched in tears as she chased his truck down the drive when he drove away. He'd promised she could come visit, but Russ never let her get on a plane.

Now she was a young teenager.

"I need more time," Alex was saying into his phone. "Then comb the property again. You know how bad this will be if she gets released on bail. Mark my words, that house will burn to the ground and we'll never find a shred of evidence."

Hearing his brother in full detective mode, Evan felt a surge of pride. When he left for Alaska, Alex was fresh out of the state patrol academy. Since he'd been gone, Alex had worked his way up the ranks from traffic services to a special investigator in the criminal division.

"Call me when you have something." Alex hung up with a stab of his finger. "Hey, you ready?"

"Everything okay?"

Alex sucked in a deep breath. "Just some obstacles with a case. Nothing I can't handle."

Evan wanted to ask who would be out on bail, but it probably didn't matter. His brother worked out of Norfolk primarily, and had jurisdiction over a large portion of northeast Nebraska. It was doubtful he'd even know who it was. "You sure this is a good idea?" Evan nodded toward the house.

"We've only got one mom."

"Easy for you to say. You're her favorite."

Alex shook his head. "Not by a long shot. Hannah's the one. Even as a brand-new teenager she can do no wrong." Alex patted him on the shoulder. "She's going to be pissed. Don't sweat it."

Evan nodded, then followed his brother to the front door.

The TV hummed in the background, someone winning a new car on *Wheel of Fortune*. From the kitchen, he heard the sound of a mixer. Evan took a deep breath and stepped into his mom's sight line.

From behind the granite-topped island, Anita Procter looked up from her prep space, black bangs falling into her eyes. The rest of her long, fine hair was tied up at the back of her head. Seasoned pork chops waited, ready for the oven, and buttered asparagus sat in a pan on the counter. In the mixer, he guessed, were mashed potatoes. "You're early."

Evan hadn't traveled thirty-three hundred miles to give up on anyone, including his mom. He walked around the counter, waited for her to shove the pan in the oven, then enveloped her in a hug. She stiffened, but eventually wrapped her arms around him, holding on as if she might otherwise drown.

Pulling away, she smacked him hard on the shoulder. "Five years?"

Hanging his head, Evan simply said, "I'm sorry."

"You're sorry?"

He glanced around the room, but Alex had disappeared, probably to search for Hannah. "I can't change anything, Mom. But I'm here now."

"And then what? You're going back to Alaska and staying away another five years?" With the back of her hand Anita wiped away a bang that fell across her eyes and stuck to her temple. She returned to her mixer, scooped a wad of butter, and slammed it into the bowl. "You might as well have stayed gone, Evan. It's worse this way."

"How?"

She clenched the metal bowl with both hands, her back toward Evan. He watched her shoulders sink. "You'll just hurt everyone all over again."

Evan shoved his hands in the front pockets of his jeans. Of course he planned to return to Alaska, but he'd be around for a few weeks, maybe a full month. "I'm hurt."

"*You're* hurt?"

"I mean I got hurt. About a month and a half ago. Fell out of a tree, hurt my leg." He'd spare her the gory details. He still limped occasionally, mostly when the weather turned. "I have to take some time off. To recover."

"What kind of sane man jumps out of a plane and into a fire?" Anita turned the mixer on top speed. "I told you it was dangerous!" The beaters' noise made conversation impossible.

Evan considered correcting her, telling her that he never jumped *into* a fire, just near them. But, figuring she'd turn her mashed potatoes into soup if he stayed in the kitchen, he decided to brave the reunion with his little sister.

"It's 'Bungee Jumping to Conclusions'!" he heard Hannah shout at the TV. She and Alex sat on the leather sofa, watching the game show from the edge of their seats. One glance at the puzzle board and Evan knew Hannah was right. "Why do they always go for more money?" she asked. "He's going to lose it all. Just watch!"

"Hey, Hannah."

From the couch, she turned. Indifference lingered in her eyes. Brown hair she'd once worn in low pigtails now sat curled around her shoulders. "Hi." With folded arms, she studied him, seeming to size him up, then returned her attention to the TV. "See!" she said to Alex. "Bankrupt. He would've won ten thousand dollars if he just solved the stupid puzzle."

Alex shrugged and tossed Evan a sympathetic look. In his own childhood home, Evan had become an outcast.

He returned to the kitchen now that the mixer was off. He spotted the potatoes in a bowl, looking fluffy and scrumptious. "How's Sue?" he asked his mom. Perhaps a change of subject would do them both good. Having been neighbors, Anita and Sue had become best friends when Evan was about Hannah's age. Plus, he could use all the help he could get when it came to Jeremy's mom. He was looking forward to that conversation about as much as a kidney stone.

"I wouldn't know. Sue doesn't talk to me anymore, since *you* left."

"Oh." He hadn't expected that.

"Do you even realize what I went through? I didn't just lose my best friend. I lost my oldest son too. You took off so fast you left a smoke trail behind you. No warning. You just abandoned everyone when we needed you the most."

Evan tried his best to keep his cool. He was here to grovel, not to argue. But damn it, it wasn't as if he ran off to some tropical island and lived on a beach for the past five years. "I went to Alaska because they offered me a job where I could save lives. A job where I'd be properly trained to save people from burning houses. I make a difference there. Here . . ." Evan rubbed his forehead.

"Life isn't all sunshine and rainbows." Evan fought rolling his eyes at his mom's favorite quote. "But it doesn't mean you have to *run*. I stayed after your father died. I dealt with life and moved on. Why couldn't you have done the same?"

"How is Russ these days?" Evan asked.

"It smells wonderful in here!" Alex was smiling like an idiot when he stepped into the kitchen, clearly trying to break up the tension. He stepped around the counter and hugged their mom, kissing her on the cheek. "I'm starving. When can we eat?"

"I need to stop at the fire hall," Alex said in the driveway. They'd stepped outdoors after the tense meal with the two unsmiling females. "Should only take a few minutes. Gotta pick up an accident report. Want to tag along?"

Evan's initial instinct was to say no. He'd been a volunteer firefighter for Willow Creek. He and Jeremy both had for four years. Evan feared stepping foot into that fire hall would only make the nightmares unbearable tonight. But his mom's words echoed, mocking him. If he didn't stop running, what was the point of being back at all?

"Sure. But doesn't this town know about email yet? You really have to stop by in person to get a report?"

"The department could use some upgrades," Alex admitted. "It's pretty much the same since you left, just a little bit more . . . worn."

Stepping into the garage bay at the fire hall, Evan's heart thudded as Alex slipped away to an office. The fire engine before him wasn't only similar to the one that showed up to Sue's house that day. It was the same one. *Engine 402.* He felt suddenly sick remembering all the times he and Jeremy rode together in this truck.

"Practically an antique now, isn't she?" Tim Hollander adjusted his Cornhusker ball cap, revealing thinning blond hair beneath. Evan towered at least four inches over him.

"This poor engine needed to be put out of commission five years ago. Maybe donated to a museum. How is she still hanging on?"

"Funds have been a little tight," Tim said, keeping his voice low. "But we keep up the maintenance. She runs all right."

Inside, Evan cringed. He'd been forced to work with some less-than-best equipment in Alaska, too. He understood every department, no matter where they were located or what they specialized in, had to abide by a budget. But this was ridiculous. The town only had one fire engine. If it died halfway to a fire, a family might perish. "Not enough from fundraisers or taxes?"

Tim shook his head and adjusted his cap again, no doubt to avoid eye contact.

"Are you Chief now?" Evan asked. He wished Alex would hurry.

"No, that's still Ron Larson. I think he'll have to croak before he plans to step down." It was meant as a joke, but Evan had to force a laugh. He'd never cared for Ron. The man had always flaunted his flashy purchases and trophy wife.

"Least there's an election every two years, right?"

Tim cleared his throat. "Who's going to run against him?" The words lingered in the air like a bad odor. "It's a tough job. Need some young buck to come along and stir things up." Tim rubbed his hands together as if they might be cold. "Don't suppose you're staying?"

Evan shook his head. "Just a couple weeks."

"That's a shame. We could really use the help. George Ballinger is down with a broken leg, and Freeman's off on an RV trip with his wife since their kids all left for college." Tim shook his head. "But by the time we put you through training again, you'd be leaving."

Alex returned and patted Evan on the shoulder. "He's fully trained," he offered. "Fought forest fires in Alaska as a smokejumper. Would that help expedite anything?"

Evan started to wonder if there even was a report, or had his brother tricked him into coming, hoping he could coax him into sticking around?

Hope lit up in Tim's eyes, as if Alex's suggestion might be some kind of answer to a desperate prayer. "I think it might. I'd have to verify your status and get you to sign some forms for Nebraska. We have extra gear of all sizes. I handle signing up new volunteers, so I can rush you through. There's a meeting Tuesday night. You'll need to be voted in, of course."

Evan wanted to say yes, but the doctor's warning hung in the air. Besides, he couldn't join a department he'd only abandon in a couple of weeks.

"Sorry, Tim. I won't be around long enough to make it worth anyone's time."

Chapter 7

An hour later, Allie drove Nick's crew cab truck downtown, Kim riding shotgun. "Figures Nick would get called in right before we're supposed to leave town." Allie pulled into a parking spot at the back of the hospital and locked her eyes on a back entrance she used to use. "Sprained ankle or something."

"Do you miss working here?" Kim asked.

Allie considered how to answer that question. She'd spent three years enduring the wrath of hospital administrator Lesley Jamison, but she'd also worked with some wonderful people. "Sometimes."

"Would you go back?"

That question was easier to answer. "No. My blog has really exploded these past couple of months. Crazy to think your little spark of an idea allowed me to be *paid* to read romance novels."

"What can I say? It was a great idea." Kim's purposefully cheesy smile made Allie laugh. "Hope The Twisted Tulip has the same success."

"It will," Allie said. "You've been working on that business plan since you started college. I know it'll be great. I can't wait to order my wed—" Allie cut herself off, blushing at what she nearly blurted. "Order flowers from you!"

"Wedding flowers?" Kim jumped in her seat. "Did you fail to tell me something, Allison Marie Jordan?"

Allie waved her arms in surrender. "No. No marriage proposals. Promise." It wasn't as if the idea hadn't crossed her mind. She practically lived in Nick's house now. But he had other things weighing on his mind, like how to handle an enormous sum of money awarded to him after a messy divorce. Money he didn't want.

"Not yet," Kim amended.

"Exactly." Allie twisted the cap off a bottle of Dr. Pepper and added a subtle warning. "I'm not in a hurry, either."

"I better be the first person you tell! And you *will* be receiving your floral services from The Twisted Tulip when that time comes. Non-negotiable."

Nick pushed open the hospital's back door, his emerald eyes weary. He glanced up long enough to notice Kim in the passenger side and immediately went for the backseat. "Everything okay?"

Meeting his eyes, Allie knew something else had come up about that money. She'd have to wait until they had some privacy to find out more. "Yes, everything is fine." Nick forced a smile that didn't reach his eyes.

Allie hated that he'd been burdened with such a big decision and an enormous secret. If the town found out he'd received millions from the settlement with his ex-wife, everyone would have an opinion how he should spend that money.

Last night on the deck, they'd talked again about whether to even keep the money as Norman chased rabbits around the spacious yard. It flattered Allie that he included her in such a decision. "Nick, if you're worried this money will change you, don't be." She'd reached for his hand and squeezed. "I know you. You're a good person."

"Which is why I should donate the whole sum to charity. Allie, I never asked for this."

"Think of the good you could do for this town," she'd countered. "You could use the money to make charitable contributions around Willow Creek. Anonymously, of course. And once you're satisfied, you can give the rest away if you want. Or put it in a college fund or two."

He'd returned the slightest smile at the hint of their future children.

As Allie turned onto Main Street and drove, she spotted Evan and his brother Alex as they entered the fire station. When she slowed as they passed the brick- and aluminum-sided building, Nick said, "Let's get to that sale."

Evan looked back over his shoulder as he held the door. His line of sight targeted the truck.

Kim ducked down in her seat as if someone had fired bullets.

"You okay?" Allie asked.

"Fine, fine." Kim banged her head on the glove box. "I dropped something."

"Sure it had nothing to do with a certain detective?" Allie teased. For years, Kim thought she had Allie fooled about which Rowe brother she really had the hots for. *But now that Evan's back in town, she's not going to get off so easily.*

"Oh, found it!" Kim popped back up. "Found my quarter. Let's go shopping!"

It was late, yet Kim couldn't wait to share her four boxes of finds from the auction with Gram. She hoped

Gram was up so she could make up for running off to the volleyball game and skipping supper.

Allie and Nick helped Kim unload the boxes into the backseat of her Little Green Car. "Good thing I don't have a dog to cart around," she said to Allie. "Poor Norman would have to ride on my roof if he was mine!"

Kim could read something in Allie's eyes that worried her. She'd have to dig the truth out of her friend when they were alone next.

"Whose truck?" Nick pointed to the one near the garage, conspicuous with its Alaska plates.

"Beats me," Kim lied, her breath constricting. The lone kitchen light might not be Gram at all. "I better get inside and see if Gram's still up. She's going to love some of these. Call me tomorrow, Al?"

"Sure."

She watched them disappear down the meandering drive.

Rearranging the boxes in the backseat of her Geo Metro for the third time, Kim glanced back toward the lit window. She'd been watching for someone to pass it, hoping to identify the lurker in the kitchen before sneaking inside. She glimpsed the east corner of the house and spotted the cracked lattice still lying on the ground. *Guess I won't be sneaking back in that way.*

"There's a piece of pumpkin pie with your name on it," Violet called from the front porch.

"Gram, you're up!" Kim took the stairs two at a time and flew right into her grandma's arms.

Violet ushered Kim inside to the kitchen. She expected to find Evan at the table eating his slice but felt relief at the empty chairs. "Rumor has it you caused quite the commotion at the volleyball game tonight."

Kim offered a weak smile. Allie's little sister, Amanda, had brought her team to victory tonight, *and* obtained a private conversation with the recruiter of her dreams. They'd finally beaten Rachel Jamison and her pathetic idea of payback.

"Someone had to stand up to that coach. She's been torturing people long enough, especially Allie. Can you believe she wasn't going to play Amanda—probably her best player—at all until we starting chanting her name?" Kim felt a beat of pride. The UCLA recruiter had yawned and looked at her watch as if she was preparing to leave—the Sabers *were* losing miserably in that set—until Kim yelled *put Amanda in* just once. The entire crowd caught on within seconds. "Coach Jamison's a bully, and it had to stop."

Gram carved a piece of pumpkin pie from the tin and set it in front of Kim. "I feel sorry for her myself."

Retrieving the Cool Whip from the fridge, Kim asked, "Why?"

"I don't think Rachel has any friends. With her sister in jail . . ." Violet intentionally trailed off, waving a dismissive hand.

"She might if she actually tried being nicer to people."

Gram settled into a chair opposite her with a mug of steaming coffee. "Look at the environment she grew up in. Mom runs off when she's just a little girl. Dad's a drunk, eventually drove himself into a ditch. Only sibling's a tyrant."

"People have choices," Kim argued between bites. "She could choose to be nice, no matter what terrible things her environment ingrained in her brain."

Sipping her coffee, Gram said, "I heard you also went to some sale with Allie. How was that?"

Kim was thankful for the change of subject. "Gram, you should have seen this estate sale! It was massive. They cut me off after I filled the fourth box. And get this—I got it all for twenty bucks! I think Allie made a mistake taking me along. She'll have to take me to all the other ones now." Kim glanced over her shoulder, her nerves starting to get the best of her. *What if Evan walks down the stairs in only a pair of shorts?*

"You always had a gift for taking something unwanted and making it shine."

"Did I tell you about the store in Norfolk? The one on the corner I've been watching forever? It's coming up for sale." Kim rambled on about how great her realtor was, getting her an exclusive opportunity to make the first offer, but omitting the need for that last chunk of loan-approval money.

"That's wonderful news!" Violet adjusted the front of her lavender robe and suppressed a yawn. "Have you told your parents?"

Kim's excitement fizzled. "I tried."

"Honey, they're both a little preoccupied right now. I'm sure they're very proud of you." Violet took a final sip of her coffee. "You have to understand the burden your mother is carrying with that store. Top that with dealing with your father when he's been ordered to stay under house arrest. If I were your mom, I'd hire a team of nurses and rent a hotel room for the next month."

"Maybe I'll make some flower arrangements for the store." Kim scraped the last bit of pie onto her fork. "Help brighten the place up."

"I think that's a lovely idea. Use the calla lilies. I'll bring in some from the garden first thing in the morning." Violet carried her empty Mount Rushmore souvenir mug to the sink. Over her shoulder, she said, "I hear Macy is coming back."

"I heard that, too," said Kim with a laugh. "Not sure what Mom used as bribery."

Gram let out a small, answering chuckle.

Rising from the table, Kim set her plate in the sink. "I think I'm going to dig a couple of flower pots out of my car. I'll put the arrangements together in the morning."

After a hug and kiss goodnight, Kim slipped outside. The wind had picked up, blowing her short blonde hair across her face. Opening her car door nearly blew it off its hinges. *Storm's coming.*

With the first light raindrops, Kim crawled out of her car, three various-sized tin pails in hand, and rushed back into the house. She left them in the mudroom off the kitchen. Excitement tingled at the thought of photographing the arrangements tomorrow so she could include them in her catalogue—the one she'd keep on the front counter of The Twisted Tulip.

Inside, a small nightlight halfway up the stairs illuminated Gram's open staircase. That hadn't been on ten minutes ago. Gram was always thoughtful like that.

Climbing the hardwood steps, Kim thought it odd that the bathroom door at the top was closed. Until she remembered Evan was in the house. Or maybe Gram shut it when she put on the nightlight. *Since there're so many of us here.*

Moonlight poured in from the window in the sitting area. For a moment, Kim stood at the top of the stairs and reminisced. She recalled many nights as a little girl, secretly slipping out of her bedroom to sit in one of those wicker chairs bathed in moonlight to gaze at the stars.

Lost in the memory, Kim shrieked in surprise when the bathroom door opened. In the doorway stood Evan Rowe, shirtless. His disheveled black hair looked damp, as if he'd recently towel-dried it. A missed droplet of water trailed down his hard stomach, running into the waistband of mesh pants.

"Kimberly?"

Her heart sped up so quickly that she thought it was trying to start its own high-speed chase. "How dare you," she hissed. "Don't *Kimberly* me."

"I didn't realize you were staying here. Violet didn't..."

She folded her arms, and managed to pull her eyes from his glorious body. "Gram didn't tell me either."

"I—uh . . . how've you—"

The first crack of thunder snapped sense back into Kim. She yearned for the safe haven of her canopied bed. "Look, we can be adults about this. Stay out of my way, and I'll stay out of yours." She stormed down the hall, fighting the urge to slam her door. Gram would surely come investigate if she did.

Kim's entire body trembled; memories from their secret passionate summer flashed through her mind like strobe lights. Afternoons spent down by the creek, nights curled up in a sea of blankets in the bed of Evan's truck, sneaking kisses, his touch as hot as fire . . . No matter how much she tried to stay mad at Evan Rowe, her anger would cave unless she kept her distance.

Chapter 8

Sleep had eluded Evan. He was no longer a stranger to the nightmares of a burning house that made sleep a mythical concept these past few years. But last night, each time he closed his eyes, Kimberly's beautiful face was before him, her hazel eyes icy, and that scowl. She was always sexiest when she was fired up. Though he'd expected a similar cold reaction from their first meeting, he hoped to have some actual words prepared.

He'd been stunned to find her staying at Violet's, especially when there'd been no trace of her before his evening shower.

When he opened the bathroom door, the rush of old feelings flooded him instantly. As if someone waved a magic wand, a dam's wall of emotion vanished at once. Moonlight bathed her voluptuous body, reminding him how soft her skin always felt beneath his rough fingertips.

He heard Kim's door open around five that morning, after the storm subsided. He listened to the hiss of the shower and tried like hell not to envision her standing beneath the water. But when it came to Kimberly Wilkerson, he was hopeless.

Deciding against the torture of lying in bed, visualizing the water trickling down her soft skin, Evan threw on a pair of shorts and running shoes. He'd obeyed his doctor and refrained from running for well over a month now. It was time to get back to it. He'd welcome the distraction of the physical pain.

It wasn't too cold out. Turning west at the top of the driveway, Evan looked forward to hills in the country. He breathed in and ran. While the town only had one hill of notable size, west of Violet's house the road could double as a rollercoaster ride. Climbing graveled hills, he noticed soybean crops on either side of the road that looked only a week or two from harvest. Deep ditches with a light trickle of water kept Evan's path in the center of the narrow road. He hoped a combine wouldn't force him off.

Evan passed the cemetery, the one where Jeremy was buried. But he wasn't ready for that visit yet.

After running two miles, he turned around. The wound at the bottom of his calf stung from the strain, but he forced himself to go the entire distance. He was a smokejumper, dammit! He'd known men—and women—who trained through much worse. A minor muscle injury wasn't about to hinder him from an easy run.

When Evan reached the clearing in Violet's driveway, Kim was setting a box of flower arrangements on top of a tiny green sedan. "Good morning."

Kim jumped backward; the box wobbled on the rounded roof. Catching it before the arrangements toppled to the ground, she snapped, "Didn't anyone ever teach you it's not nice to sneak up on people? And put on a shirt!"

"I didn't mean to startle you." He'd reached a hand out, but at her tone he instantly withdrew it. He hadn't expected it to be so hard to fight the most natural urges around her. "Kim, I really would like the chance to talk to you."

"Sorry, really busy. I have to get to the store to help my mom. I probably won't be back until really late. Dad needs some company tonight, too."

"Sorry to hear about his heart attack. I hope he's okay."

"He's been trying to escape house arrest."

Evan raised an eyebrow. "Oh?"

Kim set the arrangement on the backseat. From where he stood, the entire backseat seemed filled with random containers—watering cans, mason jars, hand-painted vases, and even glass Coke bottles.

"He's doing okay," she added, closing the car door. "Just bored. And stubborn." Yanking open the driver's door and falling into her seat, Kim said, "Gotta go. Mom's waiting."

"Maybe we can talk tomorrow?"

"I'm pretty busy. For the rest of the week." She reached for the door handle. "Actually, I'm pretty busy for the rest of my life." She tugged the door closed and sped off.

With a sigh, Evan headed inside to gather the hardware he picked up yesterday. He promised to join Violet for breakfast just as soon as he repaired the broken lattice on the north side of the house. Kimberly might be stubborn, but he had worn her down once. He could do it again.

At six forty-five that morning, Kim slipped inside Wilkerson's back door, carrying three artsy arrangements of purple lilies and white roses in painted metal buckets, feeling victorious. The bucket's chipped white texture gave the flowers the perfect contrast.

"Kim, these are gorgeous!" The smile illuminating Penny's thin face made waking up two hours early worth it for Kim. But she refused to admit her entire effort was fueled by the desire to get out of the house before Evan woke up.

Weaving purple ribbon and twine together now, she knotted the combination around the bucket with a bow. She had hundreds of little handmade logos for her brand and tied one to each bucket handle. *Might as well get some free advertising.*

Penny helped herself to a Hershey bar. The chocolate candy reminded Kim of the color of Evan's eyes. She fidgeted with a box of magazines; one slipped from her hands and slapped the tile floor.

"You okay, Kimmie?" Penny asked. She took one of the arrangements and stationed it at the edge of the checkout counter. "You seem a little distracted."

"I'm peachy." Kim had tried so hard not to notice, but whatever he'd been doing in Alaska these past few years, Evan's sculpted chest and Adonis muscles agreed with it. Didn't he know how cruel it was this morning, showing up unannounced and bare-chested?

At the sight of a crew cab truck crawling past the store, Kim ducked behind the counter.

"Peachy, huh?" Penny repeated, her eyebrow cocked in seeming amusement.

Kim offered a crooked smile as she stood. "I'm a little tired." She caught the taillights of a red truck out the window. *Not Evan.* Surely he'd be leaving in a couple of days. She only had to avoid him long enough for him to go back north. "We got back late from the game, and then there was that sale."

"From what I heard, you bought half of it."

Kim smirked. "They kicked me out after I tried to sneak a fifth box."

"You always had that knack to turn something plain into something beautiful and desired. You give these ratty, unwanted buckets second chances." Penny placed an arrangement on a stand near the door. "How much are you selling these for?"

"Selling them?" Kim flipped the tag on the largest arrangement, displaying her dangling logo. "I just thought they'd brighten the place up. I didn't plan to sell them."

"Why not? With your store opening soon, this is a good way to let people know."

Kim beamed a smile so wide her cheeks hurt. It was the first hint in weeks, maybe even months, that Penny had taken any interest in her business. "I guess I could add a price tag. How should Wilma ring them up?"

Penny shrugged, unlocking the front door. "Why don't you have them pay cash or write a check to The Twisted Tulip?"

"What's going on?" Kim asked, eyeing her mom. Her hair shimmered in the reflection of the halogen lights, and she'd worn a silk lavender blouse. "You got your hair done yesterday." The shorter chin-length hairdo suited Penny, now dyed a dark coppery color that complemented her hazel eyes.

"You like it?"

"Something's definitely going on." Compared to the frazzled woman Kim found yesterday, Penny looked radiant—even her eyes twinkled—and, well, she looked relieved. "You're awfully chipper today. New hairstyle, you're willing to sell my arrangements . . ."

"I don't know what you're talking about."

"Sure." Kim straightened a stack of coupons on the counter. "Did you drug Dad again?"

"No!"

"You did!"

"Melatonin is *not* a drug, Kimmie." She patted her daughter's shoulder. "The main truck should be here in about fifteen minutes. Fred called out sick today, so looks like it'll just be the two of us unloading."

"Who's Fred?" Kim wondered if maybe this *Fred* warranted her mom's extra effort on her appearance today.

Penny snatched a Snickers mixed in with the Milky Way box and tucked it back where it belonged. "A part-timer who helps unload the trucks."

"You have a lot of those part-timers."

"More economical that way."

"Noted." Kim glanced toward the saloon doors in the back. "There's really no one else to help?"

"Well, your father can't, obviously."

"Because you drugged him."

Penny exhaled. "And Wilma couldn't lift a single box in that truck without it crushing her. Even if she didn't have to check out customers." Penny adjusted an arrangement an inch toward the light. "These really are beautiful. They brighten the place up. Bring more tomorrow."

The day flew by, Penny and Kim spending the first half unloading the biggest truck Kim had ever seen. How one little grocery store could house so much merchandise, she'd never comprehend. She felt lucky she'd never have to carry boxes of laundry detergent around in her own store.

Halfway through the work on the truck, Kim mentally cursed her sister. She'd arrive around lunchtime tomorrow. Her flight had already landed, Kim saw on Facebook, but Macy conveniently decided to stay the night in Omaha with friends. *And miss freight day.*

"You should get going," Penny said later that afternoon, seemingly shooing Kim out of the store.

"Are you sure? I don't mind—"

"Go!"

"Is there anything else I can do?" Kim glanced at the clock; it wasn't even three yet. If she went back to Gram's now, she'd probably find Evan on a ladder, fixing things without his damn shirt on. If she kept running into him like that, she'd attack him like a spider monkey finding its first banana.

And that would completely undermine her plan to stay mad at him for the rest of her life.

"You agreed to check on your father."

Kim grumbled.

"You offered." Penny tried to hide her smile but failed. "Just stop by unannounced so I can see if he's actually taking his medication. I suspect he might be on to me."

"It's only day two!"

"If he's awake, he outsmarted me." Penny hopped up one step toward her office, then stopped. "Why don't you make some more flower arrangements for tomorrow? Maybe a couple more this time since those three all sold before noon."

Sending a salute to her mom, Kim reluctantly left the grocery store. Truth was, she didn't hate it as much as she'd thought she would. It was actually interesting learning the ins and outs of running a business. She'd not appreciated all the details that went into running a small-town store before. It sure beat that stupid office job.

Not having her dad around criticizing every wrong move certainly added to the appeal. The half dozen compliments she'd received for her floral arrangements hadn't hurt, either.

"This is so beautiful, Kim!" said Abigail Adams, an elderly lady who was Aunt Ruby's partner in crime. Despite the hot, dry temperature, Abigail had sported a soft pink sweatshirt with a white cat pawing at a ball of yarn. "This would look perfect on my kitchen table." She studied the logo tag. "Are you starting your own business?"

"Hopefully within a couple months, in Norfolk."

"Norfolk?" Abigail's nose had wrinkled, like the word tasted sour. "Too bad. Willow Creek could use a place like this."

But Kim knew she'd never be able to break even opening a shop in such a small place.

She pulled into the graveled parking area at the back of her parents' house. As she stepped from her car, she noticed Drifus' large chocolate-colored head appear in the kitchen window, his droopy ears flopping with excitement.

How many birthdays and anniversaries could a town of less than eight hundred people generate that were flower-worthy? *No, I could never open The Twisted Tulip in Willow Creek.*

Evan needed a break. His leg ached from the overexertion. He'd spent the morning repairing the lattice on the north side of the house, cutting down overgrown branches that were encroaching on the roof, and cleaning out part of the old barn in the pasture near the creek. He'd found a few containers Kim might be able to use for her flower arrangements. He'd cleaned them up, leaving a box outside her bedroom door.

After rinsing off, he decided it was time to pay Jeremy's mom, Sue, a visit.

He hadn't spoken to her since the funeral. Evan had tried reaching out a couple of times with phone calls, but Sue never seemed to be home to answer. He knew now that he was back, he should have tried harder.

Dipping back into town, heading east toward the next gravel road, Evan heard the whistle sound. He glanced at his dash, wondering if it was later than he thought. The whistle in Willow Creek blew every day at noon and six in the evening. But it was only two in the afternoon.

Evan's chest constricted as he realized it was the fire whistle. He scanned the sky for a smoke trail. Had he taken Tim up on his offer last night, he might've been able to help. With the department being shorthanded and forced to use subpar, worn equipment, there might be complications.

Evan detoured down Main Street and sped through the north part of town. The fire engine rolled out of the station, lights and siren blaring.

Flipping a U-turn, Evan promised himself he'd reconsider joining the department, even if temporarily. He became a career firefighter because he wanted to protect people. Right now though, he wouldn't let his inability to help with a fire give him an excuse to avoid Sue. She deserved an apology.

On Sue's doorstep, Evan felt sweat trickle down his neck. Would she be as angry as his mom had been last night? Would she blame him for the dissolving friendship those two once had as well as for leaving her completely alone in this world?

"Evan, I heard you were in town." A slow smile lit Sue's face. "Are these for me?" She eyed the arrangement of purple and white flowers he brought. It was one of the arrangements from the grocery store this morning. He'd stopped by before lunch, hoping to talk to Kim. But the petite elderly woman at the counter informed him that she was busy unloading stock in the back. With the line of customers behind him, he couldn't ask her to fetch Kim.

"Yes, they are," he finally answered.

"These are beautiful! Please, come inside."

Taking a deep breath, Evan followed her through the back door that led to her kitchen. The room was predominately white, but there were little yellow accents everywhere. Though it wasn't the same kitchen from five years ago, it looked eerily familiar, down to the white subway tile backsplash with yellow diamonds.

The original house site sat a quarter mile further east, closer to what was now an abandoned cattle yard.

When Sue's husband passed from lung cancer almost eight years ago, she sold all their livestock to keep the property. The life insurance had barely covered that funeral. Wanting to help his mom get back on her feet was one of the reasons Jeremy moved back home.

"As much as I'd like to take the credit for the flowers," Evan said mostly to distract himself, "this is your niece's handiwork."

"Kim. I should've known." Sue reached for the dangling cardstock label. "The Twisted Tulip. How creative." She set the flowers on the kitchen table, against the wall. "Would you like something to drink?"

Evan wanted to ask for a beer. Instead, he settled for a glass of water.

"You know, I haven't seen you since Jeremy's funeral."

Folding his hands in his lap beneath the table, Evan nodded. "I'm sorry about that."

"Heard you've been in Alaska putting out forest fires. Is that true?"

"It is." Evan reached for his glass of iced water. *Get to it,* he told himself. "I'm also sorry about the rift I caused—between you and my mom."

Sue, filling a glass of iced tea for herself, slid into a chair beside him. "She tried to blame you for that, did she?" Leaning back and crossing her legs, she continued. "Look, your mom and I never fought because you left."

"Then what happened?"

"It's complicated."

An uncomfortable silence lingered in the air. Evan's eyes roamed the kitchen that looked a little too much like the one he blacked out in five years ago. In the demented reality of his recurring nightmares, the yellow of the diamonds in the backsplash bled down the walls.

Sue placed a soft hand on his wrist. "I know you must feel an enormous amount of guilt, Evan. But it wasn't your fault. I know you did everything you could to save him."

He'd heard that a lot after Jeremy's death. It was one of the reasons he left Willow Creek.

But here he was, back again. Though he still couldn't tell anyone what he admitted to Jeremy that morning before the fire. He couldn't confess his affair with Kim. It would be selfish of him to put that out there for the whole town to know. Kim would be incredibly embarrassed, and her dad . . .

"I asked him for a favor," Evan said. This was probably the safest approach. "We were supposed to grab lunch at the Saber Saloon, but I insisted."

"Evan," Sue said, warning in her voice. "Whatever favor you asked of him, you didn't hold him at gunpoint and force him back to the house. Nor did you insist he take a nap before coming back to work."

He'd tried those same excuses on himself for years, but they never ridded the nightmares. "I don't know why he decided to take a nap. He went back to the house to get something for me. I don't even remember him being tired. Of course, a lot of memories from that day are blurry at best. I should've told him it could wait until after work."

"If you want to play the blame game, then I'm playing too." Sue took a sip of her tea. "It was my stupid curling iron. One I apparently plugged in and never even used that morning because I was late to work. I don't remember pulling the damn thing out of the drawer."

"You can't blame yourself for that."

"No? I was too cheap to buy a modern one that had one of those shut-off timers. If I'd forked out the twenty dollars, the iron never would've been hot enough to *cause* a fire." She rose from the table, grabbed the pitcher of iced tea, and carried it to the table. "Look, we can both sit here and speculate and blame ourselves all day long, but that won't get us anywhere."

Evan hung his head low.

"But if there is one thing I know about my son, it's that he'd be disappointed in you, Evan. You've been harboring guilt for years instead of living your life. You're not married; you've stayed thousands of miles away from everyone you care about, including your family. And all for what? To live dangerously trying to save others? Jeremy would slap you upside the head and tell you to start living." Sue covered his hand with hers. "He would tell you to live the life that he doesn't get to."

Chapter 9

Kim was helping Agnes Billings reach a yellow cake mix from the top shelf when Macy finally made her entrance. Kim considered herself outgoing and outspoken, but she was a dim light in a cellar compared to Macy's lighthouse beacon personality.

Walking Agnes to the checkout counter, Kim watched her older sister throw her arms around Wilma Gentry as if they were old friends. As far as Kim could remember, Macy had never done anything for Wilma, not even sent the woman a Christmas card the way Kim did. But Wilma acted as if Macy was a celebrity.

"Macy Wilkerson, you are one beautiful little lady!" Wilma stood, exclaiming. "Guess the Army didn't take *that* away from you."

"Army?" Agnes repeated in the checkout line, unable to keep from eavesdropping. With only one checkout line, it was impossible not to participate in every customer's conversation.

"Kimmie!" Macy patted Wilma on the shoulder, then slipped around the woman to hug her. "It's so good to see you." Long, wavy blonde hair and an orange, flowery perfume enveloped Kim. Judging the strength of her sister's grip, she made a mental note not to start a brawl. With Macy, she'd probably lose.

This hugging thing was newer. Until Macy left the house after she graduated high school, she and Kim had fought constantly. "I'm a little surprised to see you," Kim teased, failing to wriggle free. Macy, with a hand on Kim's shoulder, had her trapped with a Hulk-like grip. "Did Mom promise to buy you a log cabin or something?"

"Ha ha," Macy retorted.

"You're in the Army?" Agnes asked. She handed a box of cake mix to Wilma to scan.

"Yes." Macy smiled, mostly with her dazzling blue eyes, a blue the color of the ocean on a clear day. "I'm stationed in Alaska."

"Alaska?" repeated Agnes, awe in her wide eyes.

"Do they really ride dog sleds to work?" Wilma asked.

"I bet you've seen the Northern Lights!" added Agnes.

"No dog sleds for me, but yes, I've seen the beautiful Aurora! They've just started to peek out now that it's fall. It's the most amazing sight I've ever seen."

Most amazing, oh please. Kim tried again to squirm away from her sister's grip, unsuccessfully.

"The greens and purples, oh they're so fluid with movement," Macy gushed. "Like they're dancing in the sky! Kimmie, you really should come back with me. It's so beautiful up there, especially from a helicopter."

And it begins. "I need to finish up some stuff in the back." Finally breaking free of Macy's vise grip, Kim retreated to the back room where plenty of stock from yesterday's haul needed unpacking.

Halfway through a carton of peanut butter, Kim heard her sister from behind. "Can I help?"

Though several pallets were still wrapped, Kim wasn't sure she could handle Macy's Alaska patter, guilting her into visiting her newfound home. Not when it would only remind her of the man she was determined to avoid. *Stupid Alaska.*

"Nope, I'm good here. Just go keep Dad occupied. He's been too well-behaved this week, even if Mom has been drugging him."

"I'll stop by Gram's later." Macy's phone buzzed. Kim watched her sister's eyes dart to the screen. A disappointed frown followed. The moment was quick and fleeting. Macy replaced it with her bright smile. "I'm parked out front." She nodded toward the saloon doors.

"Let me guess," Kim said. "That bright red car is yours."

Hand on the swinging door, Macy shrugged. "You only live once." She whisked off toward the front of the store, greeting another customer on her way.

About to push her cart out to restock the peanut butter and jelly aisle, Kim heard the back door creak. A sliver of light poured into the dimly lit storeroom, gradually widening until Chip's head appeared in the gap.

"Dad, I swear if you don't get your butt out of here, I'm going to call Mom on you!" Kim was at the door in a heartbeat, pushing him back outside.

"I just need to get one thing from the office—"

"No, you don't." Kim latched onto his arm and forcefully ushered him to his motorcycle, discreetly parked between two storage sheds. "Are you even supposed to be riding that thing?"

Chip gave her a nasty look. "I'm recovering from stress. I'm not senile, you know!"

"Then get on your bike and drive yourself back home. I'm calling the house in ten minutes. If you don't answer, I'm telling Mom and Kid Doctor on you."

"But—"

"Now." When he didn't budge, she added a snappy, "Go!"

"You won't tell your mother?"

"Not yet."

"Did Macy make it in?" Chip asked once his helmet was properly adjusted.

"Stop stalling or I'll send her back to Alaska." With folded arms, Kim watched her dad drive away and disappear down the alley.

She'd noted the expression in his eyes when he spotted Evan's truck turning a corner in their direction as he mounted his motorcycle. It reminded Kim of yet another thing to worry about besides keeping their dad from returning to the store.

Halfway through the restocking, she heard Macy greet another customer with such pomp and circumstance anyone might've thought the president had shown up. She set the jumbo jar of grape jelly back in the cart, prepared to usher Macy out of the store with as much vigor as she used on Chip.

"Why, if it isn't the one and only Evan Rowe!"

At that, Kim reconsidered abandoning her restocking chore and drove the cart to the back of the store. Jars of jelly rattled—like her nerves.

She searched for the scanner, deciding to switch tasks. She'd come to rely on it like a sort of all-knowing robot for the store's shelves. *Dammit, it's out front.* If anyone other than Macy had been out at the checkout counter, Kim would've found something else to occupy her time. But Macy might unknowingly tell their dad about the fancy scanner and cause a second heart attack.

"Hi, Kimberly." Evan greeted her the second she came into his view. His cognac eyes slowly scanned her body, forcing Kim to look away. "I bought one of your arrangements yesterday for your aunt Sue. Just wanted to let you know, she loved it."

"Thanks." She tried to hide it, but the compliment sent excited tingles through her. "I didn't realize you went to see her."

"Don't know why that surprises you, Kimmie. He was always at Aunt Sue's house growing up. You remember, don't you?"

How could Kim forget? Growing up, people used to joke that Evan was more a Wilkerson than a Rowe for all the time he spent with their family. "Kimmie?" Evan repeated, a smirk forming. "I didn't realize anyone called you that anymore."

"Well, you haven't exactly been around to notice." The icy edge she intended didn't come across. Instead her words sounded closer to pouting.

"You're right."

Kim spotted the scanner at the edge of the checkout counter. If she slowly stepped around, she'd be able to grab it without Macy noticing. Her sister was busy eyeing Evan like a delectable dessert.

Reaching for the scanner, her hand froze halfway when Macy said, "I hear we're practically neighbors, Evan. In Alaska, I mean."

"You're stationed up there?"

"Fort Wainwright."

"How have we never bumped into each other?"

Kim felt something hot and fiery flowing into her veins. Something like annoyance, making her grip on the scanner turn her knuckles white. She refused to admit it was jealousy.

"We'll have to grab a drink one night soon," her sister suggested. "Not everyone appreciates Alaska." Macy touched his arm. "It'd be nice to talk to someone who does."

Evan opened his mouth, about to reply. Then he closed his lips. Lips that Kim couldn't seem to keep her stupid eyes off of. No matter how hard she fought the memories, she couldn't will herself to forget all the wonderful things those lips had done. *Giant emotional barrier wall, where are you?*

"Um, sure," Evan finally said through a blush.

"How about tomorrow night?" Macy suggested.

Whatever fiery substance had entered Kim's veins was now coursing through like lava. *Is she asking him out on a date?*

"Uh—tomorrow there's football. Up at the high school. I told Alex I'd go watch the game. With him."

"High school football! How could I say no to that?" Macy practically cooed.

"I don't believe he invited you," Kim said, scanner forgotten.

"Do you two want to come?" Evan's eyes lingered on Kim, challenge flashing through them. "Or are you too busy?"

"Busy?" Macy hooted. "I can't imagine with what, Kimmie. Heard you got fired from your full-time job."

About to snap back, the bells over the front door jingled. A couple of elderly ladies entered. Both were known for sharing gossip worse than their husbands.

"Kim Wilkerson, we need to talk to you about putting together some flower arrangements for the upcoming Turkey Supper. Do you do centerpieces? We'd like to hire you."

"I'm sure I could whip up something. Let's go find somewhere to talk in the back." She led them, scanner clutched tightly, away from her overbearing sister. Macy couldn't know how her shameless flirting with Evan was like a kick in the stomach to Kim. She also needed distance from the man who was launching his heaviest arsenal at her wall of spite. "What's the theme?" she heard herself ask.

"She didn't get *fired*," Macy said to Evan once Kim left. "Mom told me she basically told her boss to go to hell."

"Sounds like a Wilkerson."

"Yep." Macy tucked her long blonde hair behind her ear. She'd forgotten just how fit and muscular those Rowe men were. And how incredibly hot. Sure beat the online dating scene, which was getting her nowhere. Except badgered by creepy men who didn't understand why she turned them down. "I was just trying to rile her up."

"I can see *that* hasn't changed."

Evan wore that familiar debonair smile. Macy had noticed how it seemed to have an effect on Kim too, despite how cold she tried being to him. Macy felt that instinct to protect her younger sister. From what she'd been told, Evan was only in town for a couple of weeks, then he was headed back to Alaska. No sense in letting her sister get tangled up with a man who'd only break her heart when he left.

But with Evan living on the same base in Alaska as she worked . . . "How long have you been in town?"

"Since Tuesday."

"First time back in a while?"

"Five years." Evan glanced at the door, then at the clock. "I better get back to Violet's. She'll want this bag of sugar. See you tomorrow night at the game?"

"Maybe even tonight. I owe Gram a visit."

Evan nodded but didn't say anything more. He rushed out the door.

Macy thought highly of Evan, even after the fire. She'd never once considered him guilty of anything but trying his best to save her cousin's life. But if she wanted to win his affection, she'd have to try a little harder.

The bells above the door jingled. Macy considered letting Wilma handle this next customer so she could head home to see her dad, but when she looked up she spotted Allie Jordan, Kimmie's best friend. "Allie!" She came around the counter and gave her a hug. "How are you?"

"I reckon she's great," Wilma offered. "She's got a pretty attractive boyfriend."

"You do?" Macy asked, waiting for Allie to fill her in.

But Wilma beat her to it. "She's dating our new doctor. He's southern!"

"Good for you, Allie."

"Macy, can you stay up front while I run to the little girls' room?"

"Of course, Wilma." *As long as no customers want anything*. She didn't have a clue how to run that ancient cash register anymore. Macy turned her attention back to Allie. "Hope this prince charming is treating you right?"

"Yes," Allie answered. "He's pretty great. You'll have to meet him sometime."

"Definitely! Name the time, and I'll be there. Tonight even."

"I think he's going to Alex's tonight." Allie grabbed a basket near the front door. "Maybe this weekend we can figure something out."

"Alex? As in Alex Rowe, the state trooper?"

"Special Investigator now."

"Interesting." Macy swiped her purse from the counter and dug for a piece of gum. "Is Alex married?"

"No," Allie said. "I can't understand why." She leaned in closer to Macy, almost whispering now. "I'm keeping my eye out for someone to fix him up with. If you think of anyone, let me know."

Macy nodded, but kept silent as Allie headed to the back of the store. Special Investigator Alex Rowe was closer to Kim's age, and unlike his brother, he wasn't leaving to go back to Alaska in a couple of weeks. *Kimmie, it's time you found happiness while you're back in town.*

"I don't have that kind of money." Chip pounded his fist on his kitchen counter for emphasis, but granite had a way of muffling the effects. He needed Ron Larson to leave before Macy showed up and started asking questions. "You can show yourself out."

"The terms of the agreement are pretty clear." Ron stood with folded arms over his rounded belly. He was balding faster than Chip, but the steel had never left his eyes in the decades the men had known each other. Odd to think they'd been friends as boys.

"I've made every payment on time for the last ten years. You can't consider giving me just a little longer? Or maybe you could let me make payments."

"You have two and a half weeks to come up with the balloon payment. It's your last one, then you're free and clear of any financial obligation to me. Chip, that should feel like a relief."

"Stop trying to sound like you're the hero here, Ron. You knew that balloon payment would be impossible to come up with." Chip knew he should stop, let Ron leave before he said something he'd regret. But all this time locked up under house arrest had given him time. Time that he was trapped with nothing but the dull murmur of the TV and his thoughts. "You think you run this town now just because Lesley Jamison is behind bars? The minute that woman is offered bail, you know she'll—"

"She's not in charge anymore." Ron headed for the door, any signs of pleasantness gone. "I don't give a flying fuck about that woman. You have two weeks to come up with the payment or you'll sign the deed for the store over to me, just like the agreement states."

Chip had tried to sneak into the store earlier today, to take a peek at the books and see if there was any place cash might be pulled from, but Kim had caught him and sent him on his way home. "And if I don't?" he called to Ron's back

"You don't want to go down that road, Chip. You wouldn't survive it." Hand on the screen door, he added, "I always win. You know that."

Chip felt his blood pressure climb as he followed Ron. "You can't threaten me."

"No?" Once down the cement stairs, Ron turned. "I hear both of your daughters are back in town for a few weeks. Would be a shame if life got a little difficult for them, wouldn't it?"

"You leave them out of this." Chip could feel the heat sizzling through his pores. His face was surely an unnatural tomato red color.

"Here comes one of them now." Ron nodded down the road, to where a red Dodge Charger sped up the block. No doubt Macy's rental car. "You know what you have to do."

Chapter 10

The following afternoon, Kim watched Macy make herself right at home in Gram's guest bedroom, stretching out on Kim's bed. "If you don't want to go to the game, then don't." Her long tanned legs were barely covered by her Daisy Dukes. She paged through the binder Kim planned to set on the front counter of The Twisted Tulip. "I can see you're pretty absorbed in this little project of yours."

Kim yanked the binder free from Macy's fingers. "This *little* project happens to be my future." She set the book back on the dresser. "I may not have any interest watching people I don't know play high school football, but I do have only a week before I meet with the bank." She left out the part about making an offer on the space she wanted to buy. She'd dodged having to ask Macy for a loan, but her sister would surely find a way to *help* that would only cause a fight.

"It's our hometown, Kimmie. We should cheer them on." Macy pushed off the bed, standing. "It'll be fun." She watched out the window, for Evan no doubt. He was working out there, clearing some dead tree branches from the tangle that guarded the smallest flower garden on the east side of the house. No doubt with his shirt off again. Kim didn't bother checking. Not with Macy there at the window.

"Not all of us were Homecoming Queen."

"Is that what this is about? It's not that big a deal."

"Maybe not to you." Kim hadn't meant to sound so jealous. But her sister had always gotten everything she wanted. Life seemed to hand her whatever she desired. Kim, on the other hand, had to work three jobs to make her dreams a possibility.

Macy leered again; the smile on her face let Kim know that Evan was definitely outside without his shirt. Maybe even naked with a look like that. She pestered, "Then I guess I'll just have to tell Evan and Alex you changed your mind."

"I never said I'd go."

"Suit yourself. That's just more Rowe hotness for me!"

"Fine. I'll go," Kim blurted, some crazy emotion—not jealousy, but something—taking over her rational senses.

"Good. I think you'll have fun. Evan's brother—that cute detective—is coming too. Where does he live now?"

"Norfolk," Kim replied.

"And so do—" The chime on Macy's phone cut her off. She dug her smartphone from her tiny denim shorts. When her eyes met the screen, she sighed.

"Did someone beat you for Alaska's number one fan?" Kim teased.

"Funny." Macy put away her phone, her demeanor transformed. She skipped to the door, then paused, hugging the frame. "I'm going to get a piece of that peach pie and chat with Gram and her garden-party ladies for a bit."

"Garden party?"

"Maybe I'll see if Evan needs any help. Be ready to leave at six-thirty."

Kim's bedroom suddenly felt claustrophobic. She retrieved an old quilt from the sitting room closet, and with her binder clutched against her chest, headed downstairs with an aim of sneaking out to the clearing by the creek.

The chatter and laughter of a half dozen women grew louder, warning Kim they were gathered on the front porch. To avoid them, she slipped out the back door instead. Gram hadn't mentioned having guests. But Kim suspected it wasn't merely a coincidence that

Evan was working in their line of sight, shirtless. *Got to hand it to those little ladies. They know a good show when they see one.*

Most of the murky water of the creek was surrounded by trees and high banks. But one clearing on the edge of her grandma's property offered a gradual slope that led down to the water.

When she arrived home from the grocery store yesterday, Kim photographed each container she picked up from the estate sale with her smartphone. Today she flipped through them as well as the collection already in her binder, hoping to find ten perfect, unique containers for the Turkey Supper arrangements. She'd have to run to Norfolk for the flowers, as her grandma didn't have any yellow bearded irises she'd need to match their theme.

"Come here often?"

Kim's heart skipped a half dozen beats, like a scratch on a CD. She'd forgotten how many times they came down to the creek to get away from prying eyes. How many kisses had they snuck away to steal in their single summer? Hundreds? Thousands? "Go away."

"I need to cool off. Not used to this heat anymore."

"Stupid Alaska," Kim muttered under her breath. Or so she thought.

"What do you have against Alaska?" Evan leaned against a large oak tree. Kim tried not to watch the drops of sweat roll down his perfect muscles.

"It takes—" She cut herself off. She didn't owe him any explanation. "I just don't see what's so great about it."

"You've never been there."

Kim buried her head in her binder and continued to scan the pictures of her catalogued arrangements. At the sound of a zipper, her head shot up. "What are you doing?" If her heart had been skipping earlier, it was now playing a drum set against her eardrums. *So not fair!*

"I told you, I need to cool off."

"You can't—" Kim couldn't find it in herself to object. Or even look away. She watched his worn, dirty jeans slip to the ground. Evan stood in nothing but a pair of navy blue boxers and solid muscle. From his smirk, he found her speechlessness amusing.

"Care to join me?"

Every physical urge within her screamed *yes!* But the only sensible one held her back. The one that knew she wasn't a great swimmer. Or even a poor swimmer. "I think you have some fans back there who would join you."

"Abigail Adams did offer me a casserole if I lost my jeans."

Kim couldn't help but stare at his bare legs now, eyeing a heavily wrapped portion on his lower calf. "What happened to your leg?"

"Nothing, just a scratch. So, you coming?"

"Busy." Kim reached for her binder. "I want this to be perfect."

"Oh, that's right. Violet was bragging about that. Your business plan." There wasn't mocking in his voice, only interest.

"No one seems to think I can do this, like it's a joke or something. Except for Gram and Allie."

Evan neared the gradual slope toward the water. "I think your sales these last few days would trump that." With one inviting smile, he stepped into the water. It seemed deep enough to dive into from where Kim sat, but everyone knew not to take that chance. Looks could be deceiving. And then there was the matter of rocks, chunks of trees, and other fun gifts of nature lurking below the cover of the cloudy water.

"You coming?" Evan called from the water.

"Don't really care to drown, thank you," Kim replied, her eyes glued to her phone.

"I thought I'd find you two here." Macy's presence should have been a shock to Kim, but she'd grown used to her sister's grand entrances. A few years apart wouldn't change that, especially since she was now a glamorous helicopter pilot. "I'm surprised you aren't in the creek too. It's so hot out here!"

Macy threw her long blonde hair into a messy bun. Damn her, it looked like chaotic perfection. Then she removed her tank top, revealing a lacy black bra.

"What are you doing?" It was one thing to flirt with Evan, but quite another to strip down in front of your sister and get in the water with him. Of course, Kim had never told Macy there'd been anything between them. And there was certainly no point now.

"Going swimming, silly. Coming?"

Kim held her breath when her sister dropped her denim shorts beside the blanket she'd brought out. *At least it's not a thong.* But the matching black bikini-style panties didn't leave much to the imagination. "I'm busy."

Shrugging, Macy made her way to the edge of the water. She called out to Evan, "How deep is it?"

"It's pretty deep over here."

Kim tried not to pay attention. She shouldn't care if her sister wanted a shot at Evan. He'd just break her heart, too. But she kept sneaking glances, not really paying attention to the photos in her binder. Until one slipped out.

She'd forgotten about the single photo she and Evan had taken five years ago. They'd been nestled in the bed of his truck at sunset, the sun's golden rays illuminating the background. Her hair had been longer back then, several inches past her shoulders. Evan looked younger, but maybe it was the absence of the dark stubble growing into a beard he had now.

She looked toward Evan to make the comparison. He caught her watching and smiled.

"If I jump, will you catch me?" Macy called.

Kim shoved the photo into the back of the binder. "Do you two want some privacy?"

As Macy took a running start to make the jump safely, Kim began packing up her things. She was not going to sit here in her favorite spot and watch her sister act like a flirty teenager. How Macy had yet to snag an Alaskan man was beyond her. Macy had more boyfriends in high school than most people had classes.

Exiting the photo app on her phone, Kim felt a shadow hovering above her. Peeling her eyes upward, Evan stood at the edge of her blanket, dripping wet. His boxers, drenched by the water, clung to his thighs. She swallowed.

"You have thirty seconds," he said, his voice gruff.

"For what?"

"To shed the clothes you want to keep dry."

"Go away." Kim continued gathering her things, closing her binder and putting her pencil back in her lily-patterned tote.

"What's up with this stick in the mud thing? That's not the Kimberly I know."

"I'm a tree, rooted in dry ground."

"Have it your way." Evan scooped down and threw Kim over his shoulder so quickly she hardly had time to drop her phone, let alone register what happened before they reached the edge of the water.

"Put me down!" She tried to kick, but he had hold of her feet. The first twinge of panic hit when she saw her sister treading water just a few yards away. The creek was much deeper than she thought.

"I believe they call that the fireman's carry," Macy's voice called. "My turn next!"

"Evan, you are *not* getting me wet!"

"You never had a problem with it before," he said quietly enough so Macy didn't hear. And seductively enough that Kim blushed. It was just the distraction he needed to plunge them both into the deepest area of the creek.

Kim barely had time to hold her breath before she was completely submerged. At first, the icy water shocked her system.

"That's better," Evan said, smirking.

She had to admit that the cool water was a nice contrast to the hot early fall day. Not that she'd admit that to *them*. Her feet barely flat on the sandy bottom of the creek, she inched closer to the shore in search of more solid footing. Kim resisted the urge to stomp off toward the house.

"Oh no!" It was Macy, hugging her arms over her bare chest. "I think I lost my bra!"

"For the love of cupcakes," murmured Kim. "Really? What are you, fifteen?"

"On that branch floating behind you." Evan pointed.

"Can you help me out?"

Before Kim could sputter another retort, Violet appeared in the clearing, calling out Macy's name. "Macy, your dad is on the phone. He says it's urgent."

"Be right there, Gram," Macy yelled back, turning her back to fetch her bra from the garment-eating branch. "I'll probably head to Mom and Dad's. Evan, I'll see you tonight. Mind picking me up?"

Turning away, Kim tried to hide the jealous fire in her eyes.

"We'll be there, won't we?" Evan turned to Kim, daring her to change her mind now.

She'd been backing up in the wrong direction, apparently. She could hardly touch the bottom with the tips of her toes. Once Macy gathered her clothes and retreated toward the house, Kim edged toward shallower water. She didn't like being this vulnerable. It wasn't as if she could swim away from him. "Don't you have work to do? Little old ladies to put on a show for?"

Evan edged closer. "The work will still be there tomorrow. Probably the ladies, too."

In her pale pink tank top, Kim couldn't very well be the first one to crawl out of the water. And from the victorious look in Evan's eyes, he knew it too. She wanted to back up as he gained on her, but one step backward and she wouldn't touch bottom without her head going under. Her arms began to ache. Not that her poor attempt at treading water was even working. *Life would be so much easier right now if I were a mermaid.*

"Kim, will you please just hear me out?"

He continued closing in on her. She tiptoed back a little further and found a whole new respect for ballerinas who mastered balance without water to hold them up. Her strained toes throbbed.

"Now?"

"Now's as good as ever."

"No," Kim said with such force that Evan stopped. "Five years ago would've been the ideal time." Her head went under the water. She pushed off the bottom right away, but panic was setting in. Her body weakened.

"Are you okay?"

Kim glared. "I'm fine."

"As much as I wish I could, I can't go back and change the past." The sound of a snapping twig caused Evan to turn his head toward the clearing.

Again, she fell below the surface. This time, pushing off the bottom was a little more exhausting. She didn't resurface as quickly, and coming up, she forced herself to spit out water. Evan was calling to someone, though Kim couldn't make out the words. She tried to slip around him, but the bottom of the creek disappeared beneath her strained toes.

"I want to fix this, Kimberly."

Tears welled at the corners of her eyes, partially from the fear of drowning and partially from the use of a name only Evan had ever used. Kimberly was on her birth certificate, but not even her parents used it. "You can't. It's too late."

"No, I refuse to believe that."

"You left me. You left *us*." Kim barely got the words out above a whisper. She was so tired from failing to tread water. Her poor attempts left her unable to touch the bottom without her nose being swallowed by the creek.

"Are you sure you're—"

"Dammit, I'm fine." The last thing she needed was Evan's concern. She could save herself. *If only I could reach the shore.*

"I am truly sorry about that."

"Sorry won't cut—" Kim couldn't hold herself up any longer. She fell below the surface again. The strength she had in her legs wasn't doing much to push her up this time, despite her sporadic kicking. Her ability to hold her breath dwindled. She flailed her arms in one last desperate attempt to find air.

Two strong arms scooped her up, shooting her to the surface like a bottle rocket. Within seconds, they were both in shallower water. Kim didn't want to appear so weak in front of him, but she couldn't help it. Her arms clung to his neck so tightly she feared he might choke.

"You never told me you couldn't swim," Evan whispered against her ear. "Kimberly, I'm so sorry."

"Don't call me that." But her words lacked conviction with her body trembling so violently.

With one arm, he scooped her up and proceeded to carry her out of the creek. When he set her down, she didn't want to let go. Aside from her drowning fear, his body felt so warm and comforting, protecting hers the way it was. She'd missed that more than she wanted to admit.

She dated off and on, but she'd never let anyone get as close to her as Evan had. She'd never felt safe in another's embrace.

For months after he left, she cried herself to sleep and begged God to bring him back. She sent dozens of emails that went unanswered, and within a week of him leaving, his phone number was disconnected.

"Why?" Kim asked, now seated on her blanket. Evan's strong arm was still wrapped around her shoulders. "Why did you leave?"

Evan turned his eyes to her, a vulnerability in them she'd never seen until now. "I was scared."

Chapter 11

Evan knocked gently on Kim's door a little before five. It hadn't occurred to him until she was in the shower that, despite the time they spent *near* the creek years ago, they'd never once gone in the water. He waited till she'd taken a hot shower after her scare and his bringing her up to the house, dripping and shaking. Had he only known Kim couldn't swim, he would never have carried her into the water at all.

Today, he thought she'd playfully swim away from him, that maybe she'd let her guard down just long enough for him to find out if she was happy. Long enough to ask for that impossible forgiveness. If she would just give him a few minutes to hear him out, he could let her go. Let her find someone who'd cherish her and was never stupid enough to walk away.

"Kimberly, you awake?"

When she didn't answer, he took a deep breath then turned the knob. To his surprise, he found it unlocked.

He glanced over his shoulder, almost afraid Violet would catch him sneaking into Kim's room. But she'd already left, taking the gaggle of ladies with her for the infamous Friday bridge night at Aunt Ruby's.

"Hey," he said, pushing the door open.

Kim was curled up on the bed, her back to him. He hated to wake her, but he needed to know she was okay. She'd clung to him so tightly. The way her body had trembled with fear and cold had shaken him.

When she didn't turn, he sat on the edge of the bed. "Kim?" He touched her shoulder. What he wouldn't give to crawl in beside her. To feel her body melded against his. But those days were long behind them. He reached a hand to brush away the short blonde hair covering her cheek. Expecting that soft skin, he was surprised to feel tears.

"Please, go away." He hardly heard the quiet words.

"I will, after I say one last thing." She turned toward him then, her eyes red. Wet streaks covered her cheeks. His heart ached, knowing he'd caused her pain. "I'm not leaving until you hear me out."

"What's the point?" Kim sat up, wiping her cheeks with the back of her hand. "You're not staying."

A part of Evan yearned for the life he walked away from five years ago. If he'd only stayed . . . "I'm here now."

Kim folded her knees to her chest, the spaghetti strap of her flimsy tank sliding off her shoulder. "I want to give you that chance, to hear you out."

Evan tried not to focus on that strap, one that revealed she wasn't wearing a bra. "But you can't." His fingers ached to help that strap and the rest of the tank top slide right off Kim's silky skin.

"Yeah."

"I tried to call once," Evan said, but it didn't matter anymore. He didn't know why he told her, other than he felt he had to.

"Once." The word felt like a dagger when Kim repeated it.

Out of reflex, Evan reached his hand to tuck her hair behind her ear. His thumb wiped away the fresh tear. "I'm so sorry, Kimberly. I never meant for any of this to happen. I never meant to hurt you. Not today at the creek, and never after Jeremy died."

"I never blamed you, you know. It wasn't your fault."

Evan sucked in a deep breath. "I know." For the first time in five years, he believed the words.

"Then why did you leave?"

If he was going to make things right, he had to start by being completely honest. "I never told you what all happened that day."

148

Tears crested in her eyes. "I don't like thinking about that day." Kim reached up with both her hands, removing his hand from her face and holding it with her own. "That morning, everything was so perfect."

Out of guilt, Evan hadn't let himself think about the happiest part of that day. But here, with Kim just inches from him, he remembered waking up with her beside him in his bed. Her blonde hair had been longer back then, covering her bare shoulders. She'd been tangled in his sheets, a smudge of red lipstick on the pillowcase beside her.

"You looked like an angel in my bed that morning." He should stop himself. It wasn't fair to bring up the happiness he'd abandoned. But he couldn't stop. "I remember thinking I was the luckiest man alive. The beautiful, bold Kimberly Wilkerson slept in *my* arms."

Sheer happiness lit up her hazel eyes. Evan couldn't help himself. He leaned in, grazing her cheek with his free hand, drawing her lips to his. The kiss began gentle, sensual. A kiss of reclaiming the past, if only for a moment.

Once those memories of their passionate affair came crashing back, their kiss deepened. Kim moaned beneath his touch. Like a forest fire, her soft skin radiated heat. He pulled that pesky strap further down.

Kim's fingers tangled in his hair and drew him down on the bed.

His hands cupped her breasts through what little fabric still covered them, her nipples pebbling between his fingers. Her tongue traced his lips, begging entry. His fingers dipped beneath the hem of her shirt.

She reached for the button of his jeans.

Evan shot back from the bed as if she'd electrocuted him. "I'm sorry. I shouldn't have kissed you. That was a mistake."

He dashed out of the room, closing the door behind him. He didn't stop until he'd flown down the stairs and was out in the fresh afternoon air.

He kicked an innocent bucket clear off the porch. It landed in a pile of brush. *Dammit!* He'd promised himself he'd say his piece and go, but here he was seducing her. He hadn't expected the past to come crashing back like it had. Not only their time together, but the deep feelings they'd shared.

Evan, if you aren't careful, you'll fall in love with Kimberly all over again.

Safely squeezed on the far side of Evan's truck, Kim asked, "Are you still working for that wildland fire department?" Even the enormous center console wasn't enough to put proper space between them. That kiss in her room, as unexpected as it was, had been equally thrilling and terrifying. Filled with passion, possibility, and disaster.

"No, I'm jumping now." Evan wasn't so great at making eye contact either, it seemed.

"Like jumping out of planes into fires?"

"Yeah."

Kim suspected he wouldn't be much for conversation, even on the short drive to pick up his brother. She should be angry with him for kissing her, and even angrier that he called it a mistake. But then she remembered the sensation of his strong, rough hands on her skin, his hands cupping her breasts through the thin fabric of her tank. During that fiery kiss, she'd expected they'd spontaneously combust.

"Why'd you come back? Why now?"

Evan pulled into the winding driveway, accelerating if she wasn't mistaken. *Avoiding the question.*

"Did something happen in Alaska?" When he didn't answer, she placed her hand on his forearm. He yanked his arm away as if she'd seared his skin.

Evan shut off the ignition and pulled out the keys. "Coming?"

"Inside?"

"Yeah."

"I've never been inside before."

They stared at each other over the hood of the truck as realization dawned. They'd talked about it often enough back then. Evan had been excited to have Kim over for his family's Thanksgiving dinner. He'd raved about his mother's cooking and her pumpkin dessert. "It's better than pumpkin pie," he'd said.

"Well, except for the man-cave when Alex had people over for a baseball game a couple months ago," Kim added.

"Alex does love his Cubs." Evan ushered her forward with a light touch on her lower back. Instantly, she felt the heat of his skin bleed through her shirt's thin cotton. She should fight her attraction. She knew that. The magnetism between them had never been the issue, but it'd certainly been easier to ward off before he kissed her.

The second Kim stepped inside, she admired the high ceilings, hardwood floors, and huge bay window. From the far edge of the room, she saw into the formal dining area. Then into the kitchen. The aroma of some delicious cake filled her senses.

On the leather sofa in the living room sat a young girl with curled hair wearing a Willow Creek Sabers sweatshirt. *Evan's little sister, Hannah.* "I'm coming to the game, too," Hannah announced, interrupted from watching a show about interior design that Kim recognized. She looked Kim up and down. "Is this your girlfriend?"

"No, just a good friend of mine," Evan answered, sparing Kim the embarrassment. "Where's Alex?"

"Upstairs on the phone again. Some *super*-secret case."

"Is someone baking a cake?" Kim asked. "It smells wonderful!"

"Mom." Hannah shot her eyes to Evan. "She bakes when she's mad."

"I bet Alex will be a few minutes. Kim, let's go say hi to my mom."

From Kim's assessment, Hannah was right. Anita seemed to be stress-baking. Her hair had fallen from its high ponytail in several places. A smudge of vanilla frosting covered her left cheek. She hugged a metal baking bowl as if she were a football player, trying to keep the ball from being stripped.

"Mom, you remember Kimber—Kim Wilkerson."

A small irrational sting struck Kim when he corrected himself.

"Hi, Kim. Haven't seen in you in almost as long as Evan. Don't suppose you moved to Alaska, too?" The sarcasm, Kim assumed, was reserved for her son.

153

Kim spotted the cooling chocolate cupcakes on the counter near the toaster. She fought the urge to ask for one. *Damn things are going to be the end of me someday.* "No, just Norfolk."

"Kim's opening a florist shop. The Twisted Tulip."

"That's nice." She slammed the bowl on the counter and planted both hands on its granite surface. "Look, hurry up and get your siblings. I'm already running behind. Kim, it was nice to see you, but I need to get going myself."

Kim watched Anita remove her apron and throw it at the sink, leaving a bowl full of cake batter on the counter. "Um, should I put that in the fridge or something?"

"Leave it," said Evan.

They stood in the kitchen, the echoes of the TV filling a small void of awkward silence.

Evan rubbed the back of his neck. "Sorry about my mom. It's been a little tense."

Kim fought the urge to wrap her arms around him. *Stupid hot kiss.* Earlier, she'd been able to keep most of her walls reinforced. Now she felt they were more like a rickety fence and she kept climbing over it. "So how about a tour?"

"I guess I could show you around. C'mon." Evan motioned for her to follow him. "My great-granddad

154

built this house. He liked twelve-foot ceilings and custom woodwork." They slipped into the dining room, and instantly Kim saw what he was talking about. Beautiful cedar molding lined the floor. The floor-to-ceiling windows faced west, toward the impending sunset.

"I imagine a few family gatherings happen here." The table in the center of the room could easily seat sixteen. Kim's heart ached, remembering how Evan had wanted her to join his family for Thanksgiving all those years ago. He was so excited about it before everything changed. *We would have sat around this table together, laughing and telling jokes.*

"Yeah."

Hannah popped into the dining room. "I just let Alex know we're leaving with or without him," she announced. "Let's get this show on the road."

"Good girl. You don't mess around," Kim said.

Hannah smiled, and the awkward tension from her conversation with Evan's mom seemed to disappear.

Evan caught Hannah's attention. "Can you hang out with Kim a second and wait for Alex? I need to talk to Mom quick."

"We'll go wait by the truck." She latched onto Kim's arm and ushered her outside. It was such a shock, having a thirteen-year-old so instantly attached to her. *Is this what it's like to have a little sister?*

"Do you ever help your mom with baking?" Kim asked.

"Not really. I want to, but everyone acts like I'm just in the way."

"I know the feeling."

"You do?" The hope in Hannah's eyes was genuine.

"I'm the youngest of three also."

"Do you have brothers or sisters?"

"One of each. Macy's coming to the game with us tonight."

"Was she bossy when you were growing up?"

Kim laughed. "I hate to break it to you, but big sisters never grow out of that. She *still* bosses me around. And big brothers . . . Well, they just think they know everything."

"You *do* understand!"

"You two look like you're conspiring," Evan said as he neared them at the truck. Alex trailed behind, talking on his cell phone.

Kim met Hannah's gaze and shared a devious smile with her. "I like her, Evan. Can I keep her?" Hannah rewarded her with a beaming smile that could've blinded the entire state of Wyoming.

"Let's go," Alex said.

"You're sure you're not his girlfriend?" Hannah asked Kim.

Kim shook her head, though a part deep inside her, dormant for years, had awakened yearning for a different answer to that question.

"Can I sit in front then?"

"Of course."

At the passenger door, Hannah stopped. "Are you really opening a florist shop?"

"Yes."

"That's so cool!" Hannah hopped inside, turning as Kim buckled her seatbelt. "I like you too, Kim."

Chapter 12

When Macy joined the crowded truck, she was happy to see Evan's little sister riding shotgun and Kim in back, chatting away with Alex. *This will be easier than I thought.* "Who are we playing tonight?" she asked, reaching for her seatbelt.

"The Pine Valley Pirates," Hannah answered from the front seat. "Kim, did you play sports in high school?"

"Volleyball."

"Me too," said Macy. "And basketball." But her answer didn't seem to have any effect on young Hannah. She felt slightly outcast with her sister talking to Alex about baseball, of all things, and Evan staring straight ahead at the road. *Good thing it's a short drive.*

Not wanting to interrupt the two potential lovebirds sitting beside her, Macy leaned forward and tried for Evan's attention. "You said you're a smokejumper, right?"

"Yes," came his answer, with a nod.

"Is that what took you to Alaska?"

"Actually, I joined the wildland department first. I didn't enter the jump program until a couple of years later."

Macy could understand the adrenaline rush of parachuting out of planes into a blazing fire. She thought they probably had some of that thrill-seeker in common. The idea of Evan returning to Alaska—to Fort Wainwright—gave her hope. Maybe this bad dating spell would finally end. She wasn't sure she could handle much more of *TrueAlaskaMan69* or *HandsomeFisherman* constantly messaging her, begging for a second date. "When are you headed back?"

As if she'd pressed a mute button, conversation in the truck halted. Hannah's head shot up from her phone, her eyes on her brother. *Wrong question, apparently.*

"I haven't figured that out yet."

"Why don't you just stay?" Hannah retorted. "You drove all the way here anyway. You could just sell your cabin and move back to Willow Creek."

A cabin? Nice. "Hannah, what would your brother do here? They don't have any paid firefighters in town. He'd be bored to tears, wouldn't you, Evan?"

"You could go back to your old job," Hannah said as they pulled into the already crowded high school lot.

"The one where you manufactured irrigation pipes. You thought it was good enough when Jeremy was still alive."

The quiet inside the truck cab seemed to stop time. *What a bold little girl.* Macy felt the need to fix this, considering it was her question that had spiraled out of control. "Your brother's a very talented firefighter. He saves lives, Hannah. It wouldn't be fair to ask him to give that up."

They piled out of the truck, no one talking as they walked together toward the admission gate. She reached for Evan's arm and pulled him back. "I'm sorry. I probably should've kept my mouth shut."

Evan shook his arm free. "Yeah, you might've waited. Things are complicated enough."

Following the group to the stands, Macy scanned the crowd hoping to find familiar faces. She'd loved high school and knew a handful of her classmates had stayed in Willow Creek. Most were married and had a kid or two. But she didn't see anyone she recognized. Even the football coach was a stranger.

Guess tonight I'll just focus on setting Kimmie up with Alex.

Finding a spot in the crowded bleachers, Kim and Hannah sat in the row in front of Macy, Evan, and Alex. The football players, sporting white jerseys with black and gold accents, tossed footballs on the south end of the field as the warm-up clock ticked down.

"Evan!" Hannah exclaimed, leaning past Macy to get his attention. "Kim says she can teach me how to make some really awesome flower arrangements! Isn't she the coolest?"

Macy tilted her head in confusion. She could think of plenty of things a thirteen-year-old girl might find more entertaining than some lady teaching her about flowers. Like boys, for instance. But she refrained from opening her foot-filled mouth again.

Earlier, she dismissed Kim's business plan as a silly dream. Guilt crept in, the truth embarrassing. Macy felt intimidated. It forced her to face the reality that a couple of years from now, she'd no longer be in the Army. She could continue flying helicopters once she got out. Plenty of pilots did just that. But there was no guarantee that a job would be waiting for her in Alaska.

"You got awfully quiet," Alex said.

"Me?" Macy nodded at Evan. "What about him?"

Evan stood at that comment, like he might be avoiding further interrogation. "I need to talk to someone." Macy still felt bad about her unintentional ambush. "Be right back."

Moments after Evan disappeared behind the bleachers, talking to some man Macy didn't recognize in a John Deere hat, Hannah snuck off to talk to a friend.

Her buzzing phone stole her attention. Another message from a member of that dating service. *Helicopter pilot? Well Sexy, you can be my Top Gun anytime.* Macy fought the urge to throw her phone, catching the middle of a conversation between her sister and Alex just in time.

"It's not my fault." Kimmie was laughing so hard she was holding her stomach. "I got stuck in that locker room. I didn't have a choice. It was hide or—"

"Be caught," Alex finished. "Didn't you know those lockers would lock you in?"

"Of course not!"

"You had to," Alex continued, a twinkle in his eyes. "Just admit it, Kim Wilkerson. You wanted so badly to see me naked that Homecoming night that you locked yourself in the locker right next to mine."

Macy was too stunned to interject. She hadn't played cupid in a while, but she was happy to see her instincts hadn't grown rusty. *They already have such great chemistry.*

"I'm going to grab some popcorn," Evan announced just as Hannah returned to the bleachers. "Anyone want anything?"

"Are you buying?" Hannah asked.

"Sure."

"I'm coming! Kim, you have to come, too."

Alex shook his head as the three wandered off. "Amazing, isn't it?"

"What's that?" Macy asked.

"Those two just met before the game. Hannah's acting like Kim's some long lost sister or something." Digging his phone from his pocket, he checked it for at least the fourth time since they found their seats. "I'm pretty good at figuring people out, but I can't tell if she's trying to punish Evan or if she really meshed with your sister so quickly."

"It did seem a little strange, her so excited about flowers."

Alex shrugged. "Actually, that part's probably genuine. When she's not solving puzzles on *Wheel of Fortune*, she binge-watches all those interior-decorating shows. She might think Kim can show her how to make some of her own stuff."

"Huh."

"I'm determined to figure this out tonight."

"Good luck." Macy's own phone vibrated again. She knew she should unsubscribe from that dating service. She'd replied to dozens of messages, and had gone on half as many failed dates. But curiosity and hope won out.

"MountainGoat23?" Alex raised an eyebrow.

Macy shoved her phone back in her pocket.

Alex bumped her with his shoulder. "Don't you want to see what he has to say?"

Retracting her phone from her hoodie, she dared to open the email. *You're hott. Wanna grab a drink at my place?* "Happy?" Deleting the email, she put her phone away.

"You're going to crush that poor boy."

"Boy? You did see his pic, right? That man has a miner's beard. He's got to be at least fifty-five."

"Sounds like your dating life's about as exciting as mine."

Macy scanned the area, ensuring that Kim, Evan, and Hannah were all far away. "Can I ask you something personal?"

"Depends on what it is."

"I'm guessing you're not seeing anyone?" From the raised eyebrow, she quickly added, "I'm not asking for me. I'm asking for a friend." His eyebrow rose higher. She smacked him playfully with the back of her hand. "I'm serious! I have a friend I'd like to set you up with, if you're interested. I promise, she's amazing."

"I don't know," Alex said. "After what happened the last time I agreed to a blind date, I swore I'd never go on one again."

"C'mon," said Macy. "You can't fault me for your last experience. And I assure you, I can top whatever dating disaster story you have." She leaned a little closer, lowering her voice. "How bad was it?"

"Let's just say I wasn't really her type."

Macy sent him a look that told him such a broad explanation wasn't going to cut it.

"Because I wasn't a girl."

"Oh! That is a bit of a disaster. Who set you up on that one?"

Alex waved his hand. "Doesn't matter. Point is, I'm a little bit jaded on the whole blind-date thing. Plus, the case I'm working on is sucking away all of my time."

"But you've been in Willow Creek for a couple days now. Surely it's given you some free time?" Then it dawned on her. "Your case is here, isn't it?"

"*Still* here is more like it."

"Please? I think she's perfect for you." She watched the struggle in his eyes and pushed her luck. "You sound like you need a break from your case, Alex. A real one."

"Okay, fine."

"Great! How about tomorrow night? I'll make a dinner reservation in Norfolk for the two of you."

Fifty yards before the metal building that housed the concession stands, Evan saw Ron Larson walking his way. The man was rounder than the last time he saw him. Ron's wrinkle lines, like gorges around his eyes, were deeper, not well hidden by the Willow Creek Volunteer Fire Department ball cap he wore.

"As I live and breathe, I feel like I'm seeing a ghost," said Ron. "Evan Rowe, is that really you?"

Something in Evan's stomach churned. The pain reminded him of his nightmares, though he didn't know why seeing Ron Larson would cause such a reaction. "It is." He took the man's outstretched hand, shaking it without a smile.

"This must be your little sister." Ron folded his arms across his belly. Looked like he might be smuggling a beach ball in there. "How old are you now, Hannah?"

Evan knew it was a small town, but he didn't like how Ron seemed to know her name without any assistance.

"Thirteen."

"Thirteen, now ain't that something?" Evan noticed how Ron's gaze made Hannah uncomfortable. She folded her arms and stepped closer to Kim, as if she might be able to camouflage herself. "And Kim Wilkerson, I presume? Heard you're helping your folks out at the store while your father's recovering."

Kim nodded.

"That's awful gracious of you." Ron adjusted his ball cap, lifting it just high enough for Evan to note a receding hairline. "Especially with that new store of yours up and coming."

"Family comes first," Kim answered, her expression blank.

"We're headed to the concessions." Evan nodded toward it just a short distance away; no one mentioned how Ron was blocking their path. "Don't want to miss too much of the game. If you'll excuse us?"

"Actually headed there myself," Ron said. "Forgot a drink."

Evan planted himself between Ron and the women and the four walked in uneasy silence. He remembered how the man could make people uncomfortable with little effort. Truth be told, he made Evan uncomfortable too. It wasn't right how much the man knew about everyone.

The moment they stepped inside the concession building, Evan was hit with a blast of heat. He'd not realized how chilly it'd gotten outside until now. He ushered Kim and Hannah to the end of the line and offered to let Ron go ahead of them. But the man insisted on waiting his turn.

Hannah tugged on Evan's jacket sleeve. "Can I just tell you what I want?" She tossed a glance in Ron's direction. Her face screamed how uncomfortable she felt. "A popcorn, some Skittles, and a Coke."

"You're not a cheap date, you know that?" He squeezed her shoulder and pulled her toward him for a side hug—one she let him have. He considered a joke about buying back her love, but with Ron behind them, he decided against it.

"Thanks."

Just as Hannah wriggled free, Tim Hollander slapped Evan on the back. "I hope this means you've decided to join the department."

That statement stopped Hannah in her tracks.

Eyeing both Evan and Ron, Tim continued. "We really could've used you on that last call. Might've saved some of that barn if you'd been there with us." Several heads turned at Tim's declaration. He wasn't a quiet man, by any means. His voice, deep as it was, carried even more in the hollow building with its high metal ceiling.

"You should do it!" Hannah's eyes filled with such excitement that Evan actually felt torn.

"Surely you're not sticking around here?" Ron asked, letting his voice carry as well. "Not with your grand job waiting for you in Alaska." He leaned in a little closer, but his voice remained at the same volume. "It *is* waiting for you, isn't it?"

"Yes." Something about his tone warned Evan to choose his words carefully. He'd only told his mom about his injury. No one else knew anything different. If he admitted the truth to Ron Larson now, in front of a crowd of people, he knew the man would find a way to twist it. Use it against him somehow.

"Well, there you go. No sense in having you on the department for just a week or two, is there."

Tim clapped Evan on the shoulder. "Ron, surely you know we could use any help we can get, even if it's just temporary." But his eyes were on Evan. "Maybe we'll even get lucky enough to keep him in Willow Creek. Can't hurt us to try, right?"

"The fire season up north will be over soon," said Evan. "Not too many forest fires once the snow flies." He wasn't sure what he was doing, picking an argument with Ron.

But he was bothered that the man obviously didn't want him to rejoin. He saw a flash of ice in the man's sea glass eyes. Something about it was eerily familiar. The twisting in Evan's stomach tightened.

A woman Evan recognized but couldn't immediately place joined in their circle. "Evan Rowe, is that really you?" She smiled and shook her head. "I hear you've been up in Alaska jumping out of airplanes to put out fires!" The admiration in her voice was almost embarrassing. Evan had never once decided on firefighting for the glory. He only wanted to ensure he'd never fail to save someone from a fire again.

"Yes, ma'am."

That flattered her all the more. "You don't have to call me ma'am. It'll always be Betty."

That helped. Betty Meyers, married to Mort Meyers last he knew. The bald, lazy man who ran the hardware store. One glance at her left hand revealed an absence of a ring and a faint tan line where one had been. Evan wondered how many other lives had been completely altered in his five-year absence. "I'll try and remember that, Betty."

"Betty, we're trying to convince Evan here to join the department while he's staying in Willow Creek," Tim said. "You have anything to add that might tip the scales in our favor?"

"Well, Evan here is debating, aren't you?" Ron interjected. "Seems he may just leave us for his beloved Alaska soon. Isn't that right?"

Evan knew what he was supposed to say. He knew everything would be better if he just went along with it, turned down the offer. It really didn't make sense to join for such a short period of time. Chances of another call were minimal, and Evan suspected Ron wouldn't be all too interested in any training he'd offer to conduct. "Well, I don't know yet. But I'll be here a few weeks. The department might need the help, especially with you down two men right now."

"A few weeks?" Kim repeated. She'd been so quiet he nearly forgot she was there. But that would be impossible. He'd always be aware of her presence whenever she walked into a room.

"I think that would be just wonderful," Betty cooed. "Even if we only get you for a little while. Chief, I bet your department could benefit quite a bit from his expertise."

"Evan, you should do it!" Hannah tugged again on his arm, drawing his attention. In her eyes, he saw the pleading little girl she was when he last left. "It would be so great to have you home. Pleeease?"

"Well now, I don't hardly see how you can say no to her," Betty said, smiling down at Hannah.

"Or her, either." Tim glanced at Kim, tipping his ball cap. "I'd sure have a hard time."

"Looks like the decision's been made for me." Evan looked at Ron. "Chief, where do I sign?"

Hannah wrapped her arms around him, jumping up and down. It even earned him an admiring smile from Kimberly.

"Wonderful!" Betty was clapping, and so were a few bystanders. "I'll do a little write-up for the paper," she added. "I'm Editor now, you know."

"Evan, meet me down at the station tomorrow. I'll get you all taken care of." Tim beamed. "Then all we have to do is get you voted in at our meeting. I better get back to the game. My wife'll be wondering what happened to her popcorn. You folks have a good night now."

At the front of the line now, Evan shelled out twenty bucks for Hannah and Kim's concession items, a small grocery store haul. As he left, he and Ron shared one brief, icy glare.

"Welcome to the department, Rowe," Ron said, his voice carrying. Evan wasn't fooled by his insincere proclamation, intended to make himself look like a good guy. "Hope you can adhere to our standards all right. We do things a little differently around here than in the Alaskan Wilderness." If there was one thing Ron Larson had never been, it was good. "Fewer bears to worry about, you know."

Chapter 13

At halftime, Kim snuck away from the game, claiming she needed to find someone. Slipping through the trees behind the school, she invited herself through Nick's front door. She found Allie snuggled in a blanket on his couch, reading a book and with a sleeping dog at her feet. "You do still live at your own house, right?" Kim was surprised the fireplace wasn't crackling. Then again, Allie was holding her book upside down. "I didn't miss some big announcement, did I?"

"Kim, hey."

Ignoring the lack of enthusiasm in her friend's voice, she plopped down on the couch. "You okay, Al?" She noticed her friend wore a hoodie and no makeup.

"Of course. I thought you were at the game." She glanced at the clock on the wall over the fireplace mantel. "Is it over already?"

"Halftime. I came to fetch you." From the looks of her sloppy ponytail and sweatpants, Kim doubted she was dragging Allie out tonight. She'd have to go back soon or Hannah might come looking for her. Odd how that girl had latched onto her so quickly and easily, like they'd known each other for years rather than just hours.

Kim scratched Norman's ears. "Where's Nick?"

"Oh, I didn't tell you?" She closed her book and set it on the end table, one Nick had no doubt brought back to life by the looks of its fresh cherry wood polish. "He flew back to Georgia for the weekend."

"Oh, to see his family?"

"Yeah, they're moving to town soon."

Eyeing the slight bags beneath Allie's usually bright eyes, Kim worried. "Is that why you're so glum?"

"What? No. I love his sister. I'm actually really excited. They aren't moving for a couple weeks yet, but Nick's helping arrange movers."

"So he had to fly to Georgia?"

Allie shrugged, reaching for a nearly empty glass of wine. "Before you ask, I'm just tired. Trying to catch up on my blogs. I've been a little . . . behind lately."

"Too much time in paradise?"

That comment elicited the first smile from Allie tonight. "You look a little flushed, Kimmie. Is there something you want to tell *me*?"

"You've been reading too much." Kim searched the room but found no signs of a wine bottle. "Where's the good stuff?"

"In the kitchen."

"Want a refill?"

Allie let out a yawn.

"Yes, you do," Kim grabbed her glass and darted for the kitchen, Norman on her heel, probably expecting a treat.

"Just half a glass," Allie called out.

The kitchen, once a blast from the seventies, was now a stunning, modern delight.

"Hey, I like this!" The orange Formica countertops were now a beautiful granite, the floor now tile, and the appliances no longer looked like they belonged in an episode of *I Love Lucy*. "Great job on the kitchen."

"Thanks. Mom helped quite a bit in here," Allie said from the doorway, yawning again. Kim noticed she was wearing an Atlanta Braves sweatshirt, several sizes too big for her. "Who's all at the game? Surely you didn't leave Macy by herself." Allie paused. "Right?"

"Miss Homecoming Queen? No, she's got Alex and Evan keeping her company." Kim retrieved a wine glass from a cabinet over the sink. "I'd say Hannah, but I don't think that girl likes Macy. It's kind of nice, in a mean way, having a fan who doesn't seem wowed by the amazing and heroic Macy Wilkerson."

"How's it been, having Evan staying at your grandma's house?"

Kim turned her back to Allie, reaching for the bottle of merlot. She took her time twisting off the busted cork and pouring their glasses almost to the brim. "Fine."

"How do you sleep at night, knowing he's just down the hall? I forgot how hot he was."

Not me. "Well, Macy obviously hasn't." She handed Allie her glass, then chugged from her own. "She's been trying to climb that man like a tree."

"Ah, so that's what it is."

"What?"

"You're jealous."

"Over Evan?" Kim laughed, probably too loudly. "Yeah, right." There was no reason to be jealous when Evan had kissed *her,* not Macy. Even if he had called it a mistake. Kim took another large drink.

"You're not driving, right?"

Kim shook her head. "Evan drove."

"I'm surprised you even left to come get me," said Allie. "I'm sure putting up with Macy can't be all that bad if you're hanging out with your high-school crush."

She'd have to tell her the truth about their past, but tonight that topic was too dangerous. Even if she did owe Allie an explanation about Evan. Her best friend still mistakenly thought she'd had the hots for Alex.

Kim eyed her empty glass. *Is there a hole in this thing?* "You have met my sister, right?" She reached for the bottle and poured herself a refill.

"Yes, and though she can be a little . . . much, I know she just wants what's best for you. Maybe this is a good time to give her a chance. Trust her a little, you know?"

"With this big secret? No thanks!" Kim realized her mistake the second the words left her mouth. *Stupid wine.* Instead of abandoning the rest of her drink, she swallowed more.

"What big secret?"

Turning away from the curious twinkle in Allie's eyes, Kim waved her hand in the air. "It's nothing." If she opened up about Evan now, she'd probably fall in love with him all over again. No, she'd have to wait until he went back to Alaska. Just because he agreed to join the volunteer fire department for a couple of weeks didn't mean anything. It's not like that would pay a mortgage.

Allie placed her untouched glass on the kitchen island. "Liar."

"I'll only tell you if you tell me what's really going on with you and Nick." Setting her glass down, Kim folded her arms. "Something is up with you, and I want to know what. You said you're not getting married yet, so I know it's not that. But you've been acting weird since we went to that estate sale the other night. Spill it, Allie Jordan, or I'm leaving." Kim vaguely realized she was rambling toward the end of her tirade, but the spew of words had their desired effect of deflection.

"I can't tell you, Kim." Allie let out a sigh, one that seemed to deflate her entire body. "Nick would *kill* me."

Damn it, now I have to leave or I'll look like an idiot. She stared at the half-empty bottle of merlot. Many would frown if she brought it back to a high school football game. "Why?" she pressed on, hoping to stall until the bottle of wine was empty. It made her feel so warm and toasty. Or maybe it was the memory of making out with Evan earlier, the taste of his tongue . . .

"Because he swore me to secrecy, that's why—are you *blushing*?"

"Well, you've been polishing off this wine all night," Kim speculated, ignoring Allie's question. "You can't be pregnant."

"Not pregnant!"

The worst-case scenarios started playing through Kim's mind. "Did something happen at the hospital?" She had images of a body being stashed in the basement or buried somewhere in the middle of the country. "He didn't kill anyone, did he?"

"What?" The look of utter shock on Allie's face sent waves of relief through Kim. "Of course not! Why would you even think that?"

"You've got all these really gory things running through my mind!" *Might be the wine.* "He is a doctor, after all." *Probably the wine.*

Taking her first sip from her glass, Allie seemed to ponder something. "It *is* killing me to keep my mouth shut. But you can never, ever tell anyone. And that might drive you crazy."

"I can talk to *you* about it."

"But not around Nick. He can't know you know."

"Okay."

"I mean it, Kim!" Allie's eyes narrowed. "Maybe I should wait. You're drunk."

"Nope, not drunk." Kim shook her head, probably too hard. "I can keep a secret, Allie. I've kept plenty. Remember?" When Allie still didn't say anything, Kim straightened, setting her glass down on the counter. "I promise to keep my yap shut, Allie. What the hell is it? Did Nick drop a clamp into someone during surgery or something?"

"He's loaded."

Kim was lost. "Come again?"

"Nick. He's the . . ." Allie looked around the kitchen, like there might be spies lurking in the cupboards. For a second, Kim considered someone might be hiding in the dishwasher. It was just so shiny and new. In a whisper, Allie finished her sentence. ". . . richest man in town."

"So? He's a doctor, living in a mansion on a hill. How is this news?"

Allie shook her head with vehemence. "No, you don't understand. Remember his ex-wife?"

"The one who wouldn't divorce him?"

Nodding, Allie continued, "She didn't want to divorce him because she was obligated to give Nick part of her inheritance. Her dad liked him so much and was somehow sure she'd dump him that he put a clause in his will to leave part of his money with Nick should she divorce him too soon."

Interesting, but not exactly scandalous enough to make the cover of the National Enquirer. "So, some old guy liked Nick better than his own spoiled daughter. What did he leave him? A hundred grand? Two hundred?"

Allie laughed, unintentionally spitting out some of her drink back in the glass. "Not even close."

"Then how much? Don't tell me it's a million dollars." Even saying that amount of money out loud seemed ludicrous to Kim. Who inherited a million dollars these days except celebrities and people in movies who tried renovating haunted houses into B&Bs?

"Try *fifty* million."

Kim choked on her final gulp. "Come again? I don't think I heard right. It's *not* because I'm drunk." She studied her glass as if it was a lab specimen. "Unless you spiked this stuff."

"You heard me perfectly fine." Allie took a gulp of wine. "See why this is such a big deal? No one can know."

"I don't get it. Wif—*with*—that much money, wouldn't it be a good thing? He could take this town back. Knock down those assholes who think they run the place." Kim found her way to a bar stool on the far side of the island, her hand missing the rounded top several times. *Damn thing keeps moving!* "People like Lesley Jamison! She'd never bother anyone—*again*. Well, she's in jail. But there're more o' them 'round here."

"It's not that easy," Allie said, her voice whisper quiet.

"Like that pompous ass Ron Larson, for starters. Did ya know he didn't even *want* Evan to join the fire department? He didn't say it like that, but I could tell.

Everyone 'round us wanted him to do it, even if he doesn't stay long. But Ron looked ready to light 'im on fire!" Kim tipped the wine bottle toward her glass, whimpering when nothing came out. "You have more of this?"

"I'm cutting you off." Allie yanked the bottle away and dropped it in the trash.

"Why?"

"Because you're drunk—"

"Am not!" Kim tipped her glass as far as it would go to taste that final drop. "How come no one know—*can know*—about the money?"

"Upsetting the power balance in this town's dangerous." Allie wrapped her arms around herself, her eyes gravely fixed on the bowl of seashells in the middle of the island. "If people knew Nick had that much money, they'd expect him to fund every little crazy idea they had. They'd want him to fix all the roads in town, redo the park, and probably build a new school." She released a heavy sigh. "That's all fine, but after that it'd just get obnoxious. And if he turned anyone down, they'd take it personally. Not exactly good for relationship-building for the town doctor, you know?"

"Makes sense, I guess."

"Plus, he might not even keep it. He's talking about donating it all. To charity."

"Dirty money and all that?" Understanding begun to sink in, the realization sobering her a bit. "So, Nick has to be very careful who knows? Especially if he decides to give it all away without letting the town have any of it?"

Allie nodded.

Rising, Kim stumbled just once before she reached the cupboards two feet away. She started searching for more wine. *I know she has a stash.* "And so far that's him, you, and me?"

"Yeah. Well, Mom knows."

"What? You told her before you told me!"

"Well, we did go a little out for this," Allie said, motioning her arm around the kitchen. "She got suspicious where the money came from."

Staring at a bottle of Jack Daniels for all of three seconds, Kim actually considered drinking the vile stuff. She slammed the cupboard shut and spun around. "But that's all?"

"Other than his sister and her family, yeah."

"So that's what was up the other day when you picked Nick up?"

"It's been a little stressful, trying to hide that much money." Allie lifted her glass, but set it back down without taking a drink. "Nick had to open an account out of town. You know people at the bank can't keep that kind of secret to save their lives. Especially with

Ron Larson as the vice president." Abandoning her wine, Allie poured herself and Kim a glass of water. "So, what's your big secret?"

Crap! I was hoping she'd forget. Kimmie, play the drunk card. "I had a secret? Can't seem t' 'member what it was."

Allie shook her head. "Nope, you're not getting out of this that easily. Spill it, Kimmie, or so help me I'll clean this town out of chocolate cupcakes and red wine until you leave."

Kim sighed, plopped down on a stool, and nearly fell off. "Fine! But you're sworn to secrecy, too." She eyed Allie until she relented and finally agreed aloud to keep quiet. Taking a deep breath, Kim considered the speech she planned five years ago. The one she'd intended to tell Allie when she thought she and Evan had a future.

Except, five years ago she hadn't been drunk. *Buzzed.* Kim watched a glass of water slide in front of her. *Just spill it.*

"Evan and I used to have crazy, passionate sex down by the creek. Like all the time. I was probably even in love with him."

Allie smiled. "That's . . . graphic."

Kim surveyed the kitchen, wishing more wine would appear. "You're not surprised." Not that she needed more wine. At this rate, she'd have to call Evan to come pick her up from Allie's. She started fantasizing about driving out into the country like they used to, spreading blankets in the back of his truck . . .

"Kim!"

Kim jumped out of her stool, smacking her head on the side of the fridge. "I'm not drunk!"

"Did you hear anything I just said?"

"The answer is seven?" She clenched the granite-topped island, sitting slowly on the stool so she wouldn't miss it again.

"What happened with Evan today?"

After all these years as friends—since kindergarten—it shouldn't surprise her how much *didn't* get by Allie. "We might've made out a little bit." She remembered the cut of his chest, beads of sweat dripping from his muscles. Muscles that hadn't gotten anything but better with age. She couldn't believe she'd been annoyed at him for not wearing a shirt. *I've wasted so much time!*

"Made out?"

"In my bed."

"Are you two sleeping together again?"

"I wish," muttered Kim. Then she realized her inner dialogue hadn't been so *inner.* "I mean, no! Of course not. He's not staying, Allie, and he broke my heart when he left." There. She said it. "I'm sorry I never told you, but you were in Omaha getting ready for college to start. When you finally came back . . . I'm not going through that again. I'm not that stupid." She twirled the empty wine glass against the counter. "Right?"

"You were in love with him, weren't you?" Allie asked, her voice soft.

Kim couldn't bring herself to talk about it. If she did, she'd surely be inviting some of those old feelings and fantasies back. "Yeah." When Kim lifted her eyes to meet Allie's, she felt the tears. *Stupid wine. I thought we were friends!* "It didn't last long. But it was . . ."

"It was what?" Allie finally asked.

"It was the happiest, craziest, most insane time of my whole life."

If one kiss could make her come undone, what would talking about their history do? Especially knowing she'd have to sleep under the same roof tonight. Gram may or may not even make it home. Sometimes she slept over at Aunt Ruby's, depending on how many margaritas she polished off.

Kim sighed. "I promise I was going to tell you, but then the fire happened, Jeremy died, and that, well, it changed everything."

"Kimmie, I knew."

"What?"

"I knew you liked him, *not* Alex. I've always known. The crazy, passionate sex was a new detail for me, but I'm not that surprised."

"You're not?"

Allie shook her head. "Tell me what happened."

"I don't think I can, Al."

"Why not?"

"Because I can't afford to fall in love with him again. He's just going to leave. And this time, I don't know if I'll survive it. It'll destroy me. I loved him *so* much."

Allie dug a mostly empty package of cookies from the cupboard and slid them toward Kim. "Why did you keep it such a big secret back then?"

"Well, it would've been a little scandalous, you know. That was right before my eighteenth birthday. My dad would've killed him since he's almost ten years older. Hell, if my dad found out now—"

"Chip would probably still kill him?"

"Especially since he thinks Jeremey's death is Evan's fault."

"Has he actually said that to you?"

Kim sighed. "Not directly. But he's muttered curses about Evan under his breath since Jeremy died."

"Was your dad the only reason back then?"

"Well, that and Evan thought the fire department might vote him off if he was dating *a minor*," she said with air quotes. *Never mind that we were completely fine under the Nebraska state law.* A tear dropped from her eye. She wiped it away with the tips of her fingers. "We, uh, we were going to pretend to hit it off at my birthday party. Let people watch us fall in love, that kind of thing."

Allie stood, and Kim let her wrap her arms around her like a favorite sweater, warm and comforting. "But Jeremy died." Squeezing her, Allie added, "Kim, I was afraid to let anyone close after Travis turned on me. I can't explain how afraid I was. It was for a different reason, but trust me. Love like you had, it's worth pushing past the fear and giving a second chance."

Kim shook out of Allie's hug and stood. "I should get back to the game. Surprised they haven't sent a search party for me."

"Um, I'm sure the game is almost over."

"Uh-oh." She whipped out her cell phone, discovering half a dozen texts from Macy.

"Before you go, Kimmie."

"Yeah?"

"You do realize you have a second chance, right? No one has to know about before—including your dad. To everyone else, you'll appear to have a brand-new blossoming romance. Your dad will come around eventually."

"Even if that's true, Evan's just going to leave again."

"But not for a few weeks."

"So?"

"Give him a reason to stay."

Chapter 14

"Do you think I should stick around?" Evan asked Alex after they dropped everyone else off. He let his brother take the wheel, not bothering to ask where they were headed.

Alex slowed near an intersection, craning his neck forward to see past the tall corn blocking both their views. "Willow Creek?"

"Yeah. That was always the plan. Before—"

"Before Jeremy died," Alex finished. "You're past this self-blame thing, right?"

"Yeah. Still got to face Chip, though." The one person he'd saved for last, not because of Chip's heart attack, but because he was afraid of that confrontation the most. Chip had been abundantly clear at the funeral that Evan had forgotten all his training, costing Jeremy his life. He understood now that Chip felt he lost a son that day, one who *wanted* to take over the family business. But it wouldn't make facing him any easier.

"Well, he's pretty stubborn. But he'll come around."

"Probably not the best time with the recent cardiac thing though, huh?"

Alex shrugged. The skitter of gravel halted while he crossed a paved road, then picked back up on the other side. "You may want to leave out that you're in love with his daughter until *after* he's taken the blame off you for Jeremy."

"I'm not—"

"It's my job to see through people, remember?" Turning another corner a mile off the country highway, Alex added, "You're about as transparent as a sheet of glass. What have you two been doing under Violet's roof? I know she's been gone a lot. I think she and Aunt Ruby are conspiring about something, but I haven't figured out what."

Evan refused to meet his brother's pensive gaze, relieved that darkness hid most of his expression. One kiss didn't qualify as anything, did it? Even if it opened floodgates to the past. *Who am I kidding? It wasn't just a kiss.*

"There's a history, isn't there?"

"What makes you think so?"

"You want me to give away all my detective secrets?" Alex shook his head, but the lights of the dashboard revealed a smirk. "Speaking of coming around, I caught Mom smiling at the flowers you left her."

"Really?"

"Yeah. But once she caught me in the kitchen she started scowling again."

It was progress. Evan would take what he could get. "How's Russ doing these days? Figured he'd be back in town since it's the weekend."

"He doesn't come home as often as he used to. If he's not driving a semi hauler across the country, he attends these business seminars that last a couple of weeks."

Evan didn't have to ask; he could hear the truth in Alex's tone. *No wonder Mom's been extra defensive.* "Does Hannah know?"

Alex slowed as a patch of trees grew closer. "I'm not sure." He applied the brake until they were practically crawling. "She's the toughest one to read. But she's smart, so I know she at least suspects something's up."

"What's out here?"

"Lesley Jamison owns this property." The glow of the nearly full moon revealed a dilapidated farmhouse on a strip of farmland. "This's where I arrested her."

Evan listened as his brother recounted the story of a kidnapping—Kim's best friend taken by her ex-boyfriend, Lesley's son. A shoot-off between Lesley and her son after she confessed to her husband's murder. "You can't convict her on that?"

Pulling to the edge of the driveway and parking, Alex cut the headlights. "Prosecutor thinks the case will fall apart if we don't have a body."

"This is why you're in town, isn't it?" Evan asked. "Not because you're thinking about settling down here, but because you can't let this case go."

Alex pulled his phone from his pocket and checked it for what had to be the nineteenth time since the beginning of the football game. "I think you should stick around. If that's what you want, I mean." He ran his hand through his hair. "You know I want you to live a real life, right? One that means something and makes you happy."

"What would I do here?"

"They need help at Loomis. I'm sure they'd hire you back in a heartbeat. It's not the most glamorous work, but manufacturing pays well. Then you could help put Ron Larson in his place, too. Someone needs to. He's become a tyrant with Lesley behind bars." Alex laughed, just slightly at first.

Then it grew, causing Evan's eyebrows to rise. "What's so funny?"

"I'm tempted to get Lesley Jamison bail just to see if those two power-hungry idiots will take each other out and solve all our problems!" Alex threw the truck in reverse and backed out of the driveway.

"You don't need to get out? Look around?"

Alex shook his head. "We've combed the property dozens of times. I just check on the place from time to time. Make sure no one's been out here to burn down the house."

They drove back to town in silence.

Pulling into Violet's driveway, Evan hoped she was home. And that Kim had passed out. When Kim stumbled back to the game with less than a minute left in the fourth quarter, she'd been drunk. Drunk enough to nearly topple down the bleachers if he hadn't caught her.

He'd been gone over two hours, enough time for her to sober up. *She might want to talk about that kiss.* Until he figured out if he was staying in Willow Creek, he wouldn't risk hurting her again. That might just lead to more kissing, heavy petting . . . Evan no longer trusted himself around her. He had to keep his distance.

"Look, I know you planned to make a life here before, probably with her," Alex said, nodding toward the green sedan parked by the house. "And I'd love to have you closer to home, as I'm sure Mom and Hannah would too. But life happens and people change. If you stay, stay because you want a future here. Not because you want to recreate the past."

At nearly two in the morning, Kim woke with a start. She'd heard what might be thunder, but one look outside at the clear sky ruled that out. Twisting the knob on the lamp, a faint glow illuminated the floral room. *No intruders here, unless* . . . Gathering the courage to look under her bed, she heard it again—some sort of scuffling somewhere down the hall.

Kim switched off her light and tiptoed to her door. Pressing her ear against the painted wood, she listened for footsteps. Had someone broken into the house?

When she didn't hear anything, she grew curious. Pushing the door open, Kim peered into the dark, empty hallway. *Maybe I'll just use the bathroom and make sure everything's okay.* She'd never forgive herself if she didn't at least scope out the area.

Before she slipped into the hall, she grabbed the only potential weapon she could find—her three-inch binder. If she had to, she'd smack any intruder and send him down the stairs. That binder was like having a bundle of bricks at the ready.

Hand on the glass doorknob to the bathroom, she heard it again. This time it sounded more like a piece of furniture sliding. Light, restless moaning echoed. Her heartbeat froze when she realized it was coming from Evan's room.

Abandoning the bathroom, Kim tiptoed as quickly as she could down the hallway. The closer she grew, the more she could hear. The legs of the bed frame dragged against the floor as if someone was constantly shuffling it from side to side. And agonizing groans, like a beast caught in some trap. The strained agony nearly split Kim.

When knocking didn't work, Kim opened the door. Creeping in, she found Evan tossing more violently than she'd ever witnessed.

Hovering over him, Kim knew her next move was crucial. If she wasn't careful, he might deck her unintentionally. "Evan!" she called in a louder voice than normal. But that did nothing. "Evan!" she repeated, even louder this time.

"Help me get him out," he mumbled, thrashing his entire body toward the wall. The twin bed slid an inch beneath the violent turn. "Help me get him out! Why're you—"

Kim prepared to throw her binder to the floor and risk waking Gram, but Evan stilled.

She didn't know whether she felt more relieved or frightened. Bravely, she took a step closer and sat on the edge of the bed. "Evan?"

He'd turned away from her, but if he rolled back he'd knock her off the bed. "Evan." Feeling courageous, she reached a hand toward his bare shoulder.

Kim was momentarily stunned as she touched his moonlit skin. A thin sheet covered only a small portion of his beautiful, illuminated body. So little that she realized he wasn't wearing anything at all. She could see his exposed hip and felt desire course through her entire body. She should leave, go back to bed now that her presence seemed to have calmed him.

Her fingers grazed his shoulder, waking him. He jumped, alarmed. "You were having a nightmare," she said, her voice barely above a whisper.

Rubbing his eyes, Evan sat up. The sheet fell a little further, and her eyes followed the trail of the V-cut muscle. She needed to leave, to go back to bed now. No matter what Allie had said about second chances, Kim couldn't risk her heart. Nothing was worth going through that kind of pain again.

"You were worried."

"Yeah." She should take her hand away, but she couldn't seem to stop herself from tracing his arm lightly with her fingertips. "Do you have them a lot?"

Evan watched her fingers. "From time to time."

"Is that why you came back?" Despite every instinct warning her to force some distance between them, Kim curled her legs on the bed and scooted closer to Evan. She continued to trace his skin, now his chest. She used to feather his skin with her fingertips when he was upset, all those years ago. It calmed him and allowed him to open up about whatever bothered him.

"I had a nightmare the same day I had a bad landing."

"Bad landing?" Kim glanced down to the foot of the bed and saw a gouge in his unwrapped lower calf. "From parachuting to a fire?"

"Yeah."

"How bad?"

"Got in a fight with a tree." He tried to smile, but it failed almost right away. "I was distracted by the nightmare. Like something was gnawing at me."

Crawling beneath the sheet, Kim curled up beside Evan, her head on his chest as her fingers grazed his other arm.

"Chief ordered me to take some time off." There was silence, with only their breathing in the dimness. "I always wake up at the same part. I'm in the kitchen, blocked by the beam that fell across the back door. I know the only way out is the front door, through a thick cloud of toxic smoke. But before I can charge through it, everything just goes blank."

The sensation of his hot skin against her body sent electricity pulsing through her. Kim kissed his shoulder. "You came back hoping to remember the rest?"

"Not at first." He wrapped an arm around her shoulders. "But maybe if I can figure out the rest, they'll stop."

"You asked someone to help you."

"What?"

Kim tilted her head up. "When you were having your nightmare. You asked someone to help you." When he tensed beneath her, she said, "I'm sorry."

"For what?"

She trailed three kisses along his collarbone toward his neck. "I'm sorry you had to go through any of it."

"You should go, Kimberly."

The words should sting. But his tone said what he really meant. *Go before something happens neither of us can take back.* "I know." She feathered kisses up his neck. His stubble tickled her lips.

"Kimberly."

Meeting his eyes was a mistake. If she'd had an ounce of control to leave, it was gone with one glimpse of the desire burning in his gaze. Caressing his neck and cheek, she drew his face to hers.

The instant their lips brushed, Kim let go of her fears that he'd hurt her. Somewhere in the back of her mind she knew he probably would, but she didn't care. What mattered was that he was here now, tangling his hand in her hair and drawing her body against his.

His hand slid beneath her cotton tank, pushing it up. Within seconds, his hands cupped her bare breasts. Kim tried to stay quiet, knowing Gram might awaken, but a moan escaped anyway.

Kicking the sheet away, Evan's desire was no longer a secret. She swung her legs over his thighs, stretching her arms over her head as she peeled the rest of her tank top away. The cotton of her shorts was all that separated her from Evan. She gently lowered herself against his length. The feeling of his hard shaft pressed against her caused her to tremble with anticipation.

It'd always been like this between them, passion almost too intense to handle from the very first touch.

Evan sat up, his arms wrapped around her bare skin. His lips crashed against hers, lustful hunger consuming them. When his tongue begged entry, Kim didn't fight. His hot hands roamed her skin, tangled in her hair, and his thumbs edged against the hem of her shorts.

His hand slid easily beneath the silky fabric of her panties. Kim whimpered as his fingers stroked her hot, wet center.

She wrapped her fingers around his rock-solid shaft . . . and he yanked her hand away as if she'd burned him.

"Evan, what's wrong?"

"We can't." He shimmied himself out from beneath her. "I can't do this to you again. I won't do it again. Please, Kimberly, you need to go."

Chapter 15

The next afternoon, Kim shuffled three stacked boxes filled with assorted ribbons and watering cans away from the front of her closet door in her Norfolk studio apartment. Despite her best efforts to ditch her sister, Macy sat on the edge of her bed.

"You, uh, certainly have a lot of stuff in this little apartment," Macy said. "Where exactly do you sleep? I feel like I should call that TV show. You might have a slight hoarding problem, Kimmie."

Kim pulled a long, narrow TV box filled with poster board from inside her closet to gain better access to her clothes. "Why don't you go get a pedicure or a find a gym?" It was bad enough that she agreed to this crazy shenanigan, but she'd not take her sister's criticism, too.

Macy dug through a box of twine and ribbon. "You'll just blow off your date if I don't stay."

At first, a blind date—one her sister set up—sounded as appealing as a root canal. How could she trust Macy to pick someone decent, someone who didn't live with his mother? "How did I let you talk me into this again?" Had it not been for Evan rejecting her advances last night, she never would've agreed. She made sure he heard all about her date before she left Gram's.

"Relax, Kimmie. I promise you'll have a good time. He's actually a great guy. Devilishly handsome, too." The more Macy rambled on about this mystery man's qualities, the more Kim suspected she might know him. "He has these sexy eyes that could turn you into a puddle with a single glance. Looks like he spends eight hours a day in a gym."

That piqued Kim's interest. With a description like that, this guy didn't sit in his mom's basement surrounded by a sea of empty takeout containers. "But he has the IQ of a toddler, right?"

Macy studied a tangled ball of ribbon caught on her fingers. "You really don't give me enough credit, you know?"

"Put that back," Kim snapped. "You're getting it all knotted."

Macy peeled the ribbon from her fingers and shoved the box away. "For your information, this guy is smart, dedicated, selfless, and not afraid to face danger."

The effort Kim exerted in emptying her closet to find that perfect outfit seemed less tedious now. She hoped her sister might finally be doing her a favor. Every quality Macy described fit Evan to a T. Maybe she'd seen the way they interacted at the game and thought she needed to give them a nudge. Though pride would keep her from throwing herself at Evan on her own, maybe an unexpected date would help them both overcome the fear holding them back.

It didn't mean she'd ever tell her sister about her past with him if this date worked out, but that had its advantages too. If Macy took credit for setting them up, no one would suspect anything else. And Kim and Evan, well, the past could be their scandalous little secret.

Tossing a dozen brightly patterned tops on her already cluttered bed, Kim climbed into the cubby-sized closet and went for her dresses. If Evan tried to turn her down tonight, she wasn't planning to make it easy.

"Want me to send in a search party if you don't resurface in an hour?" Macy called.

Kim flung a purple dress at her sister.

"No, Kimmie." Kim caught her sister's horror-struck expression as she examined the dress. "Just, *no!*"

"I'm not wearing that one." Kim reached for the slimming black dress in the back. It was a sexy little thing, elegant and not too aggressive. Once reemerged from the depths of her closet, she held it out for Macy's approval.

"Better. Much better."

Slipping into her bathroom, Kim changed.

It fit—a plus. The stretchy silk material hugged her body in all the right spots, dropping to just above her knees. The sleeves hung off the top of her shoulders and the girls were properly represented without trying to steal the show. She twisted to the right, then the left. "Little black dress, you are my new favorite cliché."

"Are you going to come out of there?" Macy yelled. "I need to make sure you're presentable."

Kim swung the door open, hands posted on her hips. "This good enough?"

"Wow, Kimmie." Macy's ocean blue eyes were wide. "You look great!"

"Glad you approve. Now I need to find my shoes." A pair of turquoise heels were here somewhere. Probably under the bed. Kim dropped to her knees and began flinging various boxes and containers filled with fake flowers and greenery in every direction until she spotted her favorite dressy shoes. The three-inch heels might make her feet hurt, but they were sparkly. She'd endure the pain.

"Have fun, Kimmie." Macy gave Kim another one of her hulk hugs. "Just give the hostess your name. She'll take you right to your future husband. You can thank me later."

Between gasps for air, Kim murmured, "I just hope I don't regret this."

Pulling into the parking lot of Franklin's, Kim checked herself in the mirror again. Throwing open her car door, she couldn't move. Her stomach seemed to have some sort of circus performing inside, all acts at once. The outfit might be a little much for a sports bar, but Macy had reassured her they had a private, romantic booth in the back.

She and Evan had never been on a date together in public. They'd had to sneak off in his truck for nights hidden in a cornfield under the stars.

Passing an expansive quartz-topped bar and several filled tables, Kim followed the hostess to a booth in the back of the restaurant. The booths nearby were mostly empty, as well as the seat across from Kim's. She spotted him then, standing with his back to her, in a deserted dark corner, talking on his cell phone. *Black hair, broad muscles.*

She slipped into her seat, her back now to the mysterious corner. "Mr. Rowe will join you shortly," the hostess said. "He asked me to tell you he's finishing up a very important phone call. Care for any wine or cocktails?"

Kim craved a little bit of merlot, but getting tipsy from nerves was the last thing she needed. "Just water for now, thanks."

Sipping her iced water, she wondered if Evan knew who he was meeting. Surely he did, or he wouldn't have agreed. Even if Macy had tried to be discreet about it, he would've figured it out. *Right?*

"I'm so sorry about that," said a deep male voice from behind. He touched her shoulder briefly, then quickly fell into his own seat. Kim wondered why she didn't feel passionate tingles at his touch until she saw the man sitting across from her for the first time.

"Alex?"

"Kim?" At first confused, he then smiled. "I should've known."

Almost as if it was choreographed, the two erupted together in laughter. Kim felt tears fill the edges of her eyes from laughing so hard. Of course Macy would think Alex was the perfect man for her. They were closer in age, both lived in Norfolk, and she'd never suspect that her dream-man description would also cover Evan.

"I'm sorry," Alex said.

Kim shook her head, emptying her glass in a gulp. "I suppose we became Macy's little pet projects. She probably thought she'd knock out two people on her list with one date." Branches decorated in white lights hung from the ceiling. Wiping her sweaty palm against her cloth napkin, she felt suddenly uncomfortable in such a romantic setting. "I'm sorry, Alex. You really don't have to buy me dinner."

"I'm not paying," he said, wearing a wicked smile. "Macy offered just so I'd come. I think the least we owe her is to enjoy our meal. She obviously put a lot of thought into it."

"In that case, I'm ordering a New York strip."

Alex laughed again. "I wonder if Evan knows."

"Is it sad to say that I thought you'd be him?" Heat crept into her cheeks as she scrambled to think, forgetting Alex didn't know about their past. "I mean, by the way Macy talked . . ."

"Kim, I know."

Why was her pulse racing as though it would surpass the speed of light? "What do you know?"

"About you two."

Alex reached for a glass of wine Kim desperately wished was hers. The second the waiter returned, Kim ordered a bottle. *Macy's buying, might as well.*

"You forget I'm a detective," Alex reminded her, and reached for a piece of steaming bread. "I figured it out." Kim watched him unwrap a small slab of butter and scoop it up with his knife. "Evan acted a lot like you're acting now. I'm good at reading people."

Normally, Kim would be devouring some delectable bread herself, but she worried even a single bite might come back up instantly. "What did Evan tell you?"

"Not much."

His words didn't have the reassuring effect she'd hoped.

"Kim, I'm not going to tell the world your little secret."

Kim welcomed the waitress' interruption. In addition to her dinner, she ordered two pieces of chocolate truffle cake to take home for later. Completing her order with a side of spinach dip, she noticed Alex pulling his phone from his pocket. Once the waitress left, Kim asked, "Expecting a call?"

"Working on a case." Alex shrugged. "Job hazard, I guess."

"You've been spending a lot of time in Willow Creek. Any chance it has to do with Lesley and Travis?"

Alex nodded "Still looking for evidence."

"A body."

After another nod, Alex reached for his wine. "Look, I promised Macy I'd try to put aside work long enough to enjoy one date, even if it is with my brother's girl. Let's talk about something else."

"You've been to Alaska, haven't you?" Kim asked, an odd urge to hear about it from someone who didn't worship its very soil. "What was it like?"

"Honestly?"

"Yeah."

"Probably the most beautiful place I've ever seen." Alex leaned his elbows on the table. "Everywhere you look, there's something that leaves you stunned. If it's not the enormous mountains and glaciers, it's the ocean and the wildlife."

Not the answer I wanted to hear. "Evan's going back, isn't he?"

Alex folded his hands before they disappeared below the table, and took a moment to answer. "Kim, I think you need to be patient with him while he sorts everything out."

Recalling Evan's nightmare the previous night, Kim could only imagine what he must be combating inside. She wished she could help him, but she couldn't change the past any more than he could. Evan needed space to make his own decision.

Sipping their wine until the food arrived left Kim alone with her thoughts. If Alaska was really anything like Alex just described, how could he *not* go back?

"He thinks he doesn't deserve to be happy," Alex said after a long stint of silence.

"Survivor's guilt?"

He didn't meet her eyes. "Yeah. Alaska's kind of an escape for him."

"He feels he can make a difference there."

"Yeah, one that doesn't leave the possibility for any emotional attachment to the victims. The chances of him knowing anyone living in a homestead away from civilianization are pretty minimal. Not like Willow Creek."

Pulling into Gram's driveway, Macy smiled victoriously. She hadn't been able to help herself, spying on the two little lovebirds at Franklin's. She caught them laughing and smiling, probably at the realization that they'd been under each other's noses the whole time.

With Kim out of town and Gram at the Legion Hall playing bingo with her little lady friends, Macy was certain she'd have Evan all to herself. There he was, just as she expected, still working on the house despite the setting sun. In the few days he'd been around, he'd practically rebuilt the place for Gram.

Evan stood on a ladder, his shirt off again, ripping up the ratty old shingles above the covered porch. Macy called up to him, "So, you're a firefighter, smokejumper, landscaper, and now you're a roofer?"

"Just helping out where I can."

"Want something to drink? I'm going to fix myself a gin and tonic."

"You know Violet isn't home, right?"

"Yep."

Still pulling off torn shingles and letting them drop on a tarp, Evan added over his shoulder, "And Kim's on that blind date you set up. With Alex."

"Brilliant, right?"

Evan's hands stopped for a moment, though he didn't turn. "I think I'll take that drink now."

Inside, Macy mixed two drinks. A little stronger than she normally made them, but she could tell Evan needed help loosening up. With a glance in the mirror and a poof of her hair, Macy headed back to the porch to sit on the stair.

"I think it's really nice what you're doing to help Gram." Shingles continued dropping to the ground, their slap echoing in the otherwise quiet evening.

"There's really no one around to do it anymore. Dad's always too busy with the store, and even now he's practically on house arrest."

"How's Chip doing?"

"He discovered *Pawn Stars*. Now he's rummaging the house, thinking everything they own is worth thousands of dollars." Macy shook her head and took her first sip. She was glad Evan was still on a ladder and couldn't see her wince at its potent content. A few sips later and it wouldn't cause her such a reaction.

"How's his heart doing?"

"Fine, as far as I can tell. He's taking some medication to help keep his blood pressure under control. Seems he still gets fired up pretty easily. Anyway, I suspect it helps. Other than that, he's itching to get back in that store." Macy was flattered that he cared about her dad, but she really wanted to change the subject, and the mood. "Do you want a hand up there? I'm not so shabby with a crowbar, you know."

"Just finished." Evan climbed down the ladder and reached for his discarded T-shirt. He stood and wiped away sweat. "I'll take that drink now."

Macy stood, stepping just a bit closer than necessary, and handed it to him. "Maybe we should go cool off in the creek?"

"I'm good." Evan's face soured at his first taste. "Did you put anything in this besides gin?" He set the glass on the railing and leaned against it.

"I like my drinks strong." She took a step closer, edging around him. She leaned against the railing beside him, just inches apart, leaving the slimmest of a gap. "Just like I like my men."

Evan laughed, then took another sip. "Did you tell Kim to use that line tonight on my brother?"

"She didn't know it was Alex." Macy emptied her glass, considered getting a refill. Instead, she turned, still leaning against the railing, moving closer to Evan. "I checked up on those two, and it seemed they were hitting it off. Just like I knew they would. I suspect Kim knew, though. You should've seen that little black dress." Macy dug out an ice cube with her finger. "She looked pretty hot."

"Little black dress?"

"I'd be surprised if Alex's able to keep his hands to himself." Setting her glass on the railing, Macy reached toward Evan's collarbone. "You have a piece of shingle." She removed it, letting her fingers trail down his hot skin.

"Why does Kim stay here with Violet if she lives in Norfolk? Couldn't she just drive the thirty-some miles each day?"

All these questions about Kimmie. "I suspect she has nowhere else to sleep. You should've seen her apartment! Every spare inch is covered in flower pots, buckets, boxes of ribbons. All kinds of junk for that little idea of hers."

Evan stiffened. "That's all you think of your own sister?" He pushed away from the railing and picked up the claw hammer again.

"That—that came out wrong."

"Can't you see how much passion—how much of herself—she's poured into this? Have you been paying any attention over the years to what she creates with all that *junk*? People can't get enough of it."

Macy took a couple of steps back, nervously eyeing the hammer as Evan rammed it in a box of tools. "I . . . I didn't mean—"

"Why you can't acknowledge that what she's doing isn't just some cute little hobby? Kimberly's pursuing her dreams. It takes real guts to do that. You should be proud, not mocking her."

Macy was caught between guilt for saying what she had and shock at Evan's passionate stance about Kim's future store. *How could I have missed it?* Evan slammed the toolbox shut and stomped off across the porch to the front door. *There's something going on with these two.* "Where are you going?"

"To shower." Hand on the door knob, Evan added, "Go home, Macy."

Chapter 16

It'd been five years since Evan donned a firefighting jacket for Willow Creek's volunteer department, but they still had his old uniform. "When's the last time the department got new gear?" Evan adjusted the heavy jacket on his shoulders. Some of the reflective tape stitched into the fabric was peeling off. A closer look suggested it'd been repaired by needle and thread at least once, maybe twice. As a jumper, he'd gotten pretty good with sewing, but he wasn't sure there was much he could do for this sad gear.

"Budget's been a little tight," Tim told him, marking down Evan's sizes on a clipboard. "We're short on volunteers as it is. It's hard to justify new equipment when what we got is still functional. Boots are new, though."

Evan eyed the box suspiciously. In Alaska, he'd purchased much of his own equipment. Though the prices could send a rich man into shock, he never skimped on quality. The gear was intended to keep him alive. The boots he stared at now seemed to have been purchased in bulk and on clearance.

"What would it take to get the department new gear?" Evan asked. "Are we looking for grants or planning any fundraisers?"

"We did a cookout in July, during the Summer Festival. That's what got us these boots."

Evan realized that a small community would hardly be able to fork out thousands to outfit a volunteer department with the best gear. Still, he hated how they went for the cheapest rather than save up for something better. *Maybe there's something I can do to help after all.*

"If those fit, I think you're outfitted and ready for a fire. Paperwork's good."

"Thanks for meeting me on your lunch break," Evan said. He'd been voted in last night at the monthly meeting. What he expected to be a simple formality turned uncomfortable when nearly half the members didn't vote to add him to the department. Though the votes were anonymous, he suspected Ron Larson had a few underlings trying to keep him out. It'd grown so unnerving that Tim suggested they outfit him the next day rather than after the meeting.

In the large bay, radio chatter picked up. Evan couldn't quite make out what they were saying—the speakers weren't the best quality—but he heard something like "crop fire" and "west of Willow Creek." He and Tim shared the briefest of glances.

Tim dropped his clipboard on the pavement and kicked it toward a corner to retrieve later. Seconds before the fire whistle sounded, they were suited up.

Stepping up to the fire engine, Evan asked, "Where do you want me?"

"In the back," Ron Larson hollered, rushing in through the side door in his business suit, pulling off his tie. "You stay out of the way and do only what I tell you to do. Understood, Rowe? This is my fire, best you remember who's in charge."

During the quick drive a mile and a half west of town, Evan caught the briefing of their situation. A farmer had been driving a combine, unaware that a bearing overheated and was dropping sparks in his soybean field until he was more than a quarter mile from where the flames started.

Evan remembered riding in a combine with his dad when he was just a little boy. He tried to watch the field out the back window, curious what the combine had done, but it was impossible to see immediately behind them. He knew the farmer hadn't had a clue until it was too late.

"What's the wind doing?" he asked Tim.

"What did I say, Rowe?" Ron barked. "I believe it was something like seen and not heard?"

Evan bit his tongue. In a forest fire, the direction and speed of the wind were crucial factors in determining the best approach to put it out. In Nebraska, where it was almost always windy, that should determine their strategy. It could be the difference between the fire dying on its own or raging toward the town.

Digging his smartphone from an inside shirt pocket, he pulled up his weather app, one that offered enough forecast information to set a pilot up for success. He knew he should keep his mouth shut, but damn it, this wasn't about appeasing Ron. "The wind is coming out of the northwest, Chief." He threw in the *chief* hoping it'd help keep the peace. "It's at a steady thirteen miles an hour, but there are gusts up to thirty."

"If you wanted to be a weather boy, you're in the wrong field."

A cloud of light gray smoke in a giant mushroom shape filled the western sky. Evan clenched and unclenched his fist, struggling to keep silent. For a mid-October day, it was almost eighty degrees and dry. Fires burned faster the hotter the temperature, making their attack plan critical to preventing a disaster. But Ron wasn't communicating with his crew.

Tim threw the fire engine into park on the edge of the gravel road. The moment Evan's sightline was clear, he assessed the situation. Fires, he knew, needed three things to burn: fuel, heat, and oxygen. Only in removing one of the three factors could it be extinguished. Considering the temperatures and open air, they needed to focus on removing the fuel.

In Alaska, the Hotshots would dig a fire line, choking the fire with nothing to burn when it reached the dirt trenches. A good wildland crew could dig a two-foot wide trench, four hundred feet long, in under an hour. Surveying the small crew and the age of most of the members, Evan determined they wouldn't be digging today. The best they could hope for was a pivot track, the ones farmers used to run irrigation systems in their fields. Find one in the right place and deep enough, and this fire might be stopped from spreading too far.

"It's already jumped the road," Ron yelled as everyone scrambled off the truck. "We need to flank it, force it toward the creek."

The crew rushed toward the flames, one hose already spraying, trying to push the flames toward the creek. The second truck, the one with the most water, slid to a halt. A two-man crew jumped out and went to work, hastening to the flames through the field of untouched soybeans.

A bad feeling twisted in the pit of Evan's stomach. From here, he could see Violet's property in the distance. If they tried to force the fire to the creek, the wind might gust and send it across the water where it could catch tree branches. Judging by the size of the flames and their speed, they might be evacuating the entire northwest corner of town.

"Wait," Evan hollered above the roaring flames.

"What?" a burly, huffing man asked. "We have orders, Rowe."

A gust of wind whooshed through the field, lifting a patch of flames thirty feet in the air. The five men in the field watched the wall of erupting fire with awe. "We need to cut it before the water," Evan said, recapturing their attention. "If that wind hits near the creek, it'll jump right into the trees on the other side."

"What should we do?" Tim asked. The three other volunteers waited for instructions. *At least I know who voted me in.*

He'd have to worry about small-town politics later. Evan knew he'd hear about this after the fire, but Ron was still by the truck, with one of his cronies no doubt, talking into his radio with a cigarette bouncing between his lips. Right now, Evan had a town to save. "There!" He pointed. "The field with the green grass. We need to force it that way."

"You're sure?" Tim asked, staring at Evan, waiting for the call. "We've got a farmer ready to dig a pivot track. Do I need to reroute him?" He pointed to the tractor, hauling ass down the field toward them, ready to dig that trench they so desperately needed.

Evan knew whatever he said next, Tim and the others would follow his orders. For the first time since his return, he felt he could make a real difference.

"Yeah, have him set the pivot track ten yards from the creek. It'll help flank the fire toward the grass." Even though he'd never trained with most of these men, it was obvious they trusted him more than Ron Larson. That fact bothered him above all else.

Over the radio, Evan heard Ron yelling curses. Tim had directed the tractor right in the path of where Ron wanted the fire to go. Evan was too busy fighting it to care what would happen once this was over. Whatever Ron's wrath would be, it would have to wait until the town was no longer in danger.

"It's working!" a volunteer called. "The grass is killing it!"

A few cheers erupted as they continued to force the fire south. Between the new pivot line and the healthy grass, the raging fire shrank until the fire hose was able to extinguish it completely. They combed the soybean rows, dousing embers.

"Rowe, we're sure happy to have you." Tim patted him on the back as the five-man crew trekked through the field back to the fire engine.

With folded arms, Ron Larson stood looking as if he might spontaneously combust, his face was so red.

"Chief, you should think about promoting this guy," Tim yelled as they got closer. "It was his idea to chase the fire to the grass. He was right. With those wind gusts, the flames would've jumped the creek for sure. We'd be evacuating half the town now if it weren't for Rowe's quick thinking."

Ron dropped a lit cigarette to the ground. "The fire's out. Let's put everything away." Sneering as he stomped out his butt, all he had to say was, "Rowe, when we get back to the fire hall, I want a word."

Ron paced in the small meeting room stationed on the side of the large bay. "You think you're better than us, do ya?" Evan sat on the edge of a table through the haranguing, his fingers gripping the edge. "Well, boy, things operate a little differently around here. We don't go jumping out of airplanes. We save lives here."

Evan felt the defense rise in his chest, but he kept his lips pursed tightly. It would do no good to belittle the man.

"I'm the chief; I give the orders. Is that understood?"

"No." Evan stood, his full six feet two inches still shorter than Ron by an inch. But it didn't cause him to cower like so many others obviously had in this town. His brother was right: someone needed to rattle this man's cage. "I made a call that saved us from evacuating the town. I will not apologize for that." He hadn't done anything wrong. He let his training take over, and made a judgment call. One that resulted in the most minimal loss of property possible.

"You deliberately disobeyed orders."

Evan folded his arms across his chest. "You're upset that your men listened to me, aren't you?"

"That kind of behavior won't be tolerated again, Rowe. This is your first and only warning. Cross me again, and you're out."

"It bothers you that I might have better training and experience. That because of *my* call in the field, we prevented a disaster. Are you intimidated by me, Chief?"

A vein along the left side of Ron's forehead throbbed. "Don't push yourself, Rowe." Evan watched it against the cherry red of Ron's face. "No one crosses me without consequence."

"If crossing you means saving lives, I'll take whatever consequences you have to throw at me."

Ron folded his arms, a smug smirk easing onto his lips. "Go ahead and get cocky, Rowe. That's what happened five years ago. You thought you could save Jeremy Wilkerson all by yourself. You couldn't just wait for help to arrive, and that piss poor decision cost you a man's life." Ron swiped his keys off the table. "How do you even live with yourself knowing Jeremy's blood is on your hands?"

"If I had waited, he would've died anyway."

"You don't know that," Ron countered. The steel in his eyes pierced Evan. "The fire never even spread to that back bedroom, did it?"

Evan wanted to argue, but this one factor never occurred to him before. Ron might as well have gut-punched him. "You know I couldn't take that chance."

"If you'd just waited for help to arrive, they'd have pulled him out through the bedroom window." Ron had his hand on the doorknob. He gave a self-satisfied grin. "Funny how you didn't think of that."

The second Ron slammed the door, Evan ran for the trash can and lost his lunch.

Chapter 17

Kim and Macy manned Wilkerson's Grocery that following Thursday while Penny escorted Chip to a follow-up appointment in Norfolk. Kim had gone to extreme lengths to avoid her sister since the failed blind date. She spent several hours in Norfolk collecting supplies to create a new floral display for the pharmacy, hid out with Allie painting buckets for her store, and even took their dad to see a movie. Though she knew Macy meant well, Kim was irritated at her for picking the wrong Rowe brother.

With Wilma on her lunch break, Kim was left at the register, filling the candy racks. Macy was supposed to be stocking the shelves in the cleaning aisle, but instead she leaned on the checkout counter, flipping through some helicopter manual.

"Aren't you supposed to be working?" Kim snapped.

Macy sighed. "You mean helping *all* these customers?" She slapped the book closed. "And don't get all snappy with me because I sent you on a date with Alex. I'm still shocked you're not planning your wedding, you know. You two are perfect for each other."

Kim set down the box of M&M's. "Look, I'll be the first to admit that Alex is a good guy. There are certainly worse people you could've set me up with. But I don't see him like that, Macy. If you'd been around at all these last few years, you'd know he's not my type."

"How can he *not* be your type?"

The bell jingled above the front door, keeping Kim from explaining a long list of reasons why not. Including the one sauntering into the store now. "Ladies."

Evan.

Kim hadn't seen much of him since their steamy encounter late Friday night. Forcing too many bags of M&M's into their slot, she busied herself with the candy stand again. The carton would probably explode.

She'd been most aggravated with Evan for pushing her away these past few days, despite her best efforts. She'd stupidly waited hours down by the creek, but Evan never showed. He also skipped most meals, claiming the old barn needed a lot of work.

"Can I help you find something?" Considering Macy had practically been throwing herself at the guy since that lost-bra incident in the creek, her question sounded somewhat cold to Kim.

"I'm supposed to pick up some cream of tartar, whatever that is."

"It's with the spices, I think. Follow me."

The front door jingled open again. Kim was working at opening a box of Reese's Pieces when she felt someone hovering behind her. A tall pencil of a man with bloodshot eyes and messed-up hair towered over her. "Todd Crawley?" *How did he find me here?* Todd was hopeless outside of Norfolk. She was sure he couldn't locate Willow Creek if he purposely searched for it. "Are you lost?"

"Oh, am I ever!" He adjusted his loose red tie, which now hung crooked. "I am so lost without you, Kim. Please say you'll come back. Please?"

Kim couldn't have hidden the malicious smirk on her face if she'd tried. "No."

"I'll give you a raise. How does an extra two thousand a year sound? I'll even throw in an extra vacation day."

"This is why no one likes you, Todd." Kim folded her arms across her chest. "You seem to think you're offering me the world on a silver platter. But what you're really offering is a pile of dog crap on a cardboard slab."

"Please!" he begged, now down on his knees to meet Kim eye-to-eye. "Five thousand, a week of vacation?

C'mon, Kim. I'll send you, all-expenses paid, to visit our new Alaska office."

"I quit for a reason." Kim resumed filling the candy display. "I'm not coming back." Under any other circumstances, she might've negotiated. She could probably get an extra ten grand a year, two more weeks of vacation, and a company car. Maybe a company apartment from the look of desperation swimming in Todd's reddened eyes.

"I'll double your salary."

"Would you please—" But the word *double* caught her off guard. "Double? You're not authorized to do that."

"Please. Say you'll come back. Those end-of-month reports are going to be the end of me. And Doris doesn't even know which dry cleaner to use. She went to that cheap place near the dealership and they shrunk my favorite suit! Well, my second favorite."

Kim felt an inkling of responsibility to return. *Damn it, Doris, we had this talk!* If only to protect those poor, spineless cubicle workers. And Jed the Janitor. Jed was probably the most underappreciated of them all.

"Double salary, double vacation. I'll put you on the payroll as two people. Just say you'll come back!" Todd begged.

"Kim, is this guy bothering you?" Evan stood at the far end of the checkout lane, arms folded, a little plastic jar in his grip. Macy peeked over his broad shoulder. He looked ready to pound Todd into the ground with a single fist. Kim had forgotten how sexy Evan could be when he was angry.

"Not anymore. Right, Todd?"

Gathering his dignity now that there were witnesses, Todd stood and dusted off his knees. "You'll regret turning down this opportunity, Kimberly Wilkerson."

Evan powered forward. "No one calls her that but me, understand?"

Todd looked him up and down. "Who the hell are you?" But his entire body trembled with the uncomfortable proximity. Though an inch taller than Evan, Todd was skin and bones compared to the linebacker blocking his path.

"I'm who you'll have to deal with if you come within ten miles of her again, understood?" Emphasizing his seriousness, Evan took another step forward.

Todd sighed and gave a weak nod.

"Beat it."

Evan set the spice container on the checkout counter. Macy asked, "*That* was your old boss, Kimmie?"

"Real swell guy, that Todd." She should be upset with Evan for interrupting like some ridiculous knight in shining armor, especially after the way he'd been blowing her off. *I had the situation under control.* Then why did she feel like taking his hand and dragging him to the back of the store?

Like a hawk scanning prey, Evan watched Todd skitter out the front door and hop into his Camaro. How Todd had managed to acquire that car, Kim didn't want to know.

Turning to Kim, Evan asked, "You all right?"

"Yep." The box of Skittles tore and packets scattered, Kim's hands couldn't quit stuffing it. "I could've handled him, though. You can knock that skeleton over with a feather."

"Can't believe you turned down a doubled salary." *Is he teasing me?* "And what was that trip to Alaska he mentioned? Sounds like a killer deal to me."

Kim felt her sister's eyes burning back and forth between her and Evan. She had to break this tension up now or risk Macy causing a scene. Surely she'd figure out the real reason Kim and Alex hadn't hit it off if this tension continued much longer.

Slipping behind the register again, Kim asked, "You planning to pay for that cream of tartar, Evan?"

He handed it to her, and Kim felt the graze of his hot fingertips against her palm. Why did her heart choose this moment to pound like tornado sirens in her ears? "What is Gram doing with this, anyway?"

"Making a lemon meringue pie."

Kim dropped the tiny container in a plastic bag and held it out. *He has to leave. He has to leave now.* Her heart pounded harder with each second he stayed. "Better get this to her. She can't start baking without it."

"That's my favorite!" Macy chimed in. "Maybe she can save us a piece?"

"Maybe. Hannah's coming over tonight. She might eat your piece, Macy."

What the hell did Macy do to piss him off?

At the exit, Evan looked back at Kim. "I meant what I said. If he comes back, he'll be answering to me, whether you like it or not."

When Evan left, Kim nearly collapsed on the wobbliest knees she'd ever felt. Surely overcooked linguini noodles were sturdier than she was right now.

Macy leaned on the opposite side of the checkout counter, her eyes boring into Kim. "What was all that about?"

Macy watched her sister breaking down empty boxes and slamming them in a cart filled with cardboard. It was the third time she asked, but Kim was doing her best to ignore her. "What are you talking about, Macy?"

Grabbing her by the arm, Macy forced Kim to look at her. "You and Evan," she growled.

"Me and Evan what?"

"Oh c'mon. Don't play stupid with me, Kimmie." Kim wriggled free of Macy's grip at that and reached for another box to tear apart. "I have eyes," Macy kept on. "It makes so much sense now, the way Evan acted the other night."

Kim dropped the box cutter. "Oh my God, you hit on him, didn't you?"

"So?"

"And he turned you down."

Macy didn't appreciate Kim's smug smile. She'd been shot down by two men that night. First Evan, then some guy online whose screen name was *rusty_nails23*. "Well, it makes sense now. The whole macho defense thing with your old boss, the way he hugged you at the game to keep you from falling when you were obviously drunk. And, of course, you're sleeping under—" Shock slapped Macy across the face. "Are you two sleeping together?"

"Shh!" Kim hissed, spotting Wilma returning from lunch. "No, we are not!"

"You totally are! Why wouldn't you tell me this after I tried to set you up with Alex? He must think I'm an idiot now."

"You are unbelievable."

"What?"

"The only person you really care about in all this is you. As usual. You care that Evan turned *you* down and that Alex thinks *you're* clueless." Kim shoved the last slab of cardboard into her cart and pushed it away.

"That's not true," Macy called after her." I want you to be happy, Kimmie."

"Sure you do," Kim hollered back from the other side of the saloon doors. "You just want to take the credit."

Macy spun around toward the register and nearly collided with Wilma. The poor woman's face looked pale and her eyebrows were indrawn. Macy was torn between asking the sweet elderly lady what was ailing her and chasing down Kim to find out what was really going on with her, but the bell above the front door jingled again.

A woman who looked straight out of a *Real Housewives* show sashayed into the store. Her tight red designer dress hugged every gorgeous curve; its deep-V neckline showcased a diamond necklace dangling above heavily exposed cleavage. Macy tried not to stare, though she couldn't help but wonder if those bazookas were real or custom made.

"Mrs. Larson, how may we help you?" Wilma asked. Her voice trembled, if Macy wasn't mistaken. Sure, with a scowl like that, the woman looked as if she might snack on small children for fun, but Macy didn't see a reason for Wilma to act with such trepidation.

Combing back her wavy auburn locks, she turned to Macy. "I'm looking for Penny." The boulder on this Mrs. Larson's ring finger caught the light, nearly blinding Macy.

"She's not here."

"She missed our appointment today."

Macy noticed Kim peeking from behind the bread aisle. "She'll be back tomorrow." Macy didn't know this woman, but she looked like she always got her way.

"I'll tell her you stopped by," Wilma promised.

But Mrs. Larson ignored that. She narrowed her eyes at Macy, adjusting the strap on her shoulder—a Louis Vuitton purse—and spoke directly to Macy. "You do that."

Once the woman left, Kim pushed past Macy to get to Wilma. "What does Valentina Larson want with my mom?"

Wilma shook her head and studied the cash register as though it might perform a trick. "I . . . I don't know." Eyes on the register, not a blink from Wilma, she cleared her throat. "But," she told the girls, "I don't expect it's anything good."

Chapter 18

Old houses were like this, and Violet's was no exception. Which was why Evan stood in her hallway, inspecting the grounding terminal in her circuit breaker box. Studying the labels next to each breaker, it dawned on him that he'd deprived his little sister of the most amazing woman he'd ever known. But now that he was back in Willow Creek, Hannah would get to know Violet Wilkerson, the toughest, most inspirational person he'd met in his lifetime.

While he let the two become well acquainted in Violet's kitchen, he moved on to tinkering with a stubborn outlet near the living room, hoping YouTube would teach him enough about being an electrician to restore power to it.

It was inevitable that spending all of his time growing up with Jeremy led to spending time at Violet's. At first, the boys just played near the creek, climbed her trees, and ate enough pie to give them stomachaches.

"This is the best lemon meringue pie I've ever had!" he overhead Hannah exclaim. Her fork clinked against her plate. She sounded so vivacious and full of life again, the way he remembered her from before he left.

As Evan and Jeremy grew older, they brought homework along after school, helped with yard work, and were rewarded with Violet's stories about her interesting life. Evan remembered her recounting her time in Europe, before she married her late husband. She spoke a little bit of French, and knew enough Italian to find the absolute best restaurants in all of Italy.

"Evan told me you used to have a motorcycle," he heard Hannah say. "Is that true?"

"Yes, I did. My parents were furious with me, but I drove that thing till it died. Guess I didn't know much about fixing it."

"Have you ever gone skydiving?" Hannah asked.

"Just once," Violet admitted. Evan dropped his screwdriver, surprised by this. She'd never shared any skydiving tales with him. "On my honeymoon in Hawaii."

"You and your husband jumped?"

Violet chuckled. "Oh, no, dear. Jim didn't even know about it until after I landed. He was so furious with me!"

"I want to try it," Hannah continued. "You know, see what the fuss is all about."

Evan smiled, certain the *fuss* had a little something to do with his Alaskan career. She was slowly warming up to him since he joined the fire department, unlike their mother who seemed intent on presenting an angry front. She reminded Evan of a wounded animal.

But he could hardly blame her for her behavior with everything she had on her plate. He'd like to punch his stepfather square in the jaw.

"You're Kim's grandma, right?"

"I am."

Evan headed back to the hall to check all the other outlets on the same breaker, just in case. He followed Hannah's excited question from there.

"I like her. She told me she'd show me how to put together some flower arrangements for my room." The hiss of the coffee pot echoed now. "Is she coming over?"

"She should be off work anytime."

At the word *work*, Evan tensed. He'd gone a little over the top with that weaseling man he'd found begging Kim to come back to her old job. If there was something Kimberly Wilkerson didn't need, it was protecting. Surely she'd remind him when she showed up.

As if his thoughts created the woman, Kim burst through the front door, calling, "I'm home!"

Evan set down his screwdriver and prepared to head her off and apologize. But she didn't see him, tucked around the staircase as he was. A whisk of ripped jeans and a stumpy blonde ponytail vanished toward the kitchen.

"Kim!"

Evan picked up his screwdriver and decided to finish this task first. He'd been trying like hell to keep his distance, mostly because he didn't trust himself around Kimberly. Bad enough he thought about her every waking minute. That lavender scent in her hair, her tender skin, soft fingers feathering his chest when she calmed him after his nightmare . . .

Having Kim in the same house now was a dangerous distraction. Like a breaker blowing and charging a curling iron enough to start a spark. Even flipped off, electricity had a mind of its own. Evan shook the horrid thought.

"I was just about to start supper," he heard Violet announce, "but I let Hannah here have a piece of pie, so fair is fair."

"Gram, I might just move in with you full time."

The mere sound of her voice had his heart racing. Evan set down his tools and slipped out the front door for some air.

He leaned against the porch railing, staring out toward the cluster of trees near the creek. The reasons to stay in Willow Creek seemed to be outweighing the ones for Alaska. *Maybe I'll go for a run.* Sneaking back inside, hoping to make it upstairs undetected, he overheard Hannah boasting.

"My room is turquoise. At least for now."

"For now?" Kim asked.

"I change it a lot. But I like to try different things. See what works." Hannah sounded like such a young woman right now. "I want to do something really cool to show my dad when he comes home."

Evan tensed at the mention of Russ Procter. When his little sister found out the truth of his constant business trips, Hannah would be crushed. What good would it do her if her big brother ran back to Alaska now?

"Do you know what color looks really cool with turquoise?" A pause. "Purple. This purple." He heard something slide along the table. *Kimberly's binder.* She never went anywhere without it.

"I love it!" Hannah's shrieks filtered out to Evan. "That gives me so many ideas!"

The girls gabbed back and forth, talking through ideas about Hannah's bedroom. Evan lurked just outside the kitchen, unable to convince himself to retrieve those running shoes. He hadn't realized she loved interior decorating so much until she confessed to spending most of her free time watching interior design shows on HGTV. From the enthusiasm with which she spoke of it, Evan sensed the same passion and vigor in his sister that Kim possessed.

"Let's go get some flowers," Kim suggested. Chairs scuffled across the floor and footsteps hurried toward the back door.

"You might as well join us," Violet called out after the door slammed shut. "You stand there any longer you might turn into a statue."

The aroma of something beefy with just a hint of garlic lured him into the kitchen. "I'm still toying with your outlet here."

Violet stood at the stove, stirring a pot. "Uh-huh." She glanced over her shoulder. "Have a seat."

"Whatever you're making smells amazing," Evan fell into a chair, eyeing the binder. *The Twisted Tulip*. He'd seen that turquoise and purple logo dangling from the arrangement he bought for Sue the other day, as well as the one for his mother. It was a funky, fun combination, Kim's personality displayed in three colorful words. Then there was her name below it: Kimberly Wilkerson.

"Beef stew and fresh bread. Sound okay?"

"Okay?" Evan nodded, his eyes glued to the logo. *Not Kim, but Kimberly.* "Violet, at this rate you'll never get me to leave!"

She turned and met his eyes, a twinkle in her own. "That's the plan."

Even as he reached for the binder, Evan knew he should leave it alone. *If Kimberly wanted to share it, she would have,* said one side of his mind. *But she left it out in the open,* said the other, and it won. What harm could a quick peek do?

In the front, he found a catalogue of arrangements—photos glued to cardstock matching her logo color scheme, all tucked into sheet protectors. A dozen pages, no two arrangements looked anything alike. Each one was a unique twist of rustic elegance with a touch of that funky ambience her logo promised.

"You'll never be able to buy her flowers, you know."

Evan stared up at Violet, busy at the stove. *Did I hear right?* "Violet, why didn't you tell me that first day that Kim was staying here too?"

The back door burst open, and Hannah and Kim rushed inside with a handful of purple flowers. There were at least three different kinds, though Evan wouldn't have been able to guess their names if his life depended on it.

"Why don't you gals start putting together your arrangement in that side room?" Violet suggested, answering Evan's earlier question with a mere twinkle in her eyes. "If you move that box of magazines, you'll have enough prep space."

Kim spotted Evan and seemed brought up short. "Hey," she said, a sparkle in her eyes. *For me?* No, he was certain it wasn't. She'd be livid with him, chasing off her old boss. She'd been handling it all just fine. The excited gleam in her eyes surely was from having Hannah just as passionate about designing something from nothing.

Hannah popped back into the kitchen. "Violet, do you have scissors?" She sent a smile to Evan. It was quick and fleeting, but it was enough to let him know Hannah approved.

"In the sewing room, there's a bucket of scissors," Violet answered. "Grab the ones with the blue handle. It's the one I use for stems." Hannah dashed around the corner.

Kim smiled at the open binder and raised an eyebrow. "Checking up on me, are you?"

"You did leave it out," Evan said.

"Well, there's only one thing left to do . . ." Kim moved to Evan. ". . . Now that you know all my secrets." She leaned toward the binder. Sliding it to her, she closed it. But she stood so close, like a nearby flame. He could feel her body heat warming his skin.

"What's that?" he asked, hearing his voice, a little shaky. He glanced to Violet. Hopefully she didn't notice.

"I guess I'll have to kill you." She started to stand, but halfway touched his shoulder with her hand and leaned her lips close to his ear and whispered, "But I think you'll be okay with my method of torture." *She's flirting. In front of Violet.*

Hannah burst back into the room, breaking the tension. Just in time, too. Evan's heart was slamming against his chest. *I'm supposed to be keeping my distance, dammit.* His voice low, he asked, "You're not mad about what happened at the store?" But even in a spacious, high-ceiling kitchen, he wasn't certain his words were muffled.

"Mad?" Kim stood and shook her head. Her hand fell from his shoulder, her fingers grazing against the cotton of his shirt. The thin material did little to extinguish the fire of her touch. "Quite the opposite."

Ron sat at his desk the next morning, waiting for his last appointment of the day to arrive. Wilma Gentry was coming into the bank to ask for a line of credit on her little pile of rotting boards. She needed a new roof and bad, thanks to a little assistance from a certain inspector. If it didn't get done soon, she'd no doubt have to abandon the house. They'd have to foreclose, and well, he didn't need that headache.

But she wouldn't qualify for what she needed to fix the roof. Hardly half, as it stood. Rick, his tame inspector, had funneled all the background Ron needed on the old woman. They seemed to like spilling it all to a seemingly sympathetic Rick.

Wilma's credit was awful, even with both her part-time jobs, she confided earlier, and that car of hers was likely on its last ten thousand miles. She'd asked to work full time at the grocery store, she said, but Rick also relayed that Penny Wilkerson had told Wilma no.

When Chip signed over the deed in a week and a half, which Ron knew he'd do—that kind of money was almost impossible to pull together quickly—Ron would offer Wilma full-time employment. Another tactic to make him the hero in all these unfortunate circumstances.

As a teller ushered Wilma in, Ron stood. His height offered intimidation. Wilma looked as if she was shaking in her little off-brand sneakers. Nearing sixty-five, her file indicated. Since her husband's death five years ago, she'd been struggling to make ends meet. Her only kid was off in New York City, too busy to offer his mother any kind of assistance. Rick had found out so much.

"Wilma, please have a seat." Ron motioned toward a cushioned chair with high arms. It seemed to swallow the frail woman. "How are you today?"

"Fine, thank you." Wilma tried several times to meet his eyes, but instead settled on the nameplate on his desk. The one reminding everyone he was Vice President of the bank. The person in charge of decisions like whether to loan.

Fine. A lie, of course. But what did he expect? Wilma liked confrontation about as much as he liked power-hungry women. He'd been so happy the day Lesley Jamison was hauled off in handcuffs that he nearly did back flips in his living room.

Ron pretended to study the file in front of him, as though he was reading its contents for the first time. "Looks like you're in need of a new roof."

"Yes. Rick says it won't last the next heavy rainstorm. He says it's rotted and a single golf ball sized hail's gonna cause the whole thing to implode." Wilma sat, near tears.

Good job, Rick. It helped, having underlings in the right places. There were those who crossed Ron and paid the price. And others who knew better and helped carry out his orders. Rick, also a member of the fire department, was one who knew that his best interest included helping an old roof expire.

"I don't have any insurance money left to cover it. I was hoping I could take out—"

"A second mortgage," Ron finished for her. "Wilma, I can do that for you."

"You can?"

She looked so hopeful in that moment. It was his favorite look, as though he was about to answer all her prayers. That glimmer of hope before someone's dreams were crushed. It was the last moment they believed they could survive without his help.

"I can, but I'm afraid your house isn't worth enough to cover more than half the estimate. I don't know what good half a roof will do you, Wilma."

The tears formed so quickly, so suddenly they instantly fell from her pale eyes. "But what am I supposed to do? I don't have anywhere to go."

"What about your son? The one in New York?"

Wilma looked as if someone ran over her precious cat. "He's busy. He has important clients. I couldn't bother him about a roof."

Ron shook his head. "I want to help you, Wilma. I wish there was something I could do to help you save your roof."

Letting out a deep breath, Wilma set her hands in her lap. Her eyes were glued to his nameplate. "I hear you help people out from time to time." She glanced up, then back down. "On the side."

"Sometimes, if the circumstance is right." He relished her description. His wife would call it unethical, but only on the rare occasion. She enjoyed her Louis Vuitton purses and spa weekends a little too much to confront him. "But it's not the kind of help I offer everyone."

"I don't want to lose it. I've lived in that house almost fifty years," Wilma said, trembling in her chair. "Please help. I can pay you back." Desperation coated her words. "It'll take time, but I can do it. I'll even get another job if needed. I hear the café might be looking for some waitressing help."

Ron sat back, pretending to take in all of this information he already knew. "It'll be an expensive loan, Wilma." *Just like the one Chip took out a decade ago.*

She nodded.

Anchoring his forearms on the desk, he leaned forward. "No one can know if I do this little favor for you. You understand that the bank would lose money, and, well, I can't have them knowing I refused your second mortgage. They don't understand the situation like you and I do. We both know that a second mortgage wouldn't be in your best interest. It'd only fix half your roof and that wouldn't do any good."

"I understand."

"I'll draft up a document tonight, when I'm off. That way you know the terms. It'll protect both of us to have it, but you mustn't show it to anyone. I can't have anyone knowing I'm doing you this favor. Bad for business, you know."

"What should I tell people? My neighbors'll notice my roof getting fixed."

That was a problem with a small town. It would be dangerous to lie and say the bank did give her that second mortgage. There were three other people who would know that wasn't true, and he didn't need anyone foiling his plans. "Tell them your son felt guilty and sent on some money."

At first, Wilma didn't seem to like that idea. But she relented and dried her eyes. "It's not like I'm at risk of him visiting anytime soon."

Chapter 19

Kim watched the full moon gradually pull free of the cloud cover, illuminating the creek and the grounds around it. She sat in the shadows of a giant oak tree on a thick quilt, and curled up in a fleece blanket. It was still reasonably warm for a fall evening, but a breeze had kicked up, rustling the leaves overhead in the trees.

"Kimberly, I need to tell you something," Evan said, appearing at the clearing.

By now, Kim was used to Evan popping up unannounced at their old spot. She tried not to think about how empty it would feel once he left for Alaska. Hopefully, winter would come early and chase away temptations to relive these days that included him. "Have a seat." She patted the blanket.

Evan fell into the spot beside her, leaving a gap between their bodies. The blanket wasn't large enough to give him more than a few inches. One elbow rested in the grass. "You come out here a lot?"

"It's one of my favorite spots. It's where I came up with the idea for The Twisted Tulip." *And where most memories of us happened.* "It's just far enough away from the house to enjoy the chirping crickets."

"But not so far away that you might get lost in the woods, climbing out your window on a dark night?"

Kim chuckled. *Busted.* She reddened. "Yeah, exactly."

"What big, important things are you pondering tonight?"

She suspected he was stalling, but she didn't mind. Just having him near, enjoying this moment, was nice. She'd prolong it as long as she could. "I meet with the bank tomorrow. In Norfolk."

"Your business loan?"

"Yeah."

"You'll blow them away," Evan said. "They'll probably offer you double."

She smiled. "I just hope they don't laugh me out the door."

"If you need some customer testimony, I'm sure there are a few people in town who'd go to bat for you, fire off an email or two." Evan folded his knees and rested his elbows there. "But I know they'll see the passion I do. This is your dream, and you've got drive behind your plan."

She nudged him with the side of her body. "Thanks." The breeze kicked up again, cutting through her fleece blanket. It had her worried Evan might want to retreat inside, him in only his short sleeves.

"Little chilly out tonight." *We're so in sync.* "Of course, this wind makes me a total wimp."

"Don't tell me they don't have wind in Alaska." Kim unwrapped herself from the fleece. Before finding a reason not to, she scooted closer to Evan and tossed the blanket over their laps.

And he let her.

"Not much," he answered. "Not in Fairbanks, anyway."

She shivered, her arms now exposed to the breeze. What she wouldn't give for Evan to pull her in close and keep her warm. "So what did you want to tell me?"

She watched the heavy rise and fall of his chest.

"Everyone keeps saying Jeremy's death isn't my fault. Think I've finally accepted that they're right."

"Because they—"

He turned toward her then, his cognac eyes pleading to let him get out what he needed to say. She felt chills, but she wasn't sure what they meant.

"I was so in love with you that I had to tell someone. Jeremy. . . That morning, at work . . . I know we were planning to wait until after your birthday party, but I had to . . ."

After all this time apart, it felt reassuring to know he hadn't reduced what they had together to some little impractical fling. "You never told me that before."

"I didn't exactly stick around long enough to, did I?"

Evan and Jeremy had both worked at Loomis Manufacturing back then, assembling irrigation pipes. Not the most glamorous job, and it often demanded long hours during the busy season. Yet, they seemed happy working there together. The future, to Kim, had always been so clear back then. "What did Jeremy think?" Kim's breath was clipped, warning her that the answer might not be one she wanted to hear. "About us?"

He stared across the creek, maybe watching the long grass sway. The same grass that would be a charred field had Evan not taken charge. The whole town was murmuring about the incident that left Ron Larson more than a little ticked off.

Evan turned his gaze to her then. He finally put his arm around her and pulled her against him. "He was so happy, Kimberly. Truly excited for us."

Tears brimmed in Kim's eyes, both for the loss of such a wonderful man and his approval of their love. "Really?" Her word escaped, barely more than a whisper, along with a tear.

"I told him about the birthday party idea, and he offered to help us pull it off." Evan's hand gently stroked her arm. "You know, good a plan as it was, we never really had a cover story figured out for what I would be doing there."

"We didn't, did we?" Kim let loose a little laugh, amazed how they'd overlooked that one small but very important detail. "Rumors would've picked that apart until people unraveled the truth."

"He knew if you and I got caught fooling around before you turned eighteen that Ron would personally kick me off the department and make quite the show, too." He shook his head, a smile across his lips. "I think Jeremy knew, even back then, that I found my calling."

"He was wonderful like that," Kim added. "Always seeing the best in people, putting them before himself."

His eyes met Kim's, and her entire body tingled. She'd missed this so much. Back then, they'd not been able to keep their hands off each other. Their many nights sitting at the creek or curled up in the bed of his truck in a sea of blankets replayed through her mind. Lust for each other had been . . . insatiable. Clothing disappearing within minutes of their stolen moments. But once they made love, they stayed curled in each other's arms and talked, much like this.

"He needed my help setting up, especially since it was supposed to be a surprise."

Daring to disrupt this intimacy, Kim slid her hand beneath the blanket and placed it on Evan's denim-covered thigh. When he didn't push her away, she asked, "What was your cover story? Just helping with food and decorations doesn't sound too convincing."

"No, you're right," said Evan. "We figured Sue would take care of that part." He rocked her playfully, pulling her closer. The heat of his body was like an electric blanket, the breeze nearly undetectable. "He was planning to have a band come. So the cover was, we had to build a stage."

"A band?"

"I know it was a little excessive, but you remember how he was. The whole 'go big or go home' mantra."

"Yeah." Her fingers slowly stroked his leg through his jeans. She'd never been able to keep her hands off him for long, and now she had no desire to try. He might leave again, probably would, in fact. But tonight, she wanted to live in the moment. "What does any of this have to do with the fire?"

"He had to get the number for that band," Evan said, and let out a deep sigh. "I was so caught up in our plan, that I begged him to go home at lunch and grab that number so he could call right away. I thought if he waited, it would be too late. That our whole plan would fail."

Kim knew Jeremy never made it back from lunch. But it still seemed as if there was a missing piece to this puzzle. "Then why would he decide to take a nap before coming back to work? If it was so urgent to call that band, why would he stall at all?"

Evan shook his head. "I've asked myself that question a lot over the years. And why I didn't check on him sooner. I guess I thought he was calling them from there, making all these grand arrangements. It wasn't until nearly two hours had gone by and the boss was asking where he was at that I sensed—" but he couldn't seem to finish.

"You've never told anyone, have you?"

"How could I without exposing our secret?"

Kim rested her head on his shoulder, her feet curled under her thighs. She let her knee drape onto his leg. "I wish you had told me before," she finally whispered, no hint of reprimand in her words. *We could've dealt with this together.*

"I wanted to," Evan admitted. "I just didn't know how. Kimberly." He turned, cupping her cheek. "I would've ruined what we had, eventually. I was so caught up in grief and guilt. I saw the train wreck I'd make of it all if I stayed. I couldn't put you through it, that hurt. Not you. If I stayed, it would've been worse. So much worse."

She didn't want to agree with him. That small, fiery part of her wanted to be angry at him forever for abandoning her. But she heard what he hadn't said, under this confession. *We wouldn't have been strong enough to survive it back then.*

Eyes still locked with his, Kim reached her hand toward Evan's neck. She pulled him down and brushed his lips so gently it was a feather kiss. And when he didn't pull away, she kissed him harder. The breeze rustled the leaves, but Kim crawled into Evan's lap undeterred. She threw the blanket around her shoulders and wrapped them in a cocoon of fleece.

Her hands tangled in his hair, his lips trailed up her neck, stubble grazing her skin. She nipped at his ear, and finally he brought her to his lips.

When she reached for the hem of his shirt, his hand came down on her wrists like a shackle. "Kimberly, wait."

She groaned, trailing kisses along his jaw. "Look, I know you can't promise me anything. And I forgive you for leaving. I know you probably won't stay. But . . ." She'd reached his ear. ". . . We have tonight. At least leave behind a memory." Tomorrow she'd feel remorse for letting him go so easily, but tonight she needed him.

"Make love to me, Evan." Her breath was already ragged. "Please."

"If you want a memory," Evan said, planting a soft kiss on her lips, "we'll make one my way." He kissed her cheek. "Kimberly, I'm going to savor every delicious inch of you." His lips brushed her other cheek. "At my leisure."

Running both hands down her arms, he stopped at the hem of her shirt and lifted it. He rolled the cotton with such patience, patience that warned he meant what he said. Inside, Kim coursed with desire. At this rate, she'd come undone and take over within minutes.

Lifting her arms, Evan peeled the shirt from her and tossed it on the blanket. She knelt before him, naked from the waist up. "You're so beautiful, Kimberly."

At his low growl of approval, Kim felt her body tingle with delight.

She yearned to grab his hands, demand they touch her heated skin. Instead, she slipped his T-shirt over his head.

He traced his fingers above the waistband of her silk pajama bottoms. They'd shared a few passionate nights all those years ago, ones where they'd barely been able to keep their hands off each other. Too consumed with need, they never discovered how to take their time about anything. This soft, prolonged build-up was new, thrilling, and equally terrifying.

Looping his fingers in her panties, he slid them down agonizingly slow, drawing out the task. She tried to roll off his lap so he could remove her pants, freeing her knees, but Evan held on, keeping her legs planted in place. "Let me." He was the one to liberate her.

She felt vulnerable, exposed to him like this, not knowing what he planned to do. His hands ushered Kim to kneel straighter. He peeled the silk bottoms away as he sank below her. Spreading her knees above him, he drew her body down, his mouth hovering beneath her center. His hot breath, mixed with the chilly breeze teasing her nipples, elicited a small moan from Kim.

His lips met her soft folds, caressing the wet flesh with his tender kisses. Had it not been for his strong hold on her hips, she would've toppled. The tip of his tongue leisurely teased her. "Mmm," he said, the rumble of his voice intensifying the sensation. A hot, full tongue slid along her center, dipping inside her between strokes.

The wave of pleasure buckled her knees, but Evan held her firmly against his mouth until her body stilled. She was on the verge of seeing stars when Evan lifted her off him. "Lay down for me, Kimberly. I'm not finished." Obeying, she reached for the button on his jeans, but he stopped her. "I didn't bring—"

"I did."

Evan raised an eyebrow. "Were you planning to seduce me?"

"Maybe," she said. She meant her response to be teasing and lighthearted, but it only caused the tension in the air to sizzle. Kim worked at the button, then the zipper, until his pants fell away.

It was her turn now.

Her fingers slipped beneath the waistband of the last remaining obstacle, carefully stretching the elastic over his length. She marveled at the size of him. Kim remembered how well they'd always fit together.

Evan kneeled above her. When his teeth scraped against her erect nipple, her back arched. "I want to taste every inch of you, Kimberly."

Just hearing him use her full name in that gravely, lusty voice had her nearly falling over the edge. His tongue traced a leisurely path from her chest to her belly button. As he moved, the blanket began falling away, but Kim hardly noticed. "Please, Evan."

"What, Kimberly? What do you want?"

"You, inside now!" She nearly yelled it.

"So impatient," he jested. "Maybe I should slow things down."

Kim lifted her head from the blanket, sitting up with her elbows. "You slow things down any more, I'll tackle you like you're harboring chocolate cupcakes!"

"In that case, I know where you can find some frosting to lick." Evan chuckled, his deep, sexy laughter rumbling.

She crawled to her knees, flipping them both over. When Evan was on his back and finally met her eyes, both in such rapture, Kim thought she might chicken out.

Spotting her discarded pants near the blanket, Kim reached over Evan's head, not surprised when his hands cupped her free breasts dangling over his face. He kneaded them, brought one to his mouth, and nearly made Kim forget what she was doing. When her fingers felt the foil packet in her pajama bottoms pocket, she was nearly dizzy from pleasure.

How can I stand any more of this? I'll pass out!

"You don't waste any time," Evan mumbled under her, his lips releasing her nipple.

Another time, Kim would want to slow down. She would want to soak it all in, memorize every inch of his body with her fingertips, eyes closed, smiling. "I've waited five years." She tore open the foil packet and quickly went to work, her hand trembling at the feel of him between her fingers. "You'll understand if I'm a little impatient."

In a flash, Kim was on her back again, Evan hovering overhead. "You're not the only one." She whimpered in anticipation.

His body wrapped around hers, his length nudging at the one place it wanted to be. Kim thought she might lose her mind if he didn't hurry and fill her. She'd never been one for patience, and tonight her limits were nearly exhausted. "Please, Evan," she managed to whisper. "I want this. I want *you*."

Lips came crashing down on hers as he entered her all at once. It was startling, thrilling, and the best feeling she'd ever experienced. "You feel perfect, Kimberly." Evan rocked slowly, his strokes almost agonizing. She wrapped her legs around him, urging him to pick up the pace, but he only chuckled. "I told you, we're doing this my way." His raspy words betrayed his weakening ability to stick to them.

Kim lifted her hips and matched each grinding thrust. Her hands tangled in his hair, their tongues intertwined. A hand slid from her shoulder, down her torso, and settled on her clit. When Evan began to stroke the swollen flesh, Kim felt herself growing so close to her release. "Evan," she said, her voice desperate. "Evan!"

His strokes went from slow and sensual to wild and desperate. Kim cried out as she fell over the edge and stars swam in her vision. Her body convulsed with an earth-shattering force. Evan was close behind; his own groan of release filled her ears.

He gently collapsed on top of her. Against her ear, he said, "I've never stopped loving you, Kimberly Wilkerson. I don't think I ever will."

Chapter 20

Kim sat in the lobby of the bank, clenching her binder so tightly she risked breaking the clips inside. With the paycheck her mom had given her just this morning, she finally had enough for the down payment on the loan. Now the only hurdle was convincing the bank that her business was worthy of funding.

"You'll do great," Debbie had told her that morning on the phone. "As soon as you have that preapproval letter in your hand, we can get your offer together!"

She'd driven by her storefront three times this morning before she finally parked. She peered in the window, leaving a nose smudge as she imagined *her* store inside its walls.

A couple of nights ago, Allie got Nick involved when Kim discovered some pieces of furniture he already had stored in his barn. Allie cheered her on, saying they would fit perfectly in The Twisted Tulip.

He'd asked, "What is it you need with these?"

"Just to add some flare," Kim explained. "They're almost perfect the way they are, all worn and rustic-looking. I just need them to have turquoise and purple accents. Fewer sharp, dangerous edges."

"It's rustic, with a twist," Allie explained.

Nick mostly shook his head, muttering things Kim couldn't hear. Apparently, he preferred to make old, neglected pieces look like new, not leave them worn, or appearing abandoned. "Okay, but no promises on how they'll turn out," he warned.

In the end, they agreed to have a few dressers, buffet tables, and odd end tables keep their rustic look, and a few others would get a complete makeover, painted a solid color with a rustic flare to match Kim's logo. It was a combination she couldn't wait to see displayed in her store.

"I'm so proud of you, Kimberly," Evan had whispered against her ear this morning before he had to slip out of her bedroom and dash down the hall for his own. Kim felt so scandalous, inviting him to sleep in her bed last night. But what else was a girl to do when the man she'd pined after since she was fifteen told her he loved her?

"Ted Johnson?" the receptionist called out. "Mr. Anders will see you now." Kim watched a man in his forties wipe sweaty palms against his suit pants. *Holy crap, I'm next.*

That morning before she left, Penny had said, "You'll do great, Kimmie," and handed her a check. "I know I haven't been supportive lately, but I am proud of you. I want you to know that. Your father and I both are."

"Mom, I need to ask you something." Kim recalled Valentina Larson's intrusive appearance in the store. "Is everything okay? Valentina—"

"Today is your day," Penny interrupted, giving Kim only more reason to feel concern. "I believe in you."

"Kimberley Wilkerson?"

Let's do this, Kimmie.

Macy waited until her dad drifted off to a drool-worthy sleep in his favorite recliner, reruns of *Pawn Stars* playing in the background. She'd been bored out of her mind today, itching to leave the house. She'd heard that Evan joined the fire department and was eager to see if that meant he was staying. It was no secret to her now that Evan and Kimmie were hot for each other, but she still didn't want to see her sister crushed if he left and returned to Alaska.

Earlier that morning, Macy remembered that Kim's future depended on what a single banker had to say, and had fired off a text.

Macy: Good luck, Kimmie. Knock 'em dead.

Kim: Stop pretending to care.

Macy: I do care! Want me to come along?

Kim: About as bad as I want to run a grocery store.

Macy: Let me know how it goes :)

Two hours later, Macy still hadn't heard anything. She felt irritated that Kim could act so childish about all this. So she messed up and sent Kim on a date with the wrong brother. This little tantrum was immature.

Drifus grumbled in his sleep, stretching his long legs until they hit the edge of the couch. Normally Macy enjoyed spending time with her dad, but the newest meds made Chip extra cranky. And a little loopy when they wore off. He started talking about aliens before he drifted off to sleep this morning.

She shot a text to her mom, letting her know she was leaving.

Macy: He's out like a happy, drooling baby. I'm off like a prom dress :)

Swiping her purse off the kitchen counter, Macy rushed out the door. With Kim in Norfolk meeting with bankers, she decided she'd be safe spending time with Gram. Macy wanted to ask Violet what she knew about Wilma Gentry. The poor woman seemed extra jumpy lately. It also gave her the perfect excuse to poke around Evan's future plans.

Macy pulled into her grandma's familiar winding driveway. She parked under the covering of thick trees, hoping that Gram had a pie baking. She was such a sucker for a good apple pie, and Gram made the best.

Violet was in the garden, holding a green watering hose. A second one sat curled next to the spigot. Mostly Macy had avoided visiting in the past because she hadn't enjoyed Gram putting her to work. But a few years in the Army changed her perspective on what constituted *work*. Watering a garden didn't seem like such a big inconvenience compared to unpacking a forty-foot Conex for inventory. Twice in one day.

"These are beautiful," Macy said, referring to the colorful array of flowers, most she didn't recognize. There were some daisies and maybe some marigolds in one corner of the elaborate garden. But otherwise, she was lost. Kim, on the other hand, could probably name them all.

"Looks like my azaleas will make it after all." Violet looked up at the trees. "I suspect we only have another week or so before the first frost hits. At least, that's what the farmers have to say."

Macy noticed Gram's vegetable patch, looking a little thirsty. "I guess it has already snowed twice in Fairbanks."

"You going to stay up there?"

"I might." Macy unwound the hose and aimed the sprayer at the vegetables. She was too timid to touch the flowers. Flowers were more precious to her grandma than anything. "I love it there." She didn't want to admit yet that she planned to buy a house and stay at least another decade. Longer if she ended up settling down someday. "You should come visit me, Gram." Of course, that meant finding the right man. *Not one with a screen name of* Maria's Hubby.

Violet seemed to consider this a moment. "Maybe. We'll have to see."

That always meant probably not. "Kim could watch your flowers next summer for a week," Macy suggested. "You know they'd be in good hands."

"True." There seemed to be genuine interest now. "But she'll be quite busy with her store. In Norfolk."

"Did she get the loan then?" Macy asked. She assumed everyone else would know before she did.

"Haven't heard yet, but I know she will. She's got that artistic talent, twice what I ever had." Violet's words were filled with admiration. "I just wish your dad would see it for the wonderful gift it is instead of some joke."

"Well, Gram, it is just a flower shop. It's not like she's going to become a millionaire."

Violet shut off the water. "You sound just like Chip." She started to wind the hose back up toward the house. "All your life your sister has been looking for your approval. She just wants you and your parents to take her dreams seriously." Violet was no longer smiling and her normal soft, gentle tone was now a lecturing one. "You treat her vision like it's a cute kindergarten drawing that belongs on some fridge."

If Macy felt a twinge of guilt before, she felt a bolt of it now. "I guess I never thought of it that way." Finished with the vegetables, she too wound up her hose. "That's a lie."

"What is?"

"Gram, the truth is, I'm jealous of Kim. There, I finally said it. I'm jealous that she has her life all figured out, that she's always had this dream to chase. It's not like I fantasized about becoming a helicopter pilot when I was little. I love my job, I do. But it fell in my lap one day. I've never had some big dream to pursue like Kimmie." She was about to tell her grandma that she would show herself out, but Violet cut her off.

"Hurry up with that and wash your hands. We have an apple pie to eat."

Macy took the stairs two at a time, opting to use the upstairs bathroom. At the top, she stopped, spotting a sketchpad on the sitting-room table. Approaching cautiously, she tipped it open with one finger. Flipping page after page, Macy found Kim's colorful drawings: flowers, single arrangements, and much grander, large-scale designs for major events. "Kimmie, I really am proud of you, you know."

Knowing Gram's ice cream would be melting if she didn't hurry, Macy flipped the book shut. The momentum slid it off the glass-topped table and onto the floor. A few photos flew from the pages, one knocking against the wood molding below the window frame.

"Macy, are you coming?" Violet called up the staircase.

"Be right down!"

She quickly collected the stray photos from the hardwood floor. Mostly, they were of gardens and flowers, but one stopped Macy. Evan had one arm wrapped around Kim, and the other outstretched toward the camera. Their smiles were infectious, the happiness in their glimmering eyes leaving a hole inside

Macy. She envied what they'd obviously found, even if they'd been hiding it from the start.

"Wait a minute," she murmured. Kimmie's hair streamed inches past her shoulders. Macy had been gone more than she'd been around, but she distinctly remembered the day Kim had her hair cut. It was her eighteenth birthday, just after Jeremy's funeral.

Flipping the photo to the back, she found a camera's date stamp from the film.

"Oh, Kimmie!"

Chapter 21

Evan spent the majority of the day at his mom's place, helping Alex repair the chicken coop. How the thing managed to stay standing was a mystery. He risked suggesting they build a new one, but one look at his mom's pleading eyes stopped all that.

Even though Anita had moved on and remarried years ago, she wasn't ready to let it go. "Please, Evan," she begged. It was the last piece of the farm, the last memory linked to his dad.

He gave in. "We'll fix it."

She offered him the first smile he'd seen from her since hitting town. "Thank you." Things were still uncomfortably tense between Evan and his mom, but he could see her trying.

Evan and Alex worked through the morning and into the early afternoon in diligent silence, stopping only to scarf down a few sandwiches Anita brought out. They were his favorite—his mom's special chicken salad

277

recipe with seedless grapes and scallions on flaky crescent rolls.

"It's looking good." Anita leaned against a stack of lumber, regarding the half-repaired coop with some emotion Evan couldn't pin. But there appeared to be the faintest trace of a smile. "I want to get some more chickens," she finally said. "Maybe a cow."

Polishing off his third sandwich, Evan swallowed. "A cow, huh?" His mom hadn't talked about adding animals to the farm since his father passed. "Mom, are you okay?"

"Of course." She offered him a dismissive smile, but he wasn't buying it.

About to press on, the screech of brakes announced Hannah's arrival home from school. "Evan!" Hannah raced toward them, her backpack bouncing from side to side. "Evan! Did you hear?"

He propped the board against the coop. It now could support a single board's weight without collapsing. "Hear what?"

"Willow Creek might hire a full-time fire chief!"

Alex stepped around the coop's opposite side and caught Hannah's announcement. "Where'd you hear that?"

"At school!" Excitement beamed through her, worrying Evan. He shared an apprehensive glance with his mom and Alex. A town the size of Willow Creek couldn't afford to pay a firefighter a salary.

"At school?" Alex repeated.

"Yeah, Mrs. Higgins told us about it today in social studies." She dropped her backpack on the ground. "Evan, you should run!"

"What?"

Hannah nearly bounced as she added, "Mrs. Higgins said they're planning to hold an election at the rural board meeting."

"Hannah," Evan warned.

"You should put your name on the ballot! Evan, don't you see how perfect this is? You could stay in Willow Creek and do what you love to do!"

"I haven't decided how long I'm staying. You understand that, right?"

"Yeah, yeah." She waved her hand, dismissing his comment as if there wasn't time to start an argument. "Everyone's still talking about how you saved the town from that soybean fire last week." Then she changed topics mid-stream, asking her mom, "There's supposed to be a big press conference at the fire hall. Can we go?"

"When?" Anita asked, seeming to have caught her daughter's excitement.

"Like, now!"

"Evan," Alex said, "maybe we should head into town, see what the deal is."

"Hurry up, already!" Hannah shouted. "We're going to miss it!"

A block from the fire hall at the north end of Main Street, Evan realized something was already stirring. Several cars parked on either side of the brick building proved Hannah's news. One of them Ron's new truck, fire engine red.

"I don't like this," Alex said, pulling into a spot half a block away. "How did we not hear about this little press conference?"

The four walked in silence toward the fire hall.

Evan found it odd how quiet the streets were. Everyone must be packed inside the fire hall's reception area. It wasn't a large space by any means, but it was sizable enough to accommodate their monthly department meetings. Vaguely, Evan wondered if the press conference would exceed their fire code limit.

Willow Creek residents sat filling rows of folding chairs. Ron Larson stood behind a podium, facing the room. Five rural board members sat in chairs to his side. He paused when he noticed them enter, long enough to let Evan know he'd been spotted.

With standing room only, Alex nodded toward the back of the room.

"As I was saying," Ron said, "we received an anonymous donation to hire a fire chief, full time. Salary and benefits included, for the next five years. There's also a lump sum for new equipment as needed during that period."

Holy shit, Hannah was right.

"No clues where the money came from?" someone asked from the center of the listeners gathered.

"No. It was delivered by a lawyer on someone's behalf. The *who* chooses not to be identified," explained Ron, his face the slightest shade of red. "The rural board will be meeting a week from next Tuesday to discuss whether this donation is in the best interest of the community."

"What's to discuss?" a deep voice called out from the front of the packed room.

"If we hire a full-time chief, the district will be responsible for maintaining that salary after the five years expires," a board member replied before Ron could.

But he got back in charge soon enough. "We need to discuss *if* that's something we can *afford*. As I'm sure many of you've seen, we're in dire need of budget funds for upgraded equipment."

"Which you'll have if you take the donation," another person called.

Heads nodded from nearly every seat.

A fiery spark flashed through Ron's eyes. Evan could tell he wasn't used to being questioned. "I assure you the board is more than capable of considering all the pros and cons, and will arrive at the best decision for the town. And the budget."

"What happens if the board decides to take the donation?" Betty Meyers inquired from the front row. She was scrawling in her notebook, probably for a newspaper article.

When Ron seemed to lag in his answer, another board member stepped up to the podium. "Then we'll accept Fire Chief candidates to place on a ballot. The stipulations of the donation state that *if* we accept it, the town will get to vote their new chief into his position."

"What happens if the board turns down the donation?" Evan hollered from his spot. "Will the lump sum for new equipment still be donated? Most of the gear we have now needs to be replaced. Some of it isn't even safe to wear to a fire anymore."

"No," the board member answered before Ron could. "It's an all-or-nothing deal."

"Why doesn't the town get a say in it?" a voice from the third row chimed in.

Ron smiled, an endearing smile that never held sincerity. Unfortunately, Evan knew several people in this very room were blinded to that. Ron patted at the air with that smile. "I assure you, the rural board is more than competent in making this decision."

Again, Betty Meyers had a question. Her pen rose from the front row. "Are there any potential candidates yet?"

"Me, of course," Ron answered.

The crowd roared at that. "But you'll have to forfeit your position at the bank," one person said. Evan barely heard his next comment through the growing noise.

"I assure you, I have no such intention. Should we choose to move forward with this donation, I will reduce my hours, of course. But I will still be at the bank to serve Willow Creek's citizens."

"I'll run, too," Tim Hollander stood from the middle of the room. "Put me on the list." A light buzz of conversation filled the packed room.

"What about Evan Rowe?" It was Abigail Adams, Aunt Ruby's best friend. She turned in her chair and stood. Even from across the crowded room, Evan noted the white cat on her purple sweatshirt. Her eyes met Evan's, hope filling them. "You'll run, won't you?"

Before Evan even knew what he was doing, the words escaped. "Sure, Abigail. Ron, add me to that list."

"Are you sure?" Evan barely heard his mother's voice, soft as it was. He met her eyes and offered her a weak smile.

Ron flushed, his fingers grabbing the podium a bit tighter, just enough to let Evan know this decision would cost him. "Perhaps you and I can discuss this offline, Mr. Rowe."

"No need."

He heard a whispered, but excited *yes!* from his sister.

Another voice called, "I heard Evan saved the town from evacuation last week. From that crop fire."

Ron ignored that. But at least he'd stopped patting the air.

"Surely you'll be returning to Alaska soon?" Ron said. "This position, should it even come to pass, is reserved for someone willing to commit a minimum of five years."

Evan folded his arms, locking eyes with Ron, and something flashed in his mind. It was like a subliminal advertisement, only it was a memory. Ron Larson, standing in the kitchen of Sue Wilkerson's burning house. Wearing a business suit with a gold tie instead of a fire suit. "Willow Creek is my home, now."

The room erupted in a cheer Evan hadn't expected. Hannah grabbed his arm and squeezed for all she was worth. His mom let her bangs hide her watery eyes, but he caught her wiping a tear.

"Too bad accepting the donation isn't up to these folks," Alex said quietly in his brother's ear. "I doubt it'll even get accepted."

Everything Evan needed to know was hidden in what his brother had left unsaid. He suspected most, if not all, members of the rural board had their hands tied. He wondered how many of them could afford to cross Ron Larson without serious repercussion.

At the cheer for Evan, Ron ended the small press conference and dismissed everyone.

Evan wanted to slip outside and avoid Ron entirely, but it was too much to hope for. "Why don't you and Hannah go wait outside?" he suggested to his mom. "We'll be right out." He wasn't afraid to face Ron alone, but having Alex as a witness might be beneficial.

Ron separated himself from the board members conversing at the front of the room and made his way to the brothers. "You'll hurt this town if you decide you can't handle it here and run back off to Alaska," Ron said loudly. Purposefully. "I don't know why you're set on torturing good people here. You've let them down once. This time, it's just cruel."

The decision to stay had been sudden, Evan would admit later. But Ron's brash grandstanding did it. Evan's mind was made up in just those few gibes. "I'm not going back."

Fire rose in Ron's eyes; the vein along the side of his forehead throbbed again. One glance at Alex, though, and he seemed to rethink what he might be willing to say. "You shouldn't write off your options just yet. The chances of this donation going through are minimal at best. This district can't afford to keep a full-time position on the department after the money runs out."

"Then why hold a press conference?" Alex asked. "Why get the town's hopes up?"

Larson turned to study Alex before he admitted, "It was in the terms that fancy lawyer sent over." He adjusted his tie. "If you're looking for someone to blame for planting false hope in this town, find your anonymous donor. He's the one at fault here, not me."

The press conference had ended more than twenty minutes ago, and finally the echo of loitering people died down. Ron Larson crushed an empty Sprite can in his fist. He'd been smiling nearly half an hour now, until it damn well hurt his jaw in his effort to appease these people.

He hadn't counted on Evan Rowe showing up unannounced. The crowd practically crowned the jerk for adding his name to the list. A list that meant next to nothing right now.

The rural board would turn down the donation without hesitation. Four out of five members owed Ron a small fortune. By the middle of next week, this entire donation nonsense would be behind them.

Tossing the crushed pop can into the trash, Ron swiped his cell phone off his desk and prepared to head back to the bank. He had another appointment in an hour with dear Wilma. It was all a formality, one in which he'd have to officially tell her the bank couldn't provide her financing. That way no one at the bank would question his decision. Later, Wilma would sign the other documents, at a hilltop restaurant a few miles from town.

Then he'd get on to dealing with Chip Wilkerson.

But all that could wait. Right this minute he needed to know why Evan Rowe had chosen *now* to come back to Willow Creek. *Surely he doesn't remember anything more from the fire?* Well, even if he did, it wouldn't stand up in a courtroom.

Scrolling through his phone, he called an old friend.

"Mr. Larson, to what do I owe the pleasure?"

"Fire Marshal Hansen, always nice to hear your voice." Ron could waste time with formalities, but it wasn't necessary. Ted owed him a favor this time. One that wouldn't cost Ron a dime. "I need a background check on a certain firefighter."

"That all?"

Ron shuffled toward the door, but waited to open it. "Not your ordinary background check. I need one of those special ones. One that tells me what happened to a certain smokejumper up in Fort Wainwright, Alaska. I suspect he was terminated. And Ted? Time is of the essence."

"Got it. Back to you as soon as I can."

Ron hung up, straightened his back, and even allowed his chest to puff out. He would handle this. Even in the unlikely event the citizens convinced the board to accept this money, he'd find the dirt he needed to take Evan Rowe down. Whatever it took, he would run him out of town by the end of the week. Before Evan remembered too much.

Chapter 22

With Nick called in to the hospital for a patient with a fractured ankle, Allie decided to absorb herself in a romance. She was drawn completely into the story about a woman in love with her brother's best friend when the doorbell rang repeatedly. Norman started barking. Grumbling at the interruption, Allie shoved a bookmark between the pages and tromped to the front door. "I'm coming!" she yelled. But the doorbell abuser didn't seem to hear.

Throwing the door open, Allie didn't bother to pull Norman back. He shoved his way to the screen door, barking louder.

"Do you mind?" Allie practically yelled. Norman quieted, and his tail began wagging the second he recognized Kim. "Hey, Kimmie! But seriously, what's with the doorbell thing? Norman's ready to tear a limb off."

"I got it!" Kim's arms flailed above her head, like those crazy inflatable things at car dealerships. "Allie, I got the loan!"

They screamed together, causing Norman to bark his own approval even louder. Kim practically took out the screen door to get inside and throw her arms around Allie. They jumped up and down, still cheering.

"We need to celebrate!" Allie announced as she closed the front door behind them. "I think you drank me out of wine, though. Is Dr. Pepper okay?" It was a lie. A stash of wine sat hidden in the basement. But Allie wanted Kim sober tonight when she heard the news about Evan.

Kim practically skipped behind her into the kitchen. "I was so nervous, but I don't know why. My loan officer, Al? She's the sweetest thing."

Allie retrieved two cans of pop from the fridge and slid them onto the kitchen island. "Did you take her one of your arrangements?"

"Yes! Thank you for the tip. I think that's what sold her!"

Norman, sprawled on the kitchen floor, still threw in the occasional *woof!* But he'd settled on terrorizing his stuffed squirrel, letting its squeaker speak his enthusiasm. "I'm so happy for you, Kimmie!"

"I'm meeting with my realtor first thing next week to write up an offer on the space. They won't accept anything earlier."

From the cupboard, Allie snatched tortilla chips and a jar of salsa. She opened the bag and set it on the island. "So now you just wait?"

"Yeah, I guess. Everything else is in order. As soon as they accept the offer, I'll place all my orders."

"Good thinking to wait." Allie had no doubt that Kim would write an offer the current owners wouldn't refuse.

Fanning herself, Kim fell onto a stool. "I can't believe how *real* all this is! I've been planning it for years, and now it's finally happening."

Cracking open her pop, Allie asked, "Did you hear the big news in town?"

"No. What?"

"There's been an anonymous donation made to the fire department." Besides Nick, Kim was the only other person who could ever know the truth. "It'll fund a full-time position for chief. A five-year position."

With her chip halfway to the salsa, Kim froze. "Wait. *What?*"

"They had a press conference down at the fire hall earlier today, when you were charming your banker in Norfolk."

"It was Nick, wasn't it?"

"Yep." Allie scooped up some salsa and added, "The rural board is having this big debate about whether to accept it. They're worried they won't be able to fund it after the five years is up. And from the sound of it, Ron Larson doesn't want them to take the money."

"Oh, guess he would just get hired on, wouldn't he?" The disappointment was evident in Kim's dimmed eyes.

"No, not unless he's voted in." Allie reached for another chip. "But Ron isn't the only one on the candidate list, *if* they take the money. Mom told me Tim Hollander stood up." She paused for dramatic effect. "And Evan did too."

Kim's chip bounced from the island and onto the floor. Norman dove for it. "He did?"

"Yep. In fact, he told the entire room that Willow Creek was his home now."

Kim threw her hands around Allie's neck, nearly suffocating her. "This is perfect!" Releasing Allie, Kim searched the kitchen and peeked through the doorway, oblivious to Norman at her feet. When she still ignored Norman's *woof!* the dog let out a loud, deep bark that echoed. Bending down to hug Norman, Kim asked, "Where's Nick, Norm? Where is he? I want to thank him!"

Allie felt relieved Nick was gone. She still hadn't admitted to him that she told Kim his secret. That conversation wouldn't go over well right now. Not when it'd been so hard to convince him to make the donation in the first place.

"I can't just use this money to help all your friends live happily ever after, you know," Nick had told her a few days earlier.

"Why not?" Allie asked. "And besides, it's not as if Evan's a bum, freeloading off the town or anything. He's Alex's brother. He's respectable, *and* he saved the town last week. You'd be doing everyone a favor. If Kim ends up marrying the guy, well, that's just a bonus." Allie'd instantly turned away, flustered, having thrown out the "m" word so easily. Nick hadn't seemed to notice, though.

"Fine," he relented. "But it's an all-or-nothing deal. No negotiating back and forth."

That night, Allie thanked Nick many times over. The memories of some of those things they did made her blush more than her steamiest novels.

"Nick got called in," Allie told Kim. "Should be home later. But Kim, you know you can't thank him."

Spinning around and darting for the chips, she asked, "Why not?"

Eyes shooting wide, Allie said, "Really?"

"Oh, oh! He's not supposed—ah. I get it."

"He wouldn't forgive me, Kim. I wasn't supposed to tell anyone. *At all.*"

"Sure, I know."

Allie emptied her Dr. Pepper into a glass and discarded the can.

"I was worried Ron Larson would try to keep it so quiet that Evan wouldn't even know about the donation until the board shot it down. But I had Nick tell the lawyer to make it mandatory that the town be informed within twenty-four hours of the offer."

"This has to be the best day ever." A dreamy look washed over Kim, her chin in her hands. "Well, best twenty-four hours, anyway."

Across the counter, Allie saw the glow radiating from Kim's face. "Something happened between you," she guessed. "Something big."

Kim looked like she might burst, despite how tightly she clenched her lips. But that smile and her twinkling eyes were a dead giveaway.

"I'm right! Tell me. Tell me right now, Kim, or I'll go ask Evan."

"We had a . . . fun night last night down by the creek."

"Fun?" Allie shook her head. "Playing with his mansnake kind of fun?"

Kim's eyes filled with mischief and sparkled with happiness. "You are never going to let me live that down, are you? Call one penis a mansnake and I'm branded for life."

"You were! Did he decide to stay in Willow Creek, then? Last night?"

When the glow dimmed, Allie was surprised.

"No, we didn't really talk about that." Kim hugged her pop can, interlocking her fingers. "But he did tell me he loved me."

"Um, what?"

A swoop of blonde hair fell over her eyes. Kim pushed it back.

"Well?" Allie insisted. "What did you say?"

Kim shrugged. "I asked him to sneak into my room and spend the night."

"You didn't say it back?"

"I couldn't, Al. I mean, I haven't let myself think that deep into it, you know?" Norman nosed Kim's hip and dropped his slobbery squirrel in her lap. Kim picked it up with two fingers and flung it across the room. "I was sure he'd go back. How could he not? He talks about Alaska with such reverence."

"Are you in love with him?"

"Um, I don't know. I mean, I—"

"You are! I knew it!"

Kim stared at Norman—who'd returned the slobbery squirrel—obviously wanting to avoid Allie's laser-beam stare. "I don't know. Norman, what do you think? Is it possible?"

"Why are we just drinking Dr. Pepper?" Allie hopped up from her stool and pulled Nick's favorite whiskey from the cupboard—the expensive stuff he sipped only on occasion. "We need a real drink!"

Half an hour later, Allie'd ushered them to the deck, leaving the chips and salsa behind. "How is your dad doing?" Fall days were hit or miss, but this one had been spectacular. They slipped into the cushy patio furniture and enjoyed the view of the gently rolling hills and sprinkles of fall colors.

"Well, he tried to sneak into the store again yesterday. Really, I wish he'd give it up. I've caught him three times now." Kim shook her head. "I know he's used to working. And sitting at home all day must drive him crazy. But if it were me, I'd love having that much time off."

"So, what are you going to do with Evan in Willow Creek?" Allie asked, "I mean, if your shop is in Norfolk, will you just drive?"

The sour expression on her friend's face seemed to provide its own answer. "I hadn't really thought about that. I mean, I guess I'm just happy Evan's staying in Nebraska, period." She shrugged. "I'm sure we'll figure it out."

"Have Evan and your dad seen each other yet?"

Kim sighed. "No, they haven't run into each other yet. I really wish the drugs made him a lovable, slightly delirious version of Chip as we know him. Seriously, he's even crankier than usual. I took him to a movie last week, but he just picked it apart our whole drive home."

"I'm sure he'll be in a better mood . . ." Allie offered a refill, but Kim declined. ". . . Once he's cleared to go back to work."

Kim crossed her ankles. "I'm not planning to tell Dad unless something actually comes of this. I can't tell him about *before*. He'd probably chase Evan out of town himself. With a shotgun."

"You really think so? It was five years ago, Kimmie."

"Joys of being the youngest. He'll never see me as an adult, capable of making wise choices or starting my own grownup business. Then there's the whole Jeremy thing. He still blames Evan for that, too." Kim stood, ignoring her drink. "I don't know if this will even turn into something, you know?"

"You have to have a little faith, Kim."

"Seems Evan has competition for that position. And that's if the donation even gets accepted. If he doesn't get it, he still might go back. Hard to have faith when there's such a high chance that history will just repeat itself."

Chapter 23

Early Monday afternoon, Macy hunted down Kim in the grocery store's back room. "Where's Mom?"

"She left for some appointment." Kim set down the scanner on top of a pallet of toilet paper and folded her arms. "I think something's weird. Do you know what's up?"

Macy had more pressing matters to discuss with Kim, but she sensed her concern. She'd been hiding that picture all weekend, but today she'd have to ask Kimmie to explain it. She hoped her speculation was wrong. "What do you mean?"

Kim glanced toward the saloon doors and lowered her voice. "She keeps leaving for these afternoon appointments, always at three. I didn't notice at first because she sent me home early."

"So?"

"Have you been paying attention to Mom at all?" Kim asked. "I mean, you *are* staying at their house.

She's been wearing makeup again. And fancy clothes. Her hair's always done. Macy, she came back to the store the other day with a fresh manicure."

Macy didn't know what to say. Penny had always been against manicures for as long as the girls could remember. It'd been a huge argument during prom season just to convince her to let Macy get one. "A manicure?"

Kim snatched the scanner and nodded toward the office for Macy to follow her. "I know she was stressed before we came to help out, but this isn't the reaction I expected. She needed help, not someone to take over so she could pamper herself all day. Since when has our mom ever been like that?"

"You're right, never," Macy answered as she followed Kim up the stairs.

Depositing the scanner in a drawer, Kim spun around and sat on the edge of Penny's old desk. "Do you think Mom's having an affair?" she whispered.

"What?"

"I don't know, Macy. What else it could be?"

"What about that whole thing with Valentina Larson the other day? Did Mom ever tell you what she wanted?"

"Maybe we should find out." Kim made Macy poke her head out to the stairway to ensure the coast was clear downstairs. "Help me look through the office. Maybe there's a clue or something."

Eyeing an old gray filing cabinet in the corner, Macy started there. After pawing halfway through the first drawer and finding nothing but printed inventory sheets, she decided to confront her sister about the photo. But Kim was flipping through the books. "What do you think you'll find in there?"

"Well, Mom told me about this feminine products order that was really for the scanner. She wanted to hide it from Dad. Maybe there's another order like that in here."

"If there is?"

Kim shrugged. "I don't have all the answers, you know."

Taking a deep breath, Macy decided now was as good a time as any. "Kimmie, I found something upstairs at Gram's house yesterday."

"About Mom?"

"No. About you."

Kim eyed her. "What're you talking about?"

If she didn't get right down to it, Kim would just deny and stonewall. "I know about you and Evan."

Blood rushed to her sister's cheeks and turned them pink. Kim slammed the ledger shut, stuck her head in a drawer, and shuffled papers around. "So? We're both adults. What's the big deal? Jealous or something?"

So it's going to be like this, is it? "How long has Evan been in town, Kimmie?"

"Why do you care?"

"He got here just a couple days before I did, right?"

Kim slammed the desk drawer so hard it echoed. "I'm sorry he's more interested in me than you, Macy. But c'mon, you've probably got dozens of boyfriends back in your precious Alaska. Why can't you just let me have one?"

"There's no need to act like a spoiled brat, you know." Macy meant the words to come out softer than they did, but damn it, she wasn't trying to steal Evan. Being shot down once by a man was more than enough cause to take a hint. "Anyway, I'm not talking about right now. I'm talking about before he left. Five years ago."

With her back to her sister, Kim's shoulders rose then sank. "Why can't you just drop it, Macy?"

But Macy had come too far to back down now. "I found the photo, Kimmie." She reached into her pocket, meaning to pull it out. But it wasn't there. "From before Jeremy died. When your hair was longer."

Kim spun around, her eyes narrowed. Ice in her tone, she demanded, "Seriously? What do you care?"

Macy had expected Kim to blush and act as though she'd been caught stealing cookies before supper. She hadn't anticipated this hostile tone. "Where is this photo, huh?"

"I . . . I misplaced it. But I'm right. You two were fooling around. You were just seventeen." She realized there was no victory in knowing. "You couldn't tell anyone because you knew Dad would kill him. Plus, I'm sure some other people in this town would've had a few opinions to offer."

Kim stiffened.

"Kimmie, I know you were young back then. But Evan wasn't. He should've known better than to take advantage of you. He should know better now, too."

Kim marched up to her, pointing her finger inches from Macy's eyes. "Stop interfering in my life. I don't need or want your overbearing, self-serving help." At the doorway, she spun around. "And if you tell Dad, I swear, you're disowned."

"Kimmie, wait!" Macy called, but she was left standing in uncomfortable silence as the back door slammed.

Chip raced through town on his motorcycle. The dark clouds threatened rain, but he wouldn't be gone from the house long. Just long enough to have that son of a bitch arrested for taking advantage of his younger daughter.

He'd already called Alex Rowe and asked him to meet at Violet's house to make an arrest.

"An arrest? Who?" Alex had asked.

Chip only commented, "It'll be me for murder if you don't get your ass over there."

He'd flown through town, not caring when he spotted the police car parked next to the school.

When he snuck into the grocery store earlier—successfully for once—he found an interesting photo on the concrete floor. He heard his daughters arguing upstairs and had only had to climb a couple of steps to overhear the most important detail. The one about Evan Rowe fooling around with his seventeen-year-old daughter. He matched the date stamp on the picture he discovered.

He arrived at Violet's just as the two brothers met in the driveway. Chip skidded to a stop, almost losing his balance in the loose gravel. Both men rushed toward him, obviously seeing his falter. "Back the hell up," Chip growled after righting himself. "I'm rusty, not dead."

"Chip, what is all this about?" Alex asked.

"I want you to arrest this one."

"For what?"

"For taking advantage of a minor."

"Excuse me?" Alex actually stuttered back a step. "That's a pretty serious accusation, Chip. Who's the minor?"

Chip appreciated the way Alex didn't defend his brother immediately, although the look in his eyes said differently. Alex was waiting to hear the facts. *Why couldn't this one have won over my youngest?* "Kimmie." Chip nodded. He hadn't missed the way Evan's muscles tensed.

"She's not a minor, Chip."

"But she was when this one stole her innocence from her!"

Alex folded his arms and shared a glance between the two. "Does Kim want to press charges?"

"Alex!" Evan growled. "You can't be serious—"

"Answer the question, Chip."

"I haven't talked to her about it yet, but—"

"Wait." Alex unfolded his arms. "Then what evidence do you have?"

Chip dug in his jacket pocket, whipped out the photo, and shoved it toward Alex. "This."

Alex studied the photo. "This isn't exactly a compromising photo, Chip."

"Look at the date stamp."

"Chip, look—"

"Don't, Rowe." He pushed his finger in Evan's face. "You were Jeremy's age, which is way the hell older than my daughter was back then. You damn well knew better."

A car flew up the driveway, a cloud of dust three stories high trailing it. "But I guess you were just full of poor judgment back then, weren't you? Like the idiotic decision to try and save Jeremy from that fire without any of your equipment. Or training, for that matter. You're done tearing apart my family. I want you out of town. Tonight. Go back to Alaska where you can't hurt anyone."

"What the hell, Dad!" Fire shot from Kim's hazel eyes. She slammed her car door.

"Get back in your car, Kimmie. I've got this."

"Don't you dare *Kimmie* me." The look in her eyes frightened Chip. He'd never seen her so angry. They'd had plenty of arguments over the years, too.

"Kim, I have to ask," Alex said. "Do you want to press charges against Evan?"

"What?" She looked ready to slap Chip. "No!"

"Now, Kimmie, I heard you and your sister. And I have that picture."

Alex held up the photo in question. Kim ripped it from his fingers.

Chip watched some silent exchange between his daughter and Evan. Kim ran into the house. Everyone waited in uncomfortable silence, wondering if she would return. Then Chip heard the front screen door screech.

"There is no picture." Kim lifted her ash stained fingers in front of his face. "I'm about to disown one family member today. Want to make it two?"

Chip felt lost for the first time. "Can we step over to the porch? Talk about this?"

"There's nothing to talk about." She marched up to Evan, threw her arms around his neck, and planted a kiss on him that would've made a stripper blush. Turning back to Chip, she said, "I love this man. He's *never* done any harm to me. I'll stand by him no matter what you try to pull."

Chip didn't miss the smile hiding in Evan's eyes. Could Kim's admission of love be news to him? "But—"

"You've got to stop blaming him for Jeremy, Dad." Chip half expected steam to shoot from Kim's ears. Maybe fire from her mouth, like a dragon. "Evan charged into that house to save him. He almost *died*. If

Evan hadn't gone to check on Jeremy, who would've called the fire department in time?"

Chip hadn't thought of that. Not once. "I guess—"

A red Dodge Charger flew into the driveway next, sending a fresh layer of dust in the air behind it. Macy ran out, racing toward the group. "Dad, what the hell did you do?"

"Him?" Kim's eyes grew two sizes wider. "Him? What the hell did *you* do, Macy? This is all your fault. I asked you to stop meddling with my life, but you just couldn't help yourself. Could you? You ran straight to Dad."

"I didn't. Kimmie, I . . . I'm trying to fix this!"

"You are dead to me."

"That's a little extreme."

Chip agreed with Macy. Things had obviously gotten a little out of hand, but this seemed a little far to push things. Even for his girls.

To drive her point home, Kim added, "You had no right to interfere. I don't know what messed up thing happened to you that you feel the need to completely ruin my life, but whatever it is, let it go. Go back to Alaska and stay there. Move on. But move on away from me. You're not my sister."

Hoping it wasn't too late to repair the damage he'd already done, Chip said, "Officer Rowe, I believe I was mistaken. I'd appreciate it if we could just forget this little embarrassing incident."

Alex nodded. "Of course."

He wanted to talk to his Kim, to understand what he had so obviously missed. He'd believed all these years that she blamed Evan, too. But now he suspected she'd never considered him guilty of killing Jeremy, accidental or not. Had she simply been suffering a broken heart at Evan's absence?

Head hung low, Chip trudged back to his motorcycle, his hands tucked into his pockets.

"You're not driving that thing," Kim called. "My car, Dad. I'll take you home."

"I'll follow on your bike," Evan offered, sounding nicer than Chip knew he deserved.

The drive remained silent until they hit pavement at the edge of Willow Creek. "Mom will kill you, you know. If she knew you were taking that motorcycle out so much, she'd have it impounded."

Kim was still snappy, irritated. He should have talked to her first.

But he had been so overcome with blinding rage he hadn't given it a second thought. And his grief-stricken anger had allowed him to place his daughter in the middle of it.

Most of all, he'd wanted a chance to tear at Evan Rowe.

Chapter 24

Kim figured she needed a new hiding spot when Evan found her. Her adrenaline still spiked in those moments she recalled the disastrous situation that had ensued over one stupid photograph she couldn't seem to part with.

Evan sat beside her at the edge of the creek and nudged her with his shoulder. "So, that was fun."

She only wanted one thing: to protect their secret past at any cost. Tears threatened to break free now that the anger had started to dissipate. Chip could jeopardize everything. If she knew Macy, the entire town would no doubt know by dawn.

And right after Evan found a reason to stay. Ron Larson would spin this, in the worst possible light, and use it to keep Evan from the chief's position.

"Hey," he whispered against her ear. He wrapped his arm around her. "They would figure it out sooner or later."

"I should've been more careful. That picture . . ."

"It wasn't really that controversial, you know. It's not like we were naked." He smiled at her. "So you burned it?"

Wiping a tear away with the back of her hand, she shook her head. "No, I hid it."

"But there was ash on your fingers."

Kim tucked her head. "Gram might be a little upset with me later when she can't find her pecan pie recipe."

"Kimberly." Evan began to laugh. "You never cease to amaze me."

"You're not mad?" She finally dared to meet his eyes. "This could cost you Fire Chief."

His fingers grazed her bare arm, the motion soothing and slightly erotic. "Don't worry about that. A lot that has to happen before there's an election. If Larson has anything to say about it, there won't even be one."

When she told Evan she'd be okay living in the moment the other night, even then, a part of her knew she was lying to herself. If he left again, it would destroy her. "Did you mean what you said at the press conference?" Kim fought the tremble inside her. The answer shouldn't matter.

"Yes," he answered, his voice confident. "This is home."

Hope tingled inside her. Maybe, just maybe, they might have a future together. "I'm glad."

They sat at the edge of water, feet dangling from their perch on a large tree trunk, watching the sun lower in the horizon. Nebraska hadn't failed in its unpredictable weather. A few nights ago they'd been nestled in blankets, but today Kim was too warm in her jeans and tank top.

"I'm sorry about the whole creek thing a while back." Evan tucked her hair behind her ear.

"You didn't know." She stared at the brown water, illuminated by the glow of the setting sun. For such a narrow stream, she couldn't believe she nearly drowned in it. She hated that the water had such power over her, though without the ability to swim, there wasn't much she could do about it. A couple of near death experiences could do that to a person, she reasoned.

"Do you trust me?"

Kim lifted her head, following the trail of his eyes back to the creek. "Of course."

Evan hopped up from the trunk and landed back on shore. "Let me prove I'll never let you drown."

She glanced nervously toward the murky water. *Too bad we don't have crocodiles.* Any excuse to say no. Anything that wouldn't make her look weaker than she already felt in front of him.

Evan was beside her again, and turned her chin with a soft touch of his fingertips. "Look at me, Kimberly. Not at the water. Trust me?"

She managed a weak nod. "Okay."

Cupping her cheek, he slowly drew her lips to his. The kiss allowed her to savor the taste of him. She felt her legs tingle, threatening to give out at any moment. It was the most sensual kiss they ever shared. One that dared to promise a future.

Realizing that any number of people—namely, the guests of yet another garden party—could come barging into their private moment at any time, Kim settled for removing her jeans alone. She was secretly happy she'd packed her favorite pair of purple lace panties. Once the water soaked her orange tank, Evan would see it was a matching set.

She tried to avert her eyes as Evan stripped down to his boxers, but she couldn't help herself. She knew exactly what lay hidden beneath them. Overcome with desire, she forgot to be afraid of the water as he led her into the stream.

The cool water wrapped itself around her ankles and created instant goose bumps. For October, they were fortunate the late afternoon was so beautiful. It had to be nearly seventy-five outside.

Before she knew it, they were nearly chest-deep in water, several feet from the safety of the shore. Kim shivered. "It's so cold."

"There's only one way to fix that," Evan said. Never letting go of Kim's hand, he dipped his head below the surface. When he reemerged, he wore a reassuring smile. "So much better." He nodded to her, urging her to do the same. "I won't let go." He pointed his eyes to their connected hands.

Kim shook her head. "I'm fine."

"You're freezing."

"No, I'm okay. Really."

Evan closed the gap between them, his arm wrapped around her waist. "I promise, I'm right here. Nothing bad will happen." The gentle words were filled with such warmth that Kim momentarily forgot her fears. He wasn't pushing her, but he wasn't letting her off the hook either.

Gripping his hand so firmly she feared she'd break a bone, Kim bent her knees and held her breath. Eyes shut tight, she sank below the surface. Within two seconds, she shot back up. Her breathing came heavy, bordering on frantic. But Evan still had her hand. Surprisingly, she did feel warmer.

"See?"

She tilted her head and let a flirtatious glint shine in her eyes as she glanced up at him. "Okay, so maybe you were right."

"I don't think I heard that." Evan wore that mischievous smile that made her stomach tingle. "Something about me being . . . what was that word?"

Kim wrapped her free arm around his neck. "Don't push your luck."

"That's exactly what I'm doing." The soft, sensual kisses from earlier were no more. Evan's lips claimed hers and sent streaks of pleasure shooting throughout her entire body. Any concerns of cold water were miles away. In one kiss, they started a fire. She bit his bottom lip, sucking it between hers. His groan filled her with such pleasure, such satisfaction, she thought she'd lose control entirely, especially with his rock-hard desire pressed against her.

His tongue demanded entry, and with little fight she let him. Her hands threaded through his thick hair, grabbing a little harder than she meant. She was so entranced in their kissing that she didn't realize she couldn't touch the bottom of the creek until water hugged their necks.

"Evan!" Her heartbeat thumped erratically.

"It's okay."

Kim kept peering around her. Her feet fluttered, and her arms wrapped so tightly around his neck she thought she might strangle him.

"Look at me, Kimberly."

Forcing herself from focusing on her terrifying surroundings, she met his eyes instead. From this close, she could see tiny gold flecks reflecting the setting sunlight.

"I won't let you go," he repeated his earlier promise. "I got you."

Her muscles relaxed.

"Sometimes you have to learn to let go. Trust that you have someone to keep you safe."

"What are you saying?" Kim hated herself for asking. He couldn't promise anything.

"Let me in, and I promise I won't let you down. Let me be there to keep you safe. I'm sorry for what I did after Jeremy died. I'm so sorry, Kimberly, but I want you in my life. Not just for a few weeks. For the long haul."

"What about Alaska?"

In the midst of talking, Evan had pulled them still deeper into the creek. Kim suspected he could no longer touch bottom either. She wanted to trust him, to believe him.

"I bought a cabin up there. We can visit." He wound his arms tighter around her back and pulled her even closer. "My life is here now. It always has been. I guess it was just waiting for me to come back."

Such happiness filled Kim that she no longer cared whether she could touch bottom.

Evan tucked a stuck strand of hair behind her ear. "Did you mean what you said earlier?"

"What?"

"That you love me?"

Kim felt heat flash up her neck, probably turning her face bright red. "Oh, I said that out loud, didn't I?"

Evan rumbled in laughter. "You sure did." He kissed the tip of her nose. "Did you mean it?"

"I did."

She kissed him deeply, finally allowing the last of her guard to drop.

His lips trailed along her jaw toward her ear, his whiskers tickling. "Want to get out of here for a while?"

Kim wound her legs around his waist, only now she held on tightly in order to feel his body pressed against hers, rather than from fear. "Take us to shore, Captain!"

They drove several miles from town, to a deserted spot they both knew well in the country. With the corn yet to be harvested, Evan's truck, though twice the size of the one he used to drive, was hidden from sight of any nosy farmers.

Evan had snuck into Violet's house through the kitchen to borrow some blankets, careful to avoid the gaggle of elderly ladies sitting on her front porch, sipping coffee.

Lost in a sea of those blankets now, Evan wrapped himself around Kim. It was nearly impossible to be close enough to her now that they'd put their clothes back on. "Just in case someone sees us," he cautioned. "Public decency and all that." But he found them intrusive.

His lips traced every exposed inch of her succulent skin. He was sure he could never quite memorize her body enough. When his lips met her fingers, he moved to her stomach, pushing the tank top up as he took his time. Exposing her purple lace bra, he mumbled his approval through his kisses. "Mmm, this is nice."

Evan trailed kisses along her collarbone, up her neck, until his lips found Kim's. With eager hands, he forced her shirt up over her bra and let their tongues mingle. As his hands hovered over the lace material, he felt her arch her hips against him. His body ached for hers.

"Please tell me you've been carrying a condom in your wallet."

"Two, actually." Evan dropped his head to her breasts. His tongue teased the skin above the fabric there. His hands slipped behind her back and worked the clip of her bra until the entire thing slackened.

Evan suckled her breast His teeth scraped the edge of her erect nipples, earning him a whimper. He might just lose what little control he had left right here, with his mouth on her breast and her hips pressed against his length, if she kept making noises like that.

His hands slid down her exposed stomach to her jeans. He yanked the zipper down and shimmied them off her hips. She kicked them away and his fingers slid beneath her panties. She rewarded him with a sexy gasp. With one quick motion he pulled them away, exposing her to him completely.

Spreading her wet folds, he covered her center with his palm and massaged in slow circles. Kim dropped her head back against a stack of folded blankets. Her look of pure ecstasy made it hard to wait. He needed to feel her, wet and hot, wrapped around him.

Her fingers trembled against his belly as she worked at the button on his jeans. *Damn it!* He couldn't take this any longer. He shoved down his boxers and kicked them away until he was completely naked on top of her. His throbbing length slid immediately into her hands and her fingers cradled his cock. He moaned at her satin touch.

He continued massaging her clit and slid two fingers inside her.

"Please, Evan." Her plea was but a swallowed whisper. "I need you," she begged as she met his gaze.

The sight of those beautiful hazel eyes drenched in desire pushed him over the edge. His fingers slowed, just barely. "Is that all?" It was all he could do to continue teasing her.

One hand wrapped around his neck, she drew him down until their foreheads rested against each other. "I love you, Evan Rowe."

Evan plunged himself deep inside her so quickly she gasped. He tortured them both with slow strokes, but desire won out within minutes. He cupped her perfect ass in his hands, and drove his hips against hers, faster and more possessively.

Kim cried out and he groaned against her neck. They came together, their worlds exploding and uniting. "I love you, Kimberly Wilkerson. I always will."

Chapter 25

Evan had ordered them a basket of fries to munch on, but neither had touched it. Kim sat beside him in a booth at a quaint restaurant in Norfolk and waited for Alex to join them, busy acting like teenagers, fighting the urge to make out in the corner. Every time Evan nuzzled her neck, she pushed him off saying, "We're going to get kicked out!" If it weren't for Alex coming, she wouldn't have cared.

"So tell me more about The Twisted Tulip," he said, finally snatching a fry. They'd driven by her storefront before heading to the restaurant. "You'll make the offer on your building next week?"

"That's the plan." The words lacked conviction, though. Kim hadn't waivered in her plan for five years, but for the first time, she felt sad at losing her enthusiastic Willow Creek patrons. Those people weren't just customers to her. She'd come to adore them and their peculiar tastes. Like Agnes Billings, always

322

dressed head to toe in her usual orange, requesting her orange orchids. Or Brenda Norbert wanting something with *elegance and just a hint of outrageous flare* for her Tuesday coffee with her cross-stitching club. And Friday afternoons, Aunt Ruby needed at least three arrangements for her bridge nights—always with daisies in the design.

"You look like you have to go to the dentist." When she didn't meet his questioning gaze, he turned her head with his finger. "You having second thoughts?"

"About the store?" She shook her head. "No, of course not. It's my dream." She checked her watch. She'd have to leave soon to make it to her last shift at Hy-Vee's floral counter. "I'll just miss some of my regulars."

"Why don't you open the store in Willow Creek?"

The idea sounded almost like a fairy tale. Whimsical and fun, but a stretch from reality. "Well, for one thing, there're no storefronts for lease. And I don't think I could keep it running. I mean, think of the population. How many people in Willow Creek need flowers? Business would be too slow."

Evan shook his head. "This isn't the Kimberly I know. There's something else."

Kim took an extra-long sip of her pop. "The business loan is only good if I get that building on Norfolk

Avenue." She had a great meeting with the loan officer, but to secure the loan she had to plug *that* location. It promised great foot traffic and the business to complement it. "The loan's actually contingent on me getting that building."

Alex slid into the booth across from them and instantly apologized for his late arrival.

"Case?" Evan asked.

Alex nodded, but seemed distracted and was evidently relieved when the waitress interrupted. Kim ordered a salad and watched the minutes tick by. It'd be the only thing besides the basket of fries she was now nervously devouring that she'd have time to eat.

"Are you coming back tonight?" Evan asked her, his voice a sexy rumble.

She had planned to stop at her apartment here in Norfolk, switch clothes, and sleep in her own bed for a night. Maybe binge-watch Netflix until the wee hours of the morning. Macy could help out at the grocery store tomorrow since she'd been avoiding it like the plague since their little spat.

"Why don't you stay at my place tonight?" she suggested, lowering her voice to spare Alex as he ordered. "I don't get off until eleven, and I wouldn't mind the company."

"I wish I could." Evan kissed her, one kiss turning into two, then three.

From across the table Alex asked, "You two want some privacy?" and caused Kim to blush. "I can leave."

"Sorry," Kim and Evan apologized in unison. Kim stirred ice cubes with her straw and whispered to Evan, "I'll be back tomorrow afternoon. At the store."

"I'd stay, but Alex and I are working on something for this vote about the donation," Evan commented.

"Do you really think Ron'll win if they move forward on the donation?" Kim asked.

"Probably," said Alex. "Sorry to rain on your parade, Evan. But if Ron wants to win, he will. Thing is, unless we do something drastic, there won't even be an election to discuss. Holding two full time positions, no matter what Ron says, would interfere with his extracurricular activities. He's got of most of the board's hands tied with that. He doesn't want that donation to be accepted."

"And here I thought the town of Willow Creek would be a happy, Mayberry place again with Lesley Jamison behind bars," Kim muttered. "I didn't realize she had a successor." She reached for a fry and dipped it in ketchup. "But if you know about his extra activities, how is he still getting away with them? Can't you arrest him?"

"I've been keeping an eye on him, but it's hard to gather any real evidence. With a man like him, it has to be solid evidence that'll stick."

Alex glanced at his brother, a look that spoke unheard volumes.

Kim wondered what the two of them had discussed. "If we try to slap him with something minor, he'll just lawyer up. Then he'll retaliate."

"Which is why we need to come up with a strategy," Evan added.

Kim wished she could head back to Willow Creek and help. "From what I heard," she offered, "If enough people want it to be a town decision, it will be. I think you just need a petition or something."

"Huh," said Alex. "A petition. Great idea, Kim!"

Evan didn't look convinced. "If Ron's got the rural board tied up, how many others does he have cowering in their homes?"

Kim squeezed his hand beneath the table. "We'll figure this out." She looked at Evan, then Alex. "People need to learn not to be afraid." With one last gulp of pop, she kissed Evan. "Gotta run."

She meant to only leave a chaste brush against his lips, but he pulled her in and teased her tongue with his own. Within seconds, her skin was on fire. She forced herself to pull away and nearly ran out the door.

It took as much bribery as he could muster, but eventually Chip got both his wife and oldest daughter out of his hair and to a movie in Norfolk. He finally had the time he needed to sell his motorcycle and meet with Ron about the balloon payment.

All his life possessions meant little to him. Some guys wanted the fastest, loudest cars. Others, an entire workshop full of the best tools. But Chip, he'd only wanted that motorcycle. The only two he had ever owned he'd been forced to sell to pay Ron Larson.

Luckily, he found a cash buyer through an Internet site. The guy had met him on the north side of the school where most of the town wasn't likely to spot them. He didn't want rumors to fly about it. Of course, eventually Penny would realize it was gone, but he'd deal with that repercussion then. After the money was handed over.

"Do you have a check for me?" Ron asked, inviting himself into the kitchen without so much as a knock.

"Better. Cash."

Ron's eyebrows rose at that. "You've come up with twenty-five thousand in *cash?*" Adjusting his ball cap, Ron took a seat across from Chip.

"No, it's just eight grand. A good-faith payment."

Ron shook his head and leaned back with his arms folded. "That's not how this works, Chip. You have until Tuesday next week to come up with the entire amount or the deed's signed over. You knew the terms when you took out the loan a decade ago."

Chip wished he'd been smarter, wiser back then. He couldn't exactly blame his youth, either. The loan had seemed too good to be true.

The payments were small enough each month that he'd disguised them in the books as a maintenance fee. Over the years, Penny never once questioned them. But the catch had always been that the bulk of the loan principle would be due at the end of ten years. He had hated keeping this from her, but he wanted to protect her from how dire their situation had grown.

"This is a sizable amount of money, Ron. You can't take it tonight? Give me a couple more months to get the rest?"

"Why would I do that?"

Chip had had it with Ron's bullying. "What the hell did I ever do to you, anyway? You seem to have a particular grudge with my name on it."

Ron pushed away from the table and helped himself to a glass from the cupboard. It made Chip slightly sick to his stomach that this man knew where to find the glasses with one try. After pouring himself a glass of whiskey from the bottle on the counter, Ron turned back toward Chip.

"You remember when we were just young shits, playing down by the creek?"

Chip nodded. A long time ago, when they were just boys, they'd been nearly best friends. They played together many times down by the creek at Chip's childhood property. "What of it?"

"Surely you remember that little incident where you thought it'd be a riot to pull a branch back and smack me with it, right?"

Chip tried remembering. Had they'd been horsing around? He searched his mind to picture whether he'd hidden behind a tree, waiting for Ron to come running through after him. If he had, that branch was only meant to smack him up a little bit, not cause any real harm. Kids' stuff. Of course, at that young age, it was hard to gauge what a branch could do to another human being if it was pulled back with enough tension.

"I didn't know it until years later, but that prank cost me something very valuable." Ron tossed down Chip's expensive whiskey in one gulp. "It cost me a family."

"But you've got your beautiful wife." *Trophy wife.* But Chip didn't say that out loud.

"Valentina?" Ron scoffed. He shook his head. After his first wife left him, Ron had taken off on a trip to Chicago. After two weeks, he returned with the beautiful Russian girl, Valentina. Half his age and the most gorgeous woman in town. No one had ever understood the match, except she seemed rather fond of her fancy purses, expensive jewelry, and designer clothing. "She never wanted any kids. Good thing too, considering."

"What does any of that have to do with me?"

"You took away my chance to ever have a real family." Ron dropped the glass in the sink, the sharp clink of glass alluding to a possible break. "I'm not going to stop until you feel my pain, Chip. I won't stop until your family completely falls apart. And *you* know what it's like to be without one."

Ron sauntered to the back door. "You have one week left. Come up with *all* the money, or that store's mine."

"I hear you're staying in town," Sue Wilkerson said from her craft table. She was creating some kind of Halloween decoration with orange fabrics and glitter. The memory of Jeremy's mom and other craft mishaps had Evan wondering if he'd be sparkling by the time he went home, even if he managed to steer clear of Sue's craft table.

"That's the plan." Removing the new kitchen faucet from the box, Evan surveyed Sue's existing setup. He wasn't a plumber by any means, but he'd learned to be handy out in the wilderness. Surely he could survive installing a single faucet.

"I also hear you're a little sweet on a certain florist."

Evan chuckled. He wasn't surprised that news had traveled so fast through town. He'd be surprised if some of the little old ladies who bought Kim's arrangements weren't already chattering about a wedding date. "You might've heard right. For once." The town was known for relaying jumbled versions of the real story.

"I'm happy for you." Sue appeared in the kitchen doorway. Her button-up denim shirt twinkled with orange bits. "You deserve to be happy, Evan."

Instead of replying, he threw himself under the sink to search for the water shutoff. He meant what he told Kim, that he loved her and always would. But until he stopped the nightmares and got to the bottom of Jeremy's death, he wasn't sure he could offer her everything she deserved.

"I'm also proud of you."

Evan pulled a wrench from a toolbox on the floor—*Jeremy's old toolbox.* "For what?"

"For standing up to Ron Larson." Sue fell onto a footstool near the fridge, her hands folded in her lap. "I never told anyone other than Jeremy, but Ron gave us a loan after Jim died. The insurance money, well, you know it didn't cover much."

Evan sat up from under the sink. "You made some sort of deal with him?"

Stress wore heavy in Sue's eyes. Lines he never remembered seeing before were now prominent and plentiful. "I thought he was doing us a favor. Until he tried to collect that last payment. One I should've known I'd never be able to come up with." Sue released a heavy sigh. "If there was anything good that came of that fire, it was that it freed me of my obligation to Ron Larson."

Evan felt as if someone had struck him over the head. Clear as day he saw it all. Standing in the kitchen with Jeremy slung over his shoulders. Ron Larson in the doorway to the living room. "Come on," Ron had hollered. "The department's on their way." Flames licked the walls all around them. It came to him— finding it curious how the fire seemed to burn only the walls.

Then he spotted something. A gas can at Ron's feet.

Ron kicked the can away, into the flames, but he knew Evan saw him. He reached for the toolbox on the kitchen table and grabbed something blunt from it.

Time was running out, and there was only one escape route. Evan tried to charge past Ron, but his first steps into the living room were his last. He felt a sharp pain at the back of his head, and everything turned black.

"Evan?" Sue was at his side, shaking his arm. "Hey, are you okay?"

Evan shook his head to clear the memory—the walking dream he'd fallen into with that crack on his head. "Wh . . . what happened?"

"You hit yourself." She pointed. "On the pipe."

Sitting up, Evan stared at the toolbox—one that had miraculously survived the fire. "Where did that come from?" he asked, pointing.

"It's Jeremy's. You must know that." Sue pulled him to his feet and ushered him to the kitchen table. She poured him a glass of water and insisted he drink it. "He must've left it outside that morning. It was the only thing of his that survived the fire."

Evan shook his head. "No."

"No, what?"

"No, it wasn't outside." Evan felt sick to his stomach again, but he forced down the water anyway. Emptying the glass, he slammed it down on the table. "It was on the kitchen table. I remember it."

Confusion lingered in her eyes at that. Sue asked, "Are you sure?"

In the five years that Evan had these reoccurring nightmares, he never once remembered the toolbox on the kitchen table, or Ron Larson in the house, for that matter. But since returning to Willow Creek, pieces seemed to be falling back into place.

He knew a jury might not believe him after all this time. They might think he was reaching for answers. But Evan knew with every fiber of his being that what he was remembering from the day was absolute fact. "Positive." He didn't want to say anything in front of Sue, but a new mission came over him. One that went beyond the donation. *I'm going to take that son of a bitch down if it's the last thing I do.*

Chapter 26

Evan loved that his youngest sister didn't hesitate to rush up to him when she spotted him in the school parking lot. A beam of excitement lit Hannah's entire face. As she ran to his truck, her backpack shuffled from side to side. During these glimpses of the little girl Hannah used to be, Evan felt everything might work out okay as she jumped into the passenger seat.

"You didn't tell me you were going to pick me up!" Hannah's eyes sparkled as she slammed her door shut. "Are we going somewhere?"

"Thought maybe we'd swing by Violet's house. She said something about an apple pie and ice cream."

Hannah nodded, but suspicion flashed in her eyes. "Will your girlfriend be there?"

The word sounded strange from his little sister's mouth. He knew he wanted a future with Kim, but he hadn't given much thought to giving them a label. As juvenile as the word sounded to him now at thirty-three, he liked how it sounded with Kim in mind. "I think she'll be by soon."

"Good! I want to tell her about my room. Maybe you should bring her over to the house."

"I'll think about it." Pulling out of the busy parking lot and heading west, Evan thought it best to bring up the subject now. "I have a confession."

"Oh?"

"Yeah, I have ulterior motive for picking you up from school today."

"I figured as much."

"You did?" This girl was too smart for her own good. He wished for the innocent child who rushed up to his truck earlier. But he'd have to face it—Hannah was a teenager now, heading for adulthood.

"The apple pie bribe? Kind of a giveaway."

Evan shook his head as they hit the gravel and closed in on Violet's driveway. "I actually need your help tonight. Mom and some others are coming too, but you're my secret weapon."

"Is it dangerous?" The look in her eyes revealed that she hoped it was.

"Sorry, kid. We're not solving a murder case or anything exciting. Just getting some signatures for a petition."

"Oh." She slumped in her seat and rolled down the window. "Probably too late to change my mind about this ride, huh?"

Evan laughed. "If it helps, the petition takes a stance to accept that donation for the fire department. If we can get forty percent of the town to sign, then the rural board will most likely side with the people and hire a new fire chief."

"You mean the town will basically get to decide instead of Ron Larson?"

She was only thirteen, much too young to get mixed up in all this. That she knew exactly who they were up against stirred something deep inside him.

Violet stood on her porch and greeted Hannah with open arms, engulfing her in a hug. All he wanted was that she never see the dark side of this town. Evan watched Hannah's ponytail bounce. If he didn't think she'd be able to pull in a lot of signatures playing the *younger sister card*, he wouldn't have involved her at all. But it had to be done if Evan was to make sure Ron Larson never interfered in anyone's life, Hannah's included. And he'd see to that at any cost.

"Come inside, you two. I just took the pie out of the oven."

By late afternoon, Kim was proud to see that a crowd had gathered in Gram's kitchen. The Rowe brothers had offered to grill burgers, and Kim had helped Gram with the sweet potato fries. They expected the petition group to be out late and didn't want to leave anyone hungry.

"How many signatures do we need?" Penny asked.

Kim pried fries from the baking sheet with a spatula and transported them to a paper towel lined basket. "Two hundred and two."

"That doesn't sound so bad," Macy said.

"That's forty percent of the adults." Chip sampled one of the fries. "If we hit that number, we can take the petition to the meeting next week. But the board still has to vote."

"They've never gone against a presented petition," Anita chimed in. Kim studied Evan's resemblance to his mom—the black hair and chiseled jaw line.

"Oh." Macy looked defeated already, but Kim didn't say anything. She was happy to have the extra body to help. It didn't mean they were on speaking terms, though.

"It'll be tricky since we have to cover the country too," added Alex. He set a platter of burgers on the table.

"Are we sure going door-to-door is the best way to go about this?" Allie swiped a fry. "I mean, couldn't we just put up signs and have people to come to us?"

"I don't think we'd get enough," Violet told them. "Ron has a lot of people too scared to come forward in a public setting."

"And you know he'd show his ugly face," Chip mumbled, splattering his burger with mustard. "It's best to do it this way. Only a few people even know we have a plan, so we might have a head start."

Kim studied her dad, and wondered what personal vendetta he had against Ron. No one in town was a diehard fan of the man, but Chip seemed extra intent on beating him over this donation. She doubted it had anything to do with Evan. Chip had been cordial since finding out, but not overly nice.

"It's also the reason we have to try and hit as many people as possible tonight," Evan added. "By tomorrow, word will have gotten around. Ron will no doubt step in."

Evan and his mom locked eyes. "And interfere," Anita added.

"You mean threatening people? Preventing them from signing?" Hannah asked. Kim just stared at the girl a moment and saw a glimpse of her younger self in thirteen-year-old Hannah. Sometimes there were perks to being an older, wiser soul at a young age. This was not one of those times.

"Here are the cheeseburgers." Evan slid a plate onto the counter, next to a package of buns. He tucked Kim's hair behind her ear. His fingers cupped her cheek and he drew her in for a quick kiss. "Thanks for helping me out, Kimberly."

She knew everyone was watching, that some in this room didn't even know they were together. But she didn't care. She'd hidden her love for Evan years ago; she was done being so secretive.

Violet teased, "Don't suppose there's something you two want to share with us?"

Kim spotted Evan's slight blush and had to stifle a laugh. It was cute to see *him* finally off his game. It felt the tables were more even this way. "Do we have all the petitions and enough pens?" She allowed attention to fall away from their little public display.

"And a plan." Chip pulled out a map from his back pocket. "It'll take most of the evening, but I have it plotted out how we can best conquer this."

"You really have been bored at home, haven't you, Dad?" Kim patted him on the shoulder. "Only a couple more weeks."

Chip talked them through his strategy, teaming them up to cover sections of the town. "We should cover those folks within the city limits first. If Ron's going to try to put the kibosh on this, he'll start internally. Once you've covered your area in town, move out to the country. I've taken the liberty of X-ing out houses that won't sign. No sense in wasting time."

Kim admired the take-charge personality her dad displayed and Chip's emerging sense of renewed energy. She went to give him a hug but stopped when he announced the pairing.

"You did *not* put me with Macy, Dad. No way."

"Kimmie, we don't have time to argue. You ladies are taking the safest houses in town. I saved the rougher areas for the men."

"Really, Dad?" Macy objected. "I've been to war. What makes you think I'm afraid of anyone in this town?"

Kim huffed. At least she and her sister agreed on something. "There aren't any rough areas of town. There's like two houses we should avoid. The rest are completely fine!"

But no matter the amount of arguing, Chip refused to change his mind. "Let's finish up eating and get to it."

As the group filtered outside, Evan came up behind Kim and wrapped his arms around her. "It'll be okay, I promise."

"Not if I end up in jail," Kim muttered.

"Family is important, Kimberly. Give her another chance."

"And you and your mom?" Kim nodded toward Anita. "How is that going?"

"It's complicated." Evan glanced toward his mom, still on the porch talking to Gram. "But we're getting there. She came, didn't she? I'm not giving up on her. You shouldn't with Macy, either."

Spotting Macy near her flashy rental car—one that was shiny and clean instead of dusty as it should've been—Kim rolled her eyes. "You are *not* driving. We're taking my car."

"I thought I could save you some gas."

Kim wasn't sure what she was insinuating, but it sure felt like Macy was calling her poor. She hadn't worked three jobs for the last two years to be thought of as poor. "Your car's too flashy. Too red. We'll stick out. You know Ron lives in town, and we have his street."

"You don't think he'll recognize yours?" Despite the argument, Macy was following Kim toward her Little Green Car.

"I plan to park a couple blocks away where no one'll care. If you park your fancy car on the street this whole town will be humming with rumors, wondering what the popular Macy Wilkerson is up to. We don't need word getting back to Ron. And you know it will."

Kim didn't wait for Macy to get in before she cranked the ignition. She did an inventory check of petitions, pens, and clipboards. "Let's hope this works," she mumbled. If they couldn't get enough people to sign, Evan didn't stand a chance. Ron would surely veto the donation, and hold a gun to the rest of the board members until they took his stance.

Speeding out of the driveway, Kim left a dust trail in her path.

"At least we already have nine signatures," Macy said.

"If you're trying to be nice, just stop. Plus, your signature doesn't count. You don't live here."

"Neither do you."

Kim turned down the gravel road headed toward town. "I didn't ask to be stuck with you."

"But you are, Kimmie."

With a deep breath, Kim eased into town. She found herself having to nearly slam down on the brakes. *I should probably get that looked at.* She kept her mouth shut. She didn't need her sister adding another reason for taking her rental instead.

Kim parked at the school parking lot. "It's a nice night, we can walk," she said when Macy complained. The less time they spent confined in a car together, the better. "I think we should split up. We'll cover more ground that way."

"No," said Macy. "We'll do better sticking together. Some people don't really like me, remember?"

"What? Miss Homecoming Queen made some enemies?" Kim grabbed the burlap bag filled with individual flowers. She'd taken the day off so she and Gram could prepare four hundred individual flowers, each tied with twine. It was their thank you gift for anyone signing the petition.

"Let's go," muttered Macy. "The sun sets in a couple hours. Did you know that in Alaska, we have like two months where we don't even see the stars?"

"I don't want to hear it."

"And why not?" Macy asked as they approached the first house on the block. Last Kim remembered, their high school chemistry teacher, Mr. Buchannan, lived in the tiny, well-kept white ranch on the corner.

Ignoring Macy's question, Kim rang the doorbell. As she suspected, Mr. Buchannan answered the door. He looked a couple decades older than he had when she was in high school. She worried that the newest bunch of students were taking their toll on one of the sweetest, most inspiring teachers she knew.

"Well, if it isn't the Wilkerson girls!" He beamed an approving smile at them both.

Good. At least Macy isn't on his shit list. "How are you, Mr. Buchannan?"

They chatted for a few minutes as Kim asked about his wife and classroom. A soft nudge from Macy reminded her they had eight full blocks to cover in town, plus a dozen farm places before dark. "Mr. Buchannan, you heard that Willow Creek received that wonderful anonymous donation for the fire department, right?"

"I did. Seems to have created quite the stir, too. Made this week's front page."

"We're here because we want the entire town to have a say on whether they accept the donation and its terms." Kim held up the pen and clipboard. "It's not that we think the board is incompetent by any means, but that donation comes with a great deal of responsibility that will affect the whole community. We think everyone should have a chance to let the board know where we stand. A full-time fire chief could do a lot of good for our town."

"I like the sound of that."

"We just need a signature on this petition if you're in favor of the board accepting the donation. If forty percent of the town signs, we can present it to the rural board next Tuesday night at their meeting."

Mr. Buchannan signed happily, then called for his wife to sign too. Kim offered them both a daisy and profuse thanks. As they walked to the next house, she felt an incredible high. This might be easier than they thought.

"This is Wilma's house," said Macy. "I asked her to come help us tonight when I saw her at the store, but she said she wouldn't be home." Both stared at the light on in the living room window. The sheer lace curtain revealed a silhouette in her recliner, watching TV.

"What's with the scaffolding?" Kim asked, peering at the roof.

"Guess she's replacing the roof?"

Something didn't sit right about this. "Where do you suppose she got the money?" Poor Wilma worked two jobs just to keep the lights on.

Macy shrugged. "Insurance? Maybe a tree fell on it or something."

The girls knocked. "Wilma, what a pleasant surprise!" exclaimed Macy, a smile beaming, when the door opened. "We thought you'd be out of town tonight."

"Last minute change of plans," she said, her words oddly nervous. Kim didn't like it. It wasn't as though Wilma should feel threatened by their presence.

"I guess you know why we're here," said Kim. "Would you mind signing?"

When Wilma shook her head and moved to close the door, Kim was stunned. Luckily Macy had the foresight to wedge her foot in the door. "Mind if we come in for a quick minute, Wilma? Please?"

Politeness won and Wilma held the door open to invite them in.

Kim glanced at a clock hanging on the cream colored wall and watched the seconds tick by. People would say no, even ones they thought they could count on. Wasn't it more important to collect as many signatures as they could as quickly as possible?

"Wilma, what's really going on, honey?" Macy asked. She draped an arm over the frail woman's shoulders. "You seem upset." She walked her toward the recliner, but Wilma, surprisingly strong for such a tiny woman, redirected them to the kitchen. She motioned for them to have a seat at the old table shoved up against the wall.

"You girls are wasting your time." She reached for her coffee pot and refilled a mug, but didn't offer any to her visitors.

Odd. She always goes out of her way to be hospitable.

"Why do you say that?" Macy asked. "We just want the people in town to have a voice. We're not rigging an election or anything."

"You won't have to if that petition succeeds," Wilma muttered. "You should just leave it alone. Everyone will be better off if you do."

Something about Macy's last sentence struck a chord with Kim. She felt her stomach tighten. "Are you afraid, Wilma? Of *someone*?"

Wilma glanced toward the stairs. "I'm just a little distracted with the roof repair going on."

"What happened?" Macy pried. "Did a tree fall during that last storm?"

"It was rotting," Wilma said without making eye contact. "My son sent me the money to fix it."

Kim caught Macy eyeing Wilma's overstuffed purse on the counter. A bundle of papers stuck out the top. When Wilma turned away from them, Macy slipped the papers out and shoved them behind her back. "Wilma, do you mind if I use the little girls' room? I had too much iced tea today."

Kim wasn't sure what her sister was up to, but she felt it important to keep Wilma preoccupied. "Your son sent you the money?" Just in the couple of weeks she'd spent at the store, Wilma had voiced her opinion about her son enough for their relationship to be crystal clear. There wasn't one. "I didn't think you'd talked to him in years."

"Well, when I reminded him of that, he felt guilty." Wilma sipped on her coffee as Macy reentered. "You two best get on home. You're wasting your time." She headed out of her kitchen, not looking to see if the girls were following or not, but switching out the light over the sink. Macy had just enough time to slip the pages back in Wilma's purse. "You know what will happen Tuesday night, no matter what efforts you make."

Kim tried offering Wilma a flower anyway, but the woman flinched like Kim meant to slap her.

"What do you think that was all about?" Kim asked when they were on the sidewalk again.

"Not sure, but I bet we can figure it out." Macy dug her cellphone from her back jeans pocket. "I took a picture of that contract I pulled from her purse. Guess who really gave her the money?"

Chapter 27

Evan was surprised when Chip announced they would be a team. He wasn't sure whether to be flattered or frightened. Kim's father seemed ready to kill him the other day. He couldn't blame the man, either. He should've kept his distance, at least until Kim's eighteenth birthday. But truth be told, the whole thing was controversial regardless. An extra few weeks wouldn't have mattered to Chip, even if Jeremy had survived that fire.

"I saved the most difficult people for us," Chip said as they pulled up to the first house. "The ones most afraid of Ron Larson. It's up to us to convince them they deserve to have a voice."

Walking up the sidewalk to a two-story square gray house, he saw a woman catch a glimpse of them through her kitchen window. She didn't smile out at them. In fact, Evan swore he caught a scowl as she abruptly turned away and marched into the other room.

"This is Howard and Marsha Darby's place," Chip explained as they approached the covered front porch. "Their ninety-one single cab Ford finally gave out a year ago. Howard'd been laid off for over for six months, and his back didn't allow him to find another job. Marsha works at the library part-time, and at the mini-mart too."

Evan waited for the twist as they walked up the steps.

"That truck . . . " Chip pointed to the silver extended cab Ford dually parked in the driveway, ". . . it appeared a couple of weeks after the old truck died."

On the porch, Chip rang the doorbell.

"You're wasting your time, Chip." The man of the house, Howard, stood in the doorway, his arms crossed. "We heard what you're doing. We're not signing."

Evan didn't want to push anyone, but dammit, he didn't understand why the people in town didn't want a say. "Signing this petition means you're welcome to vote for whomever you think will do the best job." He saw the slightest waver in the eyes of the woman who'd scowled at him through the window. Her hair was pulled into a hasty ponytail, and bags sat under her eyes.

"We have full confidence in the board," Howard continued. "That's why we elected *them*."

Evan watched the struggle in Chip's expression. He surely knew these people better than most. Evan imagined in a grocery store business, you saw everyone in town at one point or another, even the ones who did most of their shopping in the city. He wanted to interject, but let Chip continue instead.

"This is a pretty historical event. Most small towns never see this happen. Don't you want a say in any of this? A full-time fire chief would have far more responsibility at a paid level than one at a volunteer level. There's a lot of good that could come from an individual *solely* dedicated to that position and his department."

Evan could see Marsha coming around, but he didn't miss her glance to the Ford in their driveway. She rested her hand on her husband's forearm. "We would get to vote for whoever we want, Howie. What's the harm?"

Howard also stole a glance at the truck. "Can my wife and I have a moment?"

Chip nodded. "Of course. We'll wait out here."

With the front door closed, Evan looked at Chip. "How did they get approved for a vehicle loan? That truck has to be worth fifty grand."

Chip rubbed the back of his neck, his stressed expression taking hold. "Ron gives out *special* loans for people who couldn't otherwise find financing."

"But isn't that illegal? The bank could—"

"They're personal loans for desperate people." Understanding washed over Evan. *The same kind of loan Sue Wilkerson took out after her husband died.*

The front door swung open. "We're sorry, Chip. We talked it over and we're more than confident the rural board can reach that decision on their own." Howard looked at Evan, pity in his eyes. "I think it's noble what you want to do, but it's pretty obvious what's going to happen."

"You folks have a good night." Marsha's feeble smile diminished as they closed the door.

"You weren't kidding," Evan said as they walked to the next house. "People are terrified." He wondered what had happened to all those brave souls who asked dozens of questions at the press conference. It was obvious they wanted a say. *Strength in numbers.*

"You have no idea."

"How?" Evan clenched the clipboard in his hand. "How did he get to this point? I don't remember him being such a tyrant."

"You weren't around much," Chip said, the slightest stab in his voice. "But no one really paid much attention with Lesley Jamison running the show around here. Hell, I suspect Ron had to pay her a portion of his profits until she got locked up." They stepped up to the next door and Chip knocked. "With her gone, he stepped out of his dark corner and took over."

"Eighty-one signatures!" exclaimed Allie. She high-fived Hannah. The two had been tasked with her own neighborhood along with Alex. Allie hadn't spent much time with the girl beforehand, but they'd made a great team tonight.

"Let's hope the others are having the same luck," Alex said.

Allie didn't miss how skeptical his tone was. "Well, they didn't have our secret weapon." She clapped Hannah on the back. "You, my dear, were brilliant!"

Anytime someone hesitated, Hannah would use that innocent juvenile charm, her eyes growing just a bit sad as she proclaimed that this opportunity could keep her brother in Willow Creek. "He's a firefighter at heart. It's a scary and dangerous job, and I don't want him moving back to Alaska. I want him home so he can watch me grow up. So he can come to my basketball games and concerts. He promised to teach me how to fish!"

By the time Hannah was done, there were nearly tears in some homeowner's eyes. "You're such a wonderful little sister, aren't you?" they'd say, taking the clipboard from Allie to sign their name. "I hope you get your wish."

"It's too bad we don't have more time tonight," Alex mused. "I bet we could change some more minds."

"Have you heard from anyone else?" Allie checked her phone for the tenth time. *Nothing.* Just a text from Nick saying he missed her. Allie wished he'd been on her team. People had an especially hard time saying no to him. But she understood why it was so important to keep his distance until the election was over.

"Nope. Let's head back to Violet's." Alex clapped Hannah on the shoulder. "We'll see if anyone needs some help from our superstar team."

Allie watched Hannah beam from her brother's compliment. The girl had all but pouted when she wasn't teamed up with Evan, but it seemed she'd been afraid to let Alex down, whereas Evan was easy to please.

The trio drove through town and down the main strip looking for any sign of the others. They spotted Penny's car a block from the mini-mart, but there wasn't anyone else. "Where is your boyfriend these days? Seems like he's been out of town for weeks."

Biting her lower lip, Allie looked out the window. "He's in Georgia, helping his sister get packed up."

"Oh, that's right. They're moving to town. I remember him saying that now."

Allie didn't like holding on to this secret. She hated it. Alex was Nick's best friend. *Will he be mad when the truth finally leaks out?* Allie shouldn't care, but if the town turned on them, what would they do then? Especially if that money ended up awarding Ron a permanent job as Fire Chief?

"When will he be back?" Alex asked.

"Wednesday."

"That's too bad," Hannah said, re-counting the signature lines. "He won't get to vote."

Alex and Allie shared a knowing look. Would enough people sign or would they let fear hold them back? They'd both witnessed enough fear from the people of Willow Creek when Lesley Jamison had been reigning as the town villainess. What Allie hadn't seen coming was a replacement.

If they somehow managed to take down Ron Larson, which seemed improbable, would someone else just take his place?

They'd been knocking on doors for what seemed like hours. Kim forgot to keep track of time, but her stomach growled. Between the two of them, they'd gotten forty-four signatures. It had been exhausting. Sweet Wilma wasn't the only one afraid to sign that piece of paper.

"Hope we have enough," Macy said. The two shared a look as they sped down a country road to head west through town. They'd been assigned the east side of the farming residences, and now were going back to Gram's house.

Kim looked straight ahead. "Me too."

"Look, Kimmie. I'm sorry this whole thing with Evan blew up, okay? I didn't tell Dad. He overhead us arguing at the store."

"Because you weren't home to keep him there," Kim grumbled. Her grip on the steering wheel tightened. Her foot fell heavier on the gas pedal that last gravel road mile into town.

"You're right, I wasn't."

Ignoring her sister, Kim focused on the lights of Willow Creek illuminating the night sky ahead, though the stars still managed to showcase themselves. Kim had been in Norfolk so long she didn't realize how long it had been since she saw more than a couple of prominent stars at night. *Willow Creek really has its perks.*

For the eighth—or maybe ninth—time that day, Kim considered opening her store in Willow Creek. There was always the power of the Internet for expanding a business outside a small town. *Could it work?* Each time she reached the same conclusion. *No.*

"I thought Evan would just hurt you. I was so damn sure he'd go back to Alaska that I never once considered he'd stay. Or that he really loved you. But I was wrong, Kimmie. I'm just hurt you didn't tell me about him when I set you up with Alex."

"You've been throwing yourself at Evan since you showed up!" For emphasis Kim hit the steering wheel. "You always get what you want! So how could I expect you to think I was anything but jealous?"

"I *am* jealous," Macy practically shouted. "You happy?"

Kim prepared to fire a retort, but when she pressed down on the brake pedal, nothing worked.

Hand braced against the dashboard, Macy yelled, "Slow down! Kim? What the hell? Are you trying to kill us?"

"Shut up! The brakes aren't working!" Panic rose in her chest, and her breath cut short. She wanted to scream. Her speedometer read sixty-five as they hit the pavement.

"Okay, take a deep breath." Macy also took her own advice, obviously finding her yoga center much quicker than Kim. "Take your foot off the gas. We're going to have to coast."

"Coast? Really, Macy? Shit! There's a car in front of us!"

"You need to focus." Macy was oddly calm. But now wasn't the time to assess her pain in the ass sister's personality. "Turn on your hazards."

Kim obeyed.

"Honk your horn and go around. Be careful, Kimmie! Mrs. Johnson and her dog! Right there on the shoulder."

Gripping the steering wheel until her knuckles screamed in agony, Kim jerked to the left side of the road, then darted back over, narrowly avoiding her second grade teacher and the tiny Yorkie, barely visible in the shadows between glowing amber streetlights.

"We're about to hit gravel. Stay in the middle of the road. Go straight."

"But what if someone drives toward us?"

"We'll see it, don't worry." If there was benefit to the night, it was that headlights would surely warm them of an oncoming vehicle. "Keep your eyes on the center of the road. I've got the intersections."

Kim chanced a glance at the dashboard—fifty-two—her tires caught a patch of thick gravel and jerked to the right.

"Easy. Don't overcorrect."

Kim righted the car, easing back to the center of the gravel road. She took the first breath since discovering the brakes had failed.

"Try the emergency brake," Macy said. "But pull it up easy."

Kim gently tugged at the lever between the two bucket seats. Nothing happened. "It's not working!"

That's when the cow appeared in the middle of Rural Road 865.

Chapter 28

Evan had highly underestimated Ron's influence in this sleepy town. He felt so unsettled about it all. He and Chip had knocked on over thirty doors but only managed fifteen signatures. People didn't act as though they were afraid on a day-to-day basis. On the surface, it appeared Willow Creek was the epitome of a happy small town.

"I hope the rest are having better luck than we are." They walked back to his truck, their plan to start at the south end of the next strip of blocks near the park and work their way back to the north edge of town. Evan ran a hand over his head. "This isn't right."

"No, it's not."

"You've never had to deal with Ron personally, have you?" Evan assumed Chip was too smart to ever broker a deal with a man as deceitful and cunning as Ron Larson. But Chip's pained silence as they rolled down the deserted street spoke volumes. "I guess even the best people hit hard spots."

When Evan parked the truck and prepared to jump out, he noticed Chip sitting stiff as a board.

"Chip?"

"I wish there'd been another way back then. I wish that every day." Chip's blue eyes glazed. His hands clenched in tight fists in his lap. Evan knew this couldn't be good for his stress level. "But we were going to lose the store. Everything."

Evan wanted to believe he was mentioning an instance decades ago, maybe when Kim was just a twinkle in Chip's eye. But the uneasiness in the cab spoke otherwise. "Chip, are you *still* mixed up with Ron?"

Chip nodded, just twice. Had Evan not been watching, he'd have missed it. The second nod forced a heavy tear from his eye that dropped and landed on his thigh. "He wants the store. Some sort of twisted punishment for something I did back when we were just kids. Hell, I didn't even know it was such a big deal until a couple of days ago. It's not like he ever said anything.

"What the hell does that man want with a grocery store his snooty wife refuses to shop at? He certainly doesn't want to run it. It's like he just wants to hold that over my head, that I was a failure who couldn't even leave my store to one of my kids." Chip cleared his throat. "Not that any of them want it."

"Jeremy did." Evan recalled that several times Jeremy had turned down an offer to grab a beer at Marley's Bar or catch the end of a game so he could meet Chip at the grocery store. He'd always envisioned Willow Creek as the place he'd live until his maker took him away, and he saw his future at Wilkerson's Grocery.

The first trace of a faint smile crossed Chip's lips. "Yeah, he did. I was so proud of that kid. So proud."

"So was I." Now Evan felt tears building. "Chip, I—"

"Look, I know I've blamed you for years." Chip sucked in a breath, his eyes following a stray cat across the street. "But I was wrong to. I know you did everything you could to save him. I was just so pissed he was gone." Chip sniffled. "It's not fair."

"No."

"Sorry about the other day, too." Chip met Evan's eyes. "Can't imagine a better man for my Kimmie."

"Thank you. I do love her, Chip. I love her more than anything."

"I know you do."

They sat in uncomfortable silence until Evan dared to ask another question. "What's this punishment about?"

"Apparently I'm the reason he couldn't have any kids of his own. We were just boys, playing down by the creek. The branch was sharp, but I didn't know what it would do."

Evan knew all about the damage sharp branches could inflict. His leg had only begun to be free of most of the pain, until tonight when they did so much walking. But he'd forced himself to walk tall rather than limping.

"We're going to get those signatures," Evan reassured him. "I know it's just a small thing, but it'll be enough to start taking back this town. If I make it in, I promise I won't back down until Ron Larson is knocked off his throne and rotting in a cell somewhere."

They neared the northern edge of town, and pulled up to the last stop sign before the country road. Less than a mile west they'd find out if their group managed to pull enough signatures tonight from the frightened people of Willow Creek.

In a blur, a green car sped down the adjacent road with its flashers blinking. It swerved around a truck, honking as it narrowly missed Mrs. Johnson and her little dog.

"Hey, that's Kim!" Chip sat up straighter. The car zipped toward them, down the country road, and then past. "Where the hell—she's going at least fifty!"

Evan stepped on the gas and followed. Up ahead it looked like—*oh, shit!*—a cow. "Something's wrong!"

With no other choice, Kim swerved to the right to miss the cow, but caught the lip of the ditch. She held her breath as the car leaned left and bounced over the rough dirt and washboards in the gravel. Safely around the cow, Kim yanked the wheel and brought the car back onto the road. They were slowing, finally, the speedometer now steady at forty-two.

"You got this, Kimmie," Macy said, her hand braced on the car's ceiling. "I know you can do this."

Kim wasn't sure if that commentary helped or drew out more frustration. "*Now* you choose to believe in me? What about The Twisted Tulip?" Kim didn't mean to yell, but she couldn't help it. All four tires were finally riding on gravel again, and a small uphill climb dropped their speed to thirty-nine.

"This isn't the time, Kim. Yell at me all you want once we're out of this."

"We're down to thirty-two." Kim felt the slightest bit of relief; they might be stopped within the next half mile. "If only this hill was steeper!"

Macy muttered something very rude as they crested the hill and saw how far the other side dropped. "Both hands on the wheel, Kim!"

Both girls screamed as the Geo dropped down one of the steepest hills within ten miles of town. "I don't remember this stupid hill being here!"

"Me neither. Nebraska's supposed to be flat!"

"How long have you been gone?" Kim hollered, mostly to keep her distracted from the speedometer. "Nebraska isn't flat!"

"Compared to the Alaska Range it is!"

"You and your *stupid* Alaska!" Kim barked. "You really hate it here so much?"

"You can't keep calling it stupid if you never come visit. I've asked like thirteen times. And I offered to buy you a ticket!"

The dip at the hill's bottom neared at a frightening pace. The orange needle gained to nearly fifty-five again. Kim was really starting to hate this ride. *Focus on the road. Focus on keeping to the middle of the road.* But she couldn't help herself. "Why would I visit? Just so you could rub your success and cool job in my face? I know your life is heroic and awesome. You probably have half a dozen hot pilots pining after you. But that doesn't give you any right to look down your nose at mine."

"I think you've mixed me up with someone else."

"Face it, Macy. You never thought I was doing anything with my life. Because I wasn't brave like you and Kyle and didn't join the military. Because I never made it farther away than Norfolk, you think my life is a joke. I don't need a snooty vacation to Alaska, thank you."

"Kimmie, I swear—" Macy cut herself off when they both saw what was coming up ahead.

"Oh my God, how am I supposed to get around that?" Kim whimpered. The bright lights of a combine warned the machine was hogging ninety percent of the gravel road. The driver wouldn't see them coming, but Kim could see the sharp incline of the ditch to her right. "We'll flip!"

"There!"

"You're crazy!"

"Drive into the ditch. Right there." Macy pointed to the left side of the road. "It's almost flat. It's that or we crash for sure."

Most hills were like rollercoasters, down then up, down then up. But not this stupid hill. *No, it has to go down then flatten, shooting us out like a damn slide!*

Their momentum held steady as Kim held her breath and aimed into the ditch. Instantly, the steering grew hard and jerky, as though she was driving through a million potholes. She cringed to think what it would cost her to fix her Little Green Car once they got out of this. *Because we* are *getting out of this.*

As they passed the combine, Macy exclaimed, "You're doing it! The driver's mouth was wide open, taken aback at seeing the Geo passing him in the deep ditch. He pointed frantically, shouting something they couldn't hear over his combine. It was then Kim realized below their tires ran a small, muddy ravine filled with murky water. *Water has to run somewhere.*

Kim fought to keep the car straight, the tires away from the water. If either side caught that mud, it'd suck the tires in and flip them. "I don't think we can leave the ditch." A half mile ahead, the headlights flickered against the round opening beneath the road overhead— a drainage pipe. "We can't make that."

"Is your seatbelt tight?" Macy asked.

"What?"

"Your seatbelt!"

"Yes, it's on!"

"Sit back against the seat and hold on to the steering wheel," Macy ordered.

"What?"

"Just do it! And don't bend your wrists!"

"When did you become a crashing expert?"

"This isn't the time. Just listen to me."

The dirt barrier grew closer. The speedometer dropped, but only to thirty-five. It felt as though they were competing in a drag race. "Macy, I'm sorry I've been such a brat."

"Get your damn hands on that steering wheel. And open your eyes! You need to keep us going straight or that mud will suck the car in—"

"Right!"

"I have an idea."

"Macy!"

"It might not work. The car might roll."

"Just tell me!"

"Ease to the right. Let the tires hit a little of the mud. Just a little. It might slow us down—"

"Lessen the impact." Kim nodded and gripped the wheel.

Kim shook away the urge to make a joke about crash test dummies. She focused instead on turning the tires *ever* so slightly. *Please don't flip. Please don't flip.* Her heart pounded violently in her ears, making Macy's directions hard to hear.

The car lost speed. Twenty-eight. At the last moment Macy yelled, "Roll down the window!"

The barrier couldn't be more than ten yards away.

Twenty-four. "It's working!" Kim yelled. "Macy, it's working!"

"Stay braced," Macy ordered. "Push yourself back against your seat. Keep your head straight. But stay relaxed. Are we going straight?"

"Yes."

"Drop your hands. Don't touch the pedals! Don't tense up!"

Twenty-one.

Kim pushed herself against the seat, and pressed her head against her headrest. Her hands gripped the edges of her seat so fiercely she expected the fabric to rip.

The car slammed into the barrier and jerked both girls into the deploying airbags.

Chapter 29

Evan's heart dropped when he saw the combine. Hazard lights flashed in the ditch. The farmer drove as fast as he could to the next intersection to get out of the way. Even from three miles out, they could hear the faint echo of the town whistle. *Good, help's on the way.*

He parked the truck a quarter mile beyond the smashed up Geo to make sure he'd be clear of the ambulance. Jumping out and charging down the hill with Chip close on his heel, he saw the airbags had activated. Both girls seemed to be moving, though. "Hey!" he called down. "Are you guys okay?"

The front end of the car was a good foot shorter, smashed up against the dirt barrier. White smoke hissed from beneath the hood, but nothing seemed threatening.

"Yes," Macy yelled. "Just a little stuck."

"Kim?" Evan called. He needed to hear her voice.

"I'm here. I'm fine."

"There's only room for them to get out on the driver's side," Chip pointed out. "But be careful. It's a mud pit down there."

Evan surveyed the terrain. He knew all too well how marshy ground could suck in your feet like quicksand. He was only wearing shoes, not his jump boots. Without a plan, he couldn't leap into the marsh.

"The ambulance is on the way," Chip yelled. His eyes scanned the horizon.

"We're good, Dad!" Macy said. "Really, we're fine. We just need some help with this muddy water. I think the tires are still sinking."

"Kimmie, what happened?" Chip sounded frantic. "How on earth—"

"Later, Dad. Once we're back on solid ground, okay?"

But Chip's question had several more reeling through Evan's mind. At the sight of the fire truck leading the convoy, he knew the time for honest questions was running short. "Kimberly, I promise we'll get you out. But answer your dad. We need to know." He met her gaze through Macy's open window and understanding seemed to wash over her.

"I couldn't stop. My brakes went out."

Evan felt as if he'd been whacked in the face by a two-by-four. Memories flashed, bouncing around his mind like ricocheting bullets. Each replaced his reality. He dropped to the ground and hugged his head between his knees. Faintly, he heard Kim screaming something, felt Chip's hand on his back. "Get them out," was all he managed before the memories consumed him and the night around him went dark.

"You're really not mad?" Evan was supposed to wait to share the news, but he hadn't been able to contain himself. He had to tell *someone*. Evan had expected his best friend to tell him off.

"Are you kidding?" Jeremy patted him on the back. "That girl deserves only the best, and I can't think of anyone better than you, bro. Even if you are old enough to be her dad!"

"Hey!" Evan laughed, overcome with joy and. . . relieved. He knew others wouldn't be so understanding, but with Jeremy in his corner, they'd come around a lot faster.

"Kimmie's an old soul at heart. She's perfect for you." Jeremy's keys jingled as he shoved them in his pocket. Evan followed his trail from the small parking lot to Sue's white Taurus. "Why didn't you drive your Chevelle?" Evan asked. "I thought you'd practically be sleeping in that car."

"Damnedest thing," Jeremy answered as he reached for his time sheet and clocked in. "The brakes are spongy. I don't get it. They're brand new."

"Evan!" Kim screamed and pulled free of the EMT's arms. "I'm fine," she told the woman. "I'm not hurt! Let me go!" Once they'd brought both girls to the road, the EMTs relented. And Kim ran to where Evan was on his knees, head dipped toward the road.

Gently, she touched his shoulder. "Evan, it's okay. I'm here."

Slowly, he lifted his head, as if shaking free of a daze. "Kimberly!" He threw his arms around her, squeezing so tightly she couldn't breathe. And that bruise on her side ached a little, though she hadn't mentioned it to the EMT.

"Are you okay? You just collapsed. I was worried." He ignored that, so she added, "I'm not bleeding. See? Nothing's broken. I don't need to get checked out at the hospital."

He glanced over her shoulder. The look in his eyes grew dark and focused on something far away from her. "I remembered something. Something important."

She didn't like the growl in his voice. Evan seemed about to do something dangerous. She touched his cheek and turned his face toward hers. "Evan, you need to talk to Alex before you do anything rash." *Is he listening?* "Please."

"Okay." He scrambled to his feet and pulled her with him. "But first, there's something I have to take care of."

Kim followed his line of sight to the tow truck heading down the road. "Do you think they can fix my Little Green Car?"

"We need to get your car back to Violet's house first. If Ron Larson has any say about it, it'll be towed to the junkyard, deemed a total. We can't let that happen." He pulled on Kim's elbow, leaving her running to catch up with him.

She wanted to ask why, but she suspected it had something to do with her brakes. They'd been acting a little wonky today.

"We're towing the car back to Violet's place," Evan told the tow driver as he hopped out of the truck. A couple of the volunteer firemen stood on either side of Ron Larson, their arms folded.

She recognized one as Rick Thelton, the local building inspector. The other's name she couldn't recall, but she remembered seeing him in the garage of the gas station a couple of days ago when she filled her car up.

"Don't be ridiculous," Ron said. "That car isn't salvageable. It'll never run again."

"It's Kim's car. And it goes straight to Violet's place."

Kim felt unsettled by the steely look in Ron's eyes. He didn't like being crossed, that much everyone knew. But that defiant stare warned her that he wasn't about to admit defeat, even if it seemed that way.

"Fine, waste your time trying to fix it."

She watched Evan purse his lips, obviously biting back something big. She'd never seen him so tense. When she mentioned her brakes had gone out, he'd nearly crumpled into a ball on the road.

"He's not exactly making friends," Chip said once he approached Kim. He folded his arms. "I hope we got enough signatures. Otherwise, Evan doesn't stand a chance in hell next week."

Kim had forgotten all about the petition. A little scrape with death could do that, she reasoned. "I think he remembers something, Dad."

Chip seemed to understand. "I just hope there's something we can do about it."

"Really, I'm fine!" Macy yelled, pushing past the gaggle of EMTs at the ambulance. She'd salvaged the signatures they worked so hard gathering. "I'm not going to the hospital, either. There's too much I have to do."

Kim met her sister's eye from across the road and smiled. Some days she really hated that overbearing, overprotective way Macy had. But tonight, that very trait had probably saved both of them several potential broken bones and punctured organs. She met her halfway and threw her arms around her. "You're a giant pain in the ass, but tonight I'm really glad you're my sister."

"You're the most stubborn person I know," Macy said against her ear. "And with the dad we have, that's saying something. But I love you, Kimmie. And I promise, I only want you to be happy." Macy turned, her gaze following Evan standing in the ditch, watching every move as the volunteer firemen helped hook up the car with tow straps. "I see how the two of you are together. He loves you, Kimmie."

At Violet's kitchen table an hour later Penny asked, "Did we get enough signatures?" The women were gathered, double and triple counting the names on the petitions while the men were outside searching the Geo for foul play. Kim wasn't sure they'd find anything wrong.

"Eighty-one on this one," Hannah said.

"Thirty-eight here," said Allie.

Kim rubbed her eyes. "Forty-four from me and Macy."

"And Dad and Evan only got nineteen."

Violet scribbled on a pad of paper, adding. "Well, that leaves us twenty-four short."

Kim was certain a collective sigh could be heard the next town over. "We're so close!"

"Some people weren't home." Anita let out a yawn. "We could try them again in the morning."

"We can bring the petition to the grocery store," Penny suggested. She slid her chair back and took her empty mug to the counter for a refill. "Maybe even visit some of the businesses."

"I can talk to my teachers," suggested Hannah. "Tell them to send people to the store."

"Aunt Ruby was out of town tonight visiting her niece in Lincoln," said Violet. "But she'll be back bright and early tomorrow. I know she'll sign, especially if it's to support her nephew. She has a little influence, too."

Kim's hopes were lifting. "It's only twenty-four."

The women clanked their cups together in unified agreement just as the front door burst open. Evan stood in the doorway, Alex and Chip coming up behind him. "Your brake lines were punctured."

Kim felt sick to her stomach. Several concerned looks suggested similar feelings from the women. "You're sure?"

"Positive," said Alex. "I've seen this type of job once before, on a case I worked in Lincoln a couple years back. It's less messy and less traceable than a drive-by." Kim suspected he kept from using the word *shooting* to protect his sister, but from the look on Hannah's face, she wasn't fooled. "The line was probably punctured earlier today, maybe last night, with something small, like a needle or pin. It wasn't meant to go out right away, just over time."

"What about my parking brake?" Kim asked.

"Cable was severed."

"So, you're going to the police station, right?" Macy asked.

"Don't anybody dare go running to Chief Gumble," Anita ordered. "That crusty old geezer is one of Ron's right-hand men."

"Who'd want to hurt me?" Kim asked. She tried to consider any enemies she might've made. Sure, Todd Crawley had been a little perturbed at her quitting, but that man wasn't sophisticated enough to pick up his own dry cleaning, much less attempt something as mafia-ish as this.

"Kim, let's go outside." Evan pulled her away from the kitchen.

Once the front door was closed and he stood alone with her, he said, "I bet anything the same thing happened to Jeremy." He told her about the flashback he had earlier at the accident scene. "But since Jeremy didn't drive the car—"

"Oh my God, the fire!" Kim pulled back from his embrace and met his eyes. "What are you saying? Are you saying it wasn't an accident?"

Evan drew her into his arms and wrapped her in his comfort and warmth. "Sue says Jeremy's car is still in that old barn. We're going to head over."

She didn't miss how he evaded her question. "What about my Geo?" Kim asked. She sounded pitiful, but damn it, she'd really come to love her Little Green Car. She'd found it for a steal three years ago. "Is it really beyond saving?" It had never once failed her.

"I'm afraid so." Evan caressed her back. "But don't worry, you can use my truck until your insurance comes through."

"I'm scared, Evan." Kim hadn't wanted to break down in front of everyone else, but with him she didn't have to put on a brave front. "I could have died today, and taken my sister with me." The first heavy tear dropped.

"But you didn't."

He held her tightly, and she finally let loose every emotion she'd been holding in. She trembled, and fought to keep her sobs quiet. She didn't want to worry her family. "I didn't think we'd make it. I thought I'd never see you again."

Evan kissed her forehead. "I promise. That son of a bitch will pay for every person he's harmed. He's going down, and he's going down very soon."

The front screen door creaked, and Alex appeared beside them. Kim quickly dried her tears, and hugged Evan again. "Are you sure it's safe for you guys to drive after what he did to my car?"

"We checked everyone's brake lines—on all the vehicles," Alex reassured her. "I promise, it's safe."

"I'll be home late tonight," said Evan. He kissed her twice, then released her, squeezing her hand. "Leave your door unlocked."

His flirty wink made Kim laugh, and it felt so good.

Chapter 30

In the middle of the night Chip Wilkerson woke in a cold sweat. It was just another night in a string of sleepless ones that had preceded him for weeks now. He knew he should tell his doctor about his insomnia, but how could he explain it? Explain that the stress had nothing to do with the store, only the man trying to steal it from under him?

"Chip?"

At the kitchen sink, he set down his empty glass. A single shot of whiskey had helped him sleep through many of these hard nights, but tonight it didn't even give him a friendly buzz. He felt sick, as though a knot was tied in the pit of his stomach.

"Tonight was quite the ordeal, wasn't it?" Instead of chastising him as he'd expected, Penny fished her own glass from the cupboard. "Might as well take that out of the sink and join me."

Chip sank into a chair at the small kitchen table. Their family had eaten most of their meals packed in at this table. He smiled, fondly remembering his boy elbowing his sisters below the table where he thought no one could see. His daughters . . . he'd never seen them agree on much, until tonight.

"What are you thinking?" Penny sipped her whiskey. Following her lead, Chip decided against tossing his shot back in one gulp.

"I didn't know what would happen, forcing our girls to work together tonight." He hadn't told Penny about his embarrassing confrontation with Evan Rowe, but someone in the family probably leaked it to her. "They've been at each other's throats."

"They're sisters." Penny sipped again. "Seems like they did okay tonight."

Chip didn't get it, how his wife could be so calm. "We could've lost them, Pen. Both of them."

She covered his hand with her own. "But we didn't. Because somehow, when the moment came, they worked together."

"Hell of a moment." Chip emptied the rest of his whiskey. He still felt sick about all of it. "I need to tell you something, Pen." For decades, this beautiful woman had stood beside him. She'd even given up her dream of backpacking the world to stay with him and run the grocery store. She deserved the truth, even if it meant he might lose her. "You're going to hate me, and I won't blame you."

She'd been calm, holding together like the strong woman he'd always known. But he didn't miss the weary look in her eyes, brought out even more by the wrinkles and the creases. She tossed back the rest of her whiskey and poured them both refills. "I'm listening."

"Do you remember ten years ago when we didn't know how we were going to make our mortgage payment?"

"Of course. Kyle was just getting ready to graduate high school." Penny's hands cupped her glass. "We wanted so badly to put him through college."

"But he enlisted instead."

"Without any warning." Penny shook her head. "Like he was doing us a favor." Meeting his eyes, she added, "I know how badly you wanted him to take over the store."

"Kyle never wanted that. He wanted his freedom. Jeremy's the only one who ever wanted anything to do with the store. I've always known it. It's just been easier to blame my own kids for their lack of interest in their family legacy." He reached for his glass but couldn't bring himself to drink more. "Well, that year I was forced to make a really hard choice."

"I know," said Penny. "You sold your motorcycle."

If only she hadn't been so damned trusting, this might be easier to spit out. "I did, Pen. I wish that was all it took, I do. But that motorcycle . . ." He let out a deep breath. "It wasn't worth even half of what I said it was."

"But you said—"

"I lied—about its uniqueness. So you wouldn't question where the money came from."

Penny sat up straighter in her chair. "Please tell me you didn't, Chip." Her words were barely a whisper, but the horror in her eyes spoke volumes.

"I had no choice. We would've lost the house, Pen. The store. Everything."

"You made a deal with the devil." Not a question, a statement. Full understanding. "The store isn't what put you in the hospital. It was Ron Larson." Penny shoved her chair back. "How could you keep this from me?" she shouted. "I'm your wife!"

Chip sat at the table and let her storm off into the next room. He had no right to ask for forgiveness.

Retrieving the bottle from the counter, he refilled his glass. The bedroom door would be locked, so what harm would it cause if he passed out here at the kitchen table? He poured another glass.

"How much?" Penny's unexpected appearance in the doorway made him jump. "How much do we still owe him?"

"Twenty-five grand."

Penny gasped and covered her mouth with her hands. For the first time that night, tears formed in her eyes. She finally asked, "Is there anything we can do?"

"I sold my motorcycle this week, but it wasn't enough. Not even by half. I tried negotiating." Chip explained how Ron's memories of that childhood incident had stuck with him for decades, and placed a target on Chip's back. "There's more."

"Oh my God, Chip. What else can there be?"

"He came by last week, threatening the girls. I didn't take him seriously."

"Kimmie's car? That's what happened? How does Ron even know how to do something like that?"

Chip shrugged. "Who says *he* did it? He's not exactly a man who has to get his hands dirty." He emptied his glass. Chip longed for a couple more, but he was tired of turning to alcohol to sleep. "Evan thinks he targeted Jeremy the same way, and that tonight he went after Kimmie."

"What are we going to do?" Penny's whisper was barely audible.

Softly, Chip moved his glass in circles against the scratched table. So scratched they always planned to replace it when money allowed, but they'd never been able to part with it. Too many good memories. "I don't know."

"Ron knows we don't have that kind of money."

"I know."

"So where does that leave us?"

"Signing over the deed next week."

"What? What on earth would Ron want it for? It's not like he knows the first thing about running a store!"

"He doesn't want to run it."

A look of disgust smeared Penny's face. "He wants to run you. Us. It's personal to him."

Chip didn't think recounting Ron's conversation would do much for Penny's frayed nerves. She'd held a brave front when the doctor insisted Chip stay away from the store, even through both girls being in an accident. But this, Chip knew, was too much for her.

Penny reached for his hand, squeezed it in her own. "We'll get through this, Chip. We won't let that monster destroy our family."

Outside the barn at Sue Wilkerson's house, Evan stole a moment with his brother. "I need some advice."

"Sure."

Evan released a heavy breath. This wasn't merely some self-righteous quest to relieve his guilt for Jeremy's death. This was about justice. Ron Larson needed to pay. "I remember what happened the day of the fire." He related everything he recalled from that dreadful day, even confessed about the band for Kim's birthday. Protecting their past seemed futile now.

"I wish I could remember everything," Evan said. "Like why I didn't try to bust a bedroom window and get Jeremy out that way. He was still breathing when I found him."

"You're sure about the toolbox?"

"Positive."

Alex leaned against the barn, and seemed to silently weigh everything Evan told him. It was something he'd always done. His way of processing and rearranging a big puzzle to make sense of the overall picture. "You think Sue would let you borrow that toolbox?"

Evan understood what his brother was suggesting. No need to tell Jeremy's mom that they wanted to investigate the toolbox and get her emotions unsettled again. But if Evan could borrow it, maybe they could lift a print from one of the tools. "You can really do that, five years later?"

Alex shrugged. "Not always. Depends how much they've been used. But it's worth a shot, don't you think?"

"Would it be enough, if there was a print?" Evan thought he knew the dismal answer, but he hoped Alex would give him a bit more hope.

"I don't know." Alex folded his arms. "You're the one who called in the fire, right?"

"Yeah." He'd seen the smoke from the road and dialed 9-1-1 before putting his truck in park. He wondered how long it would've been had he waited on a neighbor to notice and make the call. His mom, as he recalled, was shopping in Omaha that day.

"It'll take some quiet digging, but let me see what I can find. Maybe there's a record of you calling 9-1-1. Could be something in what you said that might help. I'll check with the fire marshal too. See what his report said."

"Thanks, Alex."

Pushing himself off the side of the barn, Alex said, "I don't want you to get your hopes up. You understand that all of this is a long shot at best, right? It's been five years. Evidence is probably a little hard to come by, especially with a fire."

Heading toward the crack of light inside the barn, Evan nodded.

"You worry about getting that toolbox from Sue. I'll handle the rest. In the meantime, you need to focus on beating that asshole in the upcoming election. Because once we're done, there *will* be an election." Alex held the barn door. "And Evan?"

"Yeah?"

"Don't confront Ron Larson. I know you want to, but you'll lose."

"Thanks for the vote of confidence."

"Let me do what I do best. Trust me, if there's a way to take that man down, I'll find it."

Two hours later, Evan drove Alex back to their mom's house, wishing he felt more empowered. He did feel just the slightest lighter, as though he'd been cleansed. He felt like shit, too, because he missed Jeremy a whole lot more than he ever had.

They'd spent hours combing the dusty Chevelle, then calling reinforcements to conduct a proper investigation and document their findings with the brakes. As they suspected, tiny pin-sized holes had also been pricked in Jeremy's brake lines.

After the state investigator—one not related to Evan—left, Alex insisted they video record Evan's eye-witness testimony. Evan spent over an hour recalling every single detail of that day, trying not to leave anything out. "A jury will be more apt to believe your testimony if they can see you telling it for the first time," Alex had reassured. "It's going to be a long shot no matter what, but this shows emotion."

When he pulled into the driveway and put his truck in park, Evan asked, "How much time do you think you'll need to take this son of a bitch down? How many more people is Ron going to threaten, hurt, maybe even kill, before this is over?"

Alex blew out a frustrated sigh before he answered. "One premature move and this guy walks. If he goes free, he'll retaliate. If you think life is bad for folks now, you don't want to be around to see the aftermath if Ron slips away from the system."

Evan understood now why he would never have made a good detective. He'd never have the patience to wait for the justice system to take its course. "You're a good man, Alexander." He clapped his brother on his shoulder.

Hand on the door handle, Alex looked at Evan. "Remember what I said. Don't confront Ron."

Kim tried sleeping, but with Evan still gone, her brain wouldn't shut down for the night. Then there was Macy. She gave Kim some space when the guys left, but she'd been hovering in the upstairs sitting area, reading some technical manual. About midnight, Macy knocked on her door, probably when she heard Kim tossing around and groaning like an impatient child.

"I know you're awake."

Kim considered tossing back an immature retort, but Macy was right about her acting like a teenaged brat lately. "Come in."

"How are you holding up?" Macy held a small plate in her hands, filled with five chocolate frosted cupcakes.

"Okay, I guess." Kim eyed the cupcakes, and wondered if Macy brought them with a catch. But when she met her eyes, Macy shrugged and set the plate on the nightstand. With everything that had happened, Kim hadn't eaten a scrap since supper. That had been hours ago.

"Pretty terrifying, huh?"

Kim peeled back the foil off the first cupcake; chocolate frosting smeared her thumb. "You missed your calling as a life coach."

"I'm proud of you, you know."

"Thanks," Kim finally said. Macy forced her to move over so she could sit on the bed. "It helped having a backseat driver. And believe me, those are words I will never say again!"

"Hey now, I think I make an excellent co-pilot. Just don't ask any of my fellow Blackhawk pilots. They think I'm bossy." The twinkle in Macy's eyes suggested she might really be an absolute terror at the flight controls.

Kim considered eating her first cupcake, but couldn't resist the urge to smear frosting against Macy's cheek first.

"Brat!" But Macy laughed and wiped the frosting away. Licking her fingers, she said, "Seriously, Kim, not everyone survives something like we just did. No broken bones. I think that's pretty amazing."

"And?"

"And what?" Macy asked.

"I'm waiting for you to badger me about Alaska. It's been at least a three hours since you have."

Macy shook her head. "If you want to miss out on the greatest state in the country, that's your loss." Grabbing a cupcake for herself, Macy stared at it. "I know you think I have some crazy, awesome life. But it's pretty lame."

"Whatever."

"I'm serious. All the hot pilots you think fawn over me are either married, total jerks, or hate me for my bossiness."

"You're lying."

"Wish I was, because then I wouldn't have signed up for online dating."

"You didn't!"

Macy tucked her head so Kim couldn't see her eyes. "In case you're wondering, that's been even more of a disaster. I had to block some guy whose screen name was *Sugar_Moose69*. He kept making these really horrifying erotic references to wildlife." Macy took a bite out of her cupcake. "Alaska's been . . . the only exciting part of my life. I love it there, and maybe I get a little carried away talking about it. But it's the most beautiful place I've ever been, and I want to make a life up there."

"Wow, Macy. I had no idea."

Her sister shrugged. "Truth be told, I envy what you and Evan have. I only hope someday I find a good one like him."

Both devoured a second cupcake. Silence filled the room. Kim's mind kept returning to the obstacles still ahead. "Do you think they'll find anything? With Jeremy's car?" For once Kim hoped her big sister had all the answers. "It's been five years."

"If anyone can, it's them."

Releasing a sigh, Kim added, "It's just that small towns have this weird system. One that revolves around power and corruption. It's hard to win when the other side doesn't fight fair."

"Lesley Jamison's behind bars." Macy swiped a splotch of frosting on the floral-patterned plate. "She pretty much ran this town, right? It only took your friend Allie to take her down, from what I hear."

Kim wanted to feel hope, but she didn't want to get ahead of herself before the meeting happened. "I really need to sleep so we can focus on getting those last signatures tomorrow. But I'm wide awake."

"Let's go for a walk," suggested Macy. "That last cupcake's for you."

Slipping on a hoodie, Kim followed her sister as they tiptoed down the stairs and out the front door. It'd been an Indian summer this week, temperatures unseasonably warm, most leaves refusing to change. But the night was chilly, as though fall might actually show its face soon.

"Where did they put my car?" Kim asked.

Macy pointed to the pasture beyond the barn. "At the far end, in that field by the creek."

"Let's go. I want to say goodbye to my Little Green Car."

"You actually call it that?"

"What should I call it? Fred?"

The girls walked in silence past the graveled clearing and into the pasture just east of the creek.

"I'm sorry about your car," Macy said as they walked around the barn and into the clearing.

"I don't know what the insurance company will offer . . ." said Kim. "Considering I willingly drove into a ditch."

"Instead of into a combine," Macy countered. "And if they can prove anything with Ron, you'll be able to sue that asshole for emotional damages." They trudged around a thick patch of trees to where the tow truck had left the car. Macy nudged Kim with her shoulder as they approached. "You might get to upgrade to a midsize."

Neither spotted the flames under the Geo until it was too late. One moment, the night was dark and uneventful. The next, a single flame rose from the hood of the car, then spread along the dried grass. Kim wished she knew more about fire because this didn't seem normal.

The flame shot into the air and caught one of the trees overhead. She screamed. The instinct to run back around the patch of trees consumed her, but everything seemed engulfed by the unnaturally spreading flames.

"Wait!" Macy yelled. She yanked Kim back. "We can't go that way."

"There's nowhere else to go!"

"The water."

"No! Macy, you know I can't—"

"Kimmie, we have to. Jump now, or I'm throwing you in. I didn't survive a car crash to die in a freak fire."

Screaming all the way down, Kim ran and jumped as close to mid-stream as she could, praying she'd miss landing on debris or slamming against a shallow bottom. She tucked her knees into her chest and hoped for the best.

Half a second before she and Macy hit the water, an explosion sounded. The creek rippled with violent waves.

Chapter 31

When Evan drove back to town, he craved a Mountain Dew. It was the damnedest thing, wanting caffeine so late at night, but there was a pop machine outside the grocery store. He didn't want to wake anyone at Violet's house snooping around for something she probably didn't have.

"Little late for you to be out, isn't it Rowe?" He didn't see Ron Larson approach until he'd inserted his last quarter.

Evan bit the inside of his lip so hard it nearly bled. There were so many things he wanted to say. It would feel so fulfilling to break this man's jaw. But he forced himself to do as Alex said. If he lost his temper now, especially with no witnesses, he'd make things worse for everyone. "Just wanted a pop."

Ron stepped closer to Evan. That crazy look Evan had started to notice more and more flickered. Or maybe it was the reflection of the streetlight. "Your days defying me on the scene are over, Rowe. Do you hear me?"

Evan retrieved his can of Mountain Dew and stepped back. "Guess I don't."

"I made a few calls. I know all about why you left Alaska."

Forcing himself to remain calm, Evan tried to tell himself that Ron could be bluffing. He cracked open his can of pop and took a drink.

"Quite the story, I have to say. Chief Benson was more than willing to fill me in on the details. How you were *relieved* from duty for the remainder of the season. Unfit and all. Hell, it sounds like you might not even have a spot there if you go back. Is that why you're hanging around here, Rowe?"

A pit started to form in Evan's stomach.

"I have a feeling Willow Creek won't be so understanding once that story spreads."

No point in arguing. Ron would spin *unfit* to his benefit, the way he always did. "What do you want?"

Ron cackled. His gold tooth caught the street light and reflected it. "I want you gone, Rowe. Leave town. Leave the department in my capable hands. You have no business here."

"This is about more than the department."

Ron took a couple of steps toward Evan. "It's about you crossing me, Rowe." His face was now only inches away. Evan stood his ground; he refused to step back. "No one crosses me without paying."

"I'm not leaving."

"Oh, I think you are."

Evan smirked. "You think I'm afraid of you, old man?"

He expected Ron to look a little taken aback, but instead the crazy flared in his eyes. "If you care anything for those you love, you'll pack your bags and leave before the election."

If only he had a witness to hear this. "You're threatening my family?"

"People who cross me pay. You best remember that." Ron turned abruptly, headed around the dark corner of the grocery store. Spinning around, he added, "If you're still here at the end of the week, you'll find I don't bluff. Aren't you tired of people dying around you?" Ron tossed one last comment over his shoulder. "Be a shame if something happened to that adorable little Hannah."

Evan lost it, charged after Ron and swung a punch. His knuckles collided with Ron's jaw and sent the man staggering back.

Before Evan could run him down and continue the beating the man deserved, he heard what sounded like a bomb going off. Tall orange flames danced above the dark trees at the northwest edge of town. *Violet's place.*

Evan beat the fire department to Violet's house. Failing to cut the engine, he shifted to park and hopped out. Flames raged in the patch of trees where they left Kim's car. Before he could reach the porch, Violet burst through the front door. "They're not inside, Evan!"

"Who?"

"Kim and Macy. They snuck out a while ago." She looked toward the flames, orange light reflecting fear in her eyes.

The fire whistle sounded in town, but Evan didn't have time to wait. He rushed toward the flames. He wished he had his jump suit with him so he wouldn't have to be so concerned with the heat. "Kim!" he called out. "Macy!"

"Evan!" Macy emerged from the edge of the field, west from the fire. "I can't find Kim!"

Evan saw Macy's dripping, shivering frame, and he scanned the area for Kim. Nothing. "Where did you see her last?" He had to forcefully keep his panic at bay. *I can't lose her now!*

She shouted across the flames, "She jumped in the water too, but I can't find her. Evan, please, you've got to help! She can't swim!"

"Get inside, Macy!"

"Not until we find Kimmie!"

Evan stripped down to his boxers and T-shirt and ran toward the clearing to the creek. Flames danced along the shore. "You keep an eye on the shore," he ordered. Jumping in, he felt the warmer temperature instantly. He counted his blessing that the water hadn't heated up enough to boil Kim and her sister alive.

He swam vigorously upstream, searching for any traces of Kim. He *wouldn't* lose her, damn it! At a bend just east of the burning car, he caught a glimpse of a single hand above the water and paddled toward it. He dove under, wrapped his arms around her chest, and pulled her up.

She wasn't breathing.

Within seconds he had her on the far shore and was administering CPR.

A few rescue breaths in, Kim coughed up water. He'd never seen her so frightened in all his life. "Evan." A weak smile flickered, then died. "How is this fair?" She clung to him; her shivering arms threatened to leave bruises from their vise-like grip. "Two near-death experiences in one night? I'll need a whole box of cupcakes to cope."

Relieved to find her sense of humor intact, Evan kissed her forehead. Sirens and flashing red lights filled the air above them. They'd have to make their way across the creek again, but he'd wait until the fire was out. "It's not fair, Kimberly. And I'm not going to stand by and watch it happen again."

No surprise that Ron Larson would make the call. Evan didn't understand how the man managed to start the fire considering they'd both been conveniently downtown when the gas tank exploded.

While the firefighters combed the dark field for any remaining embers, Evan marched up to Ron.

"You son of a bitch—"

Ron interrupted, "There's no need for that."

Evan spotted the swollen knot on Ron's jaw and felt at least one thing had gone right tonight. "What the hell is it going to take?"

Ron patted Evan on the shoulder, then led him around the side of the fire engine, away from eavesdroppers. "You could make this easy, Rowe. Just pack your bags and leave."

"Never."

"Then you'll continue to witness the consequences of your poorly decided actions. It's your choice."

"How would I know you'd leave them alone?"

"Because if I don't, I know you'll be back."

Evan couldn't argue that. "If I go, you leave them alone." Tomorrow he'd have to deal with the aftermath of his decision. Hannah would hate him, probably for years if not for the rest of her life. Kimberly would never forgive him. But at least they, and everyone he cared about, would be safe.

"You have my word."

"That includes the Wilkersons, too."

"That's an awfully tall order, Rowe. I can promise to leave the women out of this, but Chip, well, he's already in it. Deeper than you can dive to save him."

"If anyone so much as gets a paper cut, I'll be back. I promise, no one will ever find your body."

"Do we have a deal, Rowe?"

"Yes."

After the fire department showed up, so did Kim's parents and Alex. It was nearly dawn before everyone dispersed. She wondered how anyone could possibly get enough sleep to face the day ahead. Their time to collect the remaining signatures continued to dwindle. With this latest fire—considering it involved an exploding car—people would be even more afraid than usual.

"It's not fair!" Kim yelled into her pillow and punched it with her fist. How could one stupid man control the emotions of an entire town?

She tried to wait up for Evan, even heard him turn on the shower. But after dealing with the endless gaggle of people and a forced hospital visit to ensure she had no internal injuries, Kim drifted off to sleep.

When the first hint of sunlight pierced through the window, Kim reached for her spare pillow. It refused to budge, like a boulder was weighing it down.

Beside her lay Evan, sleeping heavily. Her sheet barely wrapped around his butt and legs. She could see through the thin material that he was naked. *I could get used to this*.

The smell of smoke sifted in through the cracked window. She imagined that smell would linger in the air for a few days unless it rained. It reminded Kim of the battles they had yet to fight.

She kissed Evan's forehead, meaning to let herself fall back asleep. But with the terrifying night they'd had . . . one kiss turned into dozens. Her lips softly cherished his neck, his shoulders, his muscular back. She knew she should stop, let him rest.

"Mmmm."

"Sorry," Kim whispered. "Go back to sleep." She slid back under her covers.

Evan turned his dark eyes toward her. "I don't need sleep." In one swift motion, his body was on top of hers, his stubble tickling her neck as his lips drowned her in ecstasy. Undressing her slowly, sensually, he kissed every inch of her skin. He entered her with gentle strokes, lingering each time he filled her. She reveled in the feel of him inside her, quietly moaning in sheer delight until they reached their climax together.

Chapter 32

Evan set a bouquet of flowers at the front of Jeremy's headstone. "I know, I know. Flowers!" He glanced around at the row of trees along the east side of the cemetery, at the geese overhead flying north, at the tall grass along the fence swaying in the breeze. He looked everywhere but at that slab of stone with Jeremy's name etched in it.

"I wish you could be here, Jeremy. I wish it every day." Evan shoved his hands in his pockets. "I'm sorry I couldn't save you. I'm sorry I ran off after you died. I just didn't know how else to deal with it." Evan felt angered when he began to choke up. He pushed his tears down. "Maybe if I'd just told you to wait that day—"

"It wouldn't have mattered." His mom's voice startled him. He'd thought himself alone in the small town cemetery, hadn't even heard her car pull up. "It wasn't an accident," Anita continued. "Ron wanted him

407

dead. If not that fire, he would've found another way." She leaned against him. Evan put his arm around her shoulders.

As hard as the words were to hear, he knew they were true. "I hope I'm doing the right thing."

"By leaving?"

"Yeah."

"I think you're doing the best you can in dire circumstances. That's all anyone can ask."

"You aren't mad?" It was a dangerous question to ask, considering things between them had finally started to feel normal again.

"I'm not happy," she said. "But I understand this time."

"What about Hannah?" Evan couldn't imagine her facing the news of her dad leaving for good without him around to dry her tears. "Have you told her about—"

"Hannah's a smart girl. Smarter than either of you boys. I think she already knows." Anita folded her arms across her chest. "She won't be too happy with you, but I think she'll understand better than you think."

Evan shook his head. "She's a teenager now. I'm not counting on it."

Despite Violet's pleas that the girls stay home from the store today, Kim and Macy both braved on. They had signatures to collect, and cowering at Gram's wouldn't do the town any good.

"So sorry I wasn't home last night when you ladies stopped by," Aunt Ruby Rowe said the next morning at the grocery store. She happily took the pen Kim offered and signed the petition. With her signature, they were up to three. *Twenty-one to go.*

Macy took the clipboard back. "Thank you so much, Aunt Ruby. Every signature matters. We're still a few short and running out of time."

"Don't you worry," advised Aunt Ruby as she adjusted her mint green sun visor. "Your grandmother filled me in this morning. I'll be sending down some reinforcements soon."

Kim finished bagging Aunt Ruby's groceries. She wondered if those *reinforcements* were the fine little ladies who played bridge till dawn on the weekends. "I'll drop by your house this afternoon with that arrangement of yellow irises and daises you wanted too," Kim added. "With all the commotion last night, I didn't get any put together this morning."

"So sorry to hear about the incidents last night. You girls okay?" Aunt Ruby dug her checkbook out of her pearl-colored purse.

Kim twirled a pen between her fingers. "A little rattled, but we'll live."

"In other commiserating news, I hear your loan approval went through for your city store." Aunt Ruby scribbled in her checkbook. "I'll be sad to see you gone. I don't make it to Norfolk too often."

"I'm working on a website. You'll be able to order online," Kim suggested.

Aunt Ruby looked up from her Vegas themed check. "Never needed those technology boxes before, not going to get one now." She shook her head and returned to filling out her check. "Too bad you don't just open the store here."

"Don't know if I'd have enough customers here in town," Kim said.

"Sure you would." Allie popped around the corner, causing Kim to jump. She hadn't even seen her best friend come in. "You'll have a website. You can stay and have all the other towns place orders online."

"See, there you go. Someone's thinking straight." Aunt Ruby assessed Kim, leaving her feeling a little self-conscious. "Of course, if I was with a handsome man like my great nephew, I'd lose my ability to tell people my own name."

Kim hid behind the clipboard to cover her blushing.

"I'll carry this out to your car," Macy volunteered. She grabbed the two paper sacks and charged for the front door.

"I'm serious, Kim," Allie said. "You told *me* to get a website. Look what it's done. You're already one step ahead. You just need to have your designer tweak some things before you go live."

"I don't even know where I'd set up shop," Kim said. "There's only that storefront next door to the butcher shop. Not exactly prime real estate, you know."

"How about that space upstairs?" Penny suggested. She set a box of gum to be restocked on the counter.

Kim wasn't sure she'd heard right. "You mean make The Twisted Tulip part of Wilkerson's?" She glanced around, expecting Chip to pop up over a display of fresh produce. It sounded too much like his idea for him not to be behind it.

"Why not? We've never used that space for anything but storage. Might be good, in fact, to go through and clean it out. I promise our rent is cheaper than any Norfolk storefront."

"That's a great idea!" Macy exclaimed. "Can we start setting up today?"

"Look," Kim said, "the loan approval is only good if I open my store in Norfolk. In that specific building, actually. One I have to *buy*. I'm putting the offer in this coming Tuesday. It's the perfect space."

"No pressure, Kimmie. Just thought I'd throw an idea your way." Penny set the box cutter on top of the carton of gum. "Just know it's a short-time offer. If you don't want that space, we're probably going to find someone who does."

"Let's just go look at it." Macy grabbed Kim's wrist. "Mom, can you watch the front? We haven't seen Wilma today."

"She called in sick. Said she came down with the flu."

Kim and Macy exchanged a glance. *The petition.* The poor woman was probably terrified they'd all gang up on her for refusing to sign. Kim wanted to help Wilma, but the woman had already signed that awful Larson contract. Hopefully with the picture Macy snapped with her phone, Alex could find something to charge Ron with before too long.

"Allie, c'mon," Macy urged.

The three sprinted up the stairs like ten-year-old girls set loose in a toy-filled attic. The wall separating the south side of the space from the north was exposed brick. At one time, from what Kim had been told, this side had been the last building on the block. The wall they were seeing was an exterior of that original building.

"Can't you just see your sign on that brick wall?" Allie spread her hands high. "*The Twisted Tulip.*"

"Doesn't do much for street exposure," Kim mused. "And customers would have to come up the back stairs. I don't think Dad would go for that."

"Wait!" Macy ran down the stairs and disappeared. Kim and Allie looked at each other and shook their heads. Before they could speculate, Macy hurried back up the steps. "There's a staircase in back. That metal one that goes to the second floor of that side."

"That's a fire escape, Macy."

"It would be cheaper to build a new staircase there than to put one inside."

"No one wants to go around back," Kim argued. "There are freight trucks there all week long. It'd be a huge liability for the store."

Kim spotted the curious twinkle in Allie's eyes. She shook her head. "No. No ideas from you." She bit her tongue about Nick's unexpected fortune as a possible solution. This was her baby and she'd see it through on her own. She was not about to take charity.

"Maybe you just need an investment partner?" Allie suggested.

"I think I'd listen to her, Kimmie. The backdoor's an option, but if you want actual street business, you need to be a little more accessible."

Kim shook her head. "It's a nice thought, but it just won't work." Everything she'd meticulously planned for years was designed to fit her own store, not a space she rented above a grocery in a small town. It mattered where she displayed her beautiful sign.

"Kimmie, don't let anyone push your decision either way. Do what feels right, what feels authentic to your dream." Macy took her by the shoulders and forced her to look her in the eyes. "But please, for the love of cupcakes, don't choose this option because of Evan. If that's meant to work out, a little commute from Norfolk won't foil it."

"You're right, Macy." She'd been thinking that, of course. Evan was in most of her thoughts these days. It'd be nice for him to swing by during his lunch, have him bring her cupcakes on those late nights she'd be working until she could afford to hire an assistant.

"You'll forgive me if I want to get that in writing," Macy said. "I don't think you've ever said that to me before!"

"It's a pretty historic event." Kim's smile broke free. "I think I'm going to run back to Gram's and grab some lunch. Be back in an hour?"

Evan had tucked the last of his clothes into his duffle bag when he spotted Kim through the window. Down in the garden, she pulled weeds, something heavy obviously weighing on her mind. He considered putting off his departure for one more day. The last thing he wanted was to add to her obvious dilemma.

But he couldn't delay. He headed down the stairs; he only hoped she understood.

"Hey!" She sat amid a sea of flowers, looking as beautiful as he'd ever seen her in her torn jeans and flimsy gray sweater rolled up at the sleeves. She was going to hate him. "Evan, what's wrong?"

He pulled her to her feet and wrapped her in his embrace for what might be the last time. If she forgave him after this, it'd be a miracle. "Yesterday I was so terrified."

"You were?"

"I almost lost you. Twice." The memories of pulling her from the creek haunted him most of the night. If he'd not found her right then, she wouldn't be here in his arms now. Amazing how full of life she looked after two brushes with death. "Kimberly, I need you to know that I love you more than life itself."

She wriggled free of his embrace and studied his expression. "What's going on?"

"I just got off the phone with my old wildland division. They want me to come back."

"Alaska." Not a question, a statement. "You're kidding me, right? Is this some kind of sick, twisted joke?"

"I wish it was." He wished he could be honest. "He threatened Hannah."

"Ron." She stepped back. "That's it? What happened to fighting back?" If there were neighbors this far out, they'd be peeking out their windows at Kim's tone. "You're just going to walk away? Who's going to stand up to Ron if you leave?"

"He's targeting the people I care about. Don't you see? If I stay, everyone I love is—" Evan tried to stay calm. Normally he was very practiced at it. But that was before this monster threatened his sister. "He'll go after Hannah next."

Kim threw her arms up, then paced around the garden path. "Who's going to be here to protect her if you leave? Who's going to seek justice for Jeremy's murder?"

The word *murder* struck a chord, and almost gave away his plan. "Alex will. If I go, Ron promised to leave everyone I love alone. Not just my family, but yours too." He wished he could tell her that he had tried to help her dad, but Chip's secret wasn't his to share.

Fire flashed through Kim's eyes. "So that's it, then. Ron's done his work and you're going to walk away. Again." The malice in her words pierced his heart. "You're abandoning the people in this town when they need you most."

The lies tasted sour in his mouth, but he had to make sure she believed he wasn't coming back. Kim was anything if convincing when she was mad and vented to the world about it. Word couldn't spread any faster. And he needed Ron to believe or the retaliation from that tyrant might be fatal. "This is the only way I can protect anyone."

"No, it's not! You can stay and fight! You can get elected Fire Chief and make a difference. As long as Ron Larson is running things, no one's ever truly safe."

Evan shook his head. "He knows about Alaska, Kim. He knows about me getting relieved from duty." He hoped she didn't see through this weak line of defense. "If I show up at that meeting, he'll tell the whole town. They'll believe whatever tale he spins and be too terrified to vote at all. Then he'll go after my family— and yours—for defying him. Can't you see how hard this is for me? You think I want to leave now?"

"Then don't."

"It's not that simple."

"Of course it is." She waited, and the last trace of hope faded from her eyes. "If you go, we're done."

Evan hadn't expected anything less. "I love you, Kimberly. I always will."

Her eyes shot daggers at him. "Go to hell." She stomped off. Kicking an empty bucket halfway across the driveway, she yelled, "Stupid Alaska!"

Chapter 33

The following Sunday, the Wilkerson family sat around Violet's kitchen table in tense silence. A peach pie sat cut on plates before them, three slices untouched. Chip picked up his fork and studied his strained reflection in the sterling silver handle.

Evan Rowe's abrupt departure had shocked the entire town, especially since they were able to get twenty more signatures than they needed. Tuesday night, they would present the petition to the rural board at their meeting, practically guaranteeing Willow Creek their first full-time fire chief.

He only hoped the town wouldn't choose to elect Ron Larson.

Finally, Chip announced, "I have some news." The sooner he got this over with, the sooner everyone could just go back to their own lives. He'd kept the secret with Penny as long as he could. But tomorrow night, everything would change. It was only right to let his daughters and mother know, too.

He watched Macy stab at her piece of pie, but she hadn't taken a bite. "Dad?"

Penny reached her hand across the table and covered his. They shared a knowing look. He had to be the luckiest man alive to have a woman like her at his side, especially now.

"What is it?" Kim's look bounced back and forth between her parents.

Chip let out a weak laugh. "Maybe it's good news for you girls." Neither of them, especially Kim, would have to worry about his pressuring about the family legacy. Hard to do when there wouldn't be one. "Three days from now, I—I'm signing over the deed to the store. Wednesday morning."

"What?" Macy, Kim, and Violet cried out in unison. Their empty forks clinked to their plates.

"Chip, you can't be serious," said Violet. "Your father slaved away day and night to make that store what it is. You're just going to walk away from it?"

"I thought you'd be the happiest," Chip countered. "You hated what the store did to Pop."

"Doesn't mean I want you to toss it away!" Violet shoved her chair back from the table, and occupied herself with the coffee pot. "Why on earth would you walk away now?"

"I guess that's what the men around here do," muttered Kim. "When things get tough, they give up."

Chip tried not to let the words sting. Much of Kim's spite was reserved for Evan Rowe. He'd like to pummel the guy for breaking his daughter's heart. Again. But he'd been on the other side of the fire truck. He heard the noble sacrifice Evan made. Damned guy even tried to help out an old geezer who spent the last five years hating him. That made all the difference, and he'd have to say so soon to his girls. Considering the personal vendetta Ron seemed to have for Chip's family in particular, he owed Evan his life.

"Kimmie, now that's not fair," Penny interjected.

"Not fair?" Kim slid her chair back with such force Chip expected her to hit the cabinets behind her. "Let me tell you a little something about what's not fair!"

"Sit, young lady." It'd been years since Chip had raised his voice, and the shock of it stunned Kim into silence. "You're going to hear me out before you start tearing me apart for what I did."

Kim slunk back into her chair just as Violet set down a fresh pot of coffee and empty mugs to go around.

"Ten years ago, I made a deal with the devil." Chip went on to explain the dire financial dilemma he and

Penny had been in. "We already owed the bank too much as it was. I had no choice."

"But that was a decade ago," Macy said. "Surely that's over, right?"

Chip shook his head, his fingers wrapped around his steaming mug. "No. There's a balloon payment, due Tuesday by midnight."

"A balloon—" Kim repeated. "Dad, why would you ever agree to something like that?"

"Because it was the only option," Penny said. She took a sip of her coffee, drinking it black.

"How much is it?" Violet asked.

"Twenty-five grand."

Stunned silence swept over the table.

"Obviously, we don't have that kind of money," Penny added. "So, in three days, your father will be signing the deed over to Ron Larson. We'll still manage the store, like always. It just won't belong to us anymore."

Later that evening the lone bartender of the Saber Saloon snuck away to the back for a break, and left the girls almost completely alone inside. The sole restaurant in town was unusually dead, even for a

Sunday night. One man sat sipping his beer at the far edge of the bar, watching *Wheel of Fortune* on mute.

"Are you sure you're okay, Kimmie?" Macy asked from across the table that evening, Cornhusker and Saber décor surrounding them.

"Stop asking me that!"

Macy dipped a fry in Ranch, feeling victorious that she'd managed to convince Kim to leave the house. "You're allowed to be hurt, you know."

"I prefer to forget all about it. He left." Kim ripped open her napkin, liberating her silverware. "Just like last time. Shouldn't you be gloating? Didn't you tell me he'd never stay? I should've listened. It would've saved me a lot of trouble."

Earlier today Macy had baked two dozen chocolate cupcakes, a sympathy offering. But she'd forgotten them at home. If Chip hadn't inhaled them yet, they could swing by the house and get them after they ate. But Kim might use them as darts if her scowl was any indication.

"I'm not taking his side," said Macy, her words cautious. "But Ron did threaten his little sister. That's kind of a big deal."

Kim's shoulders lifted at her sharp intake of breath. She looked like a volcano about ready to explode.

Macy braved on. "The man did try to kill you twice in one night. Who knows what could've happened to Hannah if Evan had stuck around."

"You just don't get it, do you?" Kim was obviously fighting to keep her voice low, despite the empty room. "Have you been gone so long that you forget how this town operates? Just because Evan left doesn't mean anyone in his family is safe." She looked around, then continued, "What's to stop Ron from going after them now? Not Evan."

"There's Alex. A state patrolman." Macy reached for another fry. "And if anything at all happens to them Evan would be back in a heartbeat. Probably end up in jail, but he'd show up. And you know it."

Kim swirled her glass around on the table; the ice cubes shuffled inside it. "It doesn't matter anymore. We've got bigger things to worry about." She lifted her head. "What do you think about Mom and Dad giving up the store?"

Macy leaned her elbows on the table. "I hate it. I mean, I know none of us ever wanted anything to do with it." She reached for another fry but found her basket empty. "But I don't want them to lose it."

"I wish there was something we could do."

"Me too."

"Are you sitting down?" Debbie, Kim's realtor, asked over the phone still later that night. "I know it's late, but I knew you'd want this big news!"

Kim wanted to feel the old thrill and excitement she'd captured just a few weeks ago, but a small sigh of enthusiasm was all she could muster. "What's up?"

"The owners are ready to sell now. Their plans have changed, and the sooner they can unload, the sooner they can pick up their life and move to sunny California."

Kim didn't understand how that was earth-shattering news, so she waited.

"The best part," Debbie added, "is that they're dropping their initial asking price by ten percent. All you have to do is write a clean offer at this reduced price and it's yours. They'll even foot most of the closing costs to expedite the sale."

On her bed, surrounded by the sheer canopy, Kim sat stunned. She studied the embroidered daisies, wishing they'd offer some words of wisdom. She should be jumping up and down, scaring Gram downstairs. Finally, she said, "That's great news."

"If you want to nominate me for Realtor of the Universe, I'd be totally prepared to accept," Debbie jested. "Can you come down to my office tomorrow? We can put this together. I'll have everything ready so all you have to do is sign. I just need you to bring your offer letter and proof of down payment."

Kim tried to say yes, but the pesky word wouldn't come. With each attempt, some memory invaded and stripped away the ability to commit to her lifelong dream. There was Aunt Ruby buying her very first arrangement. Her mom encouraging her to sell her arrangements instead of just displaying them. The Women's Auxiliary requesting her services to create their centerpieces. And just two days ago, a mother asked if Kim could put together the arrangements for her daughter's wedding.

At first, merging her store with her parents' grocery store seemed to defy every plan she ever made to avoid being sucked into the family business. But at the thought of them losing it, she faltered. She'd been practically running her store out of Wilkerson's Grocery already. So why was the idea so farfetched?

"Something's wrong," Debbie said in her ear. "Either you've fainted from the sheer delight of this stunning news or you're having second thoughts."

In her cupcake pajama bottoms, Kim drove Gram's Impala to her parents' house.

"Kimmie, is everything okay?" Penny asked when Kim burst through the front door. Three sets of eyes—four if you counted Drifus on the couch—stared at her. She was probably a wreck, her hair in a messy lopsided ponytail, her mascara streaked on her cheeks from the latest bout of crying. If she wasn't mistaken, there was also chocolate frosting on the side of her mouth.

"Dad, you're not signing over the deed."

"Sweetie, come have a seat." He patted the spot on the couch adjacent to his recliner. Drifus, the goofball, thought it meant him and stole the spot. But Kim didn't plan to sit.

"Mom, is that offer still open?"

"Kim, I think it's incredibly generous of you to want to sacrifice your dreams, but you can't rent a space we won't own. It's not going to save the store."

"You have something else in mind, don't you?" Macy asked, her excitement riling Drifus. He jumped up and barked once at Kim.

"I'm not going to rent the space," Kim said. "I'm going to become a partial owner."

"What?" Chip sat up straight in his recliner. "What are you saying, Kimmie?"

"I've been saving the money for my down payment. I can clear your debt with it, but only if you'll make me a partner in the store."

The light in her dad's eyes nearly illuminated the room, but like a dying candle, it flickered out. "No."

"What?"

"I'm not letting you give up on your dreams, Kimmie. I know I haven't been the most supportive, but that's because I was being selfish. Ever since Jeremy died, I've been trying to coerce you into taking over the store someday." Kim tried to interrupt, but Chip kept going. "But that's not fair. You don't want anything to do with it, and I won't let you back yourself into a corner now."

"Look, I already have enough business in town to keep a store running. But I can't do it on my own. If I tried to open a place myself, it'd fail in a heartbeat. It's hard for me to admit that because I love this little quirky town, despite all its doom and villains. But The Twisted Tulip will only be successful if it becomes part of the family legacy."

"I thought you said the bank wouldn't give you a loan unless you opened your store in that building in Norfolk?" Macy asked.

"They won't."

"But if you give us your down payment, you won't have any funding left for equipment and supplies." Penny rubbed Chip's shoulder from the armrest of his chair. "Kimmie, we love that you want to do this. But we can't let you make this kind of sacrifice to right a poor decision we made ten years ago."

"I'll have a little left over," Kim pushed on. "But you're right. It won't be enough. That's why I also have an investment partner."

"Who?" Chip asked.

"Allie!" Macy exclaimed.

"Um, honey," said Penny, "she's not even working."

"She has her blog." Kim knew exposing Allie and Nick's big secret right now wouldn't be the thing to do if she wanted to keep that investment partner, but they'd talked about a plausible cover story. One that would have to do until Nick was ready to come forward and let the town know about his newfound wealth. "She's actually doing quite well. And she's going to offer to sell some of the books she reads in my space."

Chip stood from his chair, walking toward Kim. "You're sure, Kimmie?"

"Yes, Dad."

Shaking her hand, he said, "Welcome to the family business."

Chapter 34

Two days later, Kim was in a hyper-focused state, filling her store with the dozens of boxes that had consumed her tiny Norfolk apartment. It'd taken several trips with Chip's truck and even a small trailer, but they towed over everything Twisted Tulip related. The distraction of her altered plans helped drown out the emptiness Evan left behind. He was probably halfway back to Alaska by now.

"Guess you'll still have to go back to get your furniture and stuff, huh?" Macy asked from a corner in Kim's soon-to-be flower shop. She was putting together one of the many display shelves Kim had found at a going out of business sale.

"Yeah. I gave my landlord my notice."

"You're moving in with Gram, then?"

"For now. Once the store is up and running I'll look for my own place." Allie had hinted that her little ranch house might be available for rent in the near future.

Kim hadn't pointed out that it pretty much sat empty now.

"When are Mom and Dad going to start the remodel?"

Kim cut the packaging tape on a box of office supplies she'd acquired on a Black Friday sale. All her squirreling and bargain shopping these past couple of years had paid off. She was thrilled that Allie would be an investor in her store—well okay, *Nick*—but she didn't want to ask for a dime more than she absolutely needed.

"You need an entrance accessible from the front door," Allie had insisted. "It's the next best thing since city zoning won't allow a set of stairs straight to the second floor from outside."

"Allie has someone lined up for next week," Kim told Macy. "I still feel bad, making Mom and Dad find a new spot to put the shopping carts. They're practically going to have to rearrange the whole south side of the store to make this work."

"You shouldn't feel bad, Kimmie. You're the reason they still own the store." Macy set down her screwdriver. "I'm very proud of you, you know that?"

For once, Kim was speechless. How long had she waited for her older sister to say those words?

"I know you just want to be the favorite," Macy teased, then ducked as Kim hurled a purple note pad in her direction. She sent a stray roll of polka dotted ribbon sailing back. Halfway across the room, it smacked into a broad shoulder and dropped to the floor.

"Ladies, ladies," Alex said from the doorway, standing next to the doctor. "Are you *still* fighting?"

"She started it!" But there was jest in Macy's voice.

"Nick, you're back," Kim said as she scanned him. She drew in her brows. "Allie said you wouldn't be in town until *after* the election."

"Well, she wanted me back a day early. How could I say no to the woman I love?"

"You wouldn't want to miss the most important election this town has seen," said Macy, who picked up her screwdriver and resumed her work on the shelving. "Willow Creek's about to elect their first paid fire chief. Kind of a big deal."

"Too bad the ballot got shorter," muttered Kim.

"Actually . . ." said Alex. ". . . It's a shame that Evan's name's still on it. No one asked anybody to remove it."

Kim yanked the box cutter off the counter and sliced through the packaging tape of another box. "How did that happen? I mean, you think that's the first thing Ron Larson would do. Strike his name from the ballot."

"Something to do with the terms of the donation," Nick explained. "To take your name off, you've got to personally make that request. Evan never did."

"Did anyone try to contact him about it?" Macy asked.

"I don't know," said Alex. "He's had his phone off since he left."

Typical Evan. Leave town, disconnect your phone. Kim wanted to feel the slightest shred of hope but she knew better. As mad as she wanted to stay at him, she understood the difficult choice he had to make. If it had been an option, Kim would've left town to barter for her family's peace, too.

"He hasn't stayed in touch?" Macy asked. "He just went off the grid?"

"He kind of does that," Alex replied.

"Why aren't you mad at him?" Kim finally asked Alex. Her curiosity was too much to taper down. "Seems he left you in the biggest bind of anyone. Now you get to deal with Ron all on your own."

Alex slipped his hands into his jeans pocket. "I'm not alone in this, Kim."

At that, like some weird Twilight Zone-meets-Leave it to Beaver cue, a group of people poured into the upstairs space. Their parents, Allie, Aunt Ruby, Gram, Allie's neighbor Ed—maybe Kim's neighbor soon—a small gaggle of old ladies she recognized from Gram's numerous garden parties, Hannah and her mom, and even Aunt Sue.

There aren't enough cupcakes in all of Willow Creek to help me process this little spurt of crazy! What's gotten into these people?

"We understand why Evan left," Anita said. "Family has always come first to him, even if he has a funny way of showing it. But we're not about to let his efforts be in vain. We're going to take back this town tonight."

"Count me in," said a voice from the back of the mob. Those around her parted.

"Wilma!" Despite the crowd, it took Wilma's appearance to rattle Kim. She finally set down the table cloth in her hands. "I . . . I thought—"

"Turns out my good for nothing son is good for one thing. He's a helluva lawyer. I sent him that contract I had to sign. If Ron tries to enforce it, I can sue him. I have a feeling lots of folks around here have signed that same kind of contract." Wilma folded her arms across her chest. "I'm done letting that man terrorize me. It's time to take a stand."

"We need everyone's help," said Nick. "We need to pack the auditorium tonight with every citizen we can find."

"The auditorium?" Kim repeated.

"There's not enough room at the fire hall. Not in that tiny conference room," said Alex. "So the rural board meeting has been relocated to accommodate a large turnout."

"Is anyone else running? Besides Tim?"

Alex shook his head. "No."

Kim wanted to join in their strength in numbers enthusiasm, but she wondered how the town would survive without Evan as their fire chief. The only other eligible candidate was Tim Hollander, and as nice a man as he was rumored to be, he'd be no better off in that position than Ron. Tim would probably still be under the thumb of Ron Larson, even if elected.

Ron Larson felt pretty smug about tonight's meeting. The petition had been a great distraction for that group of pests. So what if the people voted for their own fire chief? They'd likely pick Ron out of fear, and if they chose Tim Hollander, he'd still be in charge.

Tim knew better than to oppose him. The poor sap owed Ron more money than most.

"Why do I have to go to this?" Valentina pouted from their spacious master bathroom. The woman's own corner was dazzling, expensive quartz countertops and the highest end fixtures money could buy. "I'm just going to be bored."

"Because, sweetheart, that's our arrangement. I buy you whatever your heart desires and you stand by my side and keep your yap shut." Lately she'd questioned him more than he cared. After this election was over, he'd have to have a little talk with her, remind Valentina of her place. She'd been living on the streets of Chicago in one of the worst neighborhoods when he'd found her. He saved her, but he could send her right back. "Besides, you need to be there when I get elected. It won't look right if you aren't."

"And if you don't win?"

"Don't you worry your pretty little head over details. I've got this under control." Ron snatched his wallet off his dresser and shoved it in his back pocket. "Hurry up, will ya? I need you there early."

Applying her red lipstick in the mirror, Valentina asked, "What about you? Surely you don't expect me to go alone. Those people hate me."

"They're just jealous that you have a better life than them."

Valentina let out a sarcastic laugh.

Ron could deal with her later. Right now, he had something important to take care of. He promised to leave the Wilkerson's alone, all except for Chip. Since that man's meddling daughter had saved his precious store, Ron determined another way to make his point.

The auditorium was crowded; many people stood packed along the walls. Kim had never been so proud of little Willow Creek in her entire life. If only Evan were here to see it. She stifled an irritated growl. She wanted to hate him for leaving, had every right to. But one glance at Hannah, and Kim felt her anger shift to depression.

"You think this will work?" Kim asked her mom as they took their seats. Seats they only managed to secure because Macy had the foresight to arrive an hour early.

"I think you'll be surprised. Our town's quite capable during desperate times."

Weaving through her row on the opposite side, Hannah waved at Kim. She forced her way through a group of preoccupied people in Kim's row.

How can she be so happy? Kim didn't get it. Wasn't she mad, too? Her big brother—the one she idolized—was probably stuck somewhere in northern Canada waiting for a buffalo herd to cross the road as they sat in these cold metal chairs.

"We did it!" Hannah beamed.

"We did. Now the good folks can make their own choice."

"Evan's name's still on the ballot!"

Kim offered a weak smile. For thirteen, Hannah was an exceptionally smart girl. But from the glow of hope in her eyes, Kim knew she expected the impossible. "Honey, he's not coming back."

"Okay." Hannah's twinkle threatened to give Kim that same stupid hope. "They're about to get started. Better go sit with Alex and your mom."

Hannah threw her arms around Kim's neck and hugged her tight. "I know you think he's gone, but I know him." She rushed back to her seat, leaving Kim feeling oddly confused. She didn't dare get optimistic. Evan was gone. He told Alex to handle whatever Ron Larson threw at his family. If Evan did get elected, he still wouldn't return. It'd put the entire safety of his family, and hers, in jeopardy. If Ron and his henchmen could tamper with her brakes and light a car on fire, what was to stop him from burning a house? *Another* house.

Kim had no doubt now that Jeremy's death was anything but accidental. "Dammit!" she muttered.

"What?" asked Macy.

"I can't hate him. I want to, but I can't."

Macy put her arm around Kim's shoulder and hugged her. "I know."

The auditorium buzzed with conversation so loud that Kim could hardly hear herself think. The board president stood on the stage behind a podium, trying to get everyone's attention. The microphone wasn't working. The rest of the board took their seats at a long table to the left of the podium. Tim Hollander sat by himself on the opposite side, the two chairs beside him empty.

"Where's Ron?" Kim asked. "You think he'd be here."

Macy shrugged. "I see his wife. Maybe he's mingling. You know, making his last-minute threats before people vote."

But that didn't explain the twisting feeling in Kim's stomach. Something was wrong. "Where's Gram?"

"She wanted to stop by the store. Said she had a special present to leave in your shop." Macy looked at Kim with apparent adoration. "Kimmie, I'm so proud of you. I wish I could be here for your grand opening, but I'm out of leave."

"I can't believe you sacrificed all your time off to stay in Nebraska. Don't you have a ton of Alaskan expeditions to do? Dog sledding into the mountains, surfing the boar tide, making an appearance on that crazy fishing TV show?"

"Ha ha." Macy clapped Kim's knee. "You, my dear sister, will visit Alaska if it kills me."

"I heard Fairbanks had a blizzard a couple days ago, while it was sunny and seventy-two here. If you want me up there, it'll have to wait until next summer." *By then, I shouldn't miss Evan so much that I avoid the whole damned state.*

"I'm holding you to that."

Ron kept a spare can of gasoline in the back of his truck. One never knew when you might run out in the middle of nowhere. *Or need a bit of liquid assistance.*

Main Street was packed three blocks north and south of the auditorium, making parking a bit of a challenge. Reassessing his options, he realized this was actually perfect. He'd park in the alley, half a block down from the grocery store and sneak inside without anyone the wiser.

Dusk was falling, which provided him with shadows. Most everyone in town was already packed into the auditorium. Reaching for the handle of the back door, he found it unlocked. *Isn't this my lucky day?*

Ron slipped inside and made haste emptying his gasoline can.

Chapter 35

It'd been torture for Evan to be holed up inside Alex's very unused condo in Norfolk, not even allowed to hit a drive-thru or go for a run. He'd been trapped in this prison with his thoughts, staring at a cell phone he couldn't risk turning on. Alex even insisted they strip off his Alaska plates.

It'd all been necessary to make Ron Larson and the majority of the town believe he abandoned them.

Ten miles from Willow Creek, Evan was running low on gas. He floored it anyway; the election was scheduled to start at any moment. Everyone would be inside that auditorium, giving him an advantage to catch Ron off guard. Returning would be like lighting a fuse to a warehouse full of dynamite where Ron Larson was concerned. But he'd take his chances.

Last night, Alex delivered the first bit of good news. "They lifted a single print from a wrench in Jeremy's toolbox. Apparently you smudged it up a good deal when you worked on Sue's kitchen sink. But one thumb print came up. It belongs to Ron Larson."

He didn't expect a single thumb print on a wrench would be enough to convince a jury of Ron's guilt, but it was a start.

He sped to town. His fuel indicator blinked on as he turned onto Main Street and hit the gas. The police chief should be in the meeting, too, especially with the number of attendees, in case fights broke out. Evan rolled down Main Street, amazed at how many cars lined the streets. He noticed some parked off in the alleys, too.

As he passed Wilkerson's Grocery, he smiled at the addition of Kim's beautiful turquoise sign, "*The Twisted Tulip—Coming Soon!*" hanging above the glass storefront on the first floor. He was so enamored with it, at first he didn't realize what was wrong.

Evan whipped his truck around the corner at the first sight of smoke. *That son of a bitch.*

Main Street was congested as residents filled all the available parking spots and some illegal ones. Forced to block an alley, he spotted Violet's car nearby.

His element of surprise would be lost. He'd have to burst through the auditorium's front door to announce the fire.

Prepared to run down the street, Evan's stomach plummeted when he reached the rear of the building and recognized Violet's yellow purse lying on the ground by the back door.

Counting on Alex's habit of checking his phone every thirty seconds, even at an important meeting, Evan fired off a text.

Fire. Grocery store. Violet inside. Going in. Call 911.

Judging by the amount of smoke, there wasn't much time. They'd need to keep those flames from jumping to the building next door, one most certainly constructed of wood, not brick.

He used the cuff of his sleeve to grip the door's metal handle, and already felt the heat through it. Swinging open the door, Evan charged into the smoke and flames.

The board president took the mic next, "Thank you, Tim, for those opening remarks." He smiled at the too-full room. "I feel like the department would certainly be in capable hands should you be voted in. Ron, you're up next."

Kim's stomach twisted at seeing that despicable man on the stage. It took all her restraint not to stand up and call him out. Maybe it was her pent up anger that gave her this inconvenient courage. Luckily, her sister was thinking straight, because the moment Kim tried standing, Macy yanked her down to her seat.

"Sit!" she hissed.

"It's amazing what this town is capable of achieving, isn't it, Marvin? I'm very proud of each and every one of you who decided the town of Willow Creek would benefit from this full time position. I think it says a lot about how much the people care about the place they call home."

"Where's he going with this?" Kim whispered. But her sister just stared straight ahead. Kim stupidly kept glancing to the doors next to the stage, hoping Evan would burst in. She loved Hannah, but that girl got so caught up in that silly concept of hope. Didn't she realize it could end up hurting people?

"Rest assured, should you elect me, I will continue my duties at the bank. I will reduce my hours to best accommodate the needs of both the bank and the fire department. I assure you I am fully qualified and highly capable of this position. My twenty-two years of service should speak for themselves."

"Thank you, Ron," said the board president. "Our third candidate does not appear to be present."

Kim chanced a look at Hannah, and sensed the defeat starting to overcome the poor girl. She kept scanning the exits too, probably hoping Evan was coming to save the day.

A few others seemed to wish for the same.

"I can speak for him," Abigail Adams said, standing.

"So can I," said the farmer with the charred soybean field.

"As can I." This time it was her dad. Kim felt so touched she nearly cried.

Hannah stood. "Me too."

Irritation was written on Ron's usually calm face. He yanked the microphone from Marvin's hands. "Now see here, folks. Evan Rowe left for good. He left in such a hurry to get back to his precious Alaska that he forgot to strike his name from the ballot. You voting him in won't bring him back. He's disobeyed orders from his first fire call. He'd be an incompetent leader at best, should you choose to elect a ghost."

"He saved the town," the farmer said. "He was the only one who knew to chase the fire to the green grass."

"Lucky call," said Ron. "I was directing the fire to the water. Water doesn't burn at all." There was strain on Ron's face. He was fighting his temper like Kim had never seen. "Grass, no matter how green, can burn if the temperature is high enough."

"Water can boil!" Macy yelled.

"It was windy that day," Tim Hollander chimed in. "The fire would've jumped the creek and caught all those trees. We would've been evacuating the entire northwest side of town."

Betty Meyers stood. "Evan Rowe saved this town!"

Ron started to pace. "Now, you all listen to me. Evan Rowe was relieved from duty in Alaska. He was *fired* because one of his all-too-common mistakes and failure to listen to his leadership nearly cost him his life on his last call. He ran back to Alaska with his tail tucked between his legs, hoping someone will take him back." Ron was fired up now, breathing heavily, but not ready to stop. "Would you want him there to save your house? One mistake is all it takes to lose everything. Just one."

Scanning the crowd, he continued his tirade. "Need I remind this town that Evan Rowe was responsible for Jeremy Wilkerson's death five years ago? He charged into that house completely unprepared, forgetting every bit of training once he was inside. If he'd recalled any of it, he would've gotten that boy out of the bedroom window."

"Maybe he didn't receive adequate training," Chip joined in. "Sounds like a failure of leadership to me."

The crowd murmured their agreement.

"Doesn't erase the fact that Evan is the reason that boy is *dead*."

"You're wrong!" Kim yelled, shooting up from her folding chair like it had charred her skin.

Ron glared so hard she thought daggers of fire might shoot from his eyes. "You weren't there."

"But it's really convenient that you were, isn't it? The first one on the scene, before the fire department arrived?" She felt a warning glare from across the room, but she ignored Alex. If someone didn't take this bastard down tonight, she might just take matters into her own hands. "And you were the only person upset that I wanted to keep my car after my accident. Funny how someone tampered with my brakes." There were collective gasps in the room. Kim felt better for a few seconds, until Ron rebutted.

"How often did you take that ratty car in for service? The way you drive it—and everyone in here can attest to your reckless techniques—it's amazing the thing didn't fall apart months ago."

"I know you blew up my car, you son of a bitch!"

"I did no such thing. That car was towed to private property, despite my request—again defied by Evan

Rowe—to have it towed to the station where a proper investigation could be conducted."

As if the commotion wasn't already stirring, beautiful, snobby—*irate*—Valentina shot up from her poised seat. Kim had seen dragons on movies less scary than this woman. She practically seethed fire. "Proper? You said it belonged in a junkyard. You disgust me."

"Valentina, honey, what do you think you're doing?"

"Look around you. These people don't trust you. They don't even *like* you. Admit you tried to destroy *more* evidence and save these good, decent folks the trouble of taking you down."

"I didn't blow up the car, goddammit!"

Valentina folded her arms. "And who do you think believes you?"

Kim had to give it to the woman, she had guts to do this, even if she had had the piss poor judgment to marry Ron in the first place. Had she spoken out against him any other time, she might've been dropped to the bottom of a river, never to be heard from again.

Alex shot up from his seat, his eyes glued to his phone. "There's a fire at the grocery store! Evan and Violet are inside!" The announcement silenced the room. Volunteer firemen scrambled from their chairs.

Kim felt faint, as if she might lose consciousness. Evan was *here*. But he might die. Gram too. She locked her eyes on Ron Larson like a sniper on a target.

"Kimmie, let's go." Macy tugged on her arm. "We need to get outside."

Kim broke free from Macy's hulk hold. She didn't know how to swing a punch, nor did she feel like breaking her knuckles right now. But she jumped on stage and charged at Ron, knocking him to the ground like a defensive tackle. The sharp scent of gasoline invaded her nose the moment he smacked the ground beneath her.

"Violet?" Evan hollered. He'd cleared the entire first floor and found no trace of her. The only other option was up. The fire had been set in different areas, mostly in corners, but some on the aisles themselves.

He raced up the stairs, calling out as much as the smoke would allow. He couldn't understand why he didn't hear sirens by now. "Violet!" He'd sent that text minutes ago. His shirt collar covered his mouth, but the smoke invaded his lungs anyway. He wasn't sure how much more he could take, but he'd die before he left Violet to the flames.

He found her, crumpled in a scared ball beneath a metal prep table. The flames licked the cardboard boxes stacked around her. Kim's flower shop. Her dream was turning to ash before his very eyes. If she ever let him speak to her again, he hoped to never describe what he witnessed now.

"Violet."

"Evan! You came back!"

"Of course." He had so much more he wanted to say, but words would have to wait.

A cough from Violet reminded him just how little time they had. He slipped his shirt off and turned it inside out. It wasn't the best solution, but it was the one he had. "Hold this over your mouth and nose. I'm going to get us out of here."

Evan gathered Violet in his arms. The sturdy, sure woman he'd known for years felt frail and tiny. He wasn't about to lose her. He reached the brick-lined doorway that led to the north side of the building. But the wooden beam overhead of the staircase dropped and crashed against the steps in a fiery rage. It forced them back into the flower shop.

The smoke started to make Evan dizzy. *Where the hell is the fire department?* He felt his limbs weakening as he backed into what was supposed to be Kim's

greatest achievement. Her dreams just might kill him—
and her grandma too.

Chapter 36

"You're not going anywhere near my store!" Chip blocked Ron's path to the fire hall. The man already looked pissed for being taken down by a girl. Chip would have to tell Kimmie how proud he was later—right now there were more pressing matters. If Ron got anywhere near the store, he'd surely destroy any evidence of who started the fire.

"I'm the damned chief." Ron shoved Chip against the wall. The aroma of gasoline hung in the air.

"You set my store on fire!" Chip fought back against Ron's restraint and broke his hold. "You son of a bitch. You couldn't handle me not losing everything, could you?" Chip swung a punch, and hit Ron in the eye. "You stay the hell away from *my* store and my family."

"Officer Gumble!" Ron called out, then stumbled back toward Chip, rage drenching his eyes. "Care to remove this man? He's interfering with official town business."

Though the police chief stepped in Chip's path, Chip had achieved his desired result. The fire engine charged down the block without their precious chief.

"Evan!" Kim screamed as she raced down the street, pushing through the growing crowd. She knew someone should usher people back. Even if the store itself was brick, that didn't mean a thing.

Someone shackled her arm and pulled her back so hard she bounced off their chest. "You can't go in there, Kim." Alex. *Of course he'd say that.*

"But the two people I love most are inside." Tears gushed like from a broken dam. "I can't let them die!"

"They'll get him out. These guys are trained, Kim." She struggled against him, "Don't make them add *you* to the rescue list. That just makes their job harder."

"Let me through, damn it!" Ron Larson shouted, buttoning his jacket as he charged up. A ring was forming around his eye, black, blue, and yellow bruising and swelling evident.

"Stop him!" Kim yelled. "He smells like gasoline!" Though she didn't expect her words to have much effect, people around her responded. A couple of them grabbed Ron's arms and pulled him back.

"What the hell is your problem?" He spun around at Kim. "When this fire is out, missy, you'll be arrested for assault. So will your dad."

Alex seemed to be staying oddly calm, and was watching for something down the road.

"If I'm going to be arrested anyway," Kim said, "you guys hold him. I've got a little more damage to do."

Sirens echoed in the air, though Kim couldn't see where they came from. "Ron Larson," Alex said, "You're under arrest for attempted murder and tampering with evidence."

"I told you, goddammit. I didn't blow up her car!"

"Prove it," Kim heard another woman say. His wife, Valentina. She looked out of place in her shimmering dark blue dress and stiletto heels.

"I imagine after a proper investigation is conducted," Alex said, "you'll also be charged with arson." Tightening the cuffs, he added, "Oh, you're also under arrest for murder in the first degree."

"You're out of your goddamn mind. I *saved* that boy's body from being turned to cremation dust. What evidence could you possibly have?" From the smug look on his face, Kim guessed Ron believed he had the upper hand. That even if he went to jail, his lawyer would probably have him out by dawn.

"Eyewitness testimony."

From the way the color drained from Ron's face, Kim knew Alex had finally managed to build a solid case.

Evan could barely stand, but he moved in a circle around the metal prep counter. He felt thankful that any opened boxes had incinerated, leaving the area a temporary fire-free zone. But the metal was heating up. Soon, they'd not be able to stand near it.

"Evan, leave me," Violet choked through the shirt. "You have to make it out of here. For Kimmie."

His heart ached at the thought of never seeing Kimberly again, at never holding her in his arms and telling her how much he loved her. But he'd never leave Violet to die. She'd taken him in when he and his stepdad fought constantly. She'd been someone he looked up to all his life. A strong woman who refused to let life win any battle over her. "You're not dying today."

Behind a fallen beam and a thick fog of toxic smoke, Evan spotted what he failed to see in his first inspection of the room—a fire escape door. "I'm going to set you down so I can move the beam. Keep that shirt at your mouth!"

"You'll burn your hands."

Spying a tear in his jeans, Evan ripped at the denim and made himself makeshift gloves. The other leg didn't have any tears, so one would have to do. With it padding his palms, he grabbed the beam and shoved it out of the way. The heavy board flew to the opposite corner of the room, but not without consequence. The denim had only absorbed some of the heat. His hands were burned, and already blistering in a couple of spots.

Evan turned to scoop up Violet. He hoped he had enough strength left to get them to the fire escape door in time.

Chapter 37

Tears flooded Kim's eyes at the sight of Evan running down the metal stairs. He was missing his shirt and half a leg of his jeans, but he was alive! She only hoped Gram was still with them, too. She ran to them, her sister and parents behind her.

Evan carried Violet to the ambulance and laid her on a stretcher. Kim saw Violet grab his wrist and squeeze. "She's alive!"

Kim ran into his arms and wrapped herself around his bare chest. A cloud of acrid smoke filled her senses. It wasn't until he winced that she realized he was in pain. "Evan, you're hurt."

He shook his head, denying it. "I'm fine. Let's meet them at hospital."

"You're hiding your hands." She gently reached for one, and turned his palm up. "You burned your hands!"

"It's just a little scrape. I'll be fine."

"You're going to the hospital." Anita pushed her way through the crowd to her son, a mixture of concern and relief in her eyes. "That's an order."

It took a big part of the night, but Nick finally cleared Evan from the hospital, listing off specific care instructions for his blistered hands. As much pain as he was in, he couldn't help but smile as he watched Kimberly take notes. To have her taking care of him? There was nothing better.

Once the doctor left, he was about to suggest they check on Violet, but Alex slipped into the room, wearing a smile.

"Is it true?" Evan asked. "Ron's been arrested?"

Alex closed the door behind him and leaned against it. "For once, this town got a rumor right."

"The thumb print," said Evan. "It was enough?"

"No, not by a long shot," Alex said. "It along with your testimony was helpful, but not exactly sufficient for pressing charges."

"Then how did you get an arrest warrant?" Kim asked.

"Got a little something more from the fire marshal's report."

Evan drew his eyebrows together. On one of his stir-crazy nights in Norfolk, he and Alex had talked for hours about why Fire Marshal Hansen might've covered for Ron. His report offered nothing even slightly beneficial to the case. "I thought you said it was a dead end."

"Turns out the fire marshal had an assistant. Some newbie with enough foresight to send a suspicious rag to the lab."

It sounded too good to be true. "You found some sealed lab report?"

"Better," said Alex. "I found the guy who was helping that day. He agreed to testify. Seems there was chloroform on that rag, but the fire marshal dismissed it. Next thing the guy knew, the evidence was missing. That report was destroyed. This guy quit shortly after, so it was hard to track him down. But I did."

"Sounds like you're about to take down two guys," said Kim.

"Things are looking that way. Just wish I could make it three."

"No body yet?" Evan asked, but he already knew the answer. His brother had been so consumed with building a case against Ron Larson that he had to set his former case aside.

"Not yet, but I'll be spending more time in Willow Creek until I figure it out." Alex pushed himself off the door. "I have to run. I'm told Aunt Ruby took in a stray, and I need to investigate."

"A cat?" Evan guessed.

"A girl." Alex twisted the doorknob. "I'm really glad you're staying, Evan."

Once alone in the room again, Evan stepped closer to Kim. How he wished he could brush back her hair with his fingers right now. He settled for pressing a soft kiss against her forehead.

"We should go check on Gram," she said, reaching for the exam room's doorknob.

"Kimberly, wait."

She spun at his words, her hands resting on his bare arms. "Evan, you don't have to apologize. I was mad. But what matters is that you came back."

"Kimberly, I'm sorry I lied."

"Wait, what?"

"I was hiding. Waiting at Alex's place."

Her eyes narrowed. "Why?" she demanded. "Why couldn't you tell me the truth?"

Though his hands were wrapped, he was doing a pretty good job of backing her into a corner with just his body. "Please, just hear me out. I couldn't risk Ron finding out. I needed him to believe it, too. You . . . you have this way—"

"What way is that?" Kim sent him a smirk, her fingers hooked in the charred belt loops of his jeans.

"A very convincing one." He lowered his head and brushed his lips against her forehead. "Let's go check on Violet before I violate doctor's orders and use these hands to show you just how much I missed you."

Chapter 38

Nearly a week had passed since the most disruptive election the town of Willow Creek had ever endured. Violet was still in the hospital, but only as a precaution. Kim had never seen a woman so irritated to be confined. "I'm fine! I have gratitude pies to bake." Dr. Nick Bryant took most of the heat for that decision, despite it being for her own good.

Evan's hands were wrapped for five days following the brave rescue. They were still sensitive, but he seemed particularly fond of the exercise that included memorizing Kim's bare skin, and she wasn't complaining.

Macy had returned to Alaska three days ago, promising to call and see how the second election went. With the ruckus of the prior week, no one even received a ballot much less cast a vote.

Linking her arm in Evan's, Kim walked him to the auditorium stage. This time, only two chairs sat off to the side. Tim Hollander looked bored. "Good luck." Kim kissed him once, forcing herself to keep it G-rated.

A woman slipped into the seat beside Kim. "I have to apologize for something," she mumbled.

Kim almost didn't recognize her without her designer dresses and expensive makeup. Even the Louis Vuitton purse was missing. "Valentina?" In her jeans and blouse, wearing her hair in a ponytail, Valentina Larson fit in with the town for the first time.

"I blew up your car."

"Wait, what?"

"I'm so sorry."

"Why would you do something like that?"

"Because I knew it would link Ron. I wanted that son of a bitch to pay for all the harm he's inflicted on everyone." She tucked her off-brand purse in her lap. "Look, I know more than anyone else in this town what he's done. I'm testifying against him."

Her heart drummed in her chest. Kim fought an outburst in the crowded auditorium. *Valentina Larson blew up my Little Green Car!*

"I know you must be questioning my sanity. I married Ron, thinking I'd have a better life. Anything seemed better than living on the streets. But we all make bad judgment calls, right?" Valentina offered her a sad smile. "I've arranged for you to pick up a new car at the dealership in Norfolk. They're expecting you, so go when you want and pick out anything you like. It's the least I can do, not just for destroying your other car, but for everything Ron's put your family through."

Kim stared, speechless.

"And I'm really sorry about the store," Valentina continued. "Both of them. If I knew he was planning to do that, I would've stopped him." When Kim stayed silent, Valentina added, "As soon as I testify, I'm planning to leave town." She glanced up, smiled at Penny sitting in the seat next to Kim. "I know no one cares much for me, and I don't blame them. But thanks to your mother, I have a chance to start over. I'll see to it that I give back as much of the money as I can, including your father's recent payment."

"Let's try this again, shall we?" The board president was saying, asking everyone to take their seats. Valentina slipped out of her chair and found another one on the opposite side of the aisle.

"What was that about?" Kim asked her mother.

"She's been going to beauty school—in secret, of course. She needed someone to practice on to pass her tests or whatever."

"That explains the manicure," mumbled Kim "And new hair color. Your makeup and pedicure?"

All Penny said was, "She's not such a bad person once you get to know her."

"And here Macy and I thought you were having an affair." Kim shook her head.

"What!"

"Shh!" said Kim. "Evan's up."

"I haven't been entirely honest with everyone. I did get relieved in Alaska. I was so haunted by Jeremy Wilkerson's death and the guilt I've carried every day that I wasn't paying attention to my surroundings when I parachuted to a fire. I landed in a tree." A few chuckles of laughter rumbled through the audience. "I didn't think it was fair that while Jeremy wouldn't live to get married or take over Wilkerson's someday, that I was still here. I didn't think I deserved a safe, comfortable life of happiness." Evan glanced at Sue Wilkerson in the audience. "But someone set me straight." Kim saw the two of them exchange a smile.

"See, Jeremy was the kind of guy who loved life. He soaked up every moment and never took a single one for granted. He knew how to live like no one I've ever met. And I know that he wouldn't want me to stop living, either. It took me returning to Willow Creek—returning home—to realize everything I've taken for granted.

"Sure, I could ramble on about my qualifications. I could tell you how many years I spent working at various departments and how many jumps I've made to fires where my team successfully saved people and their property, but that's not the most important thing to focus on. The most important thing—I love this town. I love the people in it. You were all so incredibly brave to take a stand, not knowing the outcome. Not knowing if even united we could take down a tyrant. But you know what, we did. I promise each and every one of you, I will never back down."

The auditorium erupted in clapping. People stood in flocks, the applause growing louder, the cheering echoing from the high ceilings.

Tim stood and motioned for the microphone. The board president handed it to him, a sympathetic look on his face.

"I hate to take away your voting privileges," Tim addressed Evan, and then the crowd in general. "But I never wanted to run. I just didn't want Ron Larson to win. Evan Rowe, he's your guy. I'm striking my name from the ballot."

The board president beamed. He grabbed the mic away from Tim and announced, "Residents of Willow Creek, let me introduce you to your new full-time fire chief, Evan Rowe."

After a visit to the hospital to check on Violet—Nick promised she could return home the next morning—Kim and Evan took a slow drive through town.

"Have you decided what you'll do about your store?" Evan asked. His hand gently grazed Kim's. She could see the slightest wince on his face, but she appreciated how hard he was trying. She only wished she could ease his pain.

"Well, my realtor says that storefront in Norfolk is still for sale."

"Really? I thought there was tons of interest."

"Me too." They shared a knowing glance as they turned down Oak Street.

"Is your loan pre-approval still valid?"

"Yes." Kim watched two kids on a corner lot raking leaves into a giant mound. Their chocolate lab charged for their pile and sent leaves flying. "But I don't want to open the store in Norfolk. The Twisted Tulip belongs in Willow Creek."

"You sound sure of yourself."

"I am. We're rebuilding the grocery store to accommodate the expansion of a floral department."

"We, huh?"

"I'm a part owner now." Kim felt the car slowing. "What're you doing?" She didn't know anyone who lived in this neighborhood.

"Allie mentioned something to me I wanted to see."

"Did she now?" When Evan turned into a driveway and parked, Kim looked at him in puzzlement. "Evan?"

"This was one of her mom's fixer upper projects. Pam Jordan's looking for a renter."

"Yeah?"

Evan threw open his door. "C'mon. Let's go check it out."

The two story square house reminded her a lot of her Gram's. They both had a covered front porch. This one sat on a corner lot and included a giant sun room off to one side, and it was painted beige instead of white. Otherwise, it looked quite similar, down to the lattice work on the east side.

"You have a key?"

"I told you I talked to Allie."

Swinging open the door, Kim's breath hitched. The house, despite all its modern upgrades—paint, trim, and definitely central air—had much of its original character. The banister was no doubt original, as were the polished hardwood floors and glass doorknobs throughout.

Kim would've stood there all day gawking just in the entrance, but Evan pulled her toward the kitchen. She barely had time to admire the high ceilings, beautiful white cabinets with sea glass fronts and high end appliances before he stepped into a room off the side. The sunroom.

"Allie said her mom decided to heat this room, so I thought it might be a suitable workspace until they rebuild the grocery store. I know it's not ideal—"

"Are you kidding? Evan, it's perfect!" She threw her arms around his neck and kissed him like she'd wanted to in the auditorium. Her insides tingled with desire. The idea of having her way with him right here in the sun room had its appeal.

"We can't christen this place yet."

Kim trailed kisses down his neck. "Why not?"

"I haven't signed the lease. I wanted to make sure you were on board."

The gravity of what Evan was saying finally sunk in. "You want to live together?"

"Of course. Did you think I was just going to let you move in without me? I have news for you Kimberly."

"Oh yeah?"

"Yeah." He kissed her again and pushed her up against the wall—the one *without* frosted glass windows. "I am never leaving you again. You're stuck with me."

"Even when you make me crazy?"

"Especially then." Evan began sliding Kim's shirt up.

"I thought you said—"

"We'll be signing the lease in the next hour. What harm will it do if we break in the place a little early?"

Kim threw her arms around his neck, wrapping a leg around his waist. Her fingers quickly found their way beneath his shirt. "I love you, Evan."

"I love you, Kimberly. I always will."

If you enjoyed this book, please consider leaving a review online. I read and appreciate every review. You guys rock!

Acknowledgements

To my amazing critique panel – Nicki L., Jules, Nikki H., Jen, Audrey, Jessica, Melissa, and Magen. Thank you all for not only providing thorough feedback, but for rushing my insane timeline.

To Nikki H. – Thank you for spending hours plotting this novel, even though much of what we conspired will end up in the next book.

To Jules – Thank you for reading SecScan not just once but insisting on a second time through. Your enthusiasm kept me going on those nights I wanted to be lazy.

To Magen – Thank you for spending hours on the phone discussing plot twists and characters. Thank you also for putting my books out at your shows.

To EJ – Thank you for your amazing insight. I learn so much each time we work together and look forward to growing as an author with your mentorship.

To Brenda – Thank you for helping me make this story shine. I hope we get to meet in Alaska!

To Michelle – Thank you for working around my crazy, short timeline and helping me publish before my deadline.

To Lindee – Thank you for providing me with amazing photos. You were an absolute pleasure to work with and really understood my vision. Thanks also to the cover models Ahmad Kawsan & Mikeala Galli – you fit my image of Evan & Kim perfectly.

To Letitia – Thank you for creating such a gorgeous cover. As always, you blow me away with your amazing designs and always manage to exceed my expectations.

To Samara – Thank you for taking me on a personal tour of the Steese Volunteer Fire Department. Thank you also to those firemen who entertained my endless questions.

To Mom – Thank you for your continual support and research assistance. I promise I'm still working on that mystery story you like, but I have to admit it makes me happy to see you so excited over a romance novel!

To Dad – Thank you for explaining all about rural boards and small town volunteer fire departments. Your insight was incredibly helpful.

To Grandma – Thank you for letting me borrow your flower magazines that I ended up keeping. And your delicious pie was of course behind the inspiration for Violet's pie baking obsession.

To my readers – Your support and enthusiasm keeps me going! I write these stories for you guys. I hope you enjoy reading them as much as I enjoy writing them.

About Jacqueline Winters

Jacqueline Winters has been writing books since she was nine when she'd sneak stacks of paper from her grandma's closet and fill them with adventure. She grew up in Small-Town Nebraska and spent a decade living in beautiful Alaska. Jacqueline writes contemporary romances, some set in small Nebraskan towns, and a series coming soon set in charming Alaskan locations.

She's a sucker for happily ever afters, has a sweet tooth that can be sated by cupcakes, and firmly believes sangria was possibly the best invention ever. On a relaxing evening, you can find her at her computer writing her next novel with her dog poking his adorable head out from beneath the desk.

Follow Jacqueline

Website: jacquelinewintersromance.com

Facebook: facebook.com/JacquelineWintersRomance/

Twitter: @jwintersak

Instagram: jwinterswriter

Made in the USA
Middletown, DE
12 June 2016